TOMORROW'S
SUN

BECKY MELBY

TOMORROW'S
SUN

LOST SANCTUARY

Book One

BARBOUR
PUBLISHING

ISBN 978-1-61626-238-9

For more information about Becky Melby, please access the author's website at the following Internet address: www.beckymelby.com

Cover credit: Studio Gearbox, www.studiogearbox.com

Published by Barbour Publishing, Inc., P.O. Box 719, Uhrichsville, OH 44683, www.barbourbooks.com

Our mission is to publish and distribute inspirational products offering exceptional value and biblical encouragement to the masses.

 Member of the
Evangelical Christian
Publishers Association

Printed in the United States of America.

Dedication/Acknowledgment

To Cathy Wienke—
I have learned more from you about faith, forgiveness, perseverance, marriage, and mothering in our thirty-six years of friendship than you will ever know, and I am more grateful for your patience, love, prayers, and encouragement than I can ever express. Your passion for our Lord simply radiates. Never doubt God's purpose for your life—He has shaped you to be an encourager and a prayer warrior, and you are fulfilling that destiny daily.

Special thanks to:
Jamie Chavez, editor extraordinaire, for fast, fantastic editing and a big dose of encouragement.

Jan Glas, for reading this through, catching goofs, offering kind words, and baking scrumptious gluten-free goodies.

Cynthia Ruchti, for prayer, laughter, critiquing, wise words, and sweet friendship—for making me a better writer. . .and a better person.

Rachael Phillips, for wise critting. Victor and Lisa, for the name Mariah.

Thank you to my amazing boys, Scott, Jeff, Aaron, and Mark, their wonderful wives, Kristen, Holly, Adrianne, and Brittany, and the sweetest grandkids ever:

Sawyer and Sage—for being twins and being twelve at just the right time.

Ethan, Peter, and Cole—for a tree frog names Squiggles who now lives in these pages.

Reagan, Lilly, Keira, Caden, Oliver, and Finley—for simply being you and making life a joy.

As always, thank you to Bill, my sweetheart of forty-four years, for loving me and all of my imaginary friends.

A heartfelt thank-you to the people who shared their time and knowledge:

Earl Squires for a tour of the English Settlement Church and cemetery. Joni Beck of the Rochester Historical Society for information on the Underground Railroad.

The Burlington Historical Society Museum.

Kerry Milkie, Manager of the Youth and Family Division of the Racine County Human Services Department for extreme patience in answering my questions on child custody laws.

Bryan Wangnoss, of the Burlington Police Department for helping me put Ben in jail.

My brother, Bob Foght, Senior Probation and Parole Agent, Wisconsin Department of Corrections, for showing me how to keep Ben in jail for just the right length of time. (And for proving he has a second career in writing.)

Dan MacVeagh and Kathy Hainstock for finding books on the Underground Railroad.

Eric R. Stancliff, Public Services Librarian & Seminary Art Curator, Concordia Seminary Library, for expertise on fiber-based paper.

Thank you to the following members of American Christian Fiction Writers for so willingly sharing their expertise: Anne Love, Deb Kinnard, Kim Zweygardt, Leslie Pfeil, and Ronda Wells, MD for medical information. Tamara Cooper, Deb Raney, Linda Rondeau and her husband, for information on child custody laws. Dave Bond and Ane Mulligan, for sharing their remodeling stories. Terry Burns, for teaching me how to disable a car from the inside.

If I say, "Surely the darkness will hide me
and the light become night around me,"
even the darkness will not be dark to you;
the night will shine like the day,
for darkness is as light to you.
PSALM 139:11–12 NIV

PROLOGUE

September 2, 1852

Hannah Shaw lingered on the last line of the letter she'd vowed to destroy, pressed her lips against the soft paper, and tucked it in her apron. As she opened the heat grate in the ceiling with the handle of her broom, she commanded the smile to leave her voice. "Biscuits or corn cakes, Papa?" she called through the opening.

Wiping the biscuit cutter on a flour-sack towel, she waited for the rhythmic sweep of the trowel to slow. Papa didn't talk and work at the same time. She lifted the blue-striped bowl from the sideboard with one hand and set the biscuit pan on the table with the other.

The swishing stopped. "Is there buttermilk left?"

Peering out the back door, Hannah winked at the cardinal on the porch railing preening himself in the dawn light. "Just enough for a batch of biscuits."

"Then you knew what I wanted before you asked."

Hannah smiled. "You are the one who taught me that every man should have the right to choose his own destiny."

Laughter rumbled through the grate. "Impertinent child. Fetch the buttermilk and—"

The front door rattled under the knock of a heavy hand. One rap, followed by two.

Hannah clutched her apron. "Someone's at the door, Papa." Her voice quivered. Too early for visitors. Too insistent for one of Papa's customers. "Should I answer?"

"No." Her father's footsteps echoed as he crossed the empty second floor. The walls seemed to shake as he thundered down the stairs.

Hannah waited in the dining room. Warning shot from her father's eyes as he reached the bottom step. "Carry on as you were." Worry etching his face, he turned to the door.

How was she to carry on when her hands trembled and her thoughts raced like the river after a hard rain? *Liam. Lord, let it not be about him. Keep him safe.* She ordered her legs to carry her to the cupboard in the corner. With whitened fingers frozen on the handles and her ears straining toward the whispers in the parlor, she could not have remembered what went into buttermilk biscuits if her life depended on it. She opened the doors. The scent of cinnamon erased the past eight months, as if Mama stepped beside her, reaching from the grave for a pinch of spice for her apple butter.

"...danger is increasing...trust no one..." Scraps of sentences fell like quilt block trimmings. "Dr. Dyer, I assure you..." Her father's voice rose then dipped again. Hannah held her breath, listening for the only name that mattered.

"...should send her to Elizabeth's sister until..."

The men spoke of the growing risk, but what should have set her on edge calmed her. Their talk had nothing to do with Liam. She smiled. Dr. Dyer did not know her well, or he would never have suggested sending her to Aunt Margaret's as if she were a child. Her grip on the cupboard handles relaxed.

Flour, salt, baking soda, lard. The recipe filled the part of her mind not occupied by deep dimples and midnight blue eyes. She pulled out the ingredients, filled the bowl with flour to the first blue line, and pressed a deep well in the center. She snatched the market basket off the hook by the back door, letting her hand graze the black iron shaped by Liam's own hand. She loved how it stood out against the pale yellow paint Mama had started and Hannah had finished.

Two rooms away, the conversation grew intense yet more hushed. She gripped the handle and stood, still as death, but couldn't decipher a single word. With a prayer-filled sigh, she opened the cellar door.

The earthy cold crept beneath her skirt. Goose pimples scampered up her arms like countless baby mice. The weak light from the only window hadn't the strength to reach the corner. In the dark, she counted out five eggs, found the lard crock, and felt for the half barrel of spring water. Plunging her hand into it, she snatched the buttermilk jar and ran up the stairs. As always, the apple tree stenciled on the cellar side of the door gave her pause. Mama's paints sat in a box atop the cupboard. If only she could paint like—

We will not speak of what might have been. Papa's words, bracing as the water in the barrel, brought her back to the moment. She set the basket and the buttermilk on the kitchen table then pinched salt into the bowl. The talk at the front door ceased, and Dr. Dyer left.

"Papa?" She darted through the dining room. "Is everything all right?"

"Everything is fine." The creases in his brow had never seemed so deep. His shoulders slumped. "Make some corn cakes, too. We will need them tonight."

With her heart choosing a tempo to rival Big Jim's fiddle, she nodded. Emotions clashed inside her. The risk was great for all of them, but fear mingled with joy. Tonight they would have guests, which meant tomorrow night she would see Liam. "How many rugs?"

"Two." He turned away and stared through the lace on the north window.

Hannah followed his gaze to the river. *Tomorrow night.*

"Hang two rugs. And pray, my dear."

CHAPTER 1

What do you call the place you live if it isn't home?

Emily Foster blew her bangs off her forehead and tapped the steering wheel to "Haven't Met You Yet" as she searched the afternoon shadows for a street sign, and the house she wouldn't call home. For the next few months. Or weeks, if she was lucky.

Rochester, Wisconsin, population 1100. She'd have eleven hundred neighbors—and she'd try to get to know as few of them as possible. Michael Bublé said it would all work out. Emily turned at the corner, hoping he was right.

The old, white clapboard house framed in her windshield had shrunk in nineteen years. Or maybe the rest of her world had gotten too big since that innocent summer. She parked in a short strip of gravel that pointed toward the river. Opening the car door, she stared at the house across the street. It occupied the spot where she'd found God, and almost missed her first kiss. A long, measured sigh bowed her cheeks. With deep, controlled breaths, she swiveled in the seat then eased her feet to the ground. Moving like a woman three times her age, she unloaded the car and hobbled up the stone walk to the paneled door. The lock complained at the twist of the key.

In the front parlor, the plank floor groaned beneath her feet. With nothing to absorb the sound of her intrusion, each tap of her paisley-covered cane echoed off the peeling plaster.

The house was as hollow and weary as its new owner.

"Counter with a positive." The ever-nagging voice of Vanessa, her therapist—the one who therapied her mind, not the one who pummeled the rest of her—whispered a warning. *"Counter with a positive thought before you teeter off the brittle edge."*

Dropping her sleeping bag and air mattress in the middle of the room, Emily turned in a slow circle. *First positive Wisconsin thought: Empty is not always bad. This place is full of potential.*

Am I?

The front parlor was no larger than a hospital room. A poor excuse for sunlight struggled through warped glass in the nine-pane windows. Pale ovals patchworked dingy beige walls where long-dead faces had once kept watch, and spider-vein cracks trailed like quilt stitching between the phantom frames.

Emily closed her eyes, envisioning the space as it would soon be. Sans claustrophobia. By knocking out the walls that divided the main floor into five rooms, she'd create an open floor plan. New windows, gleaming floors, rich colors. Modern. Roomy. Sellable.

In the dining room, she unzipped her fleece jacket and yanked open a window. Storm-scrubbed air transfused the staleness with hints of apple blossom and made her hungry for more. On her way to the back door, she checked her watch. Fifteen minutes to kill until the first contractor arrived. Fifteen minutes best spent without walls. She hung the key ring on a black hook by the door. Kicking off her shoes, she stepped onto the porch.

The swollen Fox River bursting the hem of her temporary backyard rushed through Rochester on its way from Menominee Falls to northern Illinois. It bubbled over a massive limb hanging at a grotesque angle from a fresh gash in an oak tree. All that anchored the limb to the trunk was a narrow strip of twisted bark.

She hadn't thought about lawn care or tree trimming. She hadn't thought about much, other than putting Lake Michigan between her and the eggshell walkers.

A flash of red drew her attention from the water to a solitary pine on the north side of the yard. A male cardinal landed on a low bough. His mate called down from the top of the tree.

Emily imagined a hammock next to the pine. Maybe the white

noise of the river would muffle the specters in her head.

A child's high-pitched wail caused her pulse to stumble. Laughter followed the squeal, and Emily breathed a sigh. She walked to the end of the porch and bent over the railing. Two young boys wrestled over a basketball in her side yard. On the ground beside them, a circus-colored beach ball rocked in the breeze.

Some things she wouldn't get away from, no matter how far she moved.

Turning back to the pine tree, Emily tried to conjure her imaginary hammock, but it wouldn't return. She opened the screechy screen door and stepped into the kitchen.

The floor sloped toward the back of the house. In front of the sink, a layer of pink-and-gray-flowered linoleum showed through a hole in the brick-patterned vinyl. She padded across the uneven surface to a white corner cupboard. Resting her cane against the windowsill, she unlatched a tall door, releasing memories mingled with cloves, cinnamon, and coriander. She'd been fifteen when she spent the summer visiting her best friend's great-grandmother. Cara's Nana Grace was the quintessential grandma. Memories of that magical summer and the big white house in Rochester chronicled all five senses—violets, fireflies, apple crisp, a cobwebby cellar, and the trill of tree frogs. Exploring the town on Nana Grace's wobbly old Schwinn bikes, giggling about the bare-chested guy washing his car down the street, dangling their feet in the river, talking for hours about that clumsy, dream-spinning kiss. Carefree.

The way young girls should be.

Her shoulders shuddered, an invisible weight constricting her lungs. Closing her eyes, she repeated the words branded in her brain. "Release. . .relax. . .let it go." With a fierce exhale, she tugged on the window next to the cupboard. It stuck. She banged on the frame with the heel of her hand and tried again. The sash gave way, sliding up so quickly she almost lost her balance.

Sweet spring air thwarted panic. *Be present in the moment.* The cardinals still sang. In the distance, the metered cadence of the basketball on cement joined the rhythm of the afternoon. She concentrated on the steady *slap, slap, slap* as she labeled the smells. Wet leaves. River mud. Charcoal smoke. Violets.

As her pulse reclaimed a normal pace, another shrill scream pierced her quiet and she slid the window down. It banged shut but didn't block the noise. The scream grew louder. Closer.

No laughter followed.

"Let it go!"

Strange to hear her therapist's advice yelled from a child's lips.

"Michael! Stop!"

The beach ball bounced toward the river, propelled by the wind. And followed by a barefoot boy. A gust whipped it against the crippled oak. The ball shot into the water.

Lord God, no. Caught in a whirlpool, the ball swirled in a tight circle. Red. . .white. . .yellow. . .blue. . .

The boy grabbed onto the broken limb with one hand and reached for the ball with the other.

Emily's pulse thundered in her ears. Her breath rasped, fast and shallow. Black walls pushed in, narrowing her vision.

The limb swayed. A *crack* split the air. "Michael!" A man's voice. "I'll get the ball. Come here. *Now.*"

The boy stopped and waved toward the voice, then glanced up at her and waved again.

The room tilted. Emily closed her eyes. *Release. Relax. Let it go.*

Her legs gave way. She slid to the floor, biting her lip against the stab of pain in her right hip. Knees to chest, arms encircling her legs, she folded. Making herself small.

A heavy knock shook the screen door. She shrank against the cupboard.

The door rattled again. "I don't think she's home."

A lighter, quieter knock followed. "I just sawed her," a small voice insisted. "Just now in the window."

"Miss Foster? Jacob Braden, Braden Improvements."

Emily rubbed her eyes with both hands. *Go away.* She'd call the contractor tomorrow, make up some excuse. A headache or phone call. Tomorrow she'd be rested, calmer, able to think.

"Go in," the small voice whispered.

"We can't just walk in. That's rude." Footsteps retreated. "Come on."

"Nuh-uh. Nana Grace lets us."

"Nana Grace is—*Michael!* You can't—"

Hinges whined. Emily raised her head from her cocoon.

Bare feet. Red shorts. Huge brown eyes. "I'm Michael."

Breathe. Emily clenched and unclenched tingling fingers. *Live in the now.* "Hi, Michael. I'm Emily." She smiled. It felt almost natural.

"Nana Grace gave us *peanuhbutter* cookies."

"I'm sorry. I haven't had time to bake."

The door opened again. A man: dusty work boots, one lace untied and trailing; faded jeans, hole on the right knee; snug, heather-blue shirt; sun-lightened brown hair curling over his collar. Eyebrows rose above inquisitive eyes. "Are you all right?"

"I'm fine." She was sitting on the floor, half-curled in a ball. Not a chance he'd believe her. "Just. . .trying to get a feel for the place."

He nodded and a chunk of gold-licked hair swung over his forehead. He looked toward the window and Emily witnessed a split-second startle. He'd seen the cane. He wiped his palms on his jeans and cleared his throat. "Can I give you a hand?"

There was only one way she could get to her feet from where she was now, and Jacob Braden's hand wouldn't help. "Why don't you go ahead and look around and I'll join you in—"

The back door moaned once again. The older boy bounded in. "Michael, Mom said you gotta get home." Eyes almost identical to his little brother's jerked to Emily then up to the man beside him. "Why is she sitting on the floor?" he asked in a hushed tone, as if she couldn't hear.

"Russell, say hi to Miss Foster. She's going to be your new neighbor. She's sitting on the floor because she's tired. Miss Foster just drove all the way from. . .Minnesota?"

"Michigan. Traverse City."

"That's a long drive." He nudged the boy.

"Hi. I'm Russell. It's nice to meet you." The words came out stilted, rehearsed. Precious. "Did you see the ghost yet?"

A chill shimmied up her spine. "Ghost?"

Jacob Braden put a hand on Russell's head. "Local legend. In a town with this much history, people mix a little truth with a lot of fantasy. This house has been around a long time." He ruffled the boy's hair. "Say good-bye, boys."

Michael took one last look at the empty counter, waved, and ran out. Russell said good-bye, turned toward the door then stopped. "My mom says maybe you will babysit us. Do you have any boys?"

Emily shook her head. "I'm sorry, I don't."

No cookies. No little boys.

Not this side of heaven.

⚜

The soles of Jake's boots whispered in the worn depressions in the steps. *If these stairs could talk. . .*A century and a half of footfalls. Newlyweds slipping off to bed. . .a worried mother walking her feverish baby. . . children's voices echoing in the steep, narrow stairwell. . . The stories this house could tell. He reached the top and ran his hand over the newel post. Smooth. Polished by countless hands.

He smiled as he walked into a bedroom. What a sentimental schmuck he was.

Looking down at the river through wavy blown glass, he listened for footsteps. Then it hit him—maybe the lady couldn't climb stairs. What was wrong with her anyway? The multicolored cane could have been left by the old woman who'd died right there in that kitchen a few months back, but he doubted it. And something about the wary look in Emily's wide-set eyes told him her problems weren't just physical. But in that area he was out of his element. Houses he could read. Women he almost always misinterpreted. He still hadn't recovered from the last mistake.

With dark blond hair pulled straight back and no makeup, he'd guess her to be an accountant or lawyer. Something dry and bookish. She'd told him on the phone this was her first house flip. He didn't like the way she'd said it. But then, he didn't like the term *flip* anyway. It sounded like something fast, cheap. Flippant. She wouldn't get fast or cheap out of him if he took the job.

If he took the job.

He waited a respectful few minutes, gazing down at trees bursting with new, bright green leaves. Skinny branches arched over the river like hundreds of fishing poles. The water was as high as he'd ever seen it. If he found a spare minute he'd get out the kayak. Another big if.

He was walking out the door when he heard her. Slow, halting steps up the stairs. He backtracked to the window and pretended to be absorbed in the flight of a fat robin toting a strip of blue plastic.

"Sorry to keep you waiting." Emily Foster stopped in the doorway. "I think I mentioned on the phone that I had the house thoroughly inspected before I bought it. The roof was replaced nine years ago. I've hired painters for the exterior and I plan on sanding the porch myself. The foundation is sound. So"—she nodded toward the wall between the two north bedrooms—"why don't we start up here? I'm thinking these two rooms, with a bath in between, will be the master suite."

Jake's jaw tightened as he glanced at the row of old hooks in a small, open closet. Knocking out that closet would be nothing short of criminal. He grunted for her to continue the torture.

"This is a weight-bearing wall." She tapped it with the tip of her cane. A triangle chunk of plaster landed between them. "But with a header, I think it'll work. If we—"

"Can we back up a sec?" Jake rubbed the back of his neck. "First of all"—he stretched out his hand—"maybe we should actually meet. Jake Braden."

"Yes. You're right." She held out a pale hand and shook his. "Nice to meet you face-to-face."

He'd seen more enthusiasm in a smoked trout.

He planted his hands on his belt. "Before we get started, tell me what you already know about the history of the house so I don't bore you with stories you've already heard."

The girl blinked. Twice, then again. Did she not understand the request?

"Most of the wiring was replaced in the seventies and, like I said, the roof—"

"I mean *history*. Like what happened here, who lived here."

"Oh." That expression could only be labeled annoyance. "It was built in the 1840s and it was a little over a hundred years old when the Ostermanns bought it. Grace's great-granddaughter told me legend has it that the man who built this house served with Abraham Lincoln in the Blackhawk War, and Lincoln stopped here once for a visit. That tidbit could come in handy as a selling point."

Selling point? The greatest president this country ever knew could have slept in this very room and she called it a *tidbit?* Jake exhaled and almost forgot to take another breath.

"The main floor was redone at some point, but the second story here is all original lath and plaster." She tapped the toe of her sandal on the chunk of plaster between them. "I've drawn up plans to open up both floors. The place pretty much needs a complete overhaul."

Overhaul? Jake's sentimental soul writhed. Her word choice summoned visions of steamrollers and wrecking balls. "It needs some cosmetics, but—"

"The layout is boxy."

Jake folded his arms to stop his elbows from jutting out like a frilled-neck lizard. *It's a Greek Revival house, lady.* He counted the boards from the door to her cane. "You're planning on selling as soon as it's done, right?"

She gave him an of-course look. "Yes. I'm hoping to have it on the market by the end of July."

Jake aspirated her last word and fought strangulation for several breaths. "I...think...that might be a bit...ambitious." He pulled a notebook from his back pocket. "Why don't we take a walk-through. You tell me exactly what you want, and I'll tell you what I'm willing to do and how long it should take."

"Fair enough." Her lips pressed against each other.

He tried to picture her with a smile.

"Nobody's looking for this many bedrooms these days." She walked out into the hall. "We can put a bath over there and enlarge that bedroom." Again, she pointed with the cane. "And then we can..."

We? Who's we? He followed her around like a trained pup, taking notes, asking for clarification.

But he wasn't a hoop jumper. As much as he needed the work, he'd already made up his mind.

Before he said no, the woman needed a history lesson.

♕

She didn't have to like him to hire him.

Emily leaned on the railing as she clunked down the stairs ahead of him. He *would* be the chivalrous type, letting her go first.

She led him to the front room, where she'd dropped her sleeping bag. A duct-taped corner of her second copy of *Flipping Houses for Dummies* peeked out of her duffel bag.

He glanced at her meager belongings. "You're not sleeping on the floor, are you?"

"I have an air mattress." She pointed toward the black vinyl bag. "On this level, I'd like to open things up. Kind of a great-room concept. The dining room—" She stopped. Jake Braden held one hand up like he was swearing on a Bible.

"That would ruin the. . ." His shoulders rose, almost to his ears. "Maybe my opinion is clouded because I live in this neighborhood, but my personal and professional opinion"—he put way too much emphasis on *professional*—"is if you hope to sell a historical landmark, you need to respect the integrity of the original design. The buyers who will be drawn to this place are looking for a trip back in time, a strong flavor of the past."

Fingers curled toward her palms. She'd spent seventeen pain-racked months trying get rid of a strong flavor of the past in every aspect of her life. This house represented her first step toward everything new. "That's a very small, niche market. My goal is to make this place appealing to a broad range of buyers. And most people like new." She held his gaze, amused at his irritation. Braden Improvements came highly recommended. She didn't have to like him to hire him, but she did have to agree with him. Or rather, he needed to agree with her. Two more contractors would walk through the house yet today, and if she needed to interview a few more, so be it. She didn't have the energy to argue with this man.

He pulled a phone out of his shirt pocket. "Maybe you've already seen this, but I found a picture of your house on the Historical Society website. Taken in 1906." He tapped and scrolled then handed it to her.

She stared at the sepia-toned photograph. A big white dog sat on the front step. *Her* front step. The house hadn't changed much in more than a hundred years, but the top of the oak tree that now stood like a wounded soldier didn't even reach the roofline in the picture.

"Mr. Braden, I do have an appreciation for history. I understand the importance of keeping a historical feel, but I want to incorporate changes that make it work for the way people live today."

His eyes narrowed.

"I suppose if I were remodeling this house for myself, I might get interested in its stories. But, frankly, this place is a means to an end."

"Can I ask what's at the end of the means?"

Restitution. That wasn't the answer she'd give him or anyone else. "I want to buy another house when this one sells."

"And then?"

The guy was nothing short of rude. "California. Eventually."

"In a paid-for house with a pool and a view, huh?" Condescension tainted his smile.

"No." The word popped out. She should have stopped it, should have let him think she was all about luxury or appearances, or whatever conclusion he'd come to.

His head dipped slightly forward, eyebrows lifted a fraction. He was waiting for more, but there was nothing more she could tell him. If she succeeded, if the house sold and she could repeat the process at least once—somewhere even farther from Traverse City—she'd reach the West Coast penniless and without a plan. But at peace. "I just—" Jake's phone buzzed in her palm. A name flashed on the screen. *Lexi.* She held it out to him.

"Excuse me. I need to take this." He turned his back to her and walked toward a window. "Lex? Can it wait?" A rumbling sound, part sigh, part growl, came from the man as he listened. "I'll pick you up." His hand went to his forehead and rubbed over his face. "It's not a problem. And it's not your fault." His shoulders lowered. "That's what I'm here for," he said quietly, with more than a hint of resignation. "Bye."

He crossed the floor in four long strides. With his hand on the door handle, he seemed to suddenly remember he wasn't alone in the room. He turned and looked at her with tired eyes. "I don't think I'm your man, Miss Foster."

CHAPTER 2

I don't think you are either, Mr. Braden.

Emily closed the door behind him and walked over to her duffel bag. Her stomach burned. She hadn't put much in it today. Rummaging through clothes and books, she found a bag of rice cakes. Nibbling on one while massaging her lower back with the other hand, she walked through the kitchen to the cellar door. She had half an hour to explore until the next contractor arrived. If the cellar was dry, she could store her few belongings there, protected from drywall dust and out of the way of whomever she ended up hiring.

The top of the door was level with the top of her head. She turned the porcelain knob, but it just kept turning. With a yank, she pulled the door open. Half-moon chips along the opened edge displayed at least five different colors of paint. Sage green, salmon, pale yellow. Did each color represent someone's fresh start?

Cool, musty air wafted up. She pushed a mother-of-pearl button on an old-fashioned switch. A dusty bulb hanging from a wire above her head came to life. Two-by-four railings flanked the open-sided wood staircase that was little more than a wide ladder. Emily hung her cane on the doorknob. Rough planks gave slightly beneath her feet, sounding as though they were pulling free of the rusty nails that held them in place.

It took a moment for her eyes to adjust to the dim light from two bare bulbs and a small, algae-covered window. Canning shelves that once bowed under Grace Ostermann's trophies stood barren. The whole unit listed slightly to the right. With a little reinforcing, they would hold her bins. The other three walls were made of field stone with wide mortared spaces between the rocks. A deep ledge ran the length of the wall beneath a small window just above her eye level. Shapes cluttered one end of the ledge, but she couldn't make out the objects. She walked closer, wishing she'd brought a flashlight.

A cricket and two spiders scurried into the shadows when she lifted a heavy, stained and tattered Havoline Motor Oil box. Emily shivered and blew off a coating of dust before she opened it. The box was filled with pint jars. Full pint jars. She lifted one to the light. Apple slices.

She could almost taste Nana Grace's apple cobbler swimming in warm, brown sugar syrup. But these jars, blue-green with mottled zinc lids, looked like they'd been filled long before that magical summer. It may have been sitting in this very place when she and Cara had come down here with armloads of canned peas or carrots or beets. She put the box back, leaving out one jar. She'd wash it off and set it on the kitchen counter—a tribute to a woman who'd made daily chores a labor of love.

Grimacing, she reached into the shadows and pulled out a tall metal container. A hairy-bodied spider ran across her hand and she jumped. She wasn't afraid of spiders. She just didn't want to keep company with them. The tin was surprisingly heavy. When she moved it closer to the window, she saw color. About four inches square and eight high, the tin was covered in a blue and green plaid. She pulled off the lid. An enormous clear glass marble with tiny bubbles suspended in its core sat near the top. She set it carefully in a divot in the ledge and pulled out a cast-iron Indian on horseback and a miniature carved wooden frog. *Who made you? Who did you belong to?*

Coins, tokens, a whistle, and a wooden matchbox. A boy's box of treasures? The picture that came to mind was a 1940s version of the little guy who'd asked for "peanuhbutter" cookies. Striped T-shirt, blue shorts, and brown tie shoes, a homemade slingshot sticking out of his back pocket.

A cricket chirped from somewhere near her feet, and she

suddenly sensed she was surrounded by crawling creatures. As she put the marble and the frog back in the can, she scanned the cellar. The floor appeared dry. After a bug bomb, a good sweeping, and a few braces on the shelves, it would once again be usable.

She lifted her foot to the bottom step then turned back to the desolate shelves.

Would she still be here when the apples ripened?

⚜

"I get your vision, but it seems kind of a shame to change things that drastically. I'll be honest with you, ma'am, you'll lose some potential buyers and"—Matt Rayburg laughed at whatever humorous thing he was about to say—"don't be surprised if the neighbors have a thing or two to say about it." His mouth twisted to one side and he nodded as if responding to a voice only he could hear.

They already have. "But you'd do it?"

"I'd do it. Might try to persuade you a bit before I take a hammer to that wall, but I'd do it. I'll write you up an estimate and get it to you Monday."

"Thank you." She shook the man's hand and opened the front door for him as the third contractor walked up the front walk.

Mr. Rayburg eyed the taller man, muttered hello, and got in his truck.

"Mr. Hansel?" Emily's neck arched to make eye contact.

He wore a dress shirt, cuffs rolled to just below his elbows, and khakis with knife-sharp creases. He held out a soft hand. "You must be Emily. You're much younger than you sounded on the phone."

More than just his hands were smooth. The compliment generated an instant distrust. When they reached the last bedroom on the second floor, he bent forward just a degree, a subtle bow. "Refreshing. It's encouraging to meet a forward thinker. French doors in place of these would be lovely, and I can envision a few skylights here in the master suite."

Emily stared at a robin's nest in a branch just beyond the window. Had her imaginary friend in the striped T-shirt held his giant, clear marble up to this same window to catch the sunlight? "I do need to keep the cost down."

22

"Of course. Our specialty. And just for you, I'll throw in some extras. We're based out of Milwaukee and just beginning to branch out."

Fatigue descended on Emily in a sudden rush. Leaning on her cane, she suppressed a yawn. "When could you start and how soon could you have it done?"

The man cupped his elbow in one hand, and tapped his cheek. "Twelve weeks from the day we start, which could be within the week. And that's a generous estimate. Chances are, we could have things wrapped up in ten. Does that suit your timeline?"

"Th-that would suit me just fine."

"Very well. I could fax an estimate yet today."

"If you could e-mail it, I should be able to get it by Monday."

"Consider it done."

Blinking away the vision of bubbles dancing in a crystal ball, she imagined skylights and French doors and nodded. *Consider it done.*

⬡

"I'll make it up to you." Lexi whipped her ponytail over her shoulder and threw her book bag into the truck. "Ice cream. Uncle Harry's."

Jake arched an eyebrow at his niece. "You're buying?"

"Of course not. You are."

He put the truck in first gear and pulled away from the school. "And this would be making it up to me how?"

"The pleasure of my company."

"Do you seriously think there's room in my packed social calendar for hanging out with a seventh-grader?"

Lexi Sutton giggled like a girl with no cares in the world. "I seeeeriously think."

Giggles could be deceptive.

"Just so you know, if I agree to this, it's because of grasshopper ice cream, not the seventh-grader."

She raised her own eyebrow mockingly and rolled down her window. "Whatever."

"Where's Adam?"

"Doing penance. He had to skip science club and go home on the bus for feeding Pansy in the middle of the night."

"Ben has rules about midnight feedings?" The name of his late sister's second husband left an acrid taste in his mouth. Strange how a man with zero self-discipline handled his stepkids like a drill sergeant.

"Ben has rules about when you can breathe."

"So he hides your inhaler on you when it's not time to breathe?" It was hard to make light of a subject like Ben Madsen, but Jake wasn't going to allow the slug to wreck the little time he could steal with the twins.

"He would if he could. I keep it locked in my safe in Mom's box."

He had to shift the focus onto something positive. "So how was school?"

"You do realize that's the lamest question in the universe, don't you?"

"Okay, so give me a better conversation starter."

Lexi opened her backpack and pulled out a large white envelope. "Well, you could ask me if anything special happened in school today."

Jake cleared his throat. "Hi, Lex. Did anything special happen in school today?"

"Funny you should ask. The track coaches awarded me the Congeniality Person of the Month award."

"Wow. That's awesome." Emotion roughened his voice. "I'm proud of you."

Lexi smiled shyly and turned to the window. "Ben will get a good laugh out of this one."

Jake let several miles pass in silence as he tried to formulate an answer that wouldn't push them into a downward Ben spiral. He turned left onto W. "Is he still bowling on Thursday nights?"

"If that's what you call sitting at a bar with maroon shoes on."

Taking his eyes off the road, Jake lifted her chin. "I'll take you and Adam out for pizza Thursday night." It was a statement intended to bring hope.

A tiny smile rewarded him. "Don't worry about us so much. We're okay."

Right. By the time he trusted his voice again, they could see the sign for Uncle Harry's. "I promised your mom I'd watch out for you two." His throat tightened with something very much the opposite of hope. "That includes worrying."

"I know." She tipped her head to one side. "You're really good at uncle-ing."

♔

Emily stared up at the leather loop that served as a handle for the door to the attic. There was probably a drop-down ladder, but it did her no good when the handle dangled at least two feet beyond her reach. Instinctively she looked around for something to stand on, a futile gesture in an empty house.

Leave it.

Common sense spoke loudly, but curiosity overruled. She had plans for that space.

On the main floor, she scanned her meager pile of essentials and headed out the back door. A small shed hid behind the lilac bushes in her backyard. She took the key ring off the black hook, hoping one of the rusty keys Cara had sent would open the shed.

The smell of rain tinged the air. How much higher could the river rise before it caused real problems for the people living along its banks?

The shed wasn't locked, but she had to grab the edge of the door with both hands to pull it over clumps of dirt and grass. Once again she wished for a flashlight. An old push lawn mower sat in one corner and an upturned barrel held a bag of sidewalk salt and an array of garden tools. In the darkest corner she found what she was looking for—a ladder. Between the rungs, a streak of light reflected on glass. Pulling the ladder aside, she found a rough-hewn shadow box lined with faded blue calico cloth. Inside, a heavy-looking dog collar hung on a square-headed nail. Emily smiled. Who would frame a dog collar? She pictured the white dog in the photo Jacob had shown her. *Was that yours, Fluff?*

This place was having a strange effect on her. Or maybe it was just the result of time to think. Since the accident, her days had been filled, first with pain then with therapy. Before that, there'd never been enough hours in the day to have time left over for her imagination to take its own course on anything.

Thoughts of life before the accident made her feel like a voyeur, peering in on a stranger's world. The laughing, confident woman

25

who had sung "Ring Around the Rosie" to preschoolers by day and sipped *sake* on a black leather couch at the Monkey Bar in Grand Rapids by night was someone else.

One hand on the ladder, she looked up at the rafters. Wrought-iron hooks hung from the beams. A small tubeless wheel swung from the highest hook, the once-white rim and spokes the right size for a tricycle. She exhaled through pursed lips and dragged the ladder out the door.

Everywhere she turned, something reminded her of little boys.

👑

She'd long since shed her sweater, and now her white T-shirt clung to her clammy skin. With a flashlight shoved in her back pocket, she propped the ladder against the trim that surrounded the trapdoor in the ceiling. A spasm clenched her low back. A stabbing pain shot through her sacrum. Leaning on the ladder, she took two slow breaths and waited it out. When the pain lessened, she tested the rungs.

The skinny planks whined as she ascended. Emily tapped her back pocket. Assured her cell phone was in place in case she needed to meet the local rescue workers, she climbed until the top of her head nudged the door. There were no hinges. She shoved the loose panel out of the way. It scraped against the attic floor, shooting echoes and dust through the opening.

She climbed the last few rungs and landed safely on gritty boards, but as she swung clumsily into a sitting position, her foot banged the ladder. She lunged for it, but the bottom of the ladder lost its grip on the floor below. The top did a strange little jump, banged once against the frame, skimmed her hand, and crashed to the floor.

"No!" Scrambling to her feet, she hobbled to the window. Across the street, Russell dribbled the basketball. Michael sat on the beach ball, crying. Relief coursed through Emily, disarming every adrenaline-activated nerve. She unlatched the window and pulled on the brass handle at the bottom.

It didn't budge. As her shoulder wrenched, she noticed the strips of furring nailing the window shut.

She whirled. Even from here, she could see the strips of wood sealing the other window.

She banged on the glass. "Russell! Up here! Michael!"

After a minute it dawned on her—if she couldn't hear the slap of the basketball on the cement, they couldn't hear her.

Don't panic. She reached for her phone. *It's not an emergency.* Back home in Traverse City, she knew several guys on the volunteer rescue squad. She'd heard their stories, and she wasn't about to become a Friday night laugh. She was resourceful. Hadn't she heard that very word from professors and coworkers? Hadn't her therapist told her over and over that she was stronger than she thought she was? She scanned the room for a rope, a hammer, anything. On the other end of the attic, a large square of gray linoleum covered the floor. It matched the flowery pattern showing through the hole in the kitchen floor. If she could find a way to secure it, she could use it as a slide.

And end up back in the hospital.

Along one wall, an old quilt covered something about ten feet long. She yanked the quilt. Dust plumes danced in the shaft of gold sunlight straining through the west window. A church pew, dark-stained and shiny. Clusters of grapes with pointy leaves and curling tendrils decorated the back. On the end of the bench sat a Bible, the edges of the black cover ragged and curled. With the quilt at her feet, Emily sank to the bench.

On the wall directly across the room from her hung a three-foot-high black iron cross.

With it, she could break a window. But the thought of breaking the old glass seemed as sacrilegious as using a cross to do it.

Who had hung it here in this silent sanctuary? And who had made the decision to leave it?

She reached into her pocket and pulled out her phone, opened to her contacts list, and scrolled it. She knew two people in this town. Matt Rayburg and Jacob Braden.

Banishing the last shred of her pride, she decided to call the arrogant man who lived in the neighborhood. When she'd finished leaving a message, she sank back on the pew and stared at the cross. This would be a perfect place to pray.

She looked down at the faded quilt and began counting stitches.

27

"We need more."

Hannah knelt in the stifling attic and dropped a buffalo robe onto the two quilts in Papa's open arms. Only one blanket remained.

"Bertha Willett said we'll find some in the buggy after church."

"Bless that woman." She put one high-laced shoe on the ladder step, straightened her skirt about her ankles, and climbed down. "She'll be blessed in eternity, and we'll get just the opposite for lying to her."

Papa stood at the top of the stairs, petting his newly plastered wall as if it were a prized heifer. He shook his head. "When faced with two moral dilemmas, always choose the greater good. We've done no harm to Mrs. Willett by letting her believe she's making quilts for orphans."

Hannah shook the dust from her skirt and held out her arms for the blankets. "What was it that made a man with a spiritual answer for everything become a shopkeeper instead of a minister?"

A sad smile crinkled the skin at the corners of his eyes. "A sweetheart who wanted to marry a man who would indulge her."

Mirroring his smile, Hannah touched the wall in the same endearing fashion. "You did well for Mama."

A long sigh echoed off the empty walls. "If only she could have seen the house finished."

She refrained from saying *We will not speak of what might have been.* It was good for them to talk of Mama, to keep her memory alive. "She had three years to enjoy her stove and the cupboard. . ." She almost added *before*, but the word didn't need to be spoken. "She was happy. You built her 'the best new house in the best new state.'" She watched Mama's phrase darken his eyes. Hard as it was, he needed to be reminded.

Papa walked into the room that would be Hannah's as soon as the wallpaper arrived—a room with an actual closet with shelves on the bottom, and Liam's hooks on all three sides—the closet she'd already covered with a gingham curtain to hide the bit of carpentry she'd done herself.

She took him by the arm and steered him away from her closet. "The pies should be cool by now."

CHAPTER 3

Taste?" Jake held his cone out to Lexi. She licked it, a splotch of green ice cream landing on her chin, another on the picnic table. He handed her a napkin.

"Mine's better. Taste?" Eyes gleaming, she proffered a heap of neon blue with colored bits.

"Not a chance. You gotta wonder how this came about. Some dude coughs a wad of gum into the custard mix and says, 'Hey, let's call it Batman Bubblegum!'"

"A stroke of genius."

Jake shook his head. "There are names for people like you. Weird, for one." He handed her a second napkin for the blue moustache sprouting on her upper lip. "You look like your mom when you smile like that."

"Like this?" She punctuated a warped grin with a blue tongue.

The sassy face, meant to make him smile, felt like a curled fist pressed to his sternum. She'd inherited Abby's comedic timing. "Yeah. Just like that."

Lexi handed her cone to him. "Okay, be serious for a sec." She pulled the band out of her ponytail and fluffed her hair over her shoulders. "Do I look more like Mom with my hair long or short?"

Jake shook his head. "Unfair question. You know I only like long hair. All men prefer long hair."

"I didn't ask if I should get it cut. I asked which way I look more like Mom."

Grasshopper custard dripped across his knuckles. "Long."

"Good." She pointed to the puddle collecting under his hand. "I think it really bugs Ben that I look like her."

In the time it took him to lick the back of his hand, Jake experienced an emotion bordering on empathy. Thankfully, it didn't linger. "So how are things at home this week?" He watched Lexi's force field slide into place. "Be honest. I promise I won't worry." *Not.* He would worry, and he would write it all down.

Lexi shrugged. "He took Adam's phone away, and I only get mine until the end of the week when the contract is up. Oh yeah, he has a girlfriend."

The cake cone crackled under Jake's fingers.

"Adam heard noises downstairs last night."

Acid rose in Jake's throat. He didn't want to ask, but he had to—for the record. "What did he hear?"

"A woman's voice. They were laughing. What kind of person would laugh at Ben's stupid jokes? Anyway, that's the real reason Adam got up to feed Pansy—so he could check it out. They were in Ben's room."

Jake turned away and slammed the rest of his ice cream at the trash can.

"Ben came out and went nuts on Adam." Lexi wiped her mouth. "Don't say anything, okay?" Her tone pleaded.

"I won't." *Not yet.* He'd reported Ben to Human Services before. The guy slid through cracks like sewer water. He had to bide his time, bite his tongue, and trust his lawyer to work it out. In the meantime, he'd keep taking notes. And keep stashing away as much money as he could. Taking these kids out of Ben Madsen's grasp could take everything he had.

"Promise?"

Jake tapped his knuckles on the table, trying to remember what he was supposed to promise. "That I won't tell? I'll promise for now, if you make one to me."

Lexi tipped her head to one side. *Déjà vu.* Jake could have been eight years old, tagging along with his big sister, eating frozen

31

custard at this very table. Lexi scrunched her nose, wrinkling pink-tinged freckled skin. "What?"

"Promise me that if Ben ever hits you or Adam or touches—"

His phone, sitting on the table between them, rang. He glanced down, expecting the electrician or someone from his drywall crew. He was *not* expecting the name on the screen.

Emily Foster.

What part of "not interested" didn't she understand? True, he hadn't said it quite that clearly, but she should have gotten the gist. Did the woman think he was just playing the business version of hard-to-get? As he shut off the sound, something in Lexi's eyes grabbed him. A shuttered look, the force field sliding back into place. "Lex, has Ben ever touched—"

"No! Don't be dumb! I'd deck the slob if he ever—" She ended with an exaggerated shiver. "Ewww."

Jake stared at her, at the way her eyes didn't return to his. Maybe she wasn't lying. But she wasn't telling the truth either.

A sense of urgency swept over him. He stared down at the silenced phone then back at Lexi's guarded expression. It would kill him to knock down a wall that was over a hundred and sixty years old, but there were things that would hurt much worse. "I need to return this call." He stood and walked across the parking lot, swallowing pride with every step, and pushed the buttons that would connect him with compromise.

"Hello?" The cool, calm house flipper sounded distraught.

"Miss Foster, this is Jake Braden returning your call." *And eating crow.*

"Thank you for calling back. I know you're probably extremely busy." Her voice crackled on the last two words. "But I don't know anyone else in town, and I've gotten myself in the strangest predicament. . . ."

⚜

Lexi held the ladder at the bottom. An ethereal sight greeted Jake as he poked his head through the opening to the attic. Emily Foster sat on a bench on the far side of the attic, hugging a blanket. A tunnel of late afternoon sunshine landed in a square of light at her feet. Jake felt as though he was climbing the stairs to holy ground.

She rose slowly, the blanket falling to the floor. "This is so embarrassing." She walked toward him with what were clearly painful steps. "Thank you so much for coming. I'll pay you for your time."

Jake stood, surprised he didn't have to duck to clear the rafters. "No problem. As my grandma would've said—'round here we do fer each other." He let the grin he'd been suppressing since she'd called have rein and took two steps toward her. Why, he wasn't sure.

On the wall across from the bench hung a large black cross, striking in its simplicity. "Kind of a peaceful place to be stuck in a predicament. Did you hang that?"

"No. It was—"

"Can I come up, Jake?" Lexi's voice echoed through the hole in the floor.

"Sorry. That's my niece. Mind if she comes up and looks around?"

Emily lifted both hands and smiled. "Might as well make it a party. Wish I had some *peanuhbutter* cookies to serve."

Looking from Emily to the cross on the wall, Jake wondered if being stuck in this place hadn't been good therapy. She was a very different woman from the all-business person he'd talked to just hours ago.

"Wait a sec, Lex." He walked back and held the top of the ladder securely. She scrambled up and he made introductions.

"Hi." Lexi nodded to Emily and surveyed the room. "Wow. Cool. It's like a church up here." She scampered over to the bench, a straight-backed church pew. "Wouldn't this be an awesome place to pray?"

Embarrassed that he was embarrassed, Jake nodded. "If Grace Ostermann put this up here, it's been years since anyone's prayed here." He snuck a quick look at Emily. *Unless you did.* "She had bad knees. I used to see her limping around with her cane"—he regretted the word as it left his mouth—"in the garden. I don't think she could have climbed up, but maybe she could have." The old saying about digging out of a hole with a shovel came to mind.

Emily shook her head and the shadow of a smile crossed her lips. Absolution? She must be used to insensitivity.

Lexi picked up the quilt and folded it, like the good little housekeeper Ben was turning her into. "Jake, did you see this?" she whispered, running her hand across the quilt.

He took a closer look and nodded, his throat tightening. He looked at Emily. "My sister, Lexi's mom, was a quilt show addict. She died almost a year ago."

"I'm sorry. For both of you."

Jake had to hand it to her for not spewing the platitudes so many people felt necessary. "Thank you."

Lexi walked to the window overlooking the river and an awkward silence descended. Jake thrust his hands into the pockets of his jeans. "About what I said earlier—have you hired anyone yet?"

"Not yet." The slightest of smiles once again teased the corner of Emily's mouth. "I haven't changed my mind about what needs to be done."

Not really feeling it, he matched her smile. "I didn't figure you had." Convictions took sides in his head, but it wasn't really a contest. "The thing is"—he kept his sigh as silent as he could—"I have."

⬥

Emily woke on Saturday morning with a sneeze that ricocheted off the high ceiling of the dining room. Not surprising, since she'd slept ten inches off a floor with cracks wide enough to house generations of dust mites. She stretched her neck and shoulders, working from top to bottom to loosen the kinks from eight hours of driving and another eight on an air mattress. Her physical therapist had told her to stop and walk around every two hours on the trip. Now she wished she'd taken his advice.

Rolling not-so-gracefully onto her yoga mat, she arched her back and rocked her pelvis, feeling every one of the shadowy lines that still showed on X-rays.

Her stomach protested her supper of caramel rice cakes and stale peanuts. She needed to find a restaurant and then a grocery store. She dipped her head toward the floor, arms parallel to her body, held the position, breathing slow and deep, then slid her arms forward in an extended puppy pose. Two breaths into the stretch, her phone rang. She sat up, staring at an inhabited cobweb on the crown molding in the corner as she reached behind her back for her phone. "Hello."

"Hi, honey."

"Hi, Mom."

"Hey, Em." Her father's "happy voice" shot across Lake Michigan as if he were in the same room. "You're on speaker phone. How was your trip?"

"Great." She tailored her tone to harmonize with her parents' hopes. "Perfect weather."

"And you're not too stiff from the drive?"

"Nope." Depending on how one defined *too*.

"Did you stay at the house or get a hotel room?"

"I slept on the floor at the house. They left it nice and clean." She narrowed her eyes at her eight-legged roomie. "I slept great." That, surprisingly, was true.

The questions continued through the cobra pose and the bridge. Her mother giggled. "You're exercising, aren't you?"

"Yeah. Sorry. Multitasking again."

"The trip didn't affect your energy level any."

The trip sapped me, Dad. I'm stretching so I can walk to the bathroom. She'd lived with her parents since rehab ended, but she'd hidden her morning routine, along with her private pharmacy and her tears, behind closed doors. "Yup. Feeling great." Another week under their roof would have driven her back to the dock and a handful of pills. Long-distance faking was far easier.

"E-mail pictures of the remodeling. Mom's going to start a scrapbook for you."

"That'll be nice."

"Sooo . . ." Her mother's voice rose to a squeal. "What did you think of Susan's news?"

"What news?"

"She didn't call you?"

"No."

Silence. And then her father cleared his throat. "You knew she was having a sonogram yesterday, didn't you?"

Emily closed her eyes. "No."

"It's a boy."

Lowering her head, she waited out the vertigo. "That's wonderful."

Her mother giggled. "We'll do a video chat when she's here on Friday. She can show you the pictures."

Emily squeezed the phone. "I don't think I'll have Internet by then." *Or ever.* "Small town, you know."

"Well, then, we'll just talk to you on speaker phone. It'll be just like you're here with us. Almost."

"Okay"—*I won't answer, but*—"call Friday."

"Love you."

"Love you, too."

With the weight of half truths adding guilt to her stiffness, she shuffled to the bathroom and flipped the switch. A lightbulb in the fixture above the de-silvering mirror burned out with a *pop*, leaving a single clear globe still working. It didn't really matter. Her makeup was packed away in a plastic bin in the van and would likely stay in the cellar ensconced in Rubbermaid the whole time she was here. By the time she'd flipped her way across the country to a time and a place where she might actually care what she looked like, every tube and bottle would be past its expiration date. Some of it should have been stamped *RIP* long before she'd finished rehab.

The bathroom didn't have a vanity. No place to set mascara and blush even if she'd wanted to. She reached for the toothpaste and knocked it onto the floor. Emily sighed. There had been a time she'd made a career out of the simple move this required. Bend, scoop up a child, wipe a nose, kiss a boo-boo, bend back down. Effortlessly.

Focus on the here and now. She had a cliché for every situation and, step by painful step, the trite phrases were getting her through, moving her beyond. Life might never again shine like it once had, but a dim light glowed at the end of her tunnel, which, in her case, ended just short of the Pacific. The closer she got to San Francisco Bay and the farther she got from the people who wanted to wrap her in cotton batting like a china doll who might fall and break again, the brighter the light became.

"Don't go." Her mother's voice whispered in the echoey room, blurring her view of the present. *"You're surrounded by people who love you."* The air compressed around her. *"We just want to help, Em."*

A year and a half and they hadn't yet realized she wasn't fixable.

Sliding the toothpaste tube to the middle of the floor with the tip of her cane, she eased onto one knee and picked it up. *Stay present in the present. Describe your surroundings.* Dim light. . .white tiles. . . octagon shaped. . .dark blue grout. . .tiles around the toilet cracked. . . mirror above sink cracked. . .plaster cracked. . .

Like lines on an X-ray.

⁂

Halfway to the van she noticed the male cardinal perched on the driver's side mirror. His call to his mate reminded Emily of her father's Sunday morning voice.

"She's a woman. Cut her some slack. You got all the natural beauty—she has to work at it." She pictured her mother running barefoot out the door to church, carrying shoes and earrings, a piece of toast in her mouth. *I'm coming, Bob.*

Karen and Bob. She'd name her little red neighbors after her parents.

Squinting against the morning sun, Emily stood still. A hundred feet behind her, the Fox River whooshed under the bridge. Water trickled in the ditch along the road. A soft breeze teased the straps on her bike rack as if beckoning her to free her Trek from its restraints. The cardinal tweeted. "You think I should go for it, don't you, Bob?"

Emily glared at the bike. Her therapist had said he didn't think she was quite ready. But that was a week ago. After all the hours she'd logged on a stationary bike in therapy, how different could this possibly be? She reached in the van for her GPS and hooked it to the handlebars as it searched for a restaurant. Looping the handles of her purse over her shoulders like a backpack, she shoved her cane crosswise beneath it and freed the bike.

"Hi." The small, disembodied voice startled her.

"Hello?"

"Hi." This time it was a little louder, but she couldn't tell where it was coming from.

"Where are you?"

"Up here."

Emily walked around the front of the van and stared at the trees that ran between her house and the bridge. A bright green shoe wiggled about five feet off the ground. Like the picture-search pages her preschoolers loved, the rest of Michael blended with the tree. "What are you doing up there?"

"Getting a frog. Wanna see?"

"Sure." She pulled out her cane and made her way across the bumpy lawn. "You're camouflaged."

"Like a tree frog?"

"Yep. All I can see is one of your Crocs." She ducked under a low branch. The bark was shiny and slightly pinkish. Growing up in Michigan, she'd spent half her childhood playing in apple trees. Would this one bear fruit? "There you are. You're a really good hider."

"Wanna hold him?" Michael sat on a branch about a foot above her head. She stood eye-to-eye with a Sponge Bob Band-Aid.

She held cupped hands up to him. "Sure."

Michael opened his hands slowly into hers. The soft little body squirmed.

"Are you going to keep him?"

"For as long as Mom says. She doesn't like animals." His eyes widened. "Could I keep him at your house?"

Something warm and wet dripped through her fingers. "Just for a day, okay? He won't live very long if he's not free."

"Okay. Just for a day." Michael reached out for the frog. "His name is Squiggles."

"He's kind of wet."

"Frogs do that." Small warm hands closed over hers.

Emily swallowed hard. "Are you getting down now?"

"Um. I can't. Can you get me down?"

"Sure." The word scraped her throat. She was no longer under lifting restrictions, but her emotions weren't knitting in sync with her bones. She took the kind of breath that empowered weight lifters. Michael and Squiggles slid into her waiting arms.

"Do you have a box or a jar or something we can put holes in?" Large brown eyes stared up at her.

"I think I have just the thing. A can I found in the cellar. Actually, there's already a frog in it."

So maybe there were a few differences between spinning in therapy and the real thing. One, she had to get on, and two, she had to get off. She eased the kickstand back then tried to figure out her next move. After a moment, she tipped it toward her and lifted her leg over the crossbar then righted it. With a deep breath for courage, she stepped on one pedal, lifted her other foot off the ground, and began pedaling. "Whoo-hoo!" She turned onto the highway with a freedom she hadn't experienced in well over a year.

Her GPS led her to a corner restaurant in Waterford. Miraculously, she dismounted without making a total fool of herself. Walking into the restaurant was another story. She had a love/hate relationship with the piece of curved metal in her right hand. At the moment, sidling to the door like a born-on-a-horse cowpoke, she was grateful for it.

A whiteboard just inside the restaurant advertised down-home specials. A potted aloe plant decorated the juice dispenser behind the cash register. Baskets filled with thick-sliced bread in plastic wrap lined the backsplash in the waitress station. It had the feel of all small-town restaurants—the kind of place where people walked in and said, "I'll have the usual."

The thought had no sooner materialized than a waitress called across the room to a man in bib overalls sitting in a booth, gnarled hands folded on the table. "Belgian waffles, Tom?"

The man nodded. "Of course."

Emily followed the hostess past the counter to a table beside a floor-to-ceiling mural. Two pillars flanked a fountain and a blue lake shimmered in the background.

The left-hand page of the menu tempted Mexican specials like *3 Tacos De Chorizo Con Huevos*. Would she someday wake up hungry for chorizo sausage first thing in the morning? Would she someday wake up hungry?

Her waitress, in black slacks, white blouse, and black apron, was the one who'd called across the room to the guy in overalls. "Morning." She flashed an enormous grin. Highlighted waves tumbled across her forehead as she poured coffee. "Ready to order?"

"I'd like the yogurt parfait. And do you happen to have a phone book?"

"No prob."

The book was in her hands in seconds. As she searched the yellow pages for resale shops, it fell open to REMODELING. On a half-page ad for Braden Improvements, the owner's picture took up most of the space. Emily raised an eyebrow. *Smart move.* Even in black-on-yellow, the man was startlingly handsome.

Remodeling, additions, sunrooms, basements. The man did it all, albeit reluctantly. Their talk in the attic had ended with him offering to make the attic habitable for her while they discussed possibilities. Gazing at the yellow face, she questioned her motives for giving him a second chance. How much did she owe him for rescuing her from the tower? And did gratitude really have anything to do with it?

"Can I help you find something?" The waitress filled a coffee mug. Dangling the pot from her fingers, she folded her arms across her waist. "I've lived in the area for thirty-one years. There, I just admitted my age."

"I'm looking for a secondhand store that sells furniture."

"There are a couple in Burlington. Can I ask what you're looking for? If you can wait a week or so, we'll be getting stuff together for an estate sale. Some antiques, some just old, but all quality."

"I'm not in a hurry and I don't need modern. I don't even need quality. I just bought an old house in Rochester. I need a table, a couple of lamps, and a window air conditioner. I'll be living there during the remodeling and then trying to sell it. I just need enough creature comforts to get by for a few months."

"Technically I live in Rochester, too, but we're out in the country. Hey." The woman tapped a fingertip on Jake Braden's eye. "Are you the one who bought the Ostermann place?"

Speechless, Emily nodded.

"My cousin Sherry lives across the street from you. Have you met Sherry and Rod yet?"

Emily shook her head as her imagination pushed PLAY on a Disney tune. *It's a small world after all.* . . . "I met two little boys. Are they—"

"Russell and Michael. Aren't they adorable?" She set the coffeepot down and pulled out a chair. "I'm Tina Palin-as-in-Sarah.

No relation. I watch the boys on my days off sometimes, so we'll probably run into each other." She tapped again, this time on Jake Braden's lips. "Did you hire Jake? I heard he was bidding on it."

"Well, I. . ." *It's a small, small world. . . .* The music warped like the background song for a scary carnival ride.

"He does amazing work. He did our family room. We couldn't find a fireplace mantel to match our woodwork, so he made one. Hand-carved. It's beautiful." She waved at two middle-aged women. "Coffee's on its way, girls." She tapped her finger on Jake's face. "I'll have to stop by and see your progress."

"Um. . ." Emily aligned the salt shaker with the pepper. "Thank you."

"Tell you what. I'll give you first dibs on the estate sale. Call me next week and tell me when you can stop over." Tina scribbled her name and number on a napkin, laughing as she did. "People think waitresses do this all the time, but I only wrote my number on a napkin once before—and I married the guy."

"Very romantic. How long have you been married?" *And why am I asking?*

"Six years next week. We have two kids and. . ." She dipped her head and looked around. "Don't tell anyone, but number three's on the way."

Emily swallowed hard. "Congratulations." She took a long, slow slurp of coffee.

"I don't want my boss treating me special or worrying that I'm going to quit. I worked up to my ninth month with the other two." Her chair scraped on the wood floor as she stood. "Anyways, give me a call and come on over, and I'll stop by your place when I'm in the neighborhood. I'll check in on your progress"—she patted her belly discreetly behind the coffeepot—"and you can check on mine."

Wrapping both hands around her cup, Emily closed her eyes. She'd left Traverse City because her sister had finally gotten pregnant.

And Emily couldn't figure out how to be happy for her.

CHAPTER 4

Adam Sutton rummaged in the back of a bathroom drawer that should have been cleaned out months ago. There had to be something in here that could camouflage the lump on his cheek.

When he found a tube labeled "concealer," he had to work up the guts to pull the cap off. Just opening the drawer made the whole room smell like Mom.

He was reading a book on the brain and how memory works. *The olfactory bulb is part of the brain's limbic system. . .closely associated with memory and feeling. . .sometimes referred to as the "emotional brain."* He looked up at the clock that used to make bird sounds every hour and the birdhouse border surrounding the room. He'd laughed at Mom for stenciling it. "Looks like little outhouses," he'd told her. The candle on the back of the toilet was covered with dust. Black crumbles of wick speckled the wax. It hadn't been lit in almost a year. He picked it up and held it to his nose. Green apple. *Smell has the power to call up memories and powerful responses almost instantaneously.*

As he pulled the cap off, he breathed through his mouth. *The olfactory bulb has intimate access to the amygdala, which processes emotion.* Science had theories and rules to explain just about everything.

But sadness didn't follow rules.

Running the tip of his finger over the rounded top of the tan concealer, he tried not to think that the last skin it had touched was his mother's. Dabbing it under his eye, he winced at the sting, and at the kind of hurt that didn't show up swollen and purple.

In movies, people talked about being afraid that the face of the person they loved wouldn't stay in their memory. Maybe that would happen to him someday, but there wasn't a night he didn't see his mother's smile—so clear that at times he actually reached out to hug her as he pulled up his own covers and tucked himself in bed.

He replaced the cap, closed the drawer and his eyes.

New smells filtered under the bathroom door. Eggs, toast, bacon.

He put his hand on the doorknob. *Smells would not trigger memories, however, if it weren't for conditioned responses.* He walked out to the kitchen, where a miniature replica of his mother stood in front of the stove, one hand on her hip, the other stirring eggs in a pan. "Morning." He took four pieces of toast out of the toaster and began buttering.

"Good morning." Lexi waved a spatula at him. "Don't do that," she whispered. "I'll get to it."

Lexi was always protecting him. Adam's mouth hadn't learned how to stay shut like hers. "If I get in trouble for butter—"

"Get out!" The floor vibrated as Ben slogged into the kitchen. "You got time on your hands? Get started on the lawn."

Adam's fingers coiled around the knife. Lexi warned him with a look. He turned away from her, stared at the chunk of butter sliding off the knife and onto the bread. He'd promised Mom he'd take care of his sister, and standing back and watching her cook every meal and wash every dish wasn't taking care of her. "I'll get out after I eat." He spread butter on the last piece of toast and reached into the cupboard for a plate.

Two heavy steps lumbered toward him. The floor groaned. The toast hit the floor. Adam's back hit the refrigerator.

He didn't care about the place on his arm that would match his cheek by the time he got to school.

He did care about the tears on Lexi's face.

crown ornament

One arm wrapped around a bundle of two-by-fours, Jake descended the rickety cellar stairs. The cool was a welcome relief from the heat of the attic.

Working around two other jobs, he'd managed to rewire and insulate Emily's third story in just over a week. Determined to convince her to put the wrecking ball away and stick her money into new fixtures and cabinets, he'd dedicated his few spare moments to drawing up plans.

Emily wanted to get involved, so he'd suggested she refinish the corner cupboard in the kitchen. The rest of the cabinets had been installed in the fifties or sixties. They had to go, but she'd grudgingly agreed to give this one original piece a second chance. She'd been on her knees, totally engrossed in sanding when he'd peeked in a moment ago. Whether or not she admitted it, she was enjoying the job.

The woman would learn to appreciate history if it killed him.

He dropped the boards and aimed his worklights at the shelves. He'd cut half a dozen braces when he heard halting steps behind him. Emily held out a glass of iced tea.

He took the glass. "Thank you. How's it coming?"

She shrugged. "It's coming."

Hands on hips, Jake studied her. Something about her tone sounded fakely bored. He waited.

The tiniest of smiles snuck across perfectly bowed lips. "I know what you're up to." One finger wagged at him. "You're hoping that cupboard and I have a bonding moment."

"And? Are you?"

She looked away. "I will admit it has potential."

"That's always the first step in a relationship." Jake took a deep draught of tea and watched as the comment sank in and her right eyebrow disappeared behind a lock of hair. "Good tea." He set the glass on the ledge under the window.

"Anything I can do to help down here?"

"Sure. An extra set of"—*pale, smooth*—"hands would be a help. Grab that board."

With an almost masked grimace, she picked it up and handed it to him.

Jake considered pretending he hadn't noticed, but he wasn't all that good at pretending. "Should you be doing that? If it hurts, don't—"

"I'm just stiff from being in one position too long. I loosen up if I move." She looked away. "I was in a skiing accident a year and a half ago. I'm basically recovered, just not as graceful as I once was."

Now what was a guy supposed to say to that? He mimicked her eyebrow arch. "You used to be graceful?"

Her eyes glittered, lit by an actual smile. "I used to glide across the dance floor. Graceful as a swan." Her arms lifted straight out, moving fluidly like soft waves.

Jake swallowed hard. What she'd intended as a goofy shtick mesmerized him. He managed a laugh. And managed not to tell her she was beautiful.

She put her hands on her hips. Every time she did that he had the impression she hadn't always been the timid woman she appeared to be now. Her head tilted, giving him a new angle from which to appraise her chin. He'd always thought "heart-shaped" was a strange way to describe a face. Until now.

"I have a confession." She rested a fingertip on her chin. As if he needed it pointed out. "A concession."

He couldn't help the grin. "You're keeping the dining room wall."

"Not a chance. But—I want to keep the old windows. The glass, anyway. Is that possible—to replace the frames but keep the old glass?"

"Of course." His grin morphed to a smirk.

"Don't go getting your hopes up. I'm not caving. I'm refining my vision."

"Whatever you want to call it."

"You've got to be the only remodeler in the country who has to be begged to do more extensive work. My vision makes you money."

He turned toward the shelf. "Oh, I'll make money off you. Don't you worry about that." He picked up a hammer. "I started working on some ideas last night."

"I'm hearing the *cha-ching* already."

"That's the sound of quality you're hearing. You get what you pay for. If you want a decent return on your investment, you won't cut corners." *And you won't desecrate a historic landmark.* "If you want cheap and fast..."

Her gaze hardened.

"Any problem with securing this to the wall?" He gestured toward the peeling bead board that showed between the boards.

"No. Whatever it takes. I've got all my earthly possessions in Rubbermaid bins."

He rapped his fist against the wood. "It looks stur—" The entire wall swung inward a good inch, banging at the bottom. "What in the. . .?" He looked up. The top edge of the wood hid behind a ceiling beam. "Do you know what's behind this?"

She shook her head. As if needing to test the wall's stability herself, she pushed the panel. Again, it banged at the bottom.

Jake stepped back. The shelves butted up to the adjacent wall on the left, but not on the right.

"Why don't you stand back a bit? I'll try moving this." He grabbed hold of the freestanding shelving unit. It swayed side-to-side, but he couldn't budge it away from the wall.

Emily stepped in front of him and placed her hands below his. Her ponytail tickled his Adam's apple. She smelled like the lemon slices floating in the glass on the ledge. "One. . .two. . .*three.*"

It didn't move. They both stepped away. Jake looked again at the way the top of the wall was hidden from view. With one finger on his lips, he tapped out a nameless tune and then suddenly stopped. He took a closer look at the bead board. His breath caught. "There are two parts." He pointed to the right side of the wall. "See if you can slide it toward me."

"The wall?"

"Yes."

Emily slid her fingers between wood and rock, pulled, and gasped. The entire thing slid, clanging into the far wall. "It's a door!"

Cool, stale air wafted through the opening. "What do you see?"

"Nothing."

Jake bent down and dug in his toolbox for a flashlight. He flicked it on and stepped behind her, lighting up the darkness.

"It's a room."

Tamping down his curiosity, he handed the flashlight to Emily. The light arced across rock walls. He tried to peer around her.

"Looks like an old cistern." She slipped through the opening. "But there are shelves." Her voice echoed.

Turning sideways, Jake squeezed through the opening and stared at the shadowy emptiness. Low, two-foot-wide boards braced with thick posts lined three walls.

Emily rubbed her bare arms. "It must be ten degrees colder in here. A root cellar maybe."

He didn't answer. The width of the bottom shelves reminded him of something altogether different—berths in the hold of an ancient ship.

The flashlight beam bounced from wall to ceiling and stopped at a square door in the wood above their heads. "Where does that lead? Wouldn't it open under the porch?"

"It would now. Maybe the porch wasn't there when the door was put in."

Emily ran the beam across high shelves and a row of black hooks. "It looks like a coatroom like you see in old schoolhouses." She lowered herself to a bench and scanned the room for a long moment then turned her eyes to him. "This feels significant. I can't explain it. I guess that sounds crazy. . . ." Her voice trailed to a whisper. She flattened her hand against a wall.

She didn't sound crazy at all. He didn't believe in ghosts, but the space almost vibrated with a sensation of—Emily had nailed it—*significance*. He reached up and touched the cold roughness of an iron hook. "I think you're right."

The flashlight painted the walls in systematic strokes. Floor to ceiling, ceiling to floor. When the beam reached the northwest corner, it stopped. The halo of light spilled onto the bench. Emily leaned forward then rose and stepped closer. The light concentrated into a plate-sized disk. She knelt. "Come here," she whispered.

Jake crouched behind her. Carved into the bench was a picture he'd seen before—four five-petal flowers with rounded petals and two concentric circles in the center of each, connected by stems with three leaves. Crude block characters curved around one side of the wreath, spelling out "MARIAH 1852."

His long, low whistle split the shadows, eclipsing Emily's gasp. "What do you know about the Underground Railroad, Miss Foster?"

September 2, 1852

Water lilies brushed the sides of the canoe with a soft whisper. Quiet, yet more noise than Liam would have liked. The night was still. A chill hung over the moonlit river in clouds of low fog, engulfing him in thick gray mist one moment then dropping like a sheet falling from a clothesline the next. Paddling just enough to steer clear of the bank, he combed the river's edge with seasoned eyes. His newly rifled musket rested on his thigh. A dozen minié balls rattled in his pocket like a handful of lead acorns. But the weapon that fit his hands as if he'd been born with two fingers attached to the string nestled beside him like a trusty hound. Balancing his paddle across his knees, he reached over his shoulder and stroked the turkey fletching of an arrow pulled out, ready and waiting, from the others in his quiver. *Soon.* A half mile ahead, a clearing created a gathering place. As the deer nibbled on the lily pads and stems, he would find the young buck that had eluded him for three nights.

He shifted his cramped legs, inadvertently grazing the traps with his boot. Chains rattled. Liam gritted his teeth. Ten more yards and he'd pass Hannah's porch. No one should have to travel at night in this dampness that seeped through buckskin like it was parchment.

With a deep breath for courage, he let his gaze travel the riverbank to the porch. Two rugs hung over the railing. His heart missed two beats. His stomach felt as though he'd swallowed the bullets in his breast pocket.

He would be back tomorrow night.

CHAPTER 5

Emily still sat on the low, scarred bench, rubbing her arms for warmth. Leaning back against the rock wall, she tried to separate logical thought from the fanciful musings of the man who had just left.

She regretted the "significance" remark. Though the feeling hadn't left, it made her sound melodramatic. And it had fed Jake's imagination. Like the ink blots framed as modern art on the walls in Vanessa's office, this room could be whatever a person wanted it to be. She, a preschool teacher in her former life, saw a coatroom filled with giggling children and muddy boots. Jake Braden, the history buff, saw it as a secret hideaway for runaway slaves. He'd rattled on and on about abolitionists known to live in Rochester, and documented letters proving the village had been a temporary sanctuary for fugitives from the South. But they'd searched every inch of the room before he left and it gave no clues of its previous life other than the flower and a woman's name.

Had Nana Grace known about this room? Emily pictured the woman who'd always reminded her of a giant pillow cinched in the middle. Shoulders wide for a woman, a puffy chest that could smother an unsuspecting child, and she was even wider at the bottom. Grace Ostermann's generous hourglass figure could never have squeezed into this space.

Jake seemed to think that none of the previous owners knew anything about it, or they'd kept its stories secret. More than likely, the room's origin and history was simply nothing worth sharing. A root cellar or storeroom dating back to the 1840s was interesting, but not something people would pay to see.

Pay to see. The thought lodged in her brain like a tree damming a river. *He wouldn't. . .* Why hadn't she told Jake not to tell anyone about this? Within hours, the place could be swarming with curious neighbors and little old ladies from the Historical Society. She suddenly saw Jake, megaphone in hand, pulling people in from the street like a sideshow barker. The house would never get finished. Or started.

Her phone stuck in her pocket. She stood, slid it out, and dropped it. With a groan, she bent, retrieved it, and stilled her hand enough to punch in his number.

"Find something?" He didn't bother with hello.

"No." *Relax. Be casual.* She exhaled melodrama and tried not to think of him as the sideshow barker who could ruin her plans. "I was just thinking. . .it probably goes without being said, but I don't want anyone to know about this just yet. Okay?"

The quick assurance she'd hoped for didn't come. Silence seeped from the phone and filled the darkness. "Jake?"

"Um. . .yeah. . .well, I only told two people. My niece and nephew. They're just kids. I'll tell them to keep it to themselves. They had an early release day, and I just picked them up at school. We're on our way to your place. They've studied the Underground Railroad, and I promised I'd show them the room. They're really excited about. . ."

Just kids? If he'd known her background, he wouldn't have used that as a defense. "Mr. Braden"—the formal address gave her a smidgeon of power—"we don't know anything for sure."

He laughed. "*I'm* sure."

"But you won't tell anyone else, will you?"

A protracted pause followed. "You are going to check this out, right? Do some research? We have to find out who Mariah is. Maybe you're right, maybe she's just a kid who used to live there, but we have to look at records and. . ."

We? "Of course." If she didn't debunk the idea, sooner or later it would bubble out of him.

"So it's okay to bring the kids over?"

Emily sighed and closed her eyes. "Sure. Bring them over."

"We're having lunch at McDonald's. Can I bring you something?"

"No. Thank you."

"Okay. Be there in about an hour."

She closed her phone and rested her hand on the bench. On top of the flower.

Mariah, who are you? Eyes still closed, she traced the name with her fingertip and tried to envision the person who'd carved it. A young girl, sent to dig carrots and potatoes from a barrel of sand, or to leave leftovers here to stay cold? Bored with her chores, she pulls a paring knife from her apron pocket. Or a runaway slave, exhausted, scared, running for her life. Huddled under a ragged blanket, waiting out the night with a shivering child in her arms. Carving a circle of flowers and her name—or her little girl's—busying her hands to stay awake on her watch, a precious piece of candle disappearing as she worked.

A dog barked, muffled and distant, but jarring in the silence. Emily's eyes opened.

The old house was getting crowded. The fluffy white dog, the boy in the striped shirt, and now the shivering woman dressed in tatters. Like an illustration in one of her favorite children's books, would she lead a parade of imaginary friends wherever she went?

With a soft groan that reverberated off the stone walls, she stood and rubbed her back. When her legs were ready to move, she slipped through the opening, nodded toward the woman in the corner, and banged the door closed.

❧

Stopping at the top of the cellar stairs, Emily surveyed the kitchen. Her watch said lunchtime. A loaf of bread and two apples sat on the counter. The fridge held a bottle of iced tea and a package of cheese. Her hand rested just above the waist of her jeans. She felt the rumble, but the pangs didn't translate into a desire for food. Grabbing her cane from the door handle, she walked over to the sink and stared out the window as she washed an apple.

Cardinal Bob landed on the roof of the shed and called to his mate. Emily shook her head. "Give it a rest. Maybe if you act like you're not interested, she'll follow you."

Like that works. That was the tactic she'd been employing when she went to Colorado seventeen months ago. Show him you don't care, you can do this alone. After a week of her silence, he'd called. To tell her she could do it alone.

Her cardinal's song floated through the screen. She kicked off her sandals and joined him outside, leaning against the railing and listening to the river. Peeling paint bit into her forearms. The whole porch needed to be sanded and repainted. Had she bought a money pit? How much could she do herself? And would she know when to say when? She padded across the boards, willing them smooth and glistening white without the effort it would take.

The inside of her forearm prickled. A thick chunk of paint pressed into her flesh. Hunter green, her least favorite color in all the world. She pried it off. It left an imprint. A pink island—Cuba or Jamaica—in a sea of white. Scraping her fingernail across the green, she found burgundy and wondered if the porch was as old as the rest of the house.

It couldn't be. The trapdoor would have been useless. Inaccessible. Unless. . . With an agility she didn't usually possess, she scrambled down the steps. White-painted lattice covered the space between the ground and the floor of the porch. In rough condition, it would have to be removed eventually. Easing to her knees, she stuck her fingers through the holes and yanked on the crisscrossed wood strips. A yard-long panel gave way and she tossed it aside. Flattening onto the grass, she pulled Jake's flashlight out of her pocket. Contorted leaves and hickory nuts littered the dirt. There was no sign of the trapdoor, and the space wasn't deep enough for her to squeeze into.

Flicking off the light, she sat on the grass and stared at the square spindles just above her eye level. Functional, not decorative, they carried on the practical theme of the house. Unknowingly constructed over the entrance to a secret, forgotten room. *Or. . .*

Grasping spindles with both hands, she pulled herself up and walked back up the steps. A large black mat, about six feet long, covered the middle of the porch in front of the back door. Emily kicked up the corner, rolled it back with the end of her cane, and sucked in a sudden breath. A paint-filled line ran across a dozen boards. Whirling around, she spotted an identical cut. Ignoring pain, she dropped to her knees. Slipping her fingers under the board at the end of the cut, she lifted. The outlined square wiggled. Years of paint wrinkled in the cracks. With every ounce of strength, she pulled again. A popping, tearing sound accompanied two small rips. She worked her way to a stand and nearly ran into the kitchen for the knife that had sliced lemons just hours ago.

The blade cut through the stretchy, dried paint like butter. Her palms grew damp against the handle. An irrational thought seemed to ascend from the space beneath the newly freed door. *Did you see the ghost yet?* She thought of the imaginary woman, cradling her child in the room below. With a shake of her head, Emily dropped the knife and slid her fingers through a crack. Gripping the end board and holding her breath, she pulled. Hidden hinges resisted, wailing against her effort. Inch by inch, the unwilling mouth opened until, at last, the hinge loosened and the door banged against the house.

But the moment was anticlimactic. Moldy leaves, a plastic straw, and a bottle cap were the archaeological treasures stirred up by the tip of her cane. No handle to a trapdoor, no footprints turned to stone. She needed the shovel from the shed.

Preparing to hoist unladylike to her feet, she drew one knee to her chest. The fingers of her right hand slid over a plank bordering the square hole. Instead of wrapping around the board, her fingers arched around something cylindrical. Lowering her knee, she leaned into the opening.

A short pipe, about a foot long, hung by two hooks. Both ends were sealed. Her hand closed around the pipe. It was rusted to the hooks. She tried dislodging it then stopped, considering for a moment that, whatever it was, she shouldn't be disturbing it without gloves or without permission. As if she were trespassing. As if the house and its contents belonged to someone else. But the very fact that the pipe seemed to serve no purpose made taking a closer look seem vital.

Shaking off the eeriness, she twisted the pipe. Rust flakes

crumbled onto her wrist and the hooks released their hold. She sat back and raised the pipe in both hands. Black and rust-pocked and heavier than it appeared. On one end, a tab of metal about half an inch long protruded from the end. She tried to turn it, tapped it against the porch floor, and then tried again. The disk sealing the pipe rotated then pulled free. She scrambled to her feet and took two long strides to the railing. Sunlight landed on yellowed paper.

Breath held, she withdrew the scrolled papers. Two words, barely legible in faded brown script, caught her eye.

Perhaps tomorrow.

CHAPTER 6

Emily stood in her attic hideaway, the three letters she'd found in the pipe nesting together on her open hand like a brittle leaf. She read the top one.

November 3, 1852

> *If you are reading this, you have come back for me. I do not deserve it, for it is my fault you had to run. If only I could do things over again, I would never have lied. I would have done just as you said. If you were here, I would be on my knees begging for forgiveness. Please wait here for me. You will be safe. They must believe Papa acted without my knowledge for even those I know to be unsympathetic show concern that I have been left alone. I cannot leave until I know what will become of him. No one tells me anything. I am leaving before dawn to talk to Jonathan. I am terrified of making the trip to Racine alone but fear is becoming my daily companion. Fear for you consumes me day and night though I try to commit it to the Lord. The first verse of the 46th Psalm is my constant prayer for you. "God is our refuge and strength, a very present help in trouble. Therefore will not we fear." May God shelter you beneath His wings until you are in my arms. Soon, I pray. Perhaps tomorrow.*

Jake was right about the room.

As the knowledge took root and coursed along nerve pathways with tingling speed, a door opened below her. Muted voices traversed the stairs. Handling the letters as if they would dissolve at her touch, she wrapped them in tissue paper and laid them in a plastic box on top of her T-shirts, eased the cover on, and latched it.

"Emily?"

Her name, echoing through the house in a man's voice, did nothing to steady her legs as she closed the door behind her like a woman with nothing to hide.

"I'll be down in a minute!" He'd assume her breathlessness came from exertion. Not telling him felt deceptive. But she needed to read all three letters before deciding whether or not to divulge her secret.

By the time she reached the bottom step, she'd slowed the adrenaline from a zinging rush to a steady drip. "Hi."

"Are you okay?" Jake's eyebrows converged. "You look all flushed."

"Just. . .the stairs." Sometimes playing the handicap card came in handy. "Hi, Lexi. Nice to see you again."

Jake nodded unconvincingly and introduced her to his nephew. "Adam's the genius in the family."

"Hey!" Lexi's lip curled. "Our IQs are identical."

"But your grades aren't." Jake's smirk didn't falter with the jab to his arm. He grinned at Emily. "They've been in a twins study since birth. Makes for interesting competition."

Emily extended her hand to the boy with wavy hair that apparently had never made friends with a brush. A greenish shadow below one eye made her wonder if he was active in sports, or a troublemaker. She glanced down at feet that seemed out of proportion to the rest of him. The bruise could have come from the junior high curse of a gangly, uncooperative body. "Glad to meet you, Adam. I haven't met too many geniuses." She winked at Lexi. "But now I know two."

"Can we see the room?" Large hazel eyes inspected the parlor, as if searching for the hidden door. Adam-the-genius clearly wasn't much for small talk.

Jake shrugged an apology, and Emily answered with a nod. "Right this way." She pointed toward the kitchen.

Adam scrambled down the steps with his sister at his heels.

Emily followed. The twins stood in the middle of the cellar, vibrating like two idling engines. "Where's the secret door?" Adam shuffled from one oversized foot to the other.

"Is that the way a trained archaeologist would enter a site?" Jake tortured his nephew with a patronizing smile then turned to Emily. "I didn't give them a lot of details."

"Okay. Survey the scene." Adam turned in a slow circle. "Look for indications of something out of the ordinary." Bending over, he retrieved a flashlight from a cargo pocket above his knee and outlined the ceiling with the beam.

"There!" Lexi pointed to one of the rock walls. "I bet those rocks aren't real."

Adam's forehead wrinkled. "Noooo." Emily had seen identical perplexity on his uncle's face. "That's. . .not. . .it." With deliberate strides, he closed in on the opposite corner. "This paneling is strange."

Leaning closer to Emily, Jake hid his mouth behind his hand. "Bingo," he whispered.

"Smart kid." Emily moved away from the scent of musk and fresh-cut wood. "What are you thinking, Adam?"

The boy laid his hand on the wood. It moved. Adam gasped. He looked over his shoulder, eyes wide with delight. "This is it!"

Emily nodded. "Open it."

The wall slid to the side, and Adam stepped back and let Lexi walk in first. Emily observed the gesture with an almost physical reaction. "That's sweet."

"They compete, but they take care of each other." Jake stood so close, his words ruffled her hair.

"Wow." Lexi's voice was tight with excitement.

"Wow," Adam echoed. "This is like the coolest thing I've ever seen." Stroking an iron hook the way Jake had, Adam dropped his professor voice and gushed like an awestruck twelve-year-old.

Lexi sat on a bench and pressed both hands to her sternum. "We read about a sixteen-year-old girl that somebody hid around here." Gaze still roaming the room, she pulled an asthma inhaler out of her back pocket.

Neither Adam nor Jake appeared to notice. Emily sat beside her. "Does the dampness in here bother you?"

"No. It's nothing." She took a second puff on the inhaler.

"Caroline Quarlls." Adam's gaze was fixed on the door in the ceiling. "She was the first passenger on the Underground Railroad in Wisconsin."

Lexi nodded, holding her breath. "Yeah." Her exhale rode on the word. "What if she was here, right where I'm sitting?"

"She wasn't in Rochester."

"We can't jump to conclusions, guys." Jake sat down opposite Lexi. "Miss Foster isn't convinced we're on the right track."

If you only knew. The words on the yellowed pages shouted from three stories above. Jake Braden would need to take an oath—on penalty of no contract—that he wasn't a sideshow barker in disguise before she'd tell him anything. She pointed to the door that had captured Adam's attention. "Want to see where that leads?"

"Yeah!"

"I found a trapdoor on the porch." Like a first-grader at show-and-tell, she couldn't disguise the pride in her voice.

Jake's eyebrow elevated. "You've been busy since I left."

You have no idea.

"Take a look at this." Jake pointed to the flower carved on the end of the bench.

The kids scrambled closer. A tiny gasp came from Adam. "That's like Grandma's quilt. The one she put over Mom's casket."

Jake nodded and looked up at Emily, his eyes faraway and glassy. "It's the same pattern as the quilt in the attic."

Adam peered over Lexi, whose face had paled. "The rose wreath is a symbol." His expression mirrored his uncle's. "It means someone died on the journey."

"The shovel would be faster." Lexi banged the broom handle on one side of the opening in the porch and then the other. Dust billowed out of the square hole.

"Be careful. Go slow." Adam chewed his thumbnail. "The wood might be rotten."

Jake stood back from the three people crowding around the

TOMORROW'S SUN

excavation site. He leaned on a post, took a picture with his phone, and tried not to appear as impatient as the kid gnawing his thumb to the bone. He studied the ceiling. Bead board, identical to the wood used for the sliding door below, painted pale blue. In the corners, dirty cobwebs dotted with shriveled egg sacks swayed in the warm breeze. He tried to imagine sitting in a rocking chair sipping lemonade on a swept-clean porch, acting natural while a runaway slave slept in the room below, waiting for cover of night.

Emily's doubts seemed to have vanished. There was no other logical explanation for the trapdoor. No one would place the entrance to a root cellar under a porch. But it wouldn't take much to turn an existing cistern into a secret hiding place.

"I see it." Adam stepped into the foot-deep hole. He brushed the remaining dirt from the door. "Give me the broom." With the care of a trained scientist, he brushed away debris then threw the broom onto the porch.

Lexi dropped to her knees. "Pull it up."

Adam looped two fingers into an iron "U" hook. One end of the square stone lifted then tipped. "Ouch! *Man!*" He stuck his finger in his mouth and looked up at Jake. "It's too stinkin' heavy." He stepped out, face pale but focused on the stone.

"Let me see that." Emily held out her hand.

Adam pulled his finger from his mouth and held it up. A right-angle tear in the skin quickly outlined in red. "It's nothin'. Jake, can you lift that?" A drop of blood splashed to the floorboards.

"I'll get something." The screen door whined as Emily opened it.

Wrapping his finger in the bottom of his shirt, Adam pressed his lips together and glared. "I'm fine!"

Jake stepped into the opening and hefted the stone. The underside was scraped and scarred. He flipped it out of the way.

Adam pulled his flashlight out of one of his numerous pockets. He'd just flicked it on when Emily returned with a washcloth and a Band-Aid. With a look of impatient resignation, Adam let her wash his wound.

Jake's gaze lingered on her fingers, on the almost artful way she tore open the bandage. "You're very skilled at that."

"I ran a preschool for three years. Before that I taught art at a

59

junior high." She aimed a smile at Adam. "We did wood carving and stained glass."

Adam's frustration seemed to morph into mere impatience at her touch. The contrast of Adam's rough, reddened skin against the ivory smoothness of hers transported Jake to a fantasy world where his life wasn't on hold. What would it feel like to—

"What's that?" Lexi pointed to something stuffed into one corner of the recess.

With slow, careful movements, Adam pulled it out with his left hand. A frayed strip of cloth, once blue or purple, now faded to a pinkish gray. Tiny, discolored flowers, just barely discernable, dotted the fabric. "Wow. This could have been part of a dress worn by a slave."

Lexi nodded. "Maybe it belonged to Mariah."

"Can I see that?" Emily slid her hand under the strip of cloth. "Wait here." She flew down the porch stairs faster than Jake had seen her move yet. The shed door whined on its hinges. She was back in seconds, carrying a wooden box. "I found this the other day. Look at the fabric on the back of this. I think it's the same." She held a crudely fashioned, glass-fronted shadow box.

"What's in it?" Lexi touched the glass. "A dog collar?"

Emily nodded. "Jake found a picture of a dog that used to..." Emily's voice faded. She angled the box toward the light. Her lips parted.

The same surge of emotion reflected on Emily's face coursed through Jake as he stared at the rounded metal—two half circles bolted together on one side, lying slightly parted on the other. Deep scratches marred the surface. Jake locked eyes with Emily.

Adam exhaled through pursed lips. "This wasn't made for a dog, was it?"

♕

The fragile pages trembled in Emily's hand. She rested the one she'd already read on the cover of her T-shirt bin and read the others.

November 17, 1852

Papa is free. Cousin Jonathan says he only intended to put the fear of the Lord in him. If he understood the fear of the

*Lord, he would know that is why we do this. If he truly knew
his cousin, he would know Papa will not stop. That is why I am
taking it upon myself to redirect our mission.*

*I know now you aren't coming back for me. I tell myself
that you left alone because you love me. It does not feel like love,
but as I sit by the window each night hoping against hope,
I sense God's hand in even this. If you were here Papa and I
would not embark on what we are about to do.*

*God alone knows what the future holds. Even if you read
this years from now, know that I will never stop loving you.*

November 21, 1852

*Tomorrow we leave. We must before it snows. I harbor
a secret hope that I have not shared with Papa. Is it possible
God is leading me to you instead of away from you? Has God
embarked us both on the same mission? My skin prickles with
anticipation at the thought. So, my love, I will open the door
one last time to search for word from you and to leave this final
message. Once we arrive, I will write weekly to the one person
I can trust. May God hold you in His everlasting arms until
the day you are safe in mine.*

Emily walked over to the church pew and stared up at the cross,
filled with a strange certainty she, too, was embarking on a new
mission.

👑

September 3, 1852

"He'll be fine. Just fine."

Hannah worried the waist of her fan-front dress as she scanned
the room that would soon be hers. On the wall to her right, freshly
painted shelves displayed her few prized possessions—a child's cup
and saucer Papa bought her in New York when he'd crossed the
ocean to scout out land in America, and the little toy stove with two
miniature pans her grandmother sent from England for her first

61

Christmas in their little one-room cabin in Wisconsin Territory. Ten years had passed, yet still she could remember the softness of the striped fabric wrapped around the tiny stove. She and Mama had cried and talked of Grandmother Yardley as they tore the cloth into strips to decorate the evergreen bough draping the mantel.

She walked to the window and flattened her hand against one of the panes. Mama had been so proud of her windows that opened and closed—Adams Glass, shipped from Pennsylvania.

Thoughts of Mama distracted her from worries of Liam only for a moment.

"There shall no evil befall thee. . .he shall give his angels charge over thee, to keep thee in all thy ways."

"They'll all be fine." It helped to say it aloud, even if the only one listening was a doll with a papier-mâché face.

It was only half past eight, still light out. Flies buzzed in and out of the window. A mosquito landed on her hand and she slapped it, leaving a trail of someone else's blood. The river gurgled in a lazy summer way. A perfect night for a walk along the riverbank, her hand tucked in the crook of Liam's arm, whispering of wedding plans.

An exasperated sigh ruffled the coppery tendrils tickling her face. Make-believe brought only emptiness. God knew what He was doing. There were more important things than dreaming of white lace and daisy bouquets.

Papa had told her to rest for a few hours, said he'd call up the stairs when it was time, and there was nothing more she could do for their guests. They were all asleep.

How could they?

"Musn't think." She stretched out on the folded quilt she'd laid on the floor. Truth be told, she'd come up here to be farther away from the sadness in the cellar. She knew she'd hear nothing down in the back parlor where she slept for now. They'd harbored seven people since spring and never had she heard a sound, even from the little ones. A child too afraid to cry was an unbearable thought.

She forced her top lids to meet her bottom. Her fingers still worried the gray muslin of her dress. If only she could catch the thoughts that flitted through her mind and seal them tight like fireflies in a canning jar. Her arm grazed Tildy. She picked up the doll by one wooden arm. Tildy had been Mama's doll when she was little. Hannah always fancied Tildy looked like Mama with her black hair, round face, and rosy cheeks. Her body was soft leather and her wood shaving stuffings made her huggable. She still wore the dark green calico dress Mama had stitched for Hannah's tenth birthday.

A tear slid to her tatting-edged pillowcase. She sat up. Eighteen was far too old for hugging dolls.

But just the right age for reading love letters.

The board at the back of her closet lifted with a soft *whoosh*. She'd promised Liam she'd destroy them. Tear them to bits and toss them in the river. Only once had she followed through. Watching his words dissolve and float away was intolerable. Someday, as they sat by the fire and reminisced on the early days of their love, she would pull them out and read them and Liam would be glad she'd saved them.

No one would find them here.

And it was only a small deception.

CHAPTER 7

Sunday morning dawned with a tease of summer. Emily opened the dining room window on her way to the coffeepot. Through the trees, she glimpsed a black convertible sailing across the bridge, a woman with platinum hair behind the wheel.

A different time, a different place, and that could have been her. Two years ago this week she'd driven her VW Eos to Sault Ste. Marie, top down the whole way, to meet up with college roomies for a spa day. She looked down at short, bare nails and ran them through tangled morning hair. Eight inches of dishwater-blond roots kept record of her apathy—half an inch for each month of not caring what she looked like.

The girl with the standing appointment at Studio 1 hadn't survived the accident.

Maneuvering around boxed cupboards in the naked kitchen, she made her way to the coffeepot on the tarp-shrouded stove and filled one of the two mugs she'd brought. As she set the pot back, the side of her hand bumped a rectangular bulge beneath the tarp. The treasure can. She'd dumped the contents into a bag so Michael could use the container for Squiggles then stuck the bag back into the can when Squiggles had gained his freedom. She hadn't found time to look through it all.

Folding her air mattress like a chair, she shoved it against the dining room wall below the open window next to her coffee, the Sunday *Racine Journal Times*, and the treasure can. Settling onto the bouncing contraption took more than one try, but she finally accomplished it. She took a sip of coffee and lifted the can.

She set the giant marble in an indentation in the mattress and parked the truck on the newspaper next to the Indian on horseback. Her imaginary friend in the striped shirt tiptoed in, sitting cross-legged on the floor, chin resting on his knuckles.

"What's next?" A crumbling red rubber ball, a miniature iron frying pan, a water-damaged lapel button with a picture that looked like it might be Harry Truman. In the middle of the treasures stood an ivory-handled knife in a leather sheath. More marbles, a handful of jacks, and the tiny frog. She fingered the rustic angles of the frog and turned it over. An *M* was carved into the belly. Maybe it was a sign she should give it to Michael.

She pulled out what appeared to be a carved wooden baseball bat about four inches long. "Eww." Not a bat, a doll's arm. She laid it on her knee and lifted a matchbox half-filled with wooden matches. "Not for little boys," she whispered.

The treasures, like pieces in a game of Clue, spread out beside her, all of them raising more questions, creating more imaginary characters to fill the empty house. Did the woman who wrote the letters play with the doll when she was a little girl? Or had the wooden arm been carved by the same person who etched the name in the bench? Did the knife belong to "Papa"? Or the man who never read the letters?

As she took another sip of coffee, her phone rang. Cara. Her timing was eerie. "Morning."

"Hey. Just cruisin' up the Big Sur on my way to work. Thought I'd see how you're settling in."

The vision sparked an authentic smile. Change the car to white and the hair to a mahogany red only available in bottles, and Cara was the convertible girl she'd seen earlier. "We're getting a lot done. I refinished the corner cupboard in the kitchen, and the guy I hired tore out the kitchen cabinets and he's starting on the walls. It's a mess, but each day there's a little more progress."

"Can't wait to see pictures."

"You're sure this doesn't bother you?"

"Absolutely sure. Luke and I were just talking about it yesterday. We have great memories, but that's what scrapbooks are for. If we'd wanted a museum, we would have kept the house. You do whatever will get you the big bucks. The sooner you do, the sooner you're here." A siren wailed. Cara waited it out. "But you know you don't have to have a suitcase of money before you show up. That room's just sitting there empty. Well, not exactly empty—I've been working on decorating it. It's totally you. Totally Toji."

A silent groan deflated Emily's lungs. Their trip to Japan three years ago had transformed the way she dressed, wore her hair, and decorated her apartment. The Japanese symbol for "Live Strong" emblazoned the front of the shirt she'd worn under her jacket the day of the accident. But cherry blossoms, warm *sake,* and the Toji Temple belonged in the scrapbooks Cara had mentioned. "Sounds"—a reflexive swallow threatened to betray her—"beautiful. It won't be anytime soon, you know."

"Yeah. Says you."

Yeah. Says me. Emily swallowed sarcasm with a mouthful of coffee. "Did you and Luke check over this place before you"— *practically gave me your inheritance out of pity*—"sold it to me?"

"Nah. Neither of us could get away. Mom and Dad and my grandma were there in February. They took a few things and hired the auction people. Is there a problem? I mean, I know there are problems with the place, but is there something you didn't expect?"

I didn't expect mysterious letters or a hidden room or an iron cross or a little boy in a striped shirt. "Well, yes. There were a few things left here."

Cara groaned. "I was afraid of that. Listen, just hire somebody to cart it out and send me the bill."

Emily cringed. "I found a tin box with a bunch of toys." She balanced the truck on her knee. "Marbles and stuff, like a little boy's collection. It all looks old enough that it could have belonged to your great-grandfather."

"Huh. Well, just toss it or give it to some little kid. Knowing you, you've already met all the kids in the neighborhood."

Knowing you. The air through the window turned strangely cold. "I've met a couple. Um, what do you know about the things in the attic?"

66

A carefree laugh glided on airwaves from Highway 1. "I didn't even know there was an attic! Sorry I'm not much help. Luke and I were actually baffled that she'd left it to us. Other than that summer with you, I'd only been there a few other times. She was my grandma's mom, you know. That's kind of distant."

"I guess."

"So whatever you found, it's all yours to keep or dump. Hey, I have to make a couple calls for work. Can I call again tomorrow? I need some guy advice."

This time, the sarcasm wouldn't fit down her throat. "Sure. Call me. I'm the go-to girl on relationships."

"Don't be like that. The past is past. Isn't that what your counselor said? You learned from the Keith mistake and that makes you an expert."

"Right. Expert."

"Stop that! Forget I ever brought him up and go have an awesome day. What are you doing today anyway?"

"Shopping for bedroom furniture."

"See? You're headed in the right direction. But don't get serious about anyone, okay? I'm scoping out the possibilities here. Love you!" With another airy California laugh, she said good-bye.

⚜

It was much cooler in the barn than in the gravel drive where she'd parked the van. Emily unrolled the thin sleeves of her blouse as she followed Tina Palin around long tables filled with linens, glassware, and knickknacks.

"Do you need a bed?"

"No. I've got that covered." No need to explain that she'd already bought a mattress—only a mattress, as the closer she was to the ground in the morning, the better.

"Over here's the air conditioner. It's kind of massive. Does it look like it'll fit?"

Calculating the weight of the behemoth partially hidden by a tarp, Emily nodded. "It'll be perfect." She envisioned Jake fighting it up the folding stairs he'd just installed.

"Good." Tina bent over and shoved a stack of flowerpots out of the way. "I should send all these with you to give to Jake. Have you met his brother-in-law? Now there's a piece of work. A friend of ours just closed her greenhouse and Ben Madsen bought, like, two hundred flowerpots from her. Weird guy." She pulled the tarp away.

"Don't you try moving that."

With a laugh that bounced from the empty stanchions on one side to the hay hook swinging overhead, Tina shrugged. "I won't. I'll have Colt, my hubby, load it all in his truck and bring it to you. Though I probably could do it. I hayed the whole season I was pregnant with my first." She prodded the slight bulge of her abdomen with one finger. "My OB says in a healthy pregnancy you'd actually have to be trying to hurt it for anything to happen."

An unseen hand stretched over Emily's windpipe. She turned away, pretending to be engrossed in the curved arm of an old rocking chair.

"That rocker belonged to my great-aunt. My mother got it when her cousin died. She was an only child and she'd never married, so there was no one to pass it on to. My mother said she was probably rocked in it when she was a baby, so it's a little sentimental, but my sisters and I don't have the room. I have my mom's chair. She rocked us girls in it and nursed all my babies in this chair." Her words used up the air Emily struggled to suck in through her closing throat.

"You said you had a little desk," she rasped. "May I see it?"

"Sure. Sorry, I know I ramble." She pointed at an oak desk with a single drawer. "You're seriously going to live in your attic?"

Following slowly, Emily breathed the spots from her eyes and the thoughts from her head. "I'll be out of the way and I won't have to move from room to room."

"Yeah, guess that makes sense." Tina pulled a cloth from her back pocket and swiped it across the top of the desk, leaving a clean path in its wake. "The lady from the Historical Society almost bought this. Will it suit you?"

"It looks like it'll fit through the attic door—that's the main thing." Emily turned a brass drawer knob. "I've been wanting to get in touch with someone from the Historical Society. I'd like some more information about the house."

"It's a one-woman show in this town. Dorothy Willett. I'll

introduce you. Hey! What are you doing on the twenty-third? It's a Friday night."

Emily opened the desk drawer and closed it again. She wasn't here to make friends. She was here to make money. "I—"

"Are you in a relationship?"

Emily blinked. The boldness was disconcerting, yet easier to deal with than the eggshells friends and family had tiptoed over in her presence since the accident. "No. I'm not."

"Wellll." Tina's voice rose up the scale. She held the single syllable until she ran out of breath. "Then it's settled. We're having a barbeque on the twenty-third. Dorothy will be there and Jake can pick you up."

"*No!*" It popped out, too loud and way too emphatically. "I hardly know him. I mean, I don't want—"

"Then this would be a great way to start."

"Tina. . ." Her exhale scraped the lining of her tight throat. "I'm not staying here. I'll be leaving Rochester at the end of the summer."

"All the more reason. It's the perfect setup for a summer romance with no strings." Her smile spread like a puddle of glue. "Kiss and run. Oh, what fun."

⚜

Emily promenaded up the sidewalk on the arm of a floor lamp. Her cane swung from the harp beneath a cockeyed shade. Clanging through her front door like a peddler, she dodged a head-on collision with the extension ladder descending the stairs. Her cane backflipped, hitting Jake in the shin.

"Ah!"

Emily gasped. "I'm sorry!"

Jake laughed. "That thing's wicked." The attic heat had tightened his disheveled waves. Rock-star tendrils skimmed his collar. Heredity and sunlight had accomplished what some guys paid dearly for, and he was probably oblivious to it.

And she shouldn't be noticing. But as she did, "Kiss and run, oh what fun" played in her head like a jingle for a low-budget commercial.

"Did it hurt?"

"No." He pointed to the lamp. "Want that in the attic?

She nodded. "This is just the beginning. I bought an air conditioner and a desk."

"It's going to be cozy up there. I tacked down that roll of vinyl I found, so half your floor is covered anyway."

"Thank you. None of this is in your job description and—" Her phone rang. She grabbed it on the fourth ring, opening it as she raised it to her ear. "Hello?"

"Emily? Hi, it's Sierra. How are you? I heard you moved."

How am I? The question crackled across four states and eighteen months, amplified by guilt. Emily turned her back on Jake and staggered toward the dining room. She should be the one asking the question, should have asked it long ago. How could the girl still sound the same? Young, joyful, as if a hope-filled life still lay ahead of her? As if Emily hadn't stolen her future. "I'm fine. How"—the question she didn't want answered lodged in her throat—"how are you doing, Sierra?"

"I'm good. Actually, I'm really, really good. Guess what?"

Leaning her elbow on the windowsill, Emily tried to stem tears. It didn't work. "What?"

"Oh! I forgot why I called. Thank you for the birthday gift. You didn't have to do that. I mean, that was *über*generous!" Her laugh tinkled like wind chimes. "So I have to tell you what I'm doing with the money. Are you ready? You won't believe this."

Through tears and regret, a sad smile tugged Emily's mouth. "Tell me."

"I'm buying a dress. For prom!"

"You're going. . .to prom?" Emily wiped the dampness from her chin. What did prom look like at her school? There couldn't be dancing.

"Yes! I met this guy, Dillon. He goes to my old school, so I guess that tells you something." Again, the silvery laugh. "He calls himself a music geek. That's how we met. He started taking lessons from my old piano teacher and she asked us to do a duet for Christmas Eve. It was so amazing. He said it was like we could read each other, like we had a soul connection. Isn't that awesome?"

God, don't let her get hurt. Don't let him use her. Prayers for Sierra were the only ones she knew these days. "That's wonderful. What does your mom say?" The image of Dawn Anne, leaning against a hospital doorway, sobbing uncontrollably, was the only one she could call up. Years of memories. Girlfriend getaways overflowing with chocolate, wine, and laughter disappeared forever with a neurologist's prognosis.

"She loves him. She should—he's taking over half her job. Dillon picks me up on weekends and brings me home and over Christmas break he took me back and forth to rehab. He's amazing. I guess I said that already. Oh, and Beacon loves him."

"Beacon?"

"Sorry. I figured you would have heard about him from Mom. He's my dog. I just got him in February. We're still training together, but he's so smart. He gets me almost as much as Dillon does."

Emily ran a finger down a wavy streak on the window. A red dot bobbed and swam on a limb of her pine tree. "That's. . .wonderful." She turned away and sat on the floor.

"Have you talked to Mom lately?"

I haven't talked to your mom since I left Colorado. Not because of Sierra's mom. Dawn Anne hadn't created the distance. Dawn Anne didn't blame her. Because she didn't know the truth. "No, I haven't."

"Cool. Then I get to tell you. But maybe you already heard about it from Aunt Susan."

Emily's sister hadn't told her anything. Susan was an eggshell-walker, and sometimes that was just fine. "I haven't heard anything."

"Mom and I and Beacon are driving back to Michigan in June for her high school reunion. We want to stop and see you on the way."

Her stomach contracted, her tongue roughened like the canvas on her sandals. Excuses flooded her mind. She didn't have a place for them, or the emotions they'd leave behind like suitcases stuffed with dirty laundry. "I don't have any furniture and the house will be torn up by then and I—"

Laughter cut her off. "We'll only be there one night. We'll find a hotel and you can stay with us and we'll take you out to eat and you can show us your new town."

Show you? A solitary tear dropped to her knee, darkening the faded denim. "There isn't much to see." Her teeth ground together. Stupid choice of words.

"Well, you just mark your calendar and we'll have fun no matter what. I'm making enough chocolate-covered pretzels to last the whole trip, so plan on getting fat."

Emily nodded, wiping her face with her sleeve. "Sounds. . .fun." Her diaphragm tightened over her twisting stomach.

"Cool. Well, I have to get to class. See you soon."

"Okay." She rested her cheek on her knees. "Bye."

Arms hugging bent legs, she groped for a mantra to banish despair, but the words that spit out of her roiling thoughts were ones her counselor had forbidden. *My fault. . .if only. . .I never should have. . .why her?*

"Excuse me."

Emily lifted her gaze from the distressed floorboards. For the second time in two weeks he'd found her in a fetal position.

Jake cleared his throat. "Colt Palin is here with your stuff. Do you want the desk upstairs, too?" He acted as if women in tears on the floor were an everyday occurrence.

Too spent to brush the tracks from her cheeks, she nodded. As his footsteps echoed through the parlor, she closed her eyes.

But even with her hands pressed against them, she couldn't make the room as dark as Sierra's world.

Chapter 8

Jake closed his bedroom door and checked to make sure the only window was open. No matter what the temperature outside, he couldn't sleep with it closed. The glow from a streetlamp filled the window well and he closed the shade. Black cement-block walls sucked the brightness from his bedside lamp. He'd painted the room when he was fifteen, right after his father died. It suited his short-lived Goth phase. And it suited him now, at thirty-three, back in his cave in his mommy's basement like all the other statistics who'd failed at playing grown-up.

He hadn't failed. But only his two closest friends knew that. He wasn't advertising his reasons for selling the house he'd put his sweat and soul into. He wasn't talking about why his work truck was now his only transportation. His friends just assumed the economy had sucker-punched Braden Improvements and he was hanging on by his fingernails like too many of the guys he'd known since he was a kid. None of it was true. In spite of refusing to cut corners, the business his father had started the year Jake was born was still growing. But human nature gravitated to the worst. He put up with the razzing and enjoyed his mom's cooking.

He sat on the bed and opened his laptop. His version of Emily's floor plan lit the room. Tomorrow would decide which one of them would cave on the two walls he was determined not to destroy. The girl was definitely falling under the house's spell. He had that on his side.

His eyes traced the double black line encompassing the dining room and stopped at the window, at the two square feet she'd occupied when he walked in on her, saw the tear streaks on her face, and did nothing. Palms sweating, mouth turning to dust, he'd merely said good-bye and left.

But even when he played the scene over, he couldn't make it end right. In his first do-over, he asked if there was anything wrong. She responded with a head shake and an awkward silence. The next remake featured him dropping to one knee beside her and brushing away tears with the back of his hand.

Slapping the laptop closed, he slumped against black pillows and turned off the light. In the thick blackness he couldn't even make out the outline of the hand that acted out the sweep of tears from a soft, damp cheek.

<hr/>

"Like this." Jake dropped the pencil onto the unsteady card table and dared Emily with an unblinking gaze.

"But you said you'd changed your mind about doing it my way." She picked up the pencil and aimed the eraser at the line he'd just sketched on the floor plan she'd drawn by hand.

"You're a very good artist." His voice dripped with intentional patronization.

"I majored in art." She chewed her bottom lip, until it slipped out with a quiet sucking sound. "And you majored in getting your own way."

Jake snickered through his nose. "You're right. I have a BS in narcissism."

In spite of the straight line of her mouth, her eyes glittered with mirth. The pencil lowered and she closed both hands around it on the table. She leaned back. "So what I need to do is figure out how to get that ego to want what I want."

If not for the telltale glint, she might have pulled off the coldhearted, ruthless act. "Exactly." He followed her lead, as if the rickety table were laden with poker chips.

74

"So what is it that will break you, Mr. Braden? Money? Fame? Your rep—"

His phone, on the table beside him, vibrated against his watch like a swarm of yellow jackets. He looked down. Ben. Or Ben's phone anyway. Any other number and he would have ignored it and let Emily play out her hand. "Sorry. I have to—"

"Take it. I'll just occupy myself. . . ." She opened her hands. The pencil rolled out. She picked it up and began erasing.

One hand lunging for the pencil, he answered the phone. "Hello?"

"Jake. Can you come get me?" Lexi was breathless, her voice hoarse, as if she'd been running and crying at the same time.

"Where are you, Lex?"

"Ben is. . . I locked him outside and I just need you to come and—"

"I'm on my way." He jumped up, knocking over a chair. "Did he hurt you?" He gestured an apology to Emily as he tossed her the pencil and strode toward the door.

"Not me. Pansy."

"You know what to do. Don't unlock the door. Call 911 and—"

"I gotta go. I gotta catch her."

The phone was silent.

⚜

"Alexis, don't be an idiot! You know who's going to suffer for this. Open the door."

Lexi swiped at her cheeks and flattened herself against the wall as her stepfather's voice sliced through the fresh gash in the window screen. Pansy mewed, rubbing against Lexi's legs. The cat had an angel. It was the only way to explain how quickly she'd recovered after Ben ripped her off the screen, threw her on the cement, and punted her into the house like a football.

It wasn't the first of her nine lives she'd lost to the fat man screaming on the front step.

"Open the door or I'll tear the whole screen off and you'll pay for it."

Gripping the phone in sweaty fingers, Lexi picked up the cat.

75

"Shh. It's okay." Her eyes darted toward the back door. Jake had told her to stay inside until the police came. But she hadn't called the police. She knew better than that.

The door rattled under huge hammering fists. "The longer you play games, the worse it's going to be. When I get my hands on that cat..." This time he didn't finish the sentence. This time he didn't say he was going to pull her claws out one by one with pliers and then smash her head on concrete.

Lexi shut her eyes and took a deep breath. *Mom, what should I do?* She'd already done the thing her mother had told her over and over. *If anything happens, any time you're scared, call Uncle Jake.* But she shouldn't have. She just wanted him to come and take Pansy, but her uncle wouldn't do that. He'd yell at Ben and tell him he had no business raising his sister's kids because he was doing it just for the money and he'd threaten to call the police and Ben would swear at him and finally Jake would leave. And then she'd get screamed at for the rest of the night, and if Adam tried to defend her he'd get locked in his room. It always went like that.

Except for the times when it was worse. The times Ben said he was calling the social worker.

Shivers snaked up her bare arms, and she wished she could close her ears the way she scrunched her eyes. She wished there was a remote to click off the stuff in her head. "Fear not. Fear not," she whispered in Pansy's ear. She'd heard once there were three hundred and sixty-five fear-not verses in the Bible. *One for every day of the year.* What was the one for today?

Taking a deep breath and pulling her shoulders back the way she did in ballet, she told the fear to leave. Jake would take the cat and Ben wouldn't call the social worker. That's how it would be this time. Pansy would be safe and Ben could use all the disgusting words in the dictionary and she wouldn't care. She looked up at the clock with the butterflies painted on it and tried to see the minute hand under the cracked glass. She remembered the day Mom bought it. *Before Ben.* And she remembered the day Ben threw the phone at it. *After Mom.*

The memories in her head were sorted out like her scrapbook. Before Dad left. After Dad. Before Ben. After Ben. Before Mom died. After Mom. Some pages were black and white, some were colored and decorated with flowers and butterflies.

There hadn't been color for a long time.

"This, too, shall pass." She breathed Mom's words into Pansy's fur. She and Adam were survivors. That was something else her mother always said. The two of them together had weighed less than five pounds when they were born. Dad could hold one of them in each hand. There were pictures of Baby Girl Sutton and Baby Boy Sutton in clear plastic cribs with tubes taped to their mouths and noses. The doctors said Adam was a fighter and Alexis was stubborn. That's why they survived. And they were still that way.

Staying in the afternoon shadows along the wall, Lexi slipped into the dining room and around the table. Dust filled the holes in Mom's lace tablecloth. Tools and wires and pieces of metal covered the cloth. Computer guts, Adam called it. Ben said he was going to start a business fixing computers. Sure he was.

"Ten seconds and I'm breaking the window!" Ben pounded on the side window in the living room.

No you won't. He wouldn't break anything he'd have to fix, because he never fixed anything.

Lexi snuck into the kitchen, praying Ben would stay where he was. He'd already tried the back door, but she'd gotten there before him. She was always faster than Fat Ben. If she could get to the garage without him seeing, she'd call Jake and tell him to meet her at Echo Park. Moving like a cat, with no more sound than Pansy's paws made on grass, she grabbed her backpack off the table and darted out the door. Once outside, she ran like a track star, down the sidewalk and to the alley. The garage door was wide open.

Forcing her fingers not to shake, she punched in Jake's number. He sounded more scared than she was when he answered. "Lex, you okay? Are the police there?"

"Not yet. I got another idea. Meet me by the lion at Echo."

"No, Lex. Stay put until—"

"I'm on my way." She tossed the phone behind a pile of flowerpots. Another one of Ben's get-rich-quick schemes—*"Aloe plants. They'll sell like hotcakes."* She dumped her shoes and clothes behind the garbage cans and set her open pack on the floor. "Get in."

Pansy obeyed. She loved bike rides. Weird cat. She didn't know they were riding for her life. Lexi kissed the silky place between Pansy's ears. "You'll be okay."

She was always faster than Fat Ben.

꙳

He didn't have what it took to be a dad.

Jake's hand cramped on the shift knob. Deciding at the last second not to challenge the grace of the yellow light, he mashed the brake pedal. His truck tires hit the crosswalk as the light changed.

Red lights. That's what his life had turned into since his sister died. One long, exasperating stoplight after another. *Abigail, if you're looking down on all this, you gotta know I'm trying.* But she couldn't be watching. Tears weren't allowed up there.

He stared at the Wendy's sign. YOU CAN'T FAKE REAL, it said. The slogan resonated in a deep place inside him. If only people came with labels declaring them real or artificial. His brother-in-law should have come with a warning on his bloated side: *People-using, cat-hating, toxic blob of humanity. Approach with caution.*

Or don't approach at all. He'd tried to warn Abby, but she was lonely and exhausted from being both parents to two spitfire kids after their dad bailed. He'd tried to warn her about that first one, too: *immature, self-absorbed, irresponsible jerk.* "I sure know how to pick 'em," she'd said the first time she landed in the hospital with a bleeding ulcer.

The red eye blinked green and he sped into town, keeping the needle a safe seven over the speed limit. He turned right into Echo Park and put the truck in neutral. He jumped out and sprinted over to the drinking fountain—a huge, openmouthed yellow lion. Water squirted from its tonsils when a little girl who looked to be about eight turned the handle.

If Lexi were still that age, he'd know how to deal with her. The little girl ran off and he leaned on the lion's mane, remembering the scary thrill of sticking his head in that immense mouth when he was a kid. He'd never been too sure the thing wouldn't come alive.

Shading his eyes, he scanned the sidewalk along Milwaukee Avenue until he saw her. Pedaling her little pink bike over the tracks and across the bridge with all she had in her, blond hair flapping on bare shoulders. She needed a bigger bike. So did Adam. They needed a lot of things he was ready, willing, but not able to provide. He waved and she smiled. Man, the girl was resilient.

"Jake! You gotta take Pansy." She skidded to a stop on the blacktop, laid the bike down, and ran up the bank to him. "Ben threw her and kicked her and. . ." Skinny arms wrapped around his chest and he hugged her, and the cat.

"Did Ben follow you?"

"Are you kidding? He's too slow."

And you're too cocky. His greatest fear was that someday she wouldn't outmaneuver Ben Madsen's temper. "Tell me what happened." He led her to a park bench facing the playground. She took off the backpack and sat down with it on her lap. Jake waited while she caught her breath.

"Ben was sleeping on the couch when I got home from track." The cat's head stuck out through an opening under the flap, and she nuzzled her face in the fur. "He locked Pansy outside. You know. . . how she. . .hates. . ." Her shoulders heaved, one hand rose to her chest and rubbed a spot just below her collarbone. "She must have heard me. . .come in. . ." Her breath rasped. The next one was clearly a struggle.

"Where's your inhaler?" Jake took a deep breath, as if it could somehow get to her lungs.

"In my pack." She fumbled the clasp on the flap, the wheezing getting louder with each inhale.

Jake grabbed the cat and shook the bag upside down. "Where?"

Green eyes widened. "I. . .dumped. . ." Shoulders rounded, cords standing out on her neck, she stood and quickly lowered her head. "Can you. . .take. . .me home?"

Eyes darting around the park, he stuffed the cat in the pack. Slinging it over his shoulder, he scooped up Lexi and ran to the truck. As he opened the passenger door, the train signal clanged. He whipped the seat belt across her. The skin around her mouth had a purple cast. "Hang on, baby. Try to relax."

Lexi nodded. The rumble of a train muffled the clanging and doubled the distance he'd have to drive. He couldn't chance taking

her home. If she couldn't find her inhaler, or it didn't work fast
enough...

Jake jumped in, started the truck, and did a U-turn, tires
squealing. He glanced right when he got to the road, thinking for
a fraction of a second about trying to beat the train. Gates lowered
on his thought. Red lights flashed. He weaved between slowing cars
and onto Bridge Street. Sunlight lasered an SOS through the spaces
between boxcars. Through the open window, wheels clacked over
the tracks. A shadow train barreled along the grass beside him. He
ran a stoplight and sped onto the overpass then barely missed a car
on Robert Street. *Lord...*

He flipped open his phone, dialed 911, and asked them to call
the ER at Aurora Memorial. His voice shook. He gave them Ben's
number.

Lexi grabbed his arm. "Take...me...home." Her words were
tight, faint. Her exhale whistled.

"No time." As he closed in on the sign for Perkins Street, he
glanced at Lexi. Looking straight ahead, white hands gripping
the seat, spine hunched, she fought for every breath. Jake's damp
palms gripped the steering wheel. Pulse hammering in his throat,
he zigzagged—Kane Street to Highland to Randolph. He took the
back way in to the hospital, praying no one got in his way. He wove
around cars and people in the parking lot and slammed the truck
into neutral under red block letters. Unfastening Lexi's seat belt, he
slid her toward him.

The hospital doors opened automatically. He ran through the
waiting area and was ushered through double doors and into the
ER. He answered questions as he laid Lexi on a bed then kissed
her forehead and stepped out of the way. She reached out for him.
A man in blue scrubs tucked her hand back at her side. Jake moved
around him. "I'm right here, Lex."

"Pulse ox eighty-nine."

"BP one-forty over eighty."

A nurse put an oxygen mask over Lexi's nose and mouth and
explained they'd be giving her Albuterol through the mask. She
lifted the tips of her stethoscope to her ears then stopped. "Are you
her father?"

Not yet. "I'm her uncle."

The nurse nodded. "I'm going to start an IV on that side. Why don't you come over here and hold her hand. Might calm her down a bit." She smiled at Lexi. "You're going to be just fine, Alexis. It's scary, isn't it?"

Lexi nodded. The weight of responsibility dropped from Jake's shoulders. She was in good hands. She was going to be fine. He walked around the bed. Her fingers wrapped around his. "Is it getting any better?"

Her chest still heaved, but she nodded again.

"Good. I'll stay right—"

"What happened?"

Ben Madsen lumbered through the curtain. His hair was greasy and he hadn't shaved in days. He wore a faded yellow shirt unbuttoned over a stretched-out undershirt, baggy jeans belted under his enormous belly. Couch-potato poster boy. Sometimes stereotypes were the only thing that fit.

"She had an asthma attack."

"She always has asthma attacks. She's allergic to that blasted cat, and I'm forking over a hundred dollars a month for an inhaler. How'd she get here? Where was she? Little twit left the phone in the garage or I wouldn't have gotten the call. She locked me out."

The LPN looked up at Ben. One eyebrow rose and she shook her head. Jake wondered if she'd be allowed to testify in court. If that day ever came.

"Looks like she's going to be just fine," Jake said, keeping his voice steady and even.

Ben nodded, eyed the young nurse, and glared at Jake. "You can leave now."

Lexi's fingers tightened around his. He squeezed back. "I think I'll stay awhile."

"If you want to be useful, go pick up Adam at the library." Beady eyes narrowed under scrubby eyebrows.

Useful. Steel fingers gripped the back of his neck. He didn't trust himself to answer or even look in the face of the man who stood with his hands on the leather belt curling under the overhang of flesh. Kissing Lexi's cheek, he whispered in her ear, "I'll get Adam and we'll both be back here in fifteen minutes. You're going to be fine."

He didn't have what it took to be a dad. But he didn't have what it took not to try with everything in him. He turned and walked out through two sets of automatic doors. Yanking open the truck door, he looked down. The backpack was empty.

The cat was gone.

♔

September 3, 1852

"Stay home tonight, Liam. I need you to help with the rendering in the morning." Mam planted reddened hands on the tie of her apron.

"I have traps set. I can't leave them."

"Traps? So early?" She held the speckled blue pot over his cup.

He kept his eyes on the murky coffee swirling like a river current. "Wolf traps."

Mam made a clucking sound and lifted the iron cornbread pan from the table. "And what are you worried about? That a rabid chicken stealer will suffer if you leave it overnight? Serves it right, I say."

Coffee scalded his throat, but he couldn't wait any longer, couldn't take the chance Da would finish in the barn and come in and enforce her request. Not to defend her, but to hurt the son he claimed was not his. Liam smiled but hid it from his mother. With each passing year, Da's denial grew more foolish. The face that looked back at him from the drinking barrel on a windless day was a young version of Da, but Liam vowed to spend the rest of his life proving any resemblance to Patrick Keegan ended there. And Da knew it. With a brush of lips on Mam's creased brow, he snatched his coat from the bench and his musket from the hooks above the door.

The fringe on his sleeves slapped his sides as he sprinted toward the woods. He'd tethered Fallon to the apple tree behind the outhouse, though he'd fought for the shelter of the barn when they'd returned from church. Avoiding Da's distrusting eyes on these nights had become a game. As he tightened the saddle, he prayed this would be the last time then repented of his prayer. *Father, You alone know when this will end. Grant me patience to do Your will. Protect us all this night.*

He rode the three miles to the river in prayer. The sky was cloudless, speckled with stars. Only a sliver of darkness at the edge of the moon betrayed its waning. Still low, it hovered over the pines. Shadows stretched from headstones in the cemetery. The light would make the going easy. And treacherous. A coyote howled. Yelps followed. Liam guessed at least five. Sweat trickled down his sides in spite of the cold.

The hair stood on his arms as he neared town, reining Fallon to a walk. "Whoa, boy." He spoke as much to his racing pulse as to the gelding. On the other side of the river, lamps burned in two of the hotel windows. He crossed the bridge. Fallon's hooves echoed like drumbeats. *Just checking traps.* He rehearsed his defense.

A bit early to be trapping, isn't it? The pelts aren't thick yet.

Wolves, sir. Fear conjured the outline of a gun. *They've become a nuisance. I get paid for each carcass.*

The jacket opened. A .45 caliber Derringer glinted in the moonlight.

Get hold of yourself, Keegan. Liam took off his hat and ran a gloved hand through his hair. God had given His angels charge over his comings and goings thus far. He chastened himself for doubting as he rode silently into the trees across the river from Hannah's house.

A candle burned in the upstairs window. Her window. But tonight she wouldn't be sitting at her desk. He slid off Fallon, tied the reins to a skinny birch then hoisted the saddlebags over his shoulders. Did Mam wonder if she was losing her mind when every few weeks a loaf of bread would disappear from the cupboard or a slab of smoked sidepork wasn't where she'd put it? He hated the deception, but there would be no place for him under his parents' roof if they thought he sympathized with the abolitionists. If Da knew what he was doing tonight, Liam might well find himself swinging from a limb of the twisted oak that shaded the chicken coop.

He lifted the pine boughs off the canoe then stood still, trying to shake the feeling he wasn't alone. Fallon's nicker broke the night silence. And a branch snapped behind him.

CHAPTER 9

Numbly brushing eraser crumbs off the side of her hand, Emily stared at the empty chair lying on its back, flat against the floor where it had fallen. *Lexi. "Did he hurt you?" Call 911.* The fragments piled one on top of the other, triggering her own haunting memories.

Sierra? Are you okay? Can you hear me? Can you. . .? Blood, orangey-red in the afternoon sun, streaked across her forehead, into her hair, and onto the snow. Eyes—brown, dull, lifeless—staring, not seeing. *Sierra!* The scream hurt, ripped along her spine, black lines slithered before her eyes, blocking the sun.

A soul-deep shudder roused her. She pulled her sleeve back from her watch. Jake had been gone half an hour. She stood and righted the chair.

Focus on what you know to be real in the here and now. Crossing her arms over her chest, she paced to the window then back to the table. Two floor plans lay side-by-side on the table. One professional, the other drawn in pencil on graph paper. One a series of little boxes, the other wide-open and airy. One old, almost unchanged, the other new, innovative.

Was she describing renovation plans or people? She didn't know all that much about Jake, the professional keeper-of-the-same. Other than college, he'd lived in Rochester all his life. She'd never lived outside of Michigan, so they had that in common. But she'd traveled, seen the world. Had he? A town this size would make her claustrophobic. She craved new tastes, smells, views. The accident had reduced her life to a series of orderly little boxes. It was time to smash some walls.

She looked at her watch. Only four more minutes had passed. What was going on? He'd told Lexi to lock the door and asked if she'd been hurt. Who was after her? Would he call her when he knew something? *Lord, take care of her. Comfort Jake.* The prayer, so much like all the others she'd uttered in the past months, came naturally. Did God tire of hearing nothing but 911 calls?

Rolling her shoulders back, she circled the table, shaking the tingling out of her hands. Damp spots on her sleeves marked the spots her hands had clamped. *"Go to your happy place, Emily."* She'd laughed every time her therapist said it. No matter what was tearing at her insides, the psychobabble brought a laugh. Leaning her forehead against a windowpane, she closed her eyes.

She had a happy place. And she'd never even been there.

California. . .Monterey. . .light and airy. . .waves hitting rocks. . . lulling, soothing. . . Where the blue-dome sky kissed the horizon. Where a beachfront room awaited her.

Someday.

She paced into the kitchen, picked up a handful of almonds. They tasted like river rock. She looked again at her watch. *"God is our refuge and strength."* The words scrolled through her mind. She needed to know the rest of it.

She climbed the stairs and lifted the lid from the bin that held the letters. She'd arranged them in order on a stack of T-shirts to avoid touching them and reread the words of the letter dated November 3, 1852.

"God is our refuge and strength, a very present help in trouble. Therefore will not we fear." She read the verse out loud. *Lord, be Lexi's refuge and Jake's strength.* With an inexplicable need to commit it to memory, she read the verse over, and then again. *"A very present help in trouble."* From the church pew, she contemplated the iron rods on the wall—converging in the center, flattened at the ends. She stood and crossed the flowered linoleum and stroked the cold metal with her thumb.

Thunder rumbled, rattling the windows, and her phone rang. BRADEN IMPROVEMENTS flashed in white letters.

"Jake?"

"Lexi's okay. She had an asthma attack and she's in the ER. She's going to be fine."

"Thank God."

"Yeah. Hey, I won't get back to your place today. I've got a situation. Lexi's cat ran off, and I think it's too scared to go home." His sigh sent a chill from her earlobe to her fingertips. "I'll explain that later. But if Lexi finds out I haven't got the cat, she's liable to have another attack. I need to hunt it down."

"Can I help?"

Several seconds passed. "Actually, you could. Do you know how to get to the hospital in Burlington?"

"I've got a GPS."

"Can you meet me near the emergency room entrance in about twenty minutes?"

"I'll be there."

Another silence. "Thank you." Roughened by emotion, his tone sent a shiver down the opposite arm. She set down her phone and found herself focusing once again on the cross. *Lord, protect that cat.*

A smile stretched the out-of-practice muscles at the sides of her mouth. She was making great strides—she'd added two people and a cat to her prayer list.

♕

"Kind of like a stakeout, isn't it?" Adam bent low and leaned toward the dashboard, gazing at the darkening pewter of the afternoon sky.

Emily turned on the defroster. "We should have coffee and doughnuts like the cops do."

"I've got peanut-butter-and-cheese crackers." He lifted the flap on a huge camouflage-print pocket near his left calf and pulled out a clear cellophane package. "They're a little squished, but it's still nourishment." A red tab zipped along the side, loosing six impossibly orange cheesy crackers.

Taking two, Emily questioned what nourishing ingredient

caused the square to glow in the cloud-choked light. "Thank you. Makes me feel like a kid again." She scanned the houses on the hill. They were parked across the road from Adam and Lexi's house, facing west, with a river on their right. "Is this part of the same river that goes through Rochester?"

"Not here. This is the White River. It joins with the Fox and Honey Creek"—he pointed to the northeast—"on the other side of Echo Lake and then flows into Illinois."

"Wow. You're a walking Wikipedia." She pressed her lips together then smacked them. "Sorry. I suppose you get tired of people picking on you because you're smart."

"Sometimes." His head tilted to one side. "People used to call me Encyclopedia Brown."

"That's a compliment. Did you read *The Case of the Secret UFO*?"

"Yeah. Do you read those 'cause you're a teacher?"

"Actually, I read that one while I was living at a rehabilitation hospital last year."

"Jake said you were in an accident. What happened?"

"I was skiing in Colorado. I lost my balance and collided with another skier." *I shouldn't have been there.*

"That must have been awful. What happened to the other person?"

"She. . .lived."

"Thank God."

"Yes." She looked over her shoulder. No cat in sight. "Don't you think she'd come through the woods?" Adam had picked the spot to wait and watch—their stakeout. "Wouldn't it make more sense to wait at your house?"

Adam shook his head, a bit more emphatically than seemed warranted. Dark eyebrows wrinkled in closer to his nose. "Pansy's a weird cat." He pointed at the sky over the water. "Cumulonimbus," he muttered.

"Not sure the river can take any more rain. You're safe up here on the hill, though."

A short, hard exhale jerked Adam's shoulders as he glanced at the white house with green shutters. "Yeah. Safe."

So much said between lines, but Emily couldn't decipher it

without more clues. "So you and Emily live with your dad, I take it."

He shrugged. "We live with my mom's husband. Our real dad ditched us. He wasn't mean, but he was lazy like Ben. Nobody knows where he is now."

"I'm sorry."

Adam shrugged.

"And Ben never legally adopted you?"

Shoulders up then down again. He wrenched his bag from the backseat. "I got some books on the Underground Railroad." He held up what appeared to be a map. "BUR SPUR" was printed in red letters outlined in white. "This shows all the places around here where runaway slaves were hid or where abolitionists lived. The BuR SPUR stands for the Burlington, Rochester, and Spring Prairie Underground Railroad Trail. There are three places in Rochester—one of them is just a block from your—" He dropped the pamphlet. "There! There she is. I knew it!"

An enormous orange cat with an uncanny resemblance to Puss from the *Shrek* movies sauntered across the highway. Half a block away, a red pickup slowed. Pansy lifted her chin in acknowledgment. Emily's relief tumbled out in laughter. "That's one confident animal."

Adam grinned. "Lexi says she's got cattitude." He threw his bag in the backseat and opened the van door as a low black convertible barreled past, horn blasting at the animal it missed by mere inches. An almost human screech came from the cat. Orange fur bristling, Pansy darted toward the water, streaked along the river's edge. Adam slammed the car door and ran after her.

Emily started the car and made a U-turn, keeping one eye on the red shirt that bounded through the underbrush along the waterline.

At the first side road, Adam leaped over a guardrail and turned left. Emily caught a streak of orange burning ahead of him. The roly-poly cat ran like a cheetah. "Catch her!" Emily yelled. Useless noise with the windows closed.

A raindrop splattered the windshield. Thunder rumbled from the south. Flipping the signal lever, she waited for a semi to pass. A green airport sign hung below one that read BIENEMANN RD. Adam stopped running at a gravel drive that ran under what appeared to be an old railroad bridge. Rust-brown ribs spanned the river. Faded letters spelled out BIENEMANN FARM. A gate closed off the drive at the end of the bridge.

Rain pelted the windshield. Emily rolled down her window. "It's private property, Adam. Get back in the car before you get soaked."

Chin bouncing on his chest, lanky arms limp at his sides, he marched to the van and got in.

"She'll find a place to hide and find her way home when the rain stops."

Adam shook his head. "She's too smart for that. Ben'll kill her if she goes home."

Kill was an overused word in junior high. But there was no questioning the tone in his voice. "You're serious."

"Yeah." Adam ran his hand through damp hair and nodded. "Lexi told Jake that Ben said he was going to kill the cat. He threw her, really hard, on the concrete." He swiped a cheek wet with more than rain.

"We'll find her." Emily gave in to the maternal nudge and rubbed his shoulder. The red shirt was steamy, coiled muscles taut beneath it.

"Look!" His window went down. Across the water, the cat ran between the trees. Lightning branched like bleached nerves above the bridge. "I know what—" Thunder crashed, swallowing his words. Adam grabbed the door handle.

"Stay—" The door closed on her plea. Emily opened hers and fished for her cane, stuck under Adam's pack. Pulling it free, she kicked the door open. Rain lashed her face. Black clouds slammed together. Jagged, blue-white light stabbed the pewter sky. "Adam!"

"There's a boat! Come on!" His left arm scooped the air, beckoning her.

"No! That's crazy. You can't—"

"Come on!" He held up an oar, shaking it in the air.

Emily tripped in the gravel, caught herself with her cane. Half-sliding down the bank, she reached the old wooden rowboat as Adam shoved it into the water. "Get out of that thing. Look at it. It's ancient." He held out his hand to her. "Adam. Please. Get out. This isn't safe."

89

"If I don't find her, Ben will, and that's not safe. I have to catch her for Lexi."

Everything in her wanted to scream, *It's just a cat!*

She took his hand.

CHAPTER 10

It took all of Adam's strength to push away from the bank. He squeezed the oar with fingers purplish-gray from the cold. Had it ever rained this hard in the history of the world? His bottom jaw clattered against the top.

"It's not like a canoe, Adam. You can't steer with only one oar."

What did she know about boats, anyway? Emily hadn't stopped yelling since she got out of the van. But she'd gotten in the boat, and now he'd show her. Squinting into the sheeting downpour, he dipped the oar deep on the left. *Port.* He knew this stuff. He'd watched a movie on the *Titanic* just two weeks ago. Right was starboard, left was port. Two strokes into the wind, the boat swerved toward the bridge. He swung the oar across the bow, one stroke to correct. Back over the bow, two starboard strokes to fight the current, one port stroke to straighten their course. He glanced behind. Fifteen, maybe twenty yards stretched between them and the bank. Three more sets zigzagged them closer to the opposite shore. He studied the highway, a blurry line dotted with trees off to the right. It was getting closer. The current was winning.

"I'll take a turn."

What could she know about boats? Still, his arms burned. He swiveled on the splintery seat and handed her the oar. The boat jerked ahead a couple yards, but they were headed for the bridge.

Adam smiled. She'd give up soon enough. Back and forth, they crept across, but they were losing the battle with the current.

He shifted position, moving away from a crack in the weathered seat. His feet felt weighted. He looked down. Water covered the tops of his shoes. His pulse quickened. *It's just rain. Just rain.*

"Here! Take it!" she yelled.

She quit sooner than he'd thought. *Women.* He didn't try to hide his grin. Taking the paddle, he quickly fell into rhythm.

The boat rocked. What was she doing back there? Adam looked over his shoulder. Emily was taking off her jacket. If she thought she was going to make him put it on, she could guess again. It would only slow him down. The boat stopped rocking.

"Keep rowing on the right!" she called over the wind.

He glanced back. She'd wrapped her Windbreaker around the curved end of her cane and was dipping it in the water. "Okay!" He stroked and she matched it. Their course straightened instantly.

"There's no earthly way of knowing. . ." Emily scream-sang Willy Wonka's "Rowing Song" over a clap of thunder.

Adam laughed and joined in. They volleyed verses about hurricanes a-blowing and danger growing as they neared the trees. Adam looked down. The water had risen at least two inches. The boat sat lower in the water.

"Log! Ahead on the right!" Panic filled Emily's voice. He felt her swing her makeshift oar to starboard. "Paddle, Adam! Hard!"

He needed a better center of gravity. Sliding off the bench, he dropped to his knees and felt a board move beneath his shins. Bending into the wind, he shoved the oar deeper, pushed harder. The log rolled, a dragon head lifting out of the water— "We're gonna hit it!"

"Stop paddling! Let the current take us around—" The boat shuddered then rose on the right side.

Adam scrambled for a hold. The oar tumbled into the river. Wood splintered. A jagged branch punched through the bow. "Emily!" Fighting terror, he fastened his gaze on the riverbank. They weren't moving. If they could hold on to the log. . . "Give me your cane!"

It landed on his arm, the jacket still wrapped around one end. He fought with the material, but couldn't untie it. He needed a knife. *Back right pocket.* Hands stiff and shaking, he pulled it out and ripped through the jacket. He swung the hook onto the dragon neck and yanked. It held. The pitching stopped.

"Hold still. I'm moving forward." Her steady voice calmed him. "When I say so, move to your right. Okay. *Move.*"

Adam made room. With a quiet groan, Emily landed beside him. "Good thinking." She pointed at the cane. "I'll take over when you get tired." She felt around behind her as she spoke and finally produced a phone. But when she flipped it open, the screen was black. Her arm rubbed against his as her shoulders fell. She turned to him with a scared-looking smile. "Can you swim?"

She should have stopped him. Or paddled against him and with the current. Such a narrow strip of water; in quiet weather they could have crossed in two minutes. But in this. . . *Lord God, get us out of here.*

Adam shivered. His lips were blue. She put one arm around his thin shoulders. "Can I borrow some heat?"

"Sh-sure. I r-read a study about mountain climbers. If two people h-huddle together, you only lose about twenty-five percent of the heat one person would alone. It works like how mittens keep you warmer than gloves. It's a g-good survival technique."

In agreement, she rubbed his back then reached for the cane. "Can you slip out of your shoes?"

With exaggeratedly slow movements, he eased out of them. Emily did the same.

"Rub your arms and move your knees up and down carefully to get some circulation."

The wind picked up. Horizontal rain pelted like blunt-end needles. Lightning gashed the ink-black clouds. Just beyond the bridge, a tree exploded. A flash of white sparks shot into the air. Orange flames glowed through the trees but were quickly doused. So close. She stared at the aluminum cane. She was a human lightning rod.

"Jake will find us. It won't be long." Doubt edged his confident words.

Emily scanned the highway. Two cars, blobs of muted color in the tempest, had pulled to the side of the road. Looking for them? Most likely waiting out the blinding rain. "He'll find us," she echoed. Could he see them from the road? Adam's shirt would look like Cardinal Bob through her handblown windows. "Any minute now. He'll see the van and find us."

Adam nodded, but his eyes reddened.

Seventeen months of training kicked in. She was the queen of distractions. "Let's play a game while we wait."

"O-k-kay. I s-spy something wet."

Emily answered with an elbow jab. "Funny. Let's play 'Yes and No.' Think of something or someone or a place that I would know of and I'll ask questions. You can only answer yes or no and if I don't get it in ten guesses, you win."

"Okay. I got it."

"Is it a person?"

"No."

"Is it a thing?"

"Yes."

"Is it in the boat?"

Jake held up three fingers. "No."

"Can I see it from here?"

"No."

"Is it within ten miles of here?"

"Um. . .yes."

"Is it bigger than a car?"

"No."

"Can I hold it in my hand?" Rain pelted her tongue as she yelled.

"Yes."

"Is it made of wood?"

Adam shielded his eyes and turned toward the road. "No."

"Is it made of plastic?"

"No." He wiggled nine bluish fingers in front of her face.

"Can we do twenty questions instead of ten?"

"No."

"Fine. You win. What is it?"

"The metal collar you found in your shed."

"Awful to imagine a human wearing that, isn't it?"

Adam nodded. "Yeah. But I wish there was something like that today."

"Like the Underground Railroad?"

"Yeah. It's not like I want slavery again, it's ju—" The boat lurched. "The log's moving!" Adam clamped onto the cane with both hands.

"Can you—" A high-pitched whine cut the air. In slow motion the bow bent around the limb, impaling it, then ruptured in a hailstorm of splintered fragments. Hot pain seared her temple. The seat lowered like a chair lift. Water rose to their shoulders in seconds. Emily tugged on Adam's arms, but couldn't break his grip on the cane. "Let go!" She shoved the cane forward until it dislodged from the branch. Adam lunged, released the cane, but grabbed her arms, pinning them together.

Panic seized her but she managed to yell, "Swim! Swim to the bridge!"

The pressure on her arms tightened. She opened her mouth. It filled with water. With a hard kick she pushed up, screaming as she spread her arms in a burst of fear. With a fierce shove, she separated from him.

Adam's breath came in short gasps. His arms smacked the water. Emily watched her hand rise above the surface and slap his cheek.

Adam blinked. His eyes focused. With a nod, he rolled onto his belly and stretched out his arm. With smooth, strong strokes he swam toward the bridge.

Emily followed. The current ripped at her shirt. Saturated jeans dragged her legs. Eyes glued to Adam, she prayed as she had never prayed. "Almost there!"

Don't miss, Adam. Be strong.

Adam neared the bank, scrabbled for a hold on the rocks, but his hand slipped off.

"Dear God, help him."

As the current tugged at the boy, his left hand shot out and latched on to a branch. Wedging it under his arm, he waved.

With renewed strength, she stretched out and kicked deep. Her right leg slammed into something solid. Pain slashed through her thigh. Water engulfed her. She fought with her left leg and finally surfaced.

"Emily!" The frantic voice came from above her. Too deep to be Adam's, the voice infused her with determination. Lashing out against the pain, she tore at the water. The bridge neared then seemed to tilt. Her arms wouldn't move. The muffled scream grew distant. Murky green filled her vision and the world turned black.

Just like Sierra's.

⁂

"I've got you. You're okay. Can you hear me?"

So cold. Snow burrowed under her collar, beneath her gloves. *Sierra? Can you hear me? It's okay. They're here. Everything will be all right now.*

"Take her first." Her voice rasped. She coughed. "I'm fine." She pushed the hands away. "Take care of her."

"Emily, it's Jake. Just relax. Can you open your eyes?"

She lifted her hand to her face and felt it dripping with blood. Her eyes burned, but she forced them open. Only water fell from her hand. No snow, no blood. She was still in the river, and Jake's arm circled her waist. Was she dreaming? She rested her head against his shoulder. Heat radiated from his chest. His heart hammered against her spine. An ambulance siren blew. "Adam. Is he okay?"

"We'll get him checked out." He bent over her, staring directly in her eyes. "You've got a cut on your forehead. Anything else hurt?"

Her thigh throbbed. "No. I'm good. Help me up." She reached for a metal support just above her head.

Muscled arms pinned her. "Let's wait for the rescue squad."

"I'm fine. I just need to get warm." Her left foot pressed against a pylon.

"Stay still. They'll bring a spine board."

"No!" *God, please, no restraints.* "Get me out. Now." Both elbows thrust against his chest.

With a gasp of surprise, Jake opened his arms.

Pulling with her arms and pushing with her good leg, she hoisted out of the water. Large hands clamped her waist, supporting, not hindering. In seconds she stood on the bridge in front of Jake's truck, using a rusted beam for balance. Lights flashing, the rescue squad drove onto the bridge. Adam called to her through the closed truck window. She took a step. Her right leg gave out.

Jake's arm wrapped around her. "Steady. Are you dizzy?"

She shook her head and once again allowed herself to lean into him. The sky lit in repetitive flashes. Seconds passed. Thunder rumbled off to the west. Rain fell steadily but without force. Two EMTs rolled a stretcher toward her. "Look at the boy in the truck first."

They opened the truck door and a third person walked toward her, a woman in a red jacket. With her on one side and Jake on the other, they helped her to the ambulance.

"Go check on Adam." She pointed toward the truck.

Jake's grasp tightened on her arm. "He's in good hands."

"So am I." The intensity of the blue eyes squinting down on her made her squirm.

He didn't move.

Teeth gritted, Emily endured the examination, answering every question with a negative. She was not going to the hospital.

With a strained expression, the EMT cleaned the cut on her head. "You could have aspirated dirty water, you may have a concussion, and this needs to be looked at. An open wound exposed to that water—"

"I'm fine. I'll take a hot shower and go straight to bed."

"Is there someone at home to keep an eye on you, to check for—"

A torrent of expletives cut her off. A balding man, yellow shirt stretched over a massive abdomen, stomped toward Jake's truck. "What were you doing in a boat? In weather like this! How stupid can you get?" He shoved past one of the EMTs and loomed over Adam. "Your sister's in the ER and—"

Without turning from the vile man, Emily sensed Jake tighten like a drawn bow.

"Get out of their way, Ben," Jake seethed.

Bloodshot eyes turned on him. The man's bloated face reddened. "Stay out of my way, Braden." Hamlike fists opened and closed. "Why is it you're always in the middle of it when my kids do something stupid?"

"They aren't your kids." He breathed the words, low and rasping, like a curse.

The EMT who'd been pushed aside raised a hand. "Back away, please, sir. You're his father?"

"Yes." He knifed Jake with a glance. "I am."

"Not for long," Jake whispered.

The EMT stripped off her gloves, pulling Emily's focus off the drama. "You're clearly in pain. You have no idea how you're going to feel later to—"

"I'll be fine. I've dealt with injuries before."

"So you do have someone at ho—"

Shooting Jake a silent message she hoped would close his open mouth, Emily stood, sucked in air, and held it. Her stomach roiled in a wave of nausea. *Breathe. Slow.* She was used to pain. A bottle of Percocet waited on the floor beside her mattress.

A warm hand cupped her shoulder. "Is it money?" Jake asked. "Do you have insurance?"

"I have insurance. I don't need to go to the hospital."

The EMT sighed. "You'll have to sign a release saying you refused transport."

Jake increased the pressure on her shoulder. "Emily, don't be—"

"Give me the pen."

⚜

September 3, 1852

Hannah flinched as a brittle stick broke beneath her shoe. "It's me, Liam." She still couldn't see him, but his name loosened the fear-hold on her throat.

"Here." His voice blended with the whispering water.

One more step and his arms slid around her. "Hannah." He buried his face in her hair. "Are you all right?"

Her ear pressed against his chest. Leather and smoke, the smells filled her nostrils. "There are men...speaking with Papa." His heartbeat increased in volume with her words. "They're looking for a man. Not the one we have, but it's not safe tonight."

"I'll check my traps and come back." His fingers dug deep in her

98

hair, loosening her braid.

"Wait until tomorrow."

"Is there a child?"

"No. An older man and his grown son." A soft moan escaped her lips. "The son is a freeman, but he stayed for his father's sake. Their master promised he could buy his father's freedom if he worked five years. When the time came, he wouldn't let him go. Their master took sick and they got away. They've been running for weeks."

Liam shook his head. His hands slid to her face. He lifted her chin. "We are blessed. Only two years until I can buy your freedom." In the moonlight his smile deepened the shadows around his eyes.

"It is your own freedom you buy, sir. Papa would hire you quick as lightning, and I would be as happy married to a clerk as a smith."

His laugh tickled her face. "And would you be as happy if that man were miserable, balancing ledgers all day instead of using the hands God shaped to fit a horse's hoof?" He spread the fingers of one large hand and held it inches from her face.

She pressed her palm against his. "These hands were not made for wielding a pen. Though I do dearly love what they do with one."

His smile straightened then faded away. "I am going to speak to your father on Sunday."

Her pulse quickened. Her smile would not obey. "About what?"

"I want you to go and stay with your aunt in Boston until this is over."

Bile rose in her throat. "I will not! My father cannot fend for himself. He could not cook an egg nor make a decent cup of tea if his life depended on it. And who is to say this will be over before I am an old maid!" She kept her words low but could do nothing to stop the speed with which they came. "Liam Keegan, if you want to be done with me, please have the decency to address the matter forthright to—"

His lips, warm and rough and more tender than she had ever imagined, covered hers. Her legs bent like green twigs, but he held her up. She drifted above the clouds, to a weightless place where stars sang along with angel choirs. He pulled away, leaving her lips cold and longing for more.

"Now, Hannah Glennis Shaw, if ever for a moment you

question my intentions or my promise, mind you remember this moment and hang those thoughts on the gallows." Deep blue eyes bored into her, hot as the iron poker she'd seen him lift from the coals. "Do you believe me?"

Her eyes closed. "Almost."

He shoved her, gently, at arm's length. "Vixen." His teeth caught the glow of the moon as he raised his head in a silent laugh. "Did the devil send you to test the strength of my convictions?"

It was a strange thing, this feeling of power. This man, strong as a bull, weakened by a kiss. *Father, let me never cause him temptation.* "I would never—"

"I know." His fingertip touched her lips. "It is your very existence that tries me, my love."

"Is it—? Are we wrong to—?" Warmth crept above the collar of her dress and spread to her face. If only Mama were still here. She had no sister or older friend to talk to. If Papa knew. . . In spite of the cold, she felt suddenly feverish.

"I don't think so. These are different times. If I were free to court you openly, I would sit on your porch and drink tea with you every night. But God knows our desires. I have known for some time that you are the gift He handpicked for me. My heart is pure toward you and before Him."

She nodded. "Is this. . .am I. . . ?"

"My first kiss?"

Turning from the laughter in his eyes, she stared down at the canoe he'd fashioned with his own hands. "Yes." Was it wrong to ask a man such a question? Didn't she need to know if she would someday be his wife? The heat she'd felt a moment ago deserted and she shivered.

Liam pulled her shawl onto her shoulders. "You can't catch a chill. I won't stand for that." The twinkle still danced in his eyes, a reflection of moonlight and amusement. "I'll be on my way as soon as you promise you'll pray about going to Boston."

"Then you and I shall both turn to icicles. You didn't answer my question and yet you expect me to promise I will pray about something I already know is not within the will of God? I think not."

He laughed again. "Are you sure you're not Irish?"

"Bite your tongue!"

His expression darkened as if a cloud blotted the moonlight.

"You know I'm not serious."

"I know." But the teasing had left his voice.

"Be proud of your heritage, Liam."

His hands dropped then folded across his chest. "There's not a lot to be proud of. Da is exactly what they say all Irishmen are."

"But *you* are not."

"By the grace of God."

"Of course, by the grace of God. But don't berate yourself because you are what you are due to the intervention of Almighty God." She stamped her foot in the dirt and the sparkle returned to his eyes.

"You are good for me, Hannah."

"And you for me."

He pulled her close. "I wish. . ."

She pressed her face into the coat that smelled of smoke from the forge, worn leather, and a man who worked hard for what he believed. "I do, too."

CHAPTER 11

The hot shower massaged her neck. Emily turned and lifted her face into the spray then angled away to protect the cut. Filling her cupped hand with shampoo, she inhaled the soap smell. As she scrubbed her hair, exhaustion overpowered her. She leaned against the wall until the last of the suds swirled down the drain then shut off the water.

A six-inch-long bruise decorated her thigh, the puffy oval now a darker purple than when she'd stepped in. Pain hammered in time with her pulse. Hair in a towel, she pulled a plaid flannel robe off the hook on the door and walked into the upstairs hall. She gripped the railing of the folding stairs leading to her attic. She might as well have been standing, as she once had, at the base of Mount Fuji.

When she reached her bed, she wasn't sure how she'd gotten there. In a tired fog, she took three pills—one for pain, two for sleep—struggled into pajamas, and lay down on her mattress.

"You let her go home?"

Jake shrugged at his mother. "I followed her. What was I supposed to do, pick her up and throw her over my shoulder?"

Straightening Adam's hospital blanket, his mother nodded. "It sounds like that's exactly what you should have done."

Adam laughed, clouding his oxygen mask. With his IV hand, he lifted the mask. "She's fierce. You should have heard her yelling at me."

"Somebody had to!" Jake smacked the blanket tented over Adam's feet. "What were you thinking?"

"That I had to find Pansy before Lexi heard she was gone because she'd get so upset she'd have another attack. Instead, we're both in the hospital and Pansy's missing. What a screw-up."

Jake twisted his mouth to one side and nodded. "Got that right. But you screwed up for a noble cause."

"You were trying to do the right thing." Blaze Braden kissed her grandson's cheek then turned to her son. "You'd better go check on that girl. She saved your nephew's life."

"Nuh-uh." Adam's protest garbled through the mask. "I saved *her*."

"She'll call if she needs anything." Emily had made it abundantly clear she could manage on her own.

Adam raised his mask. "Her phone's wrecked. It got wet."

Great. He held his mother's pointed gaze. "Fine. I'll go check on her. I'm going to check on Lexi first."

"They're just waiting on discharge papers."

"I know. I just want to—"

"Stall."

"Yeah. Stall."

⚜

Stupid idea. Jake glared at the door handle. It was nine o'clock at night. Emily was exhausted. She'd be in bed in the attic. If he made her hobble down two flights of stairs to tell him she was all right, it would probably be accompanied by a slap.

He had a key. He fingered its outline in his back pocket. He should have brought someone with him. Who? His mother was tied up. The guys on his crew were home with their families. Or at the bar. Like calling them would have been an option anyway. *Hey, Topher, put that beer down and come with me while I break into this girl's house and go up to her bedroom.* With a massive inhale, he stuck the key in the lock and turned it.

He cracked the door open. "Emily?"

103

He sent his voice ahead of him through a two-inch slit. She could be in the downstairs bathroom. She could be. . . He shut his eyes. "Emily? It's me. Just checking up on you."

If she screamed at him and told him to get out, he'd obey before the next word left her mouth. He didn't want to be there any more than she wanted him. But no sound came from above.

With intentionally heavy steps that echoed through the empty house, he climbed to the second floor and repeated his plea for a response. Any answer would do.

He walked up the steps to the attic, pausing after every step, calling her name again. Four steps up, fear set in. No one slept that soundly. He ran up the last few steps and poked his head through the opening.

Emily lay on a mattress on the floor on the west end of the attic. Thankfully, fully clothed. The right leg of her pajamas, pushed above her knee, exposed an ugly, dark purple bruise. He didn't need to step too close to hear strong, steady breathing. She was alive. Was she conscious? "Emily?"

Just talk to me and I'll leave. Wake up, throw a pillow in my face, and I'm out of here. He kneeled beside her, sending a brown plastic bottle skittering across the floor. Bending sideways, he caught it. Percocet. A second bottle lay on its side, half-covered by a blanket. He'd picked up enough prescriptions for his mother to be familiar with both drugs—one for pain, one for sleep. If she'd taken both, she'd be a zombie.

One look at your pupils and I'll say good-bye. He lifted a limp hand. Smooth skin, tapered fingers. An artistic hand. It fit snugly in his. Rubbing the back with his thumb, he said her name again.

"Hmm?" Eyelids twitched. He let go of her hand. She rolled on her side, hugging her pillow, facing him.

So she wasn't brain-dead. Jake crossed his legs and picked up her hand again. "How are you feeling?"

"Tired." Her lips barely moved.

"Does your leg hurt?"

"Mm-hm."

"How 'bout your head?"

Her forehead crinkled. Very cute. "No." The creases deepened.

One eye popped open then the other. Equal and reactive. "Is Adam okay?"

"He's fine. He'll be in overnight for observation. Just like you should be."

"And Lexi?"

"On her way home."

"Good." Eyes fluttering shut, she shook her head. Her hair spilled across her face. Jake brushed it away, skimming her warm cheek. "Hate hospitals," she mumbled.

"I imagine you do. How long were you in?"

"Three weeks. . .first. Long time second."

"Did you need surgery after your accident?"

Her pillow rustled as she nodded. "Lots." She was silent for several seconds. "MRSA."

"That's an infection, right?" The name had something to do with antibiotic resistance. That's all he knew about it.

"Mm-hm. Evil. God punishes."

Leaning closer, he enclosed her hand in both of his. "What do you mean?"

"I deserved it."

"You deserved an infection?"

"If I hadn't. . ." Eyes squinched shut. Her breathing grew slow and deep again.

Jake lifted her hand. And kissed it.

He reached the first floor before the sensation left his lips. Common sense returned about the same time. She didn't have a phone. With that leg, it was doubtful she could even climb down to use the bathroom. Pulling out his phone, he pushed "2" and waited for his mother's voice.

"Is she okay, honey?"

"She's conscious. It looks like she took a pain pill and a sleeping pill—"

"Bring her here."

Scuffing his heel against the floor, he smiled. "You're sure?"

"That's what you called about, isn't it?"

Unnerving. "Yes."

"Then do what you should have done in the first place and sling her over your shoulder and bring her here. Unless you think she should see a doctor first."

"*I* think she should, but the ER wouldn't be a safe place if I took her against her will."

"A girl with spunk, huh?"

He cringed. One word, spoken in casual conversation, and it would follow him forever. "Mo*ther*."

"Ja*cob*. Bring her here. Lexi and I can go back for her things tomorrow."

"Okay. Thank you."

"Thank *you*." A smile tinged her voice.

He closed his phone and his eyes. This was going to be bad. His mother, who claimed her job wouldn't be complete until she found him a wife, was about to meet a girl with spunk.

☗

"That's ridiculous." Emily propped up on pillows and yawned. "I feel great and I have everything I need."

"Except a phone."

She laughed at him. "I'll run across the street if I need to call someone."

"You'll what?" He laughed right back. "No offense, but you weren't exactly running before your leg turned into a purple eggplant."

"So I'll hobble across the street." Her somewhat sheepish smile made his shirt cling to his back. The air conditioner wasn't doing its job.

"You'll like my mom."

"I'm sure I would. I'd love to meet her. Sometime."

Unfolding his legs, Jake stood. "Humor me. Get up and walk me down to the door. If you make it look effortless, I'll leave you alone."

Her next laugh sounded like a popping balloon. "I haven't made anything look effortless in almost two years!"

Way to go. "Is it constant pain?"

"It's constant something." She moved her focus to the opposite end of the room.

106

He sat back down. Above the air conditioner, feeble moonlight filtered through the window.

"Most of the time it's just stiffness and a dull ache. If I overdo it, I'll feel pain."

"So by morning you're going to be a mess."

She graced him with a tiny laugh. "That's what medication is for." Her top lashes rested again on cheeks dusted with freckles.

Jake took full advantage of her sleeping pill. Bracing his hands on the floor, he studied her face. The tips of her hair—pale, spun-gold—helped him imagine a different image than the one in front of him. Makeup, designer clothes, expensive jewelry. He could see her being high maintenance. If he'd met her two years ago, would he have looked twice? *Duh.* Probably even a third time.

While plastering a ceiling several weeks ago, Topher had asked him to describe the perfect woman. He couldn't do it. "I'll know her when I see her," he'd answered.

"There isn't just one out there, you know. What's the closest you've seen?"

No one had come to mind. His lack of answers had bugged him ever since. Was there something wrong with him that he was still unentangled? He traced the curve of Emily's chin with his eyes then stared at the natural pink of her lips. No denying the attraction but that meant nothing. He did the look-twice-and-then-again thing on a daily basis but still stuck to "I'll know her when I see her."

For now, he was grateful "she" hadn't appeared. His life was too messy. Though laying it all out on the table would be the perfect test. *Nice to meet you. Hope you don't mind that I invited two twelve-year-olds along on our date.*

Puppies and kitties were chick magnets. Preteens not so much.

Emily's breath shuddered. Did she have nightmares from the accident? The only serious accident he'd ever been in gave him some idea. He was sixteen and drunk, though maybe not as much as the driver. Her car, a gold Z28 Camaro, was a birthday present from her parents on the morning of the accident. To this day, he could close his eyes and see the patch of ice, hear himself screaming at her to pull her foot off the brake. The semi looming. . .the car spinning like a child's top in the middle of the road. . .the slam. . .shoulder harness ripping into his shoulder. . .glass shattering. . . The girl had walked away with cuts and bruises. He'd walked out of the ER with nothing but a brace for a busted collarbone. The nightmares had diminished with time, but he could still conjure the sounds and smells at will.

Emily moaned softly. Eyelids rose then lowered. "I'm really tired. Maybe I should go back to sleep."

You just were. Jake smiled. "What's your favorite food?"

"Pasta Alfredo." Her answer mingled with a yawn.

"What a coincidence. We're having a late supper tonight. Pasta Alfredo."

Her eyelids struggled open. She sat up straighter and simply stared. For a moment he wondered if she'd fallen back to sleep and forgotten to pull the shades. Finally her head tipped to one side. "Why are you doing this?"

"Why am I inviting you to dinner? It's the neighborly thing to do. You're new in the neighborhood, and my mom would like to welcome you. Did I tell you I live around the corner?"

"Little redbrick house. You told me." She rubbed her nose with a short-nailed hand, like a little girl. "I meant, why are you here?"

"I—" Why was he there? He'd climbed the stairs to satisfy his mother. He'd stayed and watched her sleep because. . . "My mother is worried about you. You saved her grandson's life."

Her hair splayed across her cheek. He restrained his hand. "Adam would have been just fine without me."

"I don't believe that for a minute. He's got a head full of book smarts and he thinks he's invincible." *If he had a father who actually took him boating or camping or anything. . .* He put the thoughts back where they belonged—on hold. "He told us how you made a paddle."

She shrugged. "My cane came in handy. It's gone, isn't it?"

"Your cane? I guess it must be."

She lifted the quilt to cover a yawn.

"Can I fix you some coffee?"

"No. Thank you. I really just need to go back to sleep. Tell your mother I appreciate her thoughtfulness."

"She'll take it out on me if I show up without you. You'd be doing her a favor, you know. Since my sister died, she hasn't had any girl talk at home."

A long sigh ruffled a loose thread on her quilt. "I wouldn't be good company." She played with the thread, wrapping it around her finger, unraveling it, and winding it again. "I don't want to sound rude, or unappreciative." Her hands slapped the sides of her mattress. Her eyes found his. "I'll just spell it out. I'm at a very self-focused time in my life. I need to get this house done and move on. If people try getting close to me, they'll be disappointed. I'll let them down because I have nothing to give. This is a great little town, and I'm sure it's full of wonderful people. Please don't take this personally, but I can't afford to get close to anyone right now."

Her eyes pleaded for understanding, but her words splashed like ice water. Jake rose to his feet. What had he expected? She'd hired him to remodel her house, not be her best friend. "I understand." His right hand made a back-off gesture, though he was the one backing away. "I'll be here tomorrow afternoon to start on the dining room wall."

"I'll see you then."

"Yeah." He'd be back in less than twenty-four hours to tear down a wall. Before that, he'd have to demolish something he'd just now identified.

The reason he'd stayed to watch her sleep.

CHAPTER 12

The water was warmer now. Rain dappled the surface above her, but sunlight pierced the cloudy green. Emily fingered the rays, played them like harp strings. Milky white hands, red nails flecked with gold, coaxed music from sunlight. Tiny bubbles tickled her arms. Thunder rumbled below her. Someone had moved the sky. The rays grew warmer. White light turned gold then orange, scorching her fingers. Her eyes burned. Thunder cracked, shaking the river bottom. The light vanished. Heat remained. Air. She needed air. Clawing to the surface...which way was up?

"Emily!"

The water muffled his voice. *Jake! I'm here!* The current spun her, wrapping her hair around her face. Her lungs screamed. *Jake! I'm—*

"Emily. Wake up."

He pulled the wet hair from her face. Sweet air filled her lungs. "Thank you." She whispered it against his hand. His touch was cool.

"I'm taking you to the hospital."

Her eyes shot open. She grabbed his hand and tore it from her face. "*No.* I told you no."

The mattress tilted. She closed her eyes. Like the boat swaying on the log, cracking beneath them, water seeping in. But she wasn't in the boat. She wasn't in the water.

Stay awake. She commanded her eyes open. Attic beams whirled

110

overhead, Jake's face blurred. Her hands clamped over her face. Just a dream.

Weightless, she rose above the floor, floating. But something held her arms. *No restraints. I told you...* Panic surged from her chest. She twisted and pushed but couldn't break free. Her feet thrashed out but found only air.

"Stop fighting." Jake's voice sounded in her ear, strained and tight.

She felt his breath on her face. But he wasn't helping, wasn't untying her. "Get me out—"

"Hold still."

Footsteps. Her body sank with them. Lower and lower until she knew she'd never find her way out.

God was punishing. And she deserved it.

♔

Jake counted the drops slipping through the tube and into Emily's arm. Eight...nine...ten... The decor was all too familiar. Hooks that looked like they belonged in a widemouth bass connected leaf-patterned privacy curtains to their aluminum tracks. A metal triangle dangled on a heavy-duty chain from a curved bar over the head of the bed. Were chin-ups a condition for early release? One tug on a white cord of mini plastic beads changed the fluorescent ambience of the room.

He stood, paced. White sheet, white blankets, white window blinds, white vinyl tiles, white walls. Blue and purple tiles interrupted the white floor at random intervals. A wallpaper border sported tan leaf-swirls on a blotchy maroon and green background—the only concessions to nonwhite.

Had no one ever done a study on the healing power of color?

Or a visitor's need to have one room different from the one down the hall where his sister had died?

A nurse walked in and pulled the beaded cord. Emily jerked then stilled. The fat-faced clock said it was ten after eight.

"Are you her husband?"

"No." *I'm the guy knocking down her walls.* He almost smiled at the dual meanings playing in his tired brain. "But she gave consent

111

for me to talk to the doctor." While she was totally drugged up. "How is she doing?"

"Everything looks good." The woman stared at a blipping monitor, arms folded across a generous-sized Scooby-Doo smock. She checked the IV needle. "The cloxacillin should neutralize any nasties she's got in her lungs. She's not as sick as she looks. We sedated her because she tried to rip out her IV." She winked. Her smile poured sympathy on his exhaustion. "We'll let it wear off and see if she's a little more willing to cooperate. Anything you can say to convince her not to fight would be helpful."

Lady, if I knew how to do that, she would have been in here yesterday. And I'd be saving myself a whole lot of frustration. "I'll see what I can do."

"Go back to sleep. I'll tiptoe when I come back."

She walked out. In what seemed like seconds he woke himself with a snore. Saliva dampened his unshaven chin. He stood and peeked through the blinds. There was still an empty space where his mother's car had been earlier. They'd released Adam after supper— an hour after Emily arrived. Jake's tongue was raw from biting back all the ugly things he'd wanted to hurl at Ben. His mother had literally begged the slug to let the kids come home with her, but he'd refused. *They're my kids, and I'll take care of them.* If only either one of those statements were true.

All the words he'd used to comfort his mother as she sobbed in the hallway were lies. Her grandkids wouldn't be fine. And she'd be in bed for days from the stress of knowing the truth.

He dozed again, waking in a semidark room. He stood and stretched and walked to the side of the bed that wasn't occupied by tubes and monitors. The head of the bed was elevated. The hand without the IV needles lay at her side. He picked it up—a habit he'd have to break when she was conscious. A habit he shouldn't have started in the first place.

What's fuelin' you? Topher's amateur psychology always came in handy. Beyond the obvious, what was the fascination? The question flipped a switch. A hundred-watt bulb illuminated the answer. *Because she's everything Heidi wasn't.* Therein lay the intrigue. He'd tried saving Heidi from drowning in herself. He liked the feel of being her hero—until her desperation wrapped around his neck and pulled him under. He still found himself gasping at times, grateful all over again for free air.

His real-life rescue of Emily Foster, on the other hand, had left him feeling anything but a hero. All he had to show for his efforts was a tender spot on his ribs.

What fueled him? Challenge. Show him a poorly planned, outdated kitchen and his adrenaline rushed like the Echo Lake dam. Give him a kayak paddle and a run of rapids and he was stoked. Emily represented yet one more challenge. And there'd be nothing wrong with it if he were a free man.

Her eyelids fluttered. Dark brown lashes with hints of gold settled back against high cheekbones. Jake's breathing quickened, tight ridges formed along the tops of his shoulders. *Ben.* Ben Madsen was the reason he couldn't pursue Emily. Ben Madsen was the reason his mother was in constant pain. His neck tensed, triggering an instant headache.

Ben Madsen was the reason his sister was dead.

Like tombstone dominoes, everything started toppling the day Abby married her second big mistake.

What was it about the way they were raised that made him and his sister want to save the world one hard-luck case at a time? He'd had the sense to walk away from Heidi. Abby never seemed to catch on until it was too late. Within six months of marrying Ben, she'd lost twenty pounds. She died a week before their third anniversary. Two days after the twins' twelfth birthday.

Ben's toxins spilled into his in-laws' lives. His mother's quick laugh silenced and, as if needing her own pain to share in Abby's suffering, she'd developed fibromyalgia.

When Abby died, no one questioned that Adam and Lexi would come to live with Abby's mother. Especially not Ben. The poor man's dreams of making it big in the computer repair business were buried with the breadwinning wife he'd put in the ground. Who could expect him to care for two children while holding down an actual job? He was prepared to surrender his rights and allow his mother-in-law to adopt the children.

And then the first Social Security check arrived.

Jake's temples pounded. Pressure built with each domino that fell in his mind. Parenting had not birthed the best in Ben.

The pale hand moved, bringing Jake out of his angry reverie. Fingers bent around his. Jake returned the pressure. In a different world, he might lift the hand once again to his lips and hope the magical kiss would wake her with a smile.

He rolled his eyes toward the ceiling. Enough with the martyrdom. No one had coerced him onto this path. Someone needed to stand in the gap for Adam and Lexi. His mother wasn't strong enough. He was determined to be the one.

He loosened his hold on Emily's hand. His time for thinking of himself would come, but it would be too late for holding hands with Emily Foster.

A shadow dappled the light from the hallway. A polite knock followed. From where he stood he couldn't see the door. "Come in."

The curtain swayed. His mother stepped through. Reddened eyes found his face and then his hand. A wisp of a smile tipped one corner of her mouth. "How is she?"

With artful nonchalance, he released the slim, soft hand. "You're supposed to be sleeping."

She shrugged.

Jake filled in her blanks. The house was too quiet.

His mother internalized and he made bad jokes. Like broken but usable gears, they'd learned how to mesh differing coping mechanisms since Abby died. Concern for the twins provided the grease.

He motioned toward the chairs. "Her fever's gone down. She's sedated because she was trying to pull out her IV. She has a hospital phobia."

Gazing at the monitor, his mother nodded. "Who doesn't?" She took a seat and smiled up at him. "You look terrible."

He smiled back. Like fragile green shoots, there were occasional signs of life in her. "You don't look so hot yourself."

Running her fingers through shoulder-length brown hair that had sprouted natural highlights in the past year, she shrugged and pulled a magazine from her purse. "Go get something to eat. I'm replacing you."

"You don't. . ." He left the thought unfinished. She needed
to be needed. "Thank you." He walked around the end of the bed
and kissed her on the cheek. The changing of the guard was all too
familiar. "Push the call light if she wakes up."

"I will." She leafed through the magazine as he walked around
the curtain. "Right after I ask her a few little questions."

⚜

The cafeteria had stopped serving an hour ago. He bought a club
sandwich from a vending machine, fought with the plastic wrap and
finally won, then zapped it in the microwave until the Swiss cheese
oozed onto the plate.

How many people have a favorite spot in a hospital cafeteria?
He had two. One in the corner, facing the wall of windows, and the
other near the cash register. It all depended on his mood and the
kind of distraction he needed. There had been days when analyzing
the lunch choices of the hospital staff had provided the perfect
respite from watching the line of red blood cells flowing into his
sister's arm. Other days, he needed to be alone with God and the
scrubby pines on the other side of the window. What he wanted
now was air. Grabbing a pile of napkins, he tossed the plate and
headed outside.

When the sandwich was gone, he broke into a run, convincing
himself with every step that from now on Emily Foster was a job
and a paycheck.

And nothing, absolutely nothing, more.

⚜

Laughter stopped him at the door to Emily's room.

". . .on my hands and knees to the bathroom. My dad had
forgotten to mention he'd called a plumber to fix the sink." Emily's
last two words dissolved with a laugh. "You can"—a fit of coughing
interrupted—"imagine the look on the guy's face, and mine, when
I crawled in."

His mother gasped for air as she cackled. "I can top that. So there
I am at Pick n' Save in an oversized shirt, standing in front of the milk
cooler, and my mind goes totally blank. Fibromyalgia fog, they call it.

115

I can't remember who I am or what I'm doing there and the cold is making the pain worse, so I fold my arms over my middle to hold in the heat and do what I always do. Lamaze breathing." She stopped to giggle. "All of a sudden, this woman throws her arms around me and tells me not to worry, she's an OB nurse. Next thing I know, she's yelling across the store for someone to call 911!"

Jake stood behind the curtain, his mouth gaping, his eyes stinging, afraid to move and break the spell. When a lull in the laughter finally came, he took several deep breaths and walked in.

"You two sharing your meds?"

His question triggered another fit of laughter, until Emily started coughing.

His mother patted Emily's knee. "This was fun, but you need to rest." She wiped her eyes and laid her hand flat against Jake's chest. "I'm outta here. Your watch." With a wink so exaggerated it looked painful, she walked out.

Jake stood helplessly as Emily held a tissue to her mouth and coughed. "Should I get someone?"

She shook her head. "No." After a moment, it stopped. She brushed her hair away from her face. "They say. . .it's good. . .for me to cough." She blew her nose and lay back on her pillow. "I like your mom. She's funny."

"She hasn't been for a long time. You seem to have brought out the best in her."

"And vice versa. Haven't laughed like that in centuries." She nestled into her pillow. "I don't think I properly thanked you for bringing me here." Pale cheeks pinked then lifted with the muscles that bowed her lips.

Properly thanked? His ribs ached and the point of contact her foot had made with his thigh on the trip down her stairs was probably the same color as the bruise on hers. "Guess I'd have to say I don't feel properly thanked."

"I'm sorry." She pushed the button to lower the head of her bed.

Did the medicine or his mother deserve the credit for this metamorphosis? "All's forgiven."

Emily yawned. "I was kind of mean."

"You were."

Her eyes closed. "I'll make it up. . .to you."

Dinner and a movie? He sneered at his own inside joke. "No need." He glanced at the chair by the window and parted the curtain. She'd be fine on her own.

⚜

September 5, 1852

Waving Mama's lace fan just inches from her face, Hannah conformed her spine to the unforgiving pew and willed her thoughts to rest on God and not on the empty space in the third row.

Liam was helping his father. She was sure of it. He'd made it home safe in the middle of the night. She'd heard the trapdoor close and tiptoed in the dark to get the letter. "All went well," it read. "I am on my way home to dream of you."

Only three miles to ride from her house. He'd made it home safe. He was just helping with the harvest. There were other empty spaces in the pews. Even the reverend said men often worshiped best in the field. When God sent the gift of a sunny Sabbath after days of rain, picking corn or harvesting wheat was a gesture of gratitude.

She pictured Liam, arms as strong as the iron he forged, grasping the plow handles. Next spring, on their own plot of land. Unlike some men, he'd talk kindly to the draft horses. Their massive feet would plod the ground, pulling the plow and turning the soil at the gentle commands from Liam's lips. Those lips. . .if they were wed she would bring him lemonade and kiss away the parchedness. He would return to the plow with a smile. When the sun rose overhead, he'd slip off his shirt. . . .

Hannah Glennis Shaw! Her fan fluttered like a nervous hummingbird. The prophet Jeremiah must have had her in mind when he penned, "The heart is deceitful above all things, and desperately wicked." Her thoughts were wicked, and how much more so that she entertained them in church!

No more. She would heed the apostle Paul's admonition and bring every thought into captivity. Like a horse with blinders, she would follow the straight and narrow furrow— She bit her tongue. *Road,* she meant road. Not for a moment would she stray to that field

117

of fresh-turned dirt or the man with the sun-bronzed back. *Lord, constrain my wayward mind!* She stared at Reverend Drummond with desperate intensity, as if her very life depended on following the rise and fall of his bushy brows.

". . .shalt love the Lord thy God with all thy heart, and with all thy soul, and with all thy strength, and with all thy mind; and thy neighbor as thyself." A hairy finger pointed directly at her. Hannah covered the smile that would not obey. She did not need to be told to love her neighbor. What she needed was a sermon on how *not* to love.

The message continued. "A certain man went down from Jerusalem to Jericho, and fell among thieves, which stripped him of his raiment, and wounded him, and departed, leaving him half dead."

Hannah pictured the men they'd hid for two days. Gaunt and tired, their feet raw and blistered. Her countenance sobered.

". . .he passed by on the other side."

How could people do that? How could they not open their homes to men and women who risked their lives to give their children freedom? She glared at the back of the bonnet in front of her. Dolly Baker's mother nodded with every verse the reverend read. The woman was a whitewashed sepulcher, sniffling and clutching her Bible to her breast as the minister described the plight of the hapless man. Yet sit beside Lucille Baker an hour from now under the shade of the cypress tree, and you'd hear a very different sermon from those primly pursed lips.

Just last Sunday Lucille had ranted, "My father cares for his darkies better than some men care for their own children. They had no use for freedom till some Yankee started fillin' their heads with crazy notions."

Lucille Baker had moved north before Dolly was born, yet whenever abolitionist views arose, her Kentucky drawl had a sudden rebirth. "Now three of 'em's run off," she'd said. "Wherever they are, they know by now how good they had it. They aren't like us, you know. They need someone ordering their time."

Hannah had left the circle of women at that point. She wasn't the first to excuse herself, and it wasn't long before Mrs. Baker and her daughter sat alone in the shade of the cypress tree.

"But a certain Samaritan, as he journeyed, came where he was: and when he saw him, he had compassion on him, and went to him, and bound up his wounds, pouring in oil and wine, and set him on his own beast, and brought him to an inn, and took care of him."

Hannah thought of her father on his knees, washing the feet of the man and his son, dressing their wounds with salve and clean bandages. Her eyes filled with tears. *Lord Jesus, let me love like that. Grant me a heart that cares more for Your children who suffer than for my own selfish wishes. Bless Papa and Liam for their kind hearts and help me to put Your kingdom above my—*

The door creaked softly as it opened. Hannah turned discreetly. Just enough to see a tall, sun-bronzed man take his seat in the third row. The heat beneath her collar grew and no amount of fanning or prayer would cool it.

CHAPTER 13

Jake stopped in front of the elevator and stared at the gift shop display case. Baskets of silk daisies in unnatural colors so bright they hurt his eyes, stuffed bunnies and bears, and slippers embellished with sparkles and pearls—all strategically located for those who wanted to arrive with full hands to complement their empty words.

He looked down at the paper bag in his hand.

Not exactly a gift, but at least he wasn't empty-handed.

He should be out looking for a scared cat. He had the perfect excuse for spending the rest of the daylight hours in a kayak, and yet here he was—in a place that felt as familiar as his basement bedroom and equally depressing. If he stopped making everyone else's problems his own he just might be able to squeeze out a couple of hours for a life.

He kicked the bottom of the wall with a plaster-splotched boot, turned around, and pushed the button.

The elevator moved too fast for his liking. He hadn't figured out what he was going to say because he hadn't figured out what he was really doing there. His mom could have made this trip for him.

The door opened on the second floor and his phone rang.

"Hey, Topher. 'Sup?"

"Who is she?"

"She who?"

"The hot chick you buzzed out of here to see. Never even said good-bye."

He hadn't? Jake rubbed the back of his neck. "No hot chick." *Really?* "Had to pick up something for the Foster job." He hadn't shared any of the details of the past forty-eight hours with the guys in his crew. In a matter of days he'd need Topher to start mudding and sanding and he'd meet the "Foster job" face-to-face.

"So you're free to hang out tonight? I'm throwing some bratwurst on. Everybody's bringing something. Six work?"

Jake glanced at his watch. "Sure. I'll grab chips and stuff."

"Bring the chick, too."

"Chicken?" Jake yelled over the static from the bag he crinkled next to his phone. "Sure, I'll bring chicken. Bye."

With a grin he couldn't repress, he walked down the hall. At the door to 254, he took off his cap and walked in. She was sitting almost upright, staring out the window. He cleared his throat. "Hi."

Her head jerked toward him. "Hi. You scared me."

He shrugged. "I scare myself sometimes." He held out the bag.

"What is…oh! A phone! You got me a…*my* phone?" She pushed a button on the side. "It works. How in the world?"

"Kitty litter."

"What?"

"I sealed it in a bag of kitty litter and left it in the hot truck all day. It's a little trick I learned after dumping my kayak."

Her face lit with a hero-worship kind of look that doubled his pulse. *There you go again, Braden.* Some guys were adrenaline junkies. His personal addiction was a wistful sigh and a you're-so-wonderful gaze. *My name is Jacob Braden and I'm a rescue addict.*

"Thank you." Emily opened her phone and let out a sigh. Of relief, not awe.

Jake sank into a chair. Maybe this was where his addiction ended. She certainly wasn't doing anything to feed it. "You're welcome."

"And *you're* wonderful."

Oh brother. "I just figured you might need it. I'd be lost without mine. Don't have anybody's number memorized."

"Me either. I know my parents' and my friend's in California. That's it." She clutched her phone to her chest. "So now I have to make this up to you, too."

We're up to two dinners and two movies now, right? "You could make it up to me by not making me knock down any more walls." *Except yours.*

Emily coughed, grabbed a tissue, and held up one finger until the spasm receded. Eyes watering, she shook her head. "Sorry about that."

Clever how she ignored his request. "I found about three pounds of rice in the dining room wall. You have, or had, mice. I know where you can get a cheap cat. Assuming we can locate it."

"I'll take her. A good watch cat is hard to find. That's only a temporary solution, but I wouldn't mind the company."

Temporary. As in not worth it. But did it have to be temporary? He counted IV drops. The antibiotics dripped healing into her veins. So different from the parade of liquid spheres he'd counted as they flowed into Abby's arm and did nothing but dull her pain.

"You must be exhausted."

He nodded. "It's been an interesting week."

"Can you take some time over the weekend to do something fun?"

"I'm hoping to get out the kayak."

"What kind do you have?" Her eyes took on a higher sheen as she leaned toward him.

The girl had active listening skills down pat. "It's just a little lightweight thing I can throw in the back of the truck."

"Sea or touring?"

"Sea. You've kayaked?"

Was there a rheostat connected to those eyes? She laughed. "I've spent some time on the water. I was on the women's rowing team in college."

His turn to laugh. "That explains a lot."

"A lot of what?"

"Adam was totally impressed with your skills—couldn't believe a female could figure out how to make a paddle. And he said you didn't row like a girl at all."

"Now there's a compliment." She held up her arm and squeezed her bicep. "There was a time I had some respectable upper body strength. I need to work on it. I plan on spending a lot of time on the water in California."

There it was again. *Temporary.* "Do you have a job waiting for you out there?" *Or a guy?*

"Nope." Her hands flipped open, palms up. "That's what makes this an adventure. I have a friend living out there, so at least I'll know one person."

He friend or she friend? "What's the draw? I mean, besides year-round summer, white beaches, incredible views, ocean air?"

Her smile seemed to tighten. Her gaze settled on the blanket hills formed by her knees. "It's far away."

"From family?"

"That. And everything." She blew out a quick breath and shot him a closed-lip smile that seemed to apologize for the break in her voice. "I used to run a preschool. I spent my days playing Freeze Tag and Leapfrog. I can't keep up with four-year-olds anymore."

"So you're starting a whole new life."

She nodded. "There's something I want to accomplish before that, but essentially, yes. California will be the beginning of the new me."

"And what about now?" He hadn't really intended to ask the question out loud. But now that she was listening in on his thoughts, why stop? "If you're not the old you or the new you, what does that make you?"

"Good question. In limbo, I guess."

"Or in transition. You can't be static. My football coach always said if you're not striving to improve, you're regressing. There's no coasting in life."

Emily nodded. "I guess flipping this house is my striving. It's moving me toward my goal."

"But what about personally? Socially?" His subconscious agenda unveiled as the words formed on his tongue. "You can't be in relationship limbo either." *Too strong.* "Don't you think people are made to be in community?"

"Yes." The single word was bathed in caution. "When we're in a place where we can put down roots. Until then, relationships don't make sense." She bit down on her bottom lip. "That didn't come out right. I so appreciate you and your mother. But I'd planned on not getting to know anyone here. What's the point when I'll be leaving?"

"Nothing wrong with long-distance friends. I have college friends from Idaho to the Bahamas. Gives me an excuse to travel." He shrugged. "Well, it did. Until my sister died. My life's in a bit of a holding pattern until we figure out what's happening with Adam and Lexi."

"What do you mean?"

"My mom and I hope to take guardianship away from Ben. If we can just prove he's the creep we know he is. I'm hoping to adopt them."

"You? Not your mother?"

"My mom's got fibromyalgia. I guess she told you about that. That and her age would work against her in a custody battle."

Her lips parted. Her eyes told him once again how amazing he was. He turned away. *Lord, kill my pride.*

She tipped her head, like a little girl watching the last scene of *Cinderella*. "That's a huge sacrifice."

He shrugged and took a mental spear to the ego monster. "Anyway, I have some understanding of putting off your life until the dominoes start falling."

"Interesting place to be, isn't it? How do we keep from regressing?"

Jake laced his fingers and stretched his arms. "Maybe it's okay to live while you're waiting for life to begin."

"Maybe. We don't want to get rusty or out of practice."

He felt his Adam's apple rise and fall like a blip on a heart monitor. "We sure don't." But rust would be safe. "Tina said she invited you to the barbecue."

"She did."

Picking up his cap, he stood. "Good place to practice living."

CHAPTER 14

This wasn't working.

Jake lay on his back, projecting his frustration onto his black ceiling.

Lexi's bed sat on the other side of the spot he'd stared at four nights in a row. Lexi's bed with Emily in it.

What had his mother been thinking?

He knew the answer to that. But how was he supposed to sleep with her right there, eight feet above him? And it wasn't just lack of sleep causing him grief. Things he'd done for thirty-three years without thought—things like chewing and swallowing—suddenly seemed to take conscious effort with those huge blue eyes across the supper table.

She wasn't his type. His parameters had changed some since he'd gotten serious about God, but he still liked the playful kind, girls who loved the cat-and-mouse, tug-of-war games of courtship. Emily Foster was beyond challenge. There were walls, and then there were walls. There wasn't a loose brick anywhere in hers. It would take the sledgehammer he'd pummeled her dining room with to make even a dent.

She was so not his type.

What about Heidi? He punched his pillow, forcing it into a U-shape to cradle his stiff neck. Okay, truth be told, there were two kinds of women he was drawn to, all still under the heading of "challenge." When it came to needy damsels, he was a total sucker.

Common sense turned to rubber right along with his knees the first time he'd looked into Heidi's eyes. She was in trouble—out of a job, out of rent money. And he'd been out of his mind to hire her. Topher told him so the first day. It took Jake another month to believe him.

He shivered, shutting his eyes against the memory of the time and money he'd sacrificed.

No more needy women.

Behind the walls, Emily was as needy as they came. Something lurked behind those eyes, some secret or loss, some reason she was all alone in a strange town, working her way toward a place where she couldn't say what she'd be doing.

But Emily was different. She wasn't asking for help.

He threw the covers off, knowing he had to get out of his house before she woke. Out of his house. . .to spend the day at hers. The upside of this ongoing torture was that he was working faster than he'd ever worked before. He grabbed his jeans off the desk chair and took one final look at the ceiling. Did she always sleep on her back the way he'd found her in her attic? Hair in a ponytail or splayed across her pillow? Pajamas? Nightgown?

He yanked the door handle. It slammed into his big toe. With a yelp, he kicked it with his good foot.

What part of "impossible" don't you understand, Braden?

Emily woke just before seven with one thing on her mind.

Pancakes.

A tiny glimmer of something akin to joy stirred inside her, a few inches above her rumbling stomach. She was hungry! And she knew what she wanted to eat.

Veronica would be ecstatic. She'd woven "How's your appetite?" into every session, as if the day Emily announced she'd eaten something just because it sounded good would be the day she was healed. No more guilt, no more panic. Hunger trumps it all.

Flat on her back in Lexi's bed, she stretched. Her hand bumped something soft and fuzzy. Her stomach grumbled again. Pancakes. Maybe with strawberries. "Celebrate the victories," she whispered to a stuffed purple hippo. "No matter how small."

In no hurry to get up, she turned on her side. Wide stripes, purple and lime green, covered the walls. Gauzy butterflies with sparkles on their wings perched on the walls and ceiling, some as small as Emily's hand, others a good two feet wide. Hot pink, bright yellow, dotted with colored glass jewels and sprinkled with glitter.

There was something magical about this house. After the second night, she hadn't needed a sleeping pill. She felt relaxed with Jake's mom. She liked Blaze's "clean enough to be healthy, dirty enough to be happy" philosophy. So unlike the atmosphere she'd grown up with. Jake's mom somehow struck the perfect balance of making her feel both at home and like an honored guest. No eggshells, no fake smiles. They'd shared a few tears and a lot of laughs.

Her stomach growled again. Would anyone be up yet? She got out of bed and, with only a few stretches, moved with relative ease. Her lungs felt clearer and the weakness she'd felt since getting out of the hospital was fading. After a trip to the bathroom, she walked out to the kitchen.

Jake stood by the back door, boots on, hat hooked on one finger, scarfing down a bowl of cereal.

"Morning." She laughed at his stance. "Where's the fire?"

"Gotta finish up a job so I can get to your place before the lumber arrives." His tone was all business.

"Sure you don't have time for pancakes? Strawberry pancakes? I know there's a box in the pantry and it won't take—"

"No." He opened the door and set his bowl on the counter. A dozen Kix still floated on the milk. "Thanks. Gotta go."

The door opened and he exited before Emily could say another word.

Rude man.

⚜

"Whoa!" Adam sat cross-legged on his grandmother's living room rug, eyes riveted to Emily's laptop. "You could have ghosts in your house!"

127

Emily leaned on a couch pillow and chewed the last bite of her BLT. She bounced her eyebrows at Adam. "Cool."

"I'm serious. Have you been to Chances yet?"

"No." The restaurant was only a block from her house, but it wasn't the kind of place to visit alone.

"It used to be the Old Union House and"—hazel eyes widened through a dramatic pause—"it was linked to the Underground Railroad Movement."

Emily shot a message-laden look toward the kitchen door and pressed her index finger to her lips.

Adam nodded. "They hid runaway slaves," he whispered. "The walls are eighteen inches thick." He estimated the width with his hands. "It was built in 1843. A plank road ran from Racine to Janesville, right through Rochester. Slaves were brought up the Fox River during the night and just before dawn they'd go back through a tunnel from the river to the hotel. The next night the slaves would be taken back through the tunnel to the river to continue their journey north."

"And their ghosts still stalk the tunnel at night." Emily wiggled her fingers in the air and let out a subdued but eerie wail.

It was good to hear the boy laugh. He was here today because tennis practice, which he claimed he hated, had been cancelled. His stepfather didn't know he was here, and Blaze felt no compunction to tell him. She'd been baking cookies and singing to herself for the past hour.

Adam squinted and cocked his head to one side. "I bet that's why you're living here. You heard the ghosts and you're scared to go back."

"I'm not living here. I'm going back this afternoon."

"Maybe." Blaze stood in the doorway. "But first she'll go to the barbecue with us." She brought something from behind her back. "Or she'll miss out on Black Forest cake."

Blaze twirled her chocolate heaven-on-a-plate under their noses. They groaned in duet. "What're you two looking at?" She peered over Adam's shoulder.

"Adam's giving me an education on Rochester history."

"Look, Grandma. When they remodeled Chances back in the

seventies, they found a crawl space that went all the way under the ground to the river. They say there are tunnels all over under Rochester, and years ago they were sealed off because of the howls and screams that came out of them in the middle of the night. The locals thought the tunnels led to hell and had them sealed with a warning sign to *never* open them."

Emily faked a shiver. "Creepy."

"We gotta go there."

"Jake did a report on the tunnels in high school. I think we still have it."

Shock registered on Adam's face. "You seriously knew about this and never told me?"

Blaze laughed. "The locals all know about it. Some people think the tunnels were used to transport runaway slaves."

"Do you think there are ghosts?"

"My grandma thought so." She tipped her head toward Emily. "She thought your house was occupied."

This time the chill was real. "The little boy across the street mentioned ghosts."

The oven timer buzzed. Blaze shrugged and walked back toward the kitchen. "Who knows?" She pursed her lips, widened her eyes, and opened the oven.

Adam stretched out on his belly. "We have to do some serious research and—ouch!" He rolled onto his back and pulled a flashlight out of a front pocket.

Emily shook her head. "Your grandma says she weighed your pants the other day."

Adam grinned. "Thirteen point two pounds."

"Unbelievable. No wonder you sank like a rock in the river."

"Hey, I'm not the one who had to be rescued."

Emily set her plate on an end table. "Touché. So is your stash all top-secret?"

"No." He got to his feet. "I guess you need to know what resources are available since you're going to be my research partner."

Emily's laugh was drowned by a rip of Velcro. "It's my house. My ghosts." She lowered her voice. "My secret room."

"True." Adam set a compass on the coffee table. "But there's no way you can carry out this investigation without my expertise." He unsnapped his back right pocket. "Or my duct tape."

"Good point."

"Or my knife."

"That already came in handy."

He reached into a patch pocket on his thigh. "Or my mirror."

"Never know when you may need to send Morse code or touch up your lipstick."

"Or start a fire or burn ants to eat."

"So true."

A ball of string, a wad of dental wax, and a pocket-sized rock-identification book lined up on the table.

"Did anything get wrecked in the river?"

Adam shrugged. "Nothing important. Jake bought me a new ball of string. I carry a different book every day. I had one about stars and that got soaked, but I have tons of those. The rest is waterproof." To prove the point, he pulled out a book of waterproof matches. "Oh! Did you hear what he brought me in the hospital?"

"No. What?"

"A GPS. It's an early birthday present. He got sick of my talking about it, I guess. So our research can take us anywhere in the world and we won't get lost."

"Think I'll start calling you Tom Sawyer."

"Nah. Just call me Sawyer. You know, from *Lost*."

"Gotcha."

From a zippered pouch hanging from his belt he withdrew a clear plastic bag, the bottom filled with crumbled dried leaves. Emily's jaw unhinged. She knew that stuff all too well. "Adam. Where in the world did you get that?"

He stuffed it back in the pocket. "The pet store. I left some food by the bridge, but—"

"Catnip!" She laughed in the wave of relief. "It's catnip. For the cat."

"Of course. What did you th—. Oh. I don't do that stuff."

"I'm sorry. I was sure you didn't, but when I first looked at it. . ."

Adam performed a reprise of her earlier eyebrow wiggle. "Evidently you know all about it, huh? Were you, like, a druggie when you were my age?"

"No!" *Not at your age.* This rabbit trail had to come to a quick end. "Absolutely not." She waved her hand to include his entire collection. "Well, Sawyer, I'm convinced I need to hire you to—"

The back door burst open, banging against the microwave stand. Jake strode through the kitchen, passing his mother without a glance. "Emily!" His eyes locked on hers, shining with an excitement he seemed to be trying to hide. "Are you up to going over to your house for a bit? I need your opinion on something." He sounded short of breath.

Emily stood. "Sure. Just need to get something on my feet." She walked toward the jumble of shoes by the front door.

Jake's sigh was controlled but audible.

"What is it? Can I come?" Adam closed the laptop. "Did you fi—"

Her back turned to Jake, Emily missed the look he must have given Adam to silence him. "Later." A boot tap accompanied his answer.

By the time she'd slipped into her sandals, Jake had his hand on the kitchen doorknob.

Blaze patted her arm as she passed. "Don't wear yourself out."

"I won't." Emily slipped through the screen door Jake held open for her. "What is it?"

He ushered her around the house to the sidewalk. "I found something"—he slowed his pace to hers—"under a hidden panel in the bedroom closet."

⚜

September 24, 1852

Hannah snapped a piece of new broom straw and opened the cookstove door. The straw pulled clean from the cake. Doubling her apron skirt, she pulled out the pan and set it on a folded flour sack towel on the table. A square of sunlight framed the gingerbread. The rounded and cracked brown top glistened.

She'd stuck faithfully to Mama's recipe, though she'd been sorely tempted to fold in a new spice with the ginger and cinnamon.

Did poison ivy lose potency when baked?

Her stomach growled like an angry bobcat. She'd not get away

131

with sampling before supper this time. Tonight there would be guests. They would sit in the dining room and eat off Mama's good dishes. They would talk of the weather and the cost of wheat. They would speak of the school for the deaf being built in Walworth County, wonder aloud at how many people now rode the train from Milwaukee to Waukesha, and talk of rumors that before long rails would connect Lake Michigan to the Mississippi.

She and Papa would bring up anything and everything to keep the conversation from steering toward politics or slavery. But their guests would do all they could to derail them.

She remembered when it was different, when a visit from Papa's cousin was something to anticipate, and not with dread. Jonathan Shaw and his wife, Victoria, were wealthy. They had come to America two years before Papa and made their money in brick making. Jonathan had asked Papa to join his business in Racine, but Mama had what she called a "gentle nudge" from the Lord and Papa turned it down.

Hannah peeked under the lid of a cast-iron pot and prodded the stewing chicken with a fork. The meat fell from the bones. With two forks, she lifted it to a platter and dumped chopped onions and carrots into the bubbling broth. Returning the cover, she looked out the back door at the three-leafed plants sprouting along the riverbank. The male cardinal perched on a sapling beside it, bobbing toward the leaves as if to tempt her. *Creamed chicken anyone? Why, that's just a touch of parsley, Cousin Victoria.*

How was it that two men who sprouted from the same branch of the family tree could see life so differently? The answer whispered over the steady *tap, tap, tap* of the pot cover. Faith made the difference. Papa saw things black or white, clear and simple, while Jonathan seemed to go through life blurring the boundaries of right and wrong and making his own rules. Even out here in Rochester, people spoke of Jonathan Shaw. A Shaw brick, they claimed, was as warped as the business dealings of the man behind it.

And now he had a side business, a way to bring in a little extra money. The Fugitive Slave Act was a boon to people like Jonathan Shaw, people who did not believe in the worth of a man.

Hannah ripped the flesh from the chicken carcass and repeated the verse Papa had read at breakfast: "The discretion of a man deferreth his anger; and it is his glory to pass over a transgression." Papa thought it would be an excellent proverb for them both to meditate on today. She'd memorized it easily enough. Putting it into practice was another matter. *Lord Jesus, guard my thoughts and put a bridle on my tongue tonight.*

Hoofbeats announced the arrival of the carriage from Racine, and she tasted the gravy. Perfect. Though it could use a dash of color.

⚜

"Lovely dinner, dear. You're as good at making do as your dear mother was."

Making do? Hannah hid a tight fist in the fold of her skirt as she cleared the twice-filled plate from in front of Victoria. What the woman had eaten could have fed her and Papa for the next three days. "Thank you, ma'am."

"You'll breakfast with us at the Union House, won't you?" Victoria patted her mouth with a linen napkin. Hannah's stomach twisted as a dark green *S* touched Victoria's pinched lips. It seemed a desecration that the initial embroidered by Mama's thin, beautiful hands should touch a mouth that spouted such ignorance.

"Of course," Papa answered.

Hannah found a genuine smile easy for the first time all evening. A meal at the inn would give her something pleasant to focus on as she ignored her dinner companions.

"Very well. Shall we say eight?" Victoria fiddled with the cameo pin at her neck.

Papa nodded. "I do apologize again for not having accommodations for you here."

Jonathan Shaw stood and grasped the back of his pudgy wife's chair. "We will be well served at the Union House. I've heard interesting things about the place lately, and I'm delighted to have the opportunity to check it out myself." Beady eyes bore into Papa as if he were looking down the barrel of a gun aimed at a rabid wolf. . . or a man running for his life.

Papa's face colored. He cleared his throat. "Hopefully by the next time you come, we'll have the upstairs finished. I lost my ambition after Elizabeth died, but I've started working on it again lately."

Jonathan nodded. "Do show me how far you've come. In fact, I'd love to see the whole house, including the cellar. We'll be building a house for Victoria's mother soon, and yours seems just about the right size." He stepped into the front parlor, and Papa had no choice but to escort him.

Hannah's other fist balled. Any other man would have been simply rude with this kind of behavior. Jonathan Shaw was not rude, he was shrewd. *Please, God, veil his eyes.* Had she been careless about concealing the door? Did it stand ajar? She smiled as naturally as possible at Victoria. "Would you like a seat in the parlor while the men look at the house? I'll just get the milk put away and—"

"Put away in the cellar?"

"Yes." Perspiration dotted Hannah's upper lip. "It's so much cooler down there."

Victoria waddled to the opposite end of the table and picked up the milk pitcher. "I'll help you carry things, dear."

CHAPTER 15

It's proof."

Jake pointed at a blue velvet bag in the middle of the card table. "I just glanced at a couple, but it's proof."

Emily sank into the chair, legs shaking from the one-block walk. The bag was about the size of her spread hand and heavier than it appeared. Tiny tufts of blue velvet stuck to her fingertips.

"Be careful."

The drawstring was already loosened. She slid her thumb and forefinger inside and pulled out a stack of letters. Yellowed, brittle, the same handwriting she'd seen on the others.

Jake pulled a chair next to hers and sat down. She unfolded the top one slowly, as if she were opening butterfly wings. She read the words out loud.

"Dearest, Autumn has always filled me with such joy. How God must delight in showering His canvas with color. But this autumn is bittersweet, for with every leaf that falls, I worry more about you. Papa says we will see few parcels when the threat of snow increases, but if there are deliveries, the danger will be so much greater. It is harder to hide without the cover of leaves. Oh, my love, I should not share my fears with you, should I? Though you never talk of it, you must be haunted by the possibility of danger lurking behind every tree as you hunt. Forgive me. What little faith I have tonight. If I

135

had the time, I would write you only in the morning when sunlight makes everything seem safe and familiar."

As she read, Jake leaned closer until his arm slid around the back of her chair. The words and his warmth did strange things to her voice. Setting the letter down, she simply stared at the feathery script. Love letters, hidden in the wall for a hundred and sixty years, probably never seen by the one for whom they were penned. "So beautiful."

Jake leaned yet closer. "His replies are not quite so flowery."

"*His?*" Her head jerked toward Jake's. She found herself staring at his full lips. She blinked and turned away. With the care of a surgeon, she lifted the second folded paper. The one beneath it bore a strikingly different handwriting. Heavy, bold lines without the rounded, feminine curls.

Emily gasped. "Did he come back?" she whispered.

"What?"

"I found three letters. All from her."

"When? Where?"

"Under the porch. The day we found the room."

Grooves appeared between his eyebrows. Thick black lashes narrowed around crystal blue eyes.

Those eyes. Why had she never noticed them quite like this before? Why was she noticing now? Again, she turned away. "I should have told you. I just don't want this place turning into a circus, you know? Before the work is done, I—"

"It's your house. You didn't have to tell me about it."

Clearly he was striving for indifference, but the disappointment edging his voice stabbed between two ribs like a miniature dagger. "No. I should have." She forced her eyes back to his. "You had a right to know. I'm sorry."

His smile was slow in appearing, but when it showed, it deepened a divot on his right cheek she was sure hadn't been there before and brought the luster back to his eyes.

"All's forgiven."

The table seemed to tip beneath her arms. *Get a grip*. She yanked her gaze back to the letter. "In the letters I found, he'd gone somewhere. She didn't know if he was coming back for her, and she blamed herself. So were these written before or after? The others were written in November of 1852. Was it the same autumn?" She took a steadying breath. "My love..." Something more off-key than a frog distorted her voice.

"Allow me." Jake's fingers grazed hers as he took it from her. "My love." He cleared his throat. "I have begun reading in the Book of Psalms every evening before I go out, as you suggested. This is the treasure I gleaned last night: 'The Lord also will be a refuge for the oppressed, a refuge in times of trouble.' Even when a full moon and barren trees allow few hiding places, I will be reminded that God alone is my refuge—and that you are my North Star."

Emily laughed, instantly lowering the temperature in the room. "Not as flowery? And 'you are my North Star'? Come on. Is that how you talk to women?"

"Of course. I'm shocked you'd even question it. I am a Renaissance man—the biceps of a contractor but the heart of a poet." He set the letter down. His hand slid over hers. "Your eyes are the stars of the midnight sky. You are the fair princess Andromeda, chained to a rock. You should not be wearing such chains as these. Tell me your name, fair princess, and I—"

She jerked her hand from his. Her cheeks burned, her pulse thundered in her ears. She knew this story. The beautiful virgin, sacrificed to appease the god Neptune, saved by dashing young Perseus, the monster-slayer. Emily's eyes burned. She was none of those things—beautiful, virgin, or able to be saved.

And now, by ruining what Jake had intended as a funny moment, she'd exposed too much. "You should be on stage." She attempted a laugh. It fell flat.

Instead of the irritation she expected, his eyes softened. The hand that had covered hers lifted her chin. "What are your chains, Emily?"

Her tears had nowhere to go but down her face and into his hand. She slid her chair away from the table and stood. "There's a box upstairs...with the other letters." She stared at him, waiting for an answer to a question she hadn't asked, not bothering to wipe away the tears. He'd seen them before.

Jake, the would-be monster slayer, nodded. "I'll put them away."

Adam leaned on the counter, eating his ninth cookie and watching the second hand sweep the black face of his Iron Man watch. Jake wasn't back yet.

"Give yourself plenty of time." Grandma Blaze sealed two bags of cookies and stuck them in his backpack. Chocolate chip for him, snickerdoodles for Lexi.

"I will. And I have to have a few minutes to hang out by the bridge before Blimpo gets home."

"Adam!"

She turned her back as she yelled at him. She probably thought it was funny, but she was too nice to say so. "I left two bowls of food for Pansy last night. One at home where Bl—*he*—can't find it and one by the bridge where we saw her last. I checked that one on my way here, but that was kind of early for her. She's used to getting fed after school, so maybe she's found it now." His voice was starting to sound weird. He didn't want his grandmother thinking he was going to cry. Pansy wasn't his cat.

"How's Lex holding up?"

"You know how girls are. She sewed Pansy a new pillow. It's purple and—" His voice crackled. Jake said that was normal for his age. "Hey, I gotta go. Thanks for the cookies." He hugged his grandma then ran outside and smack into Emily. "Oops. Sorry."

"Where's the fire?" Her mouth kind of smiled, but her eyes were all red.

Whatever Jake had found, she wasn't happy about it, or maybe she was just sad. Maybe they found out who Mariah was. Adam glanced at his bike. He was dying to know what it was, but if he took the time to ask, he'd have to forget about stopping at the bridge. And he had to find Pansy. He couldn't handle too many more days of hearing Lexi cry at night. "Gotta get back before Blim—my stepfather figures something's up."

Emily stepped aside. "Ride safe."

"Yeah. I will."

The back roads were faster than the bike trail and he'd avoid going through town. He pedaled onto Highway D and strained to see Emily's house. The trees were filling in and it was almost totally camouflaged from the road now, but he got a quick glimpse of Jake, hunched over with his head down.

He was in the middle of the bridge when it hit him. Jake and Emily liked each other! Sure, she'd been crying and he was slumped over like Eeyore on a really bad day, but that probably meant they liked each other a lot. Practically everybody in seventh grade was going out with somebody, and remembering who was with who was like watching a magician doing a ball and cup trick. He didn't get it, but he'd learned enough to know that if a guy was mad and not talking to a girl and she was crying and saying bad things about him, they were probably in love.

Jake and Emily. Now that was cool. He let out a wild-cheetah yell. Lexi would absolutely freak. She'd probably start drawing the dress she wanted to wear for the wedding. Maybe it would help her forget about Pansy.

'Cause he had a scary feeling the cat might not be coming back.

✤

Pansy hadn't touched her food. But he'd no sooner turned the corner than the orange cat appeared on the opposite side of the road, padding proudly, head held high, with a mouse in her mouth.

Relief hit so hard, it stung his eyes.

The next thing he saw was blue. Big and blue and waddling along the roadside like a gigantic Weeble. In Ben's hand was Adam's pellet gun.

Adam skidded to a stop, tossed his bike into the bushes, and hid. He had to do something. He patted his pants legs and an idea hit. He grabbed his mirror, shined it at the sun and angled the reflection onto the road about two yards in front of Pansy.

Look, you stupid cat!

Adam slunk deeper into the bushes and rested his arm on a branch. With just a slight twist of his wrist, he made the patch of light quiver on the gravel. Pansy slowed. Her head lowered. Her whole body crouched. The mouse dropped. Adam checked for cars then moved the light, inch by inch, into the street. Pansy followed.

Ben took aim.

139

"Keep moving." Adam mouthed the command and dragged the light closer, faster. Just two yards to go. Still no cars from either direction. A miracle.

The air rifle pumped. The noise should have scared the cat, but she was mesmerized by the traveling, trembling light. One more yard and Adam would grab her, run for the bike, and—

"Pansy!" Lexi screamed from the house. The cat startled. The gun fired. Pansy shrieked. Her body lurched, landing within inches of Adam's feet.

Oh God, please. Adam burst out of the bushes. Tears blurring his vision, he crouched. Lexi's screams and Ben's curses filled his ears. He laid one hand on the sun-warmed fur. "She's breathing, Lex!"

Lexi slid in the gravel on the steep driveway and dashed into the road. A car horn blared, brakes squealed. She didn't look up. Sobs shook her as she dove to the shoulder, landing hard on her knees. "Pansy. Wake up. Wake up, baby. I'm here. God, let her be okay."

Amber eyes opened. A soft mew. A tiny pink tongue licked Lexi's fingertip. Lexi laughed, but it still sounded like a sob. "She's okay."

Adam wasn't so sure. The only thing he knew was they needed to get her far away from the cursing man with the air gun. "Try to pick her up. We gotta get out of here."

Lexi nodded, running her hands over the orange fur. She gasped. Blood covered her fingers. "Her front leg. It's broken."

On the other side of the highway, Ben spat in the gravel. "Get away from the stupid cat or I'll shoot you, too!" He added a string of hate-filled words.

"She might try to fight you." Adam slipped his backpack off. "We'll have to put her in here so we can both get on the bike. We'll be halfway to Grandma's before he makes it back up the driveway."

Lexi's face contorted as she slid her hands under Pansy. The cat moaned. "We're going for a ride, sweetkins, just like always. We'll take you to the doctor and he'll fix you up and—" Pansy hissed. The claws on her good paw splayed and raked Lexi's arm. Lexi flinched but didn't pull away. "Come on, girl, I know it hurts, but we have to do this to make you better." As she talked, Pansy settled like a wilting flower. Lexi eased her into the pack. "It won't be long, baby, we'll get you—"

The gun fired. A pellet grazed the gravel less than a yard behind Lexi's feet. Lexi's eyes shot wide.

"You two get away from that blasted cat or—"

"Madsen! Are you insane?" A screen door slammed. Herb Klein stomped out of the house next door. "I just called the police, and I hope they slam your stupid hide in jail. Of all the crazy. . . Adam? Lexi? You okay?"

"We're fine. Pansy's hurt. Could you call my uncle and tell him to come get us?"

"You bet. You two come over here until he gets here. Madsen, put the gun down or I'll go get mine."

The gun clattered to the sidewalk. "It's just a stupid toy."

"Tell that to the cat. And the cops."

⚜

Finally. A witness. Jake stood with his arms around Adam and Lexi, staring at the broken butterfly clock and listening with quiet joy as Herb regaled the blue-uniformed officers with tales of Ben's rages. He'd witnessed Ben smacking the cat onto the concrete and repeated numerous threats he'd heard through the screens in the past week.

"You guys know I've called before, and I know you can't do much if all he's doing is yelling, but I always said if that"—he stopped, clearly searching for a cleaned-up word—"if I ever saw him hurt a hair on either one of those kids I'd—"

"We appreciate your call, Mr. Klein."

Ben played down every accusation. He spoke to the officers as if they were old drinking buddies. "You know what the pressure of single parenting is like. Sure, I lose it once in awhile." He painted a picture of a poor, bereaved man doing his best to raise his late wife's children to be upstanding citizens. "I wasn't shooting to hit the cat. It's my daughter's pet, why would I want to hurt it? I was just putting a little fear into it. Not like I used a shotgun, you know. I shot it off just for the noise and the st—cat turned at the last second and got in the way. I'd never hurt a fly. Just ask my kids."

The female officer nodded. "We will."

Jake couldn't read their faces. He had no idea if they were

141

buying the story. He gave his address and phone number and said the social workers could pop in anytime. They'd find the kids happy and cared for.

Finally.

Maybe there wouldn't even be a trial. Maybe the county would just step in and award the kids to him.

"Jake?" Lexi leaned into him. The tears that dampened his shirt were for the cat alone. "Can we take Pansy to the vet now?"

The female officer nodded. "No more questions for now." She gave Lexi a maternal smile. "Hope Pansy's good as new in a few days." She looked up at Jake. "And I hope things go their way."

The officer pointed to the front door. "Let's go, Mr. Madsen."

CHAPTER 16

Lexi walked through her grandparents' back door and into Grandma Blaze's outstretched arms. "We had to leave her until Monday."

Pansy's surgery had lasted almost an hour. Jake left in the middle of it to take Adam home, but Lexi wasn't budging. The vet promised she could see Pansy as soon as the operation was finished. So she'd waited. She had to be the first face Pansy saw when she came to. And she was.

Next to Mom dying, walking away from Pansy was the hardest thing she'd ever done. When the anesthesia fully wore off, Pansy would wake up in a cage. She'd never been caged before. She'd be terrified, and Lexi wouldn't be there to tell her everything was going to be fine.

"Thank goodness you found her and she's going to be okay." Grandma Blaze lifted her chin. "And thank goodness you're here. And safe."

"But what if—"

"We'll cross that bridge when we come to it. Why don't you take a shower and get some rest before the barbecue. Emily's clearing her stuff out of your room so—"

Lexi pulled away. "Emily? She's here?"

Her grandmother grinned. "I thought you knew. I invited her to stay here when she left the hospital."

"I knew, but I thought she'd be gone by now." *And no one said she took my room.* With long strides she walked through the dining room and turned the corner. Laughter came from her room.

Adam sat cross-legged in the middle of her bed, holding his mirror over his head. A blob of light danced on Emily's face as she stuffed clothes into a bag. Emily turned. "Lexi! Adam's been telling me what happened. Poor Pansy."

Lexi stared at a gray T-shirt on the floor. She never threw clothes on the floor. The bed was made, but the quilt was lower on one side than the other.

Emily reached toward her and rested a pasty-pale hand on her shoulder. "And how are you?"

Tears she thought she'd run out of pressed against the backs of her eyes. She didn't know why. Emily's voice was kind, her touch gentle. Adam liked her. And if Adam could be believed, so did Jake.

But Lexi didn't. "Fine." She would not shed those tears.

"What are you wearing to the barbeque?"

Her best friend was lying in a cage, her leg in a cast. What she wore to a silly barbeque wasn't important. "Nothing special." She reached behind the door, yanked her robe off its hook, and folded it in her arms, just the way she'd held Pansy only hours ago. "I'm going to take a shower."

And you'd better be gone when I get back.

❧

Emily stepped out of the shower in her own bathroom. She'd showered at the Bradens' early this morning, but if she was going to do anything with her hair for the barbeque, washing it again was a necessity.

Head wrapped in a giant terry-cloth turban, she stared at her reflection with a more critical eye than she had since before the accident. Her skin looked dry and blotchy from eighteen months without moisturizer. Skin that had once been accustomed to monthly facials had done a poor job of fending for itself while she'd been preoccupied with deciding if life was worth living. The split ends hidden by the towel had fared much worse. She wrote "hot oil treatment" on a Post-It note on the mirror, right under "moisturizer". Looking up at the burned-out bulbs, she thought back to a matter of days ago when none of this mattered.

Jake was right. Someday the new, freed Emily Foster would actually want to be part of the real world. She'd want friends, maybe even dates. Until then, she needed to polish her rusty social skills and relearn confidence.

She needed life practice. Not "kiss and run," but maybe "have fun and run." So there it was—a new, rhyming life philosophy.

And what better place to start than here, where everyone knew she wasn't staying and relationships were temporary. Like Post-It notes. Not too sticky.

She glanced at the time on her phone. She had two and a half hours before Blaze would pick her up. Enough time to replace the makeup and nail polish expiring in bins in her basement, pick up salad ingredients and a tub of peanut butter cookie dough, and do something drastic with her hair.

As she picked up her keys from the kitchen counter, an idea took shape. Lexi could use some cheering up. She pulled out her phone and stared at it. She didn't have Blaze's number.

She *did* have Jake's.

Walking into what had once been the dining room, she nodded with approval. The wall the room had shared with the front parlor was gone. The openness was freeing. It confirmed what she'd known all along—she was right, and Renaissance Man, the guy with the biceps of a contractor but the heart of a poet, was wrong. She smiled, her gaze drifting to the dust-coated card table. Two imprints in the plaster dust marked the places he'd rested his arms. *"Your eyes are the stars of the midnight sky. Tell me your name, fair princess."*

She'd overreacted, let her baggage get in the way again. His reaction had startled her. *"What are your chains, Emily?"* She needed to explain. But how much? How many links of her chain could he handle? Would he even answer her call? She walked to the window and stared out at her spruce tree. Karen twittered on a high branch. Cardinal Bob was nowhere to be seen or heard. For once, the song of the red-brown bird didn't sound scolding or commanding. She sounded lonely. "Sure, you chase him away and miss him when he's gone."

Emily leaned her forehead against the window frame and dialed.

It rang four times then went to voice mail. "Hi, this is Jake with Braden Improvements. We're here to make your space a better place. Leave a message and I'll return your call ASAP. God bless."

Had the last two words always been part of his message? She had no idea. *"God bless."* His smile came through in the soft benediction. It caught her off guard. When the tone sounded, she scrambled to remember why she'd called.

"Jake. This is Emily. I was just heading to Walmart and thought maybe Lexi would like to ride along, but I don't have your mom's number. If you could give me a call and—"

Chimes announced an incoming call. "Hello?"

"Emily? It's Jake. Sorry I missed your call." No disgust or condemnation colored his greeting.

She explained why she'd called.

A long pause followed. She was about to say maybe it wasn't such a good idea, when he cleared his throat. "That would be so good for her. Thank you." He gave her the number. She wrote it in the plaster dust next to his arm prints. "I'll warn you, though, she gets pretty silly when she's happy."

"I could use some silly about now." She turned back to the window, back to Karen and her lonely song. "I'm sorry I didn't respond the way I should have earlier. Sometimes I—"

"These apologies are going to have to stop, Miss Foster. Let's make a deal. When you do something that genuinely offends me, I'll let you know, okay?"

Cardinal Bob swooped onto a low branch. Emily smiled. "I think you're far too ni—polite to do that."

His laugh widened her smile. "I heard that. You almost called me nice."

"I did no such thing."

"So you don't think I'm nice?"

Her mouth opened. Nothing came out.

Jake laughed again. "I'll expect an answer to that question tonight. Have fun with my niece." The connection ended—before she could tell him she wasn't going to read the letters without him.

Lexi threw her brush at her dresser. "Without asking me? Why would you do that?"

The brush smacked the pen Emily had left there and projected it into the waste basket. "I don't need a haircut."

"That's just an option, Lexi." Her grandmother's hands left her hips. She fished the pen out of the basket. "Emily's getting her hair cut and she said if you wanted a trim at the same time. . ." A heavy sigh puffed her cheeks. "She thought it would be fun if you picked out nail polish together."

"I don't wear nail polish."

"Lex. Emily just wants—"

"I know what she wants!" Every muscle in her body turned to steel like the strings on her guitar. Pressure built in her chest, demanding to be screamed out. "We don't even know her. You let some stranger sleep in my bed and use my things and now you want me to go off with her to who knows where!"

"Walmart." Grandma Blaze swooped her gaze to the ceiling and back to the floor. "Just Walmart, Lex, not Timbuktu."

"What if she's a kidnapper? What if she's going to run off with me and send you ransom notes?"

The hands went back on the hips. "Then I'll gladly give her every one of the three hundred and forty-two dollars in my checking account just to get you back." Eyebrows lifted the same distance as the corners of her mouth.

"Sure, laugh." Lexi shoved her feet into yellow flip-flops. "You probably wouldn't pay anything to get me back."

Her grandmother stepped toward the door. "You're right, we probably wouldn't. Funny, though, that such hard-hearted people are willing to shell out eight hundred and fourteen dollars to put a pin in a cat's leg. Especially a cat that makes me sneeze."

The doorbell rang. Grandma Blaze walked out.

Lexi crumpled on her bed in tears.

Who was the hateful girl taking over her body? Was she possessed? She'd heard that demons couldn't take over your body if you believed in Jesus. Maybe that wasn't true. Or maybe she just thought she believed but she really didn't. *Lord, what's happening to me?*

No answer came. Not even God wanted to spend time with a girl who hissed like an angry cat.

Her mouth jarred open. She looked down at her right hand, at the three red stripes she'd hidden from Jake and her grandma. Pansy had scratched because she was in pain and scared.

Just like her.

She hurt because Pansy hurt and because she missed her mom. She hurt because Adam thought it would be cool if Jake and Emily fell in love and got married and because her grandma laughed with Emily the way she used to laugh with Mom.

And that's why she was scared. Life wasn't good the way it used to be. Life would never be good for her again. But what if everyone around her got happy because Emily was there to make them laugh?

And make them forget.

Think. Nobody else was making sense. It was up to her. She took a deep breath, dried her tears, and went to the bathroom and washed her face. With a smile brighter than anyone had ever smiled, she walked into the living room.

"Hi, Emily. Thank you for thinking of me. This sounds like so much fun."

Without a twinge of sadness Emily watched the faded ends—the last vestiges of her former self—drift to the floor. At the stylist station perpendicular to hers, Lexi leafed through a hair magazine.

Sophia, a short, round Italian with purple highlights in her black hair, held a chunk of Emily's tarnished platinum over her head. "Say good-bye to the old you."

Was the woman eavesdropping on her thoughts? "Good riddance."

"I think you should do something really dramatic." Lexi smiled at her in the mirror. "A wedge. You'd look pretty in really short hair."

"You think so?" Strange that the opinion of a twelve-year-old actually mattered. "Okay, Sophia, you heard the boss. Let's go shorter."

Sophia's scissors slid an inch closer to her scalp.

"What are you going to have done, Lexi?"

"I want bangs. And layers." She pointed to a picture and handed the magazine to a tall, skinny redhead in a maroon smock.

The redhead nodded. "You two are going to a barbeque tonight?"

"Yep." A purple cape settled over Lexi's shoulders. "It's in a barn where they've had dances every year since before the Civil War."

The tingle scooting along Emily's spine was becoming familiar. It was the visceral equivalent of the *Twilight Zone* theme. Would she dance tonight on the same floorboards as the writers of the letters? "I didn't know that."

"You didn't know it was a dance, or you didn't know they started doing them so long ago?"

"Neither. I thought we were going to eat."

"We are. But there's a band, too. Can you line dance?"

Could she line dance? *Oh yeah*. And, for some strange reason, none of the boxes and bags she'd donated to Goodwill before leaving Michigan had contained her gold-toed black boots. Also amazing was the fact that she knew which Rubbermaid bin they'd retired to. "Yeah. Pretty fair."

"Jake hates dancing." Lexi's expression faded to blank.

What did that mean? It was more than just conversation, Emily was sure of it. There was meaning hidden somewhere in the comment.

Maybe she could blame it on the antibiotics, but the truth dawned embarrassingly slowly. She remembered being Lexi's age— one foot in childhood, the other flailing around in the scary abyss of grown-up land. Fairy tales still seemed possible in that in-between age. And Emily had more than a hunch that Lexi was dreaming of an impossible happily-ever-after.

For Jake.

Not good. This fantasy had to stop before it began. In lieu of shaking her head, Emily tsked. Though she felt a kinship with the stone-cold Snow White, she wasn't awaiting a magical kiss. "That's too bad." Did her voice convey the impossibility of her ever falling for a man who couldn't do the electric slide? "Dancing is like breathing. It's necessary for life, don't you think?"

The redhead nodded. "Absolutely. Do you two have dates for tonight?"

"No." They answered in unison, with equal enthusiasm.

"Okay, then."

"What do you look for in a guy, Emily?" Lexi's gaze hid her hopes well.

Sophia tipped Emily's chin down to her chest. The timing was perfect. It gave her a moment to inventory Jake's good qualities and come up with their polar opposites. She thought of the first time he'd found her in tears. *Non-judging.* The battle over her floor plan. *Patient.* Carrying her down the stairs. *Strong, compassionate, unwavering.* *"What are your chains, Emily?"* Intuitive, caring. *"I'll expect your answer tonight."* Funny. Eyes the color of a mountain lake. A truant groan leapt through her lips.

"Something hurt?"

The truth? "No. Just coughing." She coughed into the cape to make it not a lie.

Sophia patted her back. "Do you need some suggestions of guy qualities?"

Emily faked a laugh. "I'm not really in the market at the moment." Still looking down, she didn't have to face the disappointment on a twelve-year-old face.

♕

"Pick a color name that describes you." Lexi waved her hand over two shelves of nail polish and smiled at Emily's too-short hair. The day was turning out way better than she'd expected. Haircut, manicure, pedicure, and realizing Adam was wrong about Jake and Emily.

"I will if you will. And we have to go with the one we pick. . . even if it's Mustard Yellow or Swamp Green."

"Deal. Let's pick two—a serious one and a fun one."

Emily picked up a bottle the color of Barney the dinosaur. "Okay. Serious for fingers, silly for toes."

"Cool."

Lexi scanned the colors. "Mad as a Hatter" would have described her a couple of hours ago.

"I've got mine." Emily held up two bottles.

Lexi took a few more minutes. "Me, too. It's purrrrfect!" She couldn't believe there was a nail color named for her. "Okay. Silly first." She showed Emily a light blue shade. "It's called 'What's with the Cattitude?'"

"That is purrrrfect!" Emily held out a bottle of pale pink polish. "Mine is 'Who Needs a Prince?'"

Way perfect. Adam was so wrong. "What's your serious one?"

"Breathe Life." Emily's bottom lip pushed against the top one. Her shoulders shrugged.

"Why did you pick—"

"Ladies pick colors now?" A short Asian woman gestured toward two open pedicure chairs.

"We're ready." Emily stepped aside and let Lexi follow the woman.

When they were seated, Lexi leaned toward Emily. "I picked my serious one because of you. It's 'Thank You Muchness.'"

❧

October 10, 1852

"Mmm." Dolly Baker batted her eyes in the general direction of Liam and two other men leaning against a wagon in front of the Settlement chapel. "I don't believe there is a more handsome man anywhere in the world."

On the blanket beside her, Hannah gnawed a chicken leg with unrefined vigor and feigned disinterest in all but the chicken. She chewed till there was nothing left of the bite in her mouth. "Can you believe what a gorgeous day this is?" She lifted her face to the sun. "Strange for October, isn't it?"

"Hannah Shaw! Are you ill? There is a man like that in our midst and you talk about the weather?"

"Which man?" She asked it so casually it came out almost like a yawn.

"Liam, silly." Fat sausage curls bounced. "Don't you just feel fluttery when he's around?"

"Hmm." She swallowed the flutters crawling up her throat. "Not really."

"You are ill. Or dead. Look at those eyes. Bluer than the bluest sky." Dolly lingered on a wistful sigh.

And up close, in the moonlight, they sparkle like stars. "Wing?" She shoved a plate beneath Dolly's nose.

151

"How can you think of food at a time like this?"

"Like what?"

"Like two weeks before the barn dance." Dolly dipped her head, shielded her face with her bonnet, and whispered, "Can you keep a secret?"

Corn bread crumbs caught in Hannah's throat, and she coughed until her eyes watered. If her best friend only knew what secrets she could keep. She nodded.

"Liam Keegan is going to ask me to the dance."

A watermelon pickle lodged in her throat. She covered her mouth with the cloth that had wrapped the corn bread and forced a calm breath.

"Of course, Mother wouldn't approve if she knew what I knew." Dolly leaned forward and looked to her right and then her left. "Last week I hid behind the lilacs just to get a closer look at him. I heard him talking to your daddy."

"Wh—what did you hear?"

Dolly laughed, fat curls skimming her shoulders. Her head dipped to one side. "You really don't know, do you? Ah, let's talk of more tasteful things." She picked up a sorghum cookie. "Like Liam Keegan."

With the inside of her mouth feeling like the bottom of her shoe, Hannah forced a laugh. "He told you he was going to ask you to the dance?"

"Don't be ridiculous. He's never said anything more to me than 'Good morning, Miss Baker.' He won't know he's taking me until you tell him."

"Wha...? Me?"

"I saw you at the smithy last week."

"I was picking up hooks for my father." Her face warmed. It was not a lie. She had been picking up coat hooks for the cellar. She had also picked up a stolen kiss.

"Did you or did you not talk to Liam when you were there?"

"I talked to Big Jim. I suppose I might have said a word or two to Liam."

"There! I knew it." Dolly picked up her reticule. "Order me a nice big hook for my father's birthday. We so rarely come to town.

And when you do, suggest that he ask me to the dance."

"I can't do—"

"You must." Her eyes gleamed with something more intense than mischief. "Because if you don't, I'll tell your daddy's not-so-little secret."

Perspiration dampened Hannah's blouse. "What secret?" Her voice was barely audible.

"The one"—Dolly rose gracefully to her feet and brushed crumbs from her skirt—"he would *die* if anyone knew."

With that, she turned and fairly skipped back to the chapel.

CHAPTER 17

"...wouldn't change a thing that changed my life..."

The man in the dirty white cowboy hat and week-old beard sang into the mic with a voice that could almost rival Kenny Chesney. Emily held an ice-filled glass of tea to the pulse points on her wrists and kept her eyes on him—and away from the man sitting in the lawn chair next to her. "The trials, the tears...it's hard to hate what got me here..."

Emily stared up at a star-flecked sky. A faint breeze wafted an intoxicating summer blend of hickory smoke and citronella across the lawn. How long would it take to not hate the things that brought her here?

And how long after she left would it take to stop liking "here"?

"Hungry?" Japanese lanterns reflected in the plastic tumbler Jake lifted toward her.

"Starving." And more than ready to get up and move and busy her hands and her mind with something other than the whistle that had greeted her exit from Blaze's car. Jake had taken her hand and twirled her in a pirouette like a ballerina in a music box. She wiggled the painted toes hidden by her gold-tipped boots. *Who needs a prince?*

Jake's hand on her back steered her to the food table. With all the insensitive jerks in the world, why did she have to hire one of the few remaining gentlemen? She picked up a heavy-duty paper plate and caught Tina staring from behind the pig roaster. A greasy thumb shot in the air.

She felt a tug on her sleeve and looked down. All she saw was the brim of a red cowboy hat. "Michael? Are you under there?" She lifted the hat. "Thought that was you."

Michael nodded, an all-business look on his tanned face. "I caught Squiggles again. He was in our garage on my dad's working bench, and I bringed him over to show you but you weren't there. I looked in your shed for the frog can, but alls I could find was a glass jar. Can I leave him there and come visit him again? For one day."

"For one day."

Jake pushed the hat over Michael's eyes and got a smile out of him. Dimples showing, the boy shoved the hat back and looked up at him. "Russell says I hafta ask if you killed any ghosts yet."

"Did I. . .wait, how do you kill a ghost?" Jake's laughing eyes locked on Emily's. "Isn't *dead* kind of the definition of a ghost?"

"But Tina says you're smashing down walls, and Russell says ghosts live in walls." The boy's eye's widened. "Maybe you 'bliterated one without seeing it and maybe—"

"Michael!" Tina called across the table. "Let the poor people eat."

"I gotta go before Russell eats my peanuhbutter cookies. Adam's grandma said you made 'em."

Emily nodded and tapped the top of his hat. "I'll take good care of Squiggles."

"Okay." Michael dropped to the floor and crawled under the table.

Jake smiled. "He likes you."

"Why do you say that?"

"It usually takes a long time for him to warm up to people. He knows you're kid-friendly."

She didn't respond. He handed her a napkin.

Two banquet tables bowed like swayback horses under the weight of fruit salads, cheese platters, vegetable trays, and desserts. Massive ice-filled troughs cradled bowls of potato salad. A Nesco roaster of bacon-loaded baked beans formed the centerpiece.

And it all looked good. Amazing. She hadn't hesitated when Jake asked if she was hungry. She was, and the fact still surprised her. *Dear Vanessa, you won't believe what happened to me this week. My stomach growled.*

"Tina and Colt make their own sauerkraut." Jake pointed to a crock as big as the pails of drywall mud lining her new great room.

"How very German. Can't wait to try it."

"Seriously?" His eyes, shadowed by a black felt hat, squinted at her.

"What? I don't look like the fermented cabbage type?"

Serving spoon suspended over the beans, he shook his head. "Not tonight, you don't."

Don't ask. Don't give in to it. Don't— "And what do you mean by that?"

"I mean. . ." He turned and graced her with a slow-and-easy country-singer smile. "Tonight you look like champagne and strawberries."

Emily stopped breathing as Who Needs a Prince? melted off her toenails.

What's the mantra for this, Vanessa? Focus on the moment. Live in the present. Nothing in her bag of emotion-stabilizing tricks fit. She needed to get out of the moment. *Happy place! That's it. Ocean breeze, sand in my toes, Coppertone, surfers skimming the—*

"Crab dip." Jake's elbow nudged her off the beach. "Mom made that. Did you taste it?"

"No. Not yet." *Though it wouldn't be hard to come by here in my happy beach place.* "I made the broccoli salad."

"You're amazing."

"Because I can chop broccoli?"

"Because you can chop broccoli, bake cookies, morph into a butterfly, and transform my cranky niece all in the same day." He nodded toward a bench swing Lexi shared with another girl about the same age. "She might not have acted like she was having fun, but it turned her day around."

Emily's chin dipped. Her head tilted. The butterfly comment slipped to the back of the queue. "We had a great time. Did she give you the idea she—"

"Emily!" Tina waved through roast pork steam. "Come meet my man."

She introduced Colt, a large man with a miniature pitchfork in one hand and foot-long knife in the other. Emily wondered if he knew she'd been curled in a corner of the dining room the day he'd delivered her air conditioner. Tina sashayed around the table and took her by the arm. "Whew, it's hot by that thing. There are so many people I want to introduce you to. Have you met Sherry and Rod or—"

Jake stuck his hand in front of Tina's face. "Stop. Look down."

Tina complied.

"What do you see?"

"Plates. Food. Oh. Bet you guys would like to eat."

"Yes, we would." He planted a noisy kiss on Tina's cheek. "Wonderful party. As soon as we're—"

"Is this her?" A little woman appeared behind Tina, hugging a book the size of an unabridged dictionary. She directed her gaze at Emily. "You're the one who bought Grace Ostermann's house, aren't you? I'm Dorothy Willett, president of the Historical Society. You go ahead and eat and then come find me. I've got some things to show you that I hope you'll find fascinating."

"How can I eat when you leave me hanging like that?"

Wise eyes crinkling, Dorothy Willett smiled and turned away then stopped and looked over her shoulder. "Have you heard the ghosts yet?"

꧁꧂

Jake swung his leg over the bench and leaned across the picnic table. "You haven't, have you?"

Emily's hair fluttered against her cheek as she sat down. His opinion about short hair on women was rapidly changing. She tucked it behind her ear, revealing a tiny square emerald on her earlobe. "I haven't what?"

"Heard the ghosts."

She laughed. "Only in the letters."

"What's in them? Learn anything?"

Emily looked down at her plate and picked up a piece of cheese. Her fingernails were painted a pale blue. "I'm waiting"—her chin lifted—"to read them with you."

"I . . ." There had been a beginning, middle, and end to the sentence when it formed in his head. Where had it gone? "Thank you."

"You found them. It's only fair that we read them together."

157

"No quotes from ancient myths this time, I promise."

She answered with a half smile. "No drama scenes, I promise."

Jake rested his fork on his plate. "You've been through a lot. I can only guess—"

"Cob!"

Topher's bullhorn voice carried across the barn. In a red plaid shirt and a white Stetson, he strode toward them like Paul Bunyan.

"Topher!"

Loose cannon, headed this way. There'd be no more referring to his time at Emily's as "the Foster job" after this. The eyebrow gymnastics zeroing in on Emily didn't bode well. Thankfully her back was turned to the approaching giant.

But something had caused a sudden change in her expression. Was it the weird glow from the little white lights overhead, or did the color just fade from her face?

Lasering a look he hoped conveyed "Keep your trap shut about the girl," Jake waved. "Emily, I'd like you to meet a friend of mine. This is Christopher Hansen. He'll be doing a lot of the drywalling at your place, unless you change your mind after tonight."

Emily offered a weak smile. She looked as if the ghosts they'd just been talking about danced along the barn walls. Topher shook the table when he plunked down next to Jake. "Glad to meet you, Em—" His black-bearded chin dropped. "Emily? *The* Emily? Cob, you been holding out on me?"

Enough with the theatrics. Whatever he was up to, it wasn't good. Jake turned from Topher's bizarre grin to Emily's frighteningly pale, wide-eyed face. What in the world was going on?

Topher doffed his hat like Hoss in an old *Bonanza* rerun. "Soooo glad to see you again." He picked up her hand and pressed his lips to it.

"What the. . .?" Jake's fingers curled into his palms. *Hands off my lady.*

A massive hand clapped his shoulder. "My Emily's back and you don't even tell me?"

"*Your.* . .?" He couldn't seem to finish a sentence. Meanwhile, Emily seemed to have forgotten how to speak altogether. "What are you talking about?"

"She's the one. For real, you don't remember? You preached at her all night. The other chick got bored and left and I had to do something to rescue this one." Topher's stupid grin widened. "So I thought of the perfect thing."

"Talked all night? I nev—" He stared at Emily's mouth opening into a perfect oval. Just as both hands slid over her face, the oval warped into a smile. In that instant, Jacob Braden was fourteen again. A short, chubby kid on fire for the Lord. A kid who witnessed to any and everyone polite enough to not walk away. A kid who didn't know his father had only three months to live, a kid a year away from a growth spurt that would propel him into sports and girls and away from God.

Topher's Emily.

His best friend's first kiss.

⚜

Fanning her face with a Dorito, Emily bit the corner of her lip and squinted at Jake. Looking at his friend was way too awkward. "You don't look anything like you did back then. You were. . ."

"Fat." Topher filled in the blank.

Emily laughed. If Jake was indeed the boy who brought her to her knees and prayed her to Jesus nineteen years ago, she had to agree. Cob. Short for Jacob. If she'd known his last name at the time, she'd forgotten it. "Braden" hadn't rung any ancient bells. Unexpected tears prickled her eyes.

Jake's warm hand covered the spot where she'd just gotten her second kiss from the guy next to him. "Are you okay?"

"You. . .prayed with me. You led me to the Lord." A thought whispered in her mind. *Are you here to lead me back?*

"I remember." His voice slid over her like satin sheets. "But I don't remember how we met."

Topher laughed. "I'm takin' the credit for that one. We were across the street from the Ostermann's, riding dirt bikes in the field, and all of a sudden there's two cute chicks standing in the road gawking at us." He winked at Emily. "I killed my engine and yelled at Tubby here to stop, but he just kept going. He was totally oblivious to females back then. So I took it upon myself to welcome you ladies to the neighborhood."

In spite of burning cheeks, Emily laughed. "You introduced yourself as Christopher and I was sure you said, 'But you can call me Gopher.'"

"And you did, as I recall."

As she bantered with Topher, she was only too aware of Jake's stunned silence. After several minutes, Topher slapped the table. "Gotta get me some food while this all sinks in. I'll be back." He stood to a height much, much taller than he'd reached nineteen years ago. She hadn't stood on tiptoes to reach his lips.

She remembered the blatant signals she'd sent that night by the fire, the tug-of-war as part of her mind hung on the chubby boy's words, while the other part wished he'd stop talking so she could be alone with his friend. The thought made her shiver. Topher was probably a nice enough guy, but—

"He kissed you." Jake stared at her with an indecipherable expression—part teasing, part accusing.

She wrinkled her nose. "That was a long, long time ago."

"It wasn't really fair, you know."

"What wasn't?"

"I present you with the keys to eternal life and he gets the kiss."

Could her face get any hotter? What was she supposed to say to that? *You're right—I'll make it up to you?* "Um. . .You were right about the sauerkraut. It's so much better than canned."

He laughed. "Sorry. That was awkward. Isn't it strange, though? That we've come full circle, meeting like this again?"

"Kind of makes you wonder."

"I don't believe in coincidence."

"You think God planned for us to meet again?"

"Of course. The question is, why?" A shimmer of mischief hinted at something not so spiritual. "It just seems—"

"How's the pig?" Tina plopped onto the bench next to Emily, her back to Jake, and nudged Emily's shoulder.

"The food is wonderful. Thank you so much for inviting me."

"Hey"—her head tipped back and her eyes rolled up as if trying to see behind her—"any friend of Jake's is a friend of mine."

With a slosh of beer, Topher set his plate and cup next to Jake and puckered his lips at Emily.

"Hey," Tina whispered. "How's the kiss-and-run plan coming along?"

Emily turned away from Topher's puckered lips and laughed. "You have no idea."

⟡

"The Shaws built your house in 1847, a year before Wisconsin was granted statehood."

Dorothy Willett ran a bony finger along the bottom of a yellowed photograph.

Seated on the other side of Dorothy, Jake leaned over the photo album for a closer look. "I found that same picture on the Historical Society website."

Dorothy nodded. "Of course, the house was more than fifty years old when this was taken."

Emily stared at the sapling oak and the big white dog. "The Shaw family lived there until the 1940s, right?"

"Yes. Several generations." Dorothy turned a page. "But there are indications that it was empty for several years before the war."

"The war?" There were several to choose from.

"The War Between the States. We have a letter." Dorothy flipped several more pages. "There's no envelope or last names, but the story passed down with it is that Big Jim was Jim Thornton, who was the town blacksmith in the 1850s. Here."

Emily's hand rose to her mouth. She locked eyes with Jake. They'd seen that scrolling, expressive script before.

Fredericktown, Missouri
May 8, 1853

Big Jim, my faithful friend,

How you must tire of me asking for news. I know how hastily you will get word to me as soon as you know anything at all.

Papa and I are doing well, though it is already as hot as July is back home. I will dearly miss the mountains when we return to Wisconsin. How gentle and quiet our little Fox

161

*will seem, but nothing will be a more welcome pastime than
watching the river roll by if I return to Rochester to marry.
God has not yet taken from me the conviction that my prayers
are not in vain, and so I continue to pray and plan for a long
and wondrous future.*

*How is your work going? It troubles Papa deeply to not
be there. I remind him daily of the magnitude of the task we
accomplished before winter. That God could use us in that way
still brings me to my knees.*

*There is much unrest here. Even more division than back
home. It is hard to hold my tongue. Working at the store exposes
me to so many opinions, but I will remain as outwardly
neutral as Missouri claims to be.*

Please give our love to anyone else you speak to.

Always,
Hannah

Emily read the letter silently and looked up, waiting for Jake to
finish. "Her name was Hannah."

Dorothy nodded. "Her mother, Elizabeth, died when Hannah
was a girl. She's buried in the cemetery at the English Settlement
Church."

"Where is that?"

"On A and J," Jake answered. "About three miles from us. The
church would have been built about the same time as the house,
right?"

Another album page turned in Dorothy's veiny hand. "Building
began on the chapel in 1846, but they ran out of money before they
could finish the interior, so the first service wasn't held there until
New Year's Day of 1849."

"What else do you know about Hannah? Did she ever marry?"

"We don't know. We have the record of her father's second
marriage. He married a widow from Burlington. They must have
had a son together because the Ostermanns did purchase the house
from someone named Shaw. Hannah may have stayed in Missouri,
or if, like the letter said, she married when she came back, it would be
hard to trace her. Maybe, if someone were curious enough to search

all the local cemeteries, that person would find some answers."

Jake looked at her over the top of Dorothy's head. Anticipation sparked in his eyes. "What are you doing on Sunday afternoon?"

"Visiting cemeteries apparently. But first I need to catch up on some letters."

Dorothy glanced from Jake to Emily, closed the album, and slid two thin booklets and a red-bound hardcover book in front of her. "I'm keeping you two from dancing." She patted Emily's hand. "Will you come and visit me soon?"

"I'd love that."

"I'm old-fashioned enough to be in the phone book. I'll get you caught up on everything we know about your house, and you can fill me in on what you've learned from the ghosts." She stood and waved with her fingertips. "See you soon."

Restraining a laugh, Emily didn't dare look at Jake until Dorothy was out of earshot.

"You have to bring her over to the house. I bet she can see them."

"Right. I'll bring her over so she can introduce me to my own ghosts." She watched the lines deepen on each side of his mouth. "They are mine, right? If I own the house, I own the ghosts."

"Absolutely. It's in the fine print of every bill of sale: 'The Seller hereby grants, bargains, sells, assigns, transfers, conveys, and sets over unto the Purchaser all ghosts, ghouls, goblins, spooks, specters, apparitions, and ethereal beings real or imaginary residing in or on the Property.'"

Emily swiped at laugh tears dampening her lashes. "I can't wait to write the listing. 'For Sale. Historic three-bedroom—'"

"Shoulda been four-bedroom."

" '*Three*-bedroom, two-bath home complete with fireplace, back porch, trapdoors, secret room, and quiet, well-mannered poltergeist.'"

"It won't be on the market more than a week." His smile waned and he reached for his hat. "Let's not talk about that now." He held out his hand. "May I have this dance?"

She slid her palm onto his. Warm, large, calloused, his hand closed around hers. She looked up at unruly sun-lightened hair peeking from under the black cowboy hat and tried to remember why she was supposed to say no. The band played the first few notes of "We Like to Party" as he pulled her to her feet and led her to the back row of dancers. As her feet began stomping in place in time to his, she remembered one of the reasons she should have declined. "I thought you hated dancing."

His forehead furrowed. Boots tapped, hands clapped, and a grin split his face. "Where'd you ever get an idea like that?"

CHAPTER 18

Lexi stared at the words of the worship chorus on the screen above the platform. She usually loved this part of a Sunday service the best, but this morning the praise lyrics wouldn't take shape in her mouth.

Adam sang the same as he did any other Sunday. Jake's voice seemed louder than usual.

She should be praising God for saving Pansy. And sticking Ben in jail. It wasn't that she wasn't grateful for both, but nothing was for sure yet. How long would Ben stay there and what would he do to her when he got out? Would he take it out on her this time or give Adam her punishment like he usually did? And where would Pansy stay when she and Adam had to go back home? Grandma was allergic to cats. She had to take pills whenever she was around them.

Jake said Emily wanted to keep Pansy.

Not a chance.

Pretending she was concentrating on the words on the screen, Lexi watched Jake's hands lifting, palms up. It wasn't God he was all joyful about. It was Emily.

So much for Who Needs a Prince? So much for "I'm not really in the market." She'd seen them Friday night, holding hands on the way to the car. Emily had come with Lexi and her grandma and left with Jake.

Lexi had no doubt God knew her every hope and dream, every wish she'd whispered on the first star of the night since Mom died. For a few hours on Friday she'd thought all her prayers were being answered. Ben was arrested and Jake came to their rescue and took them home, just the way she'd prayed it would happen.

And then he danced with Emily and wrecked everything.

Jake would marry Emily and they'd move into her house—a house with lots of rooms to fill with kids. But the kids would be Jake and Emily's.

In her daydreams, Jake built a big house and she got to design her own room. They'd go on trips every summer. Boating and hiking and skiing all over the country, maybe even the world.

She'd never told anyone about her prayer. People would laugh. What were the chances a single guy Jake's age would want to raise two kids who were almost teenagers? But God could do miracles. Even though he hadn't healed Mom, Lexi still believed God answered prayers. Pansy was alive. That was a miracle.

But sometimes He said no. And it looked like this was one of those times.

꧁꧂

When was the last time he raised his hands in worship? Jake couldn't remember. But they seemed to lift of their own accord this morning as he sang "The Heart of Worship."

Lord, it's all about You.

The song ended. The worship leader prayed. Jake felt his shoulders relax as he sat down. He rested his hands on his knees, still open in surrender. The peace that swelled in him was almost foreign, and with it came a sense of expectation, a tingly feeling he'd experienced daily as an on-fire-for-Jesus fourteen-year-old. Before his father died and he turned Goth and then jock and then simply distracted with life. He'd once labeled the tingles Holy Spirit vibes. In that one close-to-God year, he'd felt the vibes every morning when he opened his eyes and yelled, "Good morning, Lord! Who are we going to save today?"

He must have said those very words the morning of the day he'd met Emily.

166

Only the dimmest memory remained of sitting in lawn chairs by a roaring fire, talking to two girls about how much Jesus loved them and what He'd done for them. Jake had been big on zeal back then but short on true caring. He'd kept a list of the people he'd prayed "the prayer" with but never followed up on a single one. Never wrote or called or cared how they were doing a week or even a day later.

What about nineteen years later?

"Many of you remember the story of Abby Sunderland, the sixteen-year-old girl who tried to sail solo around the world." Pastor Karl began his sermon before reaching the podium. "There are many lessons to be learned from her story, but the one I want to focus on today is how she unexpectedly needed someone to rescue her."

Okay, Lord, You have my attention. The name, the water, the rescue. Who was it who'd just said last night, "I don't believe in coincidence"?

Pastor Karl folded his arms across his chest. "When Abby set sail on January 23 in 2010, she had every expectation that she was going to successfully sail around the world. However, she unexpectedly drifted into a massive storm. . . ."

Unexpectedly drifted. That could explain an entire decade of his life.

". . .the sailboat began to take on water. She was experiencing winds—"

Adam's elbow made contact with Jake's ribs. "That's just like us!" he whispered.

Jake nodded. "Listen," he whispered back as the pastor told about the French fishing vessel that rescued the girl forty hours after a plane spotted her debilitated boat.

"This morning Jesus is going to tell us a parable about a different kind of search-and-rescue mission, and the hope underlying this story is far greater than the world's most qualified search-and-rescue crews. The hope Jesus fixes our eyes on this morning is the hope of His Father in heaven, who lovingly rescues everyone who belongs to Him. Listen to the parable Jesus teaches His disciples in Matthew 18."

Jake opened his Bible and found the passage.

" 'What do you think? If a man owns a hundred sheep, and one
of them wanders away, will he not leave the ninety-nine on the hills
and go to look for the one?' "

The one. As if highlighted in neon orange, the words blazed.

" 'If he finds it, I tell you the truth, he is happier about that one
sheep than about the ninety-nine that did not wander off. In the
same way your Father in heaven is not willing that any of these little
ones should be lost.' God pursues us relentlessly. We need to join
Him in relentlessly pursuing the lost."

The tingles increased like energy droplets trickling into his
veins.

Had he missed the cues? Maybe Emily was the one he was
supposed to pursue but not in the way he'd thought or hoped. Was
it too late for a follow-up call on a girl he'd witnessed to nineteen
years ago?

None of the zeal he'd possessed at fourteen had survived his
years of Christless living. Maybe that wasn't all bad. The fanaticism
was gone, but his faith had returned one night in a sterile white-
walled room. No angel choirs or bright lights, just a quiet certainty
that God was present in the midst of Abby's pain.

What he'd lost sight of was that God was also present in the
midst of Ben's vileness.

⁂

"We need crayons." Adam dunked a French fry into Lexi's chocolate
shake and offered it to her.

It wasn't the grossest thing he'd ever done, but it came close.
Lexi dipped half a chicken strip into barbeque sauce and plunged it
into his cup.

"Yum. Thanks." Without even blinking, Adam pulled it out,
dripping with strawberry shake, and popped it into his mouth. "Like
I was saying," he garbled, "we need to take crayons and paper."

"You want to color pretty pictures at the cemetery?" Her voice
was angrier than she wanted it to be.

Adam did the slow head-shake thing that said he was way
smarter than her.

"For rubbings, right?" Jake asked. Her uncle never intentionally made her feel dumb. Sometimes it just happened.

Adam swirled the barbeque sauce with his straw. "Right." The top of his shake turned brownish pink. He slurped it off.

"I'm not going." She didn't need a reason for not wanting to walk over places where people were buried.

"Why?" Her brother and her uncle asked at the same time.

"It's creepy."

Adam pointed an onion ring at her. "It's history. I looked it up. There are tombstones there from the 1840s. I love finding kids who died when they were like our age and trying to guess what killed them."

"Ewww." This time Jake said the same thing she did. She grabbed the onion pointed at her and took a massive bite. "That's disgusting."

"No it isn't. It makes you glad to be living in the twenty-first century. Imagine not having all the medical breakthroughs we have now. A hundred and fifty years ago if you'd had an asthma attack you wouldn't have—"

"Adam. Eat." Jake sounded tough but he was smiling. *Men.*

"You guys are both disgusting."

Adam pointed to her shake. "Theobromine in chocolate can help relax your bronchial tubes, so you'd have been okay if you lived near a cacao—"

"Adam. Eat." Jake laid his hand on her arm. "I understand your not wanting to go."

It took her a second to figure it out. Jake thought she wouldn't want to go because it would make her think of Mom. Good. She'd play that up. "Thank you. It would be difficult."

"I know. You don't—"

"Wait." Adam shook his head. "That's not why, is it? You don't want to go 'cause Em—" Adam made a face like he'd just bit into a lemon.

Jake's eyebrows scrunched together. "What is it with you and Emily?"

Lexi wadded her catsup-smeared napkin and threw it at Adam's face. He was supposed to be the person she could trust with secrets. "Nothing."

"Emily said you had fun yesterday."

Lexi shrugged. She'd had fun. But that was yesterday. Before Emily changed her mind about wanting a prince.

Her uncle studied her like she was some newly discovered bug species. And then he pulled his hand away and picked up two French fries. As he swished them in catsup, he said, "Emily's moving to California as soon as her house sells. Did you know that?"

She'd heard it, but she didn't *know* it. Hearing him say it made it seem like it would really happen. Jake wasn't planning on keeping Emily here. So maybe he'd still build the dream house. In that case, she could stand a couple of hours of walking on dead people. She wiped her hands on her napkin. "I have crayons."

👑

October 13, 1852

The shop was empty. The coals glowed white as he pumped the bellows then blazed red when he stopped. Liam worked alone today but didn't know why. Just before ten this morning, Big Jim had jiggled his cot with an urgency that jolted him upright. "Sorry to wake you, boy. I need to talk with someone about getting a delivery from Spring Prairie."

Liam held his questions. Too many spaces between the wall boards. Too many ears. "I'll go."

"Not this time. Going to take some money changing hands to get this one on its way. Are you free tonight?"

"Always."

The man smiled wryly and nodded. "If there is a God, may He shine on you for it."

"What'll you have me do while you're away?" He wasn't skilled enough to handle a big job on his own.

"Make nails. Tell the busybodies I'm delivering a harrow to Spring Prairie should they ask, and they will. Act like you slept last night."

Now, four hours later, the sun was high and sweat ran from his brow. His pile of square nails had grown to two inches and he'd made two hooks the length of his hand for Hannah, adding a fancy

170

twist in one that would impress Jim.

His thoughts danced on the tune played by his hammer as he tickled the anvil with extra strikes between blows to a nail rod. Another year under his belt and he'd be making fine music. Like Jim said often, "I'd dread this job like sin if I couldn't put a song to it."

The beat took on a life of its own and soon became a hymn. "Rock of Ages, cleft for me, let me hide myself in Thee. . ." In the heat and the smoke and the grime, he led a one-man choir. "Not the labors of my hands can fulfill thy law's commands; could my zeal no respite know, could my tears forever flow, all for sin could not atone; Thou must—"

"Where's Jim?"

Two words, and the worship died on his lips. Da stood in the doorway, making a scrawny shadow on the dirt floor. Liam's hammer missed the rod and hit his thumb. He bit back the sting.

Da laughed. "*Amadán.*"

Had there been a day in his life when he hadn't been called a fool? Had his father stood over his cradle and labeled him *amadán* the day he was born? *God, be my strength, restrain my hands.* "Are you needing something?"

Again the laugh, hissing as though birthed in the bowels of the forge. "I'm needing a real smith to fix a harness and a real son to plow the corn under. Can't have neither it appears."

"Let me look at it." Liam held out a black-streaked hand.

Da stroked his rusty beard. Icy eyes stared him down. Finally he shrugged and held out a bent bar and broken harness. "Better you than that negro-loving thief. If—"

"Can I help you, Mr. Keegan?"

A crimson blush rose from the sweat-stained collar of Da's coat to the brim of his tattered hat. The red clashed with the orange of his beard. Liam forgot all about the pain in his thumb as he nodded his thanks for Jim's timely appearance. He held up the bar and traces in his hand. "He's gone and snapped a harness and bent a whippletree. Askin' more of his horses than they're made to deliver again."

Da glared. Liam drew strength from Jim's presence.

Jim nodded in his usual patient way. "We can fix that." He turned his back on Da and walked to a far corner where a tangle of harness leather hung from hooks. "Liam? Can I get your opinion on this?"

The question was for show, a subtle knife jab at the man who thought his son less than worthless, but Liam responded with all the seriousness of a seasoned smith with an opinion to share. "Of course." He strode with wide, firm steps to the corner.

Jim held the stub of a pencil in one meaty hand, a dirty scrap of paper in the other. *Pack tools 4 tonight,* he wrote then drew a thick black circle and casually pointed to his neck.

Liam's stomach rose in his throat. He'd heard of such things, never seen it. His hands shook with fear and rage. *God, why do You allow this?* Without an ounce of confidence, he nodded.

The paper crumbled in the massive hand. Jim cleared his throat. "Go work on packing the order in the back room," he commanded too loud, for Da's benefit. Another code, this one for sleep that wasn't likely to come.

With or without sleep, he'd be up at midnight.

Chapter 19

"Hush you two. It's Sunday."

Emily lounged on her inflatable bed-turned-chair on the back porch and listened to Cardinal Bob and his significant other battle it out. Karen was nagging again. Why was she always several boughs higher on the tree than her man? Emily lifted her coffee mug. "You guys need counseling."

Her flippant remark left a bitter taste that French vanilla coffee couldn't wash away. She'd broached the subject of counseling the day before she left for Colorado. The day Keith offered to pay for her "problem."

In retrospect, she couldn't fathom why she'd tried.

Stupid. The definition of insanity is pursuing a guy who's losing interest. Doing it the way she had was nothing short of evil.

Cardinal Bob took flight. The empty pine branch bobbed. He landed on the porch rail. Bright red against a green backdrop. Black eyes in a black face gave him a stern expression, but the Cosmo Kramer 'do made it impossible to take Cardinal Bob too seriously. Maybe that was Karen's whole problem.

Bob's head swiveled. One eye stared directly at her. Emily had the eerie sense he was trying to tell her something. She didn't move, just stared in awe at the amazing creature so close she could count his feathers. *Lord, he's so beautiful.* She breathed the prayer as easily as the morning air.

Karen called from the tree—*dweeb, dweeb, dweeb*. Unruffled, Bob nodded, as if to say, "Watch this." His wings opened and he glided back to his branch. *Purdy, purdy, purdy*, he answered.

Emily laughed. "Killing her with kindness, huh? How's that working for ya?"

A rhythmic screech, like steady bleats on a wooden whistle, interrupted. A blue jay swept from behind the shed and landed on the wounded oak. Karen stopped complaining. Bob began a loud *chip, chip, chip*—a warning cry—as he fluttered to a branch a foot away from her. Karen was anything but lovable today, but there he was, defending her.

The way a man should.

Leave it in the past. What's done is done. She pulled everything she could think of from Vanessa's bag of tricks and said them out loud. Keith wasn't worth the time she'd spent on him back then, so why was she giving him a piece of her day now?

Because it was all his fault. Everything that happened wouldn't have happened if Keith Miller had just come out and told her he wasn't a one-woman kind of man.

Emily reached down and grabbed the top book from a stack of things she wanted to skim before Jake showed up. *An English Settler in Pioneer Wisconsin—The Letters of Edwin Bottomley 1842–1850.* She opened the cover and stared at an Alfred Hitchcock–like silhouette of a portly gentleman in a waistcoat with tails. The caption identified him as Captain Thomas Bottomley, the recipient of the letters bound in the book. Was the cane in his hand functional or fashionable? How convenient to live in a time when no one would know.

She flipped past the introduction. The first entry was headed *LIVERPOLL, May 11, 1842…the Shipe is very Clean and the Captain appears a Sober and intelligent man.*

Misspellings were frequent, and the lack of punctuation made it hard to separate sentences as she read about the Bottomley family's departure from England.

Emily leaned back and sipped her coffee. The cardinals clamored on. The blue jay made sporadic swoops in front of the pine tree as she read. *Sunday May 15 5 0 Clock This morning we are being towed out into the Irish Chanel by a Steamer.*

Lost in the past, she left her own past behind.

❦

Emily arranged eighteen letters in two rows on the now clean card table. Jake laid out the three letters Emily had found in the pipe above the others. Only those had dates, all from November 1852. And now they knew who'd written them.

Hannah Shaw.

Emily pointed to one penned by the man, or boy, and read the short note out loud. " 'The stationmaster asked me to retrieve the parcel I picked up last night and bring it back to you. He has no room for it at present. Can you take it tomorrow night? I am confident you will, and that means I will see you again. God does, indeed, smile upon us.'" Something about the last few words roughened her voice. "It's all so coded."

Hands on his waist, Jake studied the letters. "Think what they were risking." In that stance, with the look of intrigue on his face, he was just an older version of his nephew. Still a fascinated—and fascinating—little boy inside.

"Adam started to say something in the boat before we hit the log. He said he wished there was something like the Underground Railroad today."

Jake nodded, moving one hand to rub his chin. "I get that." A slow smile took over his face and he winked at her. "Every guy wants to be a rescuer."

"Preferably rescuing damsels who don't fight back."

"Nah. That just adds to the challenge." His smile lost a bit of its lift and he picked up a letter. "I think our Hannah is a bit like you." He cleared his throat and read, " 'I have long kicked against the goads of society's expectations of a woman. Why is it that you can hunt possum in the dark of night and paddle the river by day, and I must stitch by candlelight and bake bread at sunrise?'" Jake tipped his head so his arched eyebrow aimed at Emily. "Well, maybe not in all things."

"Hey! I can bake bread."

"Have you ever?"

She nodded toward the kitchen that now formed one end of the great room. "Right here. Nana Grace taught us. When the kitchen's finished I'll bake you a loaf."

"I'd like that." His tone was serious, his eyes slightly shaded.

"Go on."

Jake focused on the letter. " 'Mama, God rest her soul, used to tell me I was cursed with restlessness. I do not consider my longing for adventure a curse. It is the very thing that drives me to pick up the standard—'" He stopped reading and pointed to the spot where Hannah had crossed out several letters.

"Looks like she started to write 'of freedom.'"

"Maybe she thought even that was giving too much away."

"Do you think they felt the excitement of being part of something so vital, or just the fear?"

"I wonder." He held the letter closer to the lamp he'd brought down from the attic. " 'It is the very thing that drives me to pick up the standard. Would Miss Prim and Proper with the fat sausage curls descend the stairs in the dark of night to tend the waiting parcels? I think not. I have come to believe of late, however, that I should be grateful for the disguise of womanhood. Who would consider an innocent young—Oh my, I have said enough for one night.'"

Jake stopped before the end of the letter. Standing so close his woodsy smell made her dizzy, Emily waited for him to continue.

" 'How glad I am that I need not even finish my thoughts and yet you will know them. May the Lord light your path tonight.'"

"I need not even finish my thoughts and yet you will know them." Hannah had voiced every woman's deepest desire—to be known so deeply, so intimately, that she didn't even need to speak her thoughts out loud. It was that desire that had started the chain of events that led to her putting on her skis for the very last time.

Be present. She took several minutes to scan the letters. "This one mentions her restlessness. Looks like his response." She swallowed twice before the words came out. " 'If restlessness is the trait that defines who you are, then I say please stay restless, my love. You have a courage that is sadly lacking even in many men. So continue to stitch and bake, both of which I am confident you do better than Miss Prim and Proper, and use your restlessness to further the cause and capture the heart of this hunter.'" She swallowed again and whispered the closing. "'Sleep well.'"

The room grew warm in the heat of Jake's gaze. Was he watching for a reaction? If so, she probably hadn't hidden the bittersweet pain the words caused. *Please stay restless, my love.* To be known so well and accepted—

"...if you changed your plans?"

"I'm sorry." She blinked and stepped away from Jake. "What did you say?"

Jake put the letter back in its place, sat down, and crossed one leg, resting his right ankle on his left knee. He chewed on his bottom lip and stared at her. "I was wondering if there's a reason why you have to end up in California. You said you didn't know what you'd be doing when you got there. Is it just something you want to do, or are you committed to something. Or someone?"

Emily pulled out a chair on the opposite side of the card table. Jake fiddled with a shoelace as he waited, but there was nothing casual about the lines forming on his forehead.

She folded her arms across her chest as if it would hold in the sudden rush of emotion that filled her lungs. *Tell him.* She argued with the voice. No one, *no one* knew the whole story. It made no sense to unburden her soul to him. He'd asked about California for an obvious reason. He wanted to know if there was a chance for something between them.

There wasn't. But not because she wanted it that way. Everything in her wanted to go back to last night when, for a few hours, she'd danced in his arms and laughed with him and pretended he was her future. But he wasn't. Because she did have a commitment, and because she couldn't be the woman he needed. And maybe telling him was the only way to squelch his hopes without hurting his feelings, without losing him as a friend. She gazed into patient eyes and took a tremulous breath.

Jake shook his head. "I know I have no business asking. But I got to thinking during church this morning about how God brought us back together."

This was going to be harder than she'd thought, but it made her even more determined to tell him everything. "Jake, I. . ."

"Just hear me out." He smiled, lopsided and awkwardly. "I know how this sounds, but that's not what I'm saying. Not that I don't wish I were in a position to pursue you." His right brow rose slightly. "But I think the reason we found each other again is more important than boy meets girl."

Emily lowered her hands and gripped the seat of the chair. "What do you mean?"

His smile grew more self-conscious. "I was a hit-and-run witnesser when I first met you. I should have stayed in touch."

The change of direction should have been expected. The letdown, an almost physical pressure on her shoulders, revealed a depth of disappointment that caught her off guard. There was no future for them, but she'd wanted him to fight for it, even just a little.

She set aside her disappointment as a dim mental picture of the pudgy kid called Cob materialized like a fuzzy hologram. So unlike the man who sat across from her—definitely not someone her fifteen-year-old cool self would have stayed in touch with. Her tall, handsome First Kiss, on the other hand, would have warranted daily letters scented with Calvin Klein Escape and sealed with iridescent pink lip gloss, but a new crush on her return home took her mind off her summer love. She smiled as she thought of the present-day Topher. God had protected her from wasting perfectly good perfume.

"I got involved in a youth group when I went home. I became just as overzealous as you were." She watched as a hint of surprise registered on his face. "Over the next three years, I went on four mission trips and worked at a church camp. And then I went to college." She wondered if he'd pick up on her implication.

"You made it further than I did. My dad died and I got mad at God. About the time I stopped blaming Him, I grew eight inches and got skinny and too cool for Jesus."

"And what about now?"

He grinned. "I'm happy to say I am no longer too cool for God." He rubbed the stubble on his chin. "I've been slowly finding my way back since my sister got sick. It feels good to be home again."

Emily rubbed one thumb with the other. "That's a good way to put it."

"I don't feel the need to sell it. This time around I just hope to live it."

"You appear to be doing that." Her voice softened unintentionally. What was it about this room, this table, that drew them into emotion-baring talks?

"Thank you." His tone played a perfect counterpart to hers. "If Ben were out of the picture I'd be a little less of a hypocrite."

"Maybe God's using him to teach you to forgive." The words came from her mouth, the wisdom unearthed from some long-buried archive.

"Maybe. If so, I'm failing. Just when I work up a drop of sincerity and manage to pray for him, he does something that makes me want to choke him."

"Was he always like this?"

"No. When Abby first met him he was simply a worthless human being." His teeth ground together in an expression part-grimace, part-seething. "See? At the very least I need to start keeping my thoughts to myself."

Emily smiled. She wasn't used to this kind of humility in a man. "You're being less of a hypocrite when you're honest. You're admitting you have a problem with the guy and you're working on it." Her shoulders relaxed. "Did your sister's death make him bitter?"

"I don't know." He put both feet flat on the floor and crossed his arms. Was he aware they were speaking the same body language? "I guess I never really asked that question. He's always had a temper, but I never feared for the kids until Abby was gone." He tipped his head to the right. "Very clever. You're trying to make me feel sorry for him."

"Only if there's good reason." She tipped her head at the same angle.

Jake laughed and uncrossed his arms. "Thank you for the nudge. I've never tried to think of Ben as having real feelings like the rest of us." He leaned back and looked up at the ceiling. "If he'd had an ounce of sensitivity in him, Abby would still be alive."

"What do you mean?"

"She died of a bleeding ulcer. The doctors said it was caused by a virus, but stress acted like gasoline on hot coals."

Emily leaned toward him and caught herself before she reached out to touch his knee. "And Ben added stress?"

"Oh yeah. But you're right, I need to attempt seeing him in a different light. Abby wasn't all that easy to live with either. Maybe they made each other miserable."

"You know all that sage advice came from you and not me. I just asked a question."

His chin lowered and he smiled at her with only his eyes. "Well, you started me thinking in the right direction. But this little talk was supposed to be about you. I'm trying to make up for lost time and you go and turn the tables. So what happened to you in college?"

Emily picked up her phone and checked the time. "We have to pick up the kids in four minutes. Just enough time to hide the letters."

"Man, you're good. But you're not off the hook. Are you going to tell Dorothy about these?"

"Yes." She added two sheets of yellowed paper to the stack. "Right before I leave."

A cord on Jake's neck stood out. "Which brings us right back to the question I probably shouldn't have asked but still want answered."

The light glinting in his eyes alluded to something more than unfinished spiritual business. She focused on the drawstring of the velvet pouch. A few more seconds under that light and she wouldn't remember her own name, let alone the reason she had to leave town. "I'll go put these away."

She reached the second floor before realizing she'd taken the steps two at a time.

Her cane was at the bottom of Honey Creek and she hadn't needed it yet.

CHAPTER 20

That one looks really old."

Adam ran to a rectangular headstone about three feet high. It leaned slightly forward, casting a stretched-out shadow.

"That's him! That's Edwin!" On Adam's heels, Emily high-fived him and turned to Jake. "That's the guy who wrote the letters to his father in England."

Shifting the drawing pad to her left arm, Lexi set the pink plastic box of peeled crayons on top of it. Her eyes narrowed as she watched Adam and Emily dashing to another grave marker. Jealousy, pure and simple. It might as well have been stenciled on her forehead. The relief on her face when Jake had assured her Emily was moving was like the sun popping through a thunderhead.

When he tried seeing the world through the eyes of an almost-teen who'd recently lost her mother, it made at least a little sense. Adam and Emily were hitting it off like they'd known each other for years. In spite of the age difference, Lexi could be looking at Emily as a threat to the bond between her and her twin. And if Lexi saw Emily as in any way usurping her mother's role, her little defensive claws would bare the way Pansy's had when she'd left the scratches Lexi thought she was hiding.

Adam waved. "Lex! Uncle Jake! Come here."

With a sigh as big as she was, Lexi marched toward them. "What?"

181

"We found the first guy buried here. He was born in 1785."

"It's not the original marker," Emily added.

"Joseph Mitchell 1785–1846." Jake read the inscription over Lexi's shoulder. "First recorded burial in English Settlement Cemetery."

"He probably just had a wooden cross when they first stuck him in there." Adam tapped the granite with the toe of his shoe. "Bet he's happy to have this thing."

Lexi did her famous "Ewww" and crinkled her nose. "You make it sound like he's still there."

"Maybe he is." Adam tortured her with a wicked laugh. "There was a guy in the eighteen hundreds who tried injecting acetate of alumina into dead people's carotid arteries. Like six quarts—that's how much blood is in the human body. Which means he must have drained all the blood out fir—"

"Adam." Jake covered a maverick smile as he told Adam to get on with the necessary facts.

"So he buried the bodies and dug them up a year later. They all looked fresh as a daisy."

"Disgusting." Emily's lips rippled in an adorable wavy line.

"What's disgusting is bodies that aren't embalmed and the worms eat through the coffins and devour the—"

"Adam!" A trio of voices ordered him to cease and desist.

With a grin and a shrug, Adam took two huge strides to another stone. "You tell me all the time how good it is that I like learning, but nobody ever wants to listen to what I learn."

"Ignore the boy." Jake stepped next to Emily. Lexi turned away and walked across the cemetery. *There goes my conscience.* He put his hand on Emily's back as he pointed to an inscription. JAMES SOTCLIFFE. DIED OCT. 28, 1856 AE 33. "Makes you grateful for modern medicine, doesn't it? A lot of these people didn't live to see their fifties."

Emily bent and put her hand on the stone. "Don't you wish you knew all their stories?"

Jake couldn't suppress a polite laugh. "If I didn't know better I'd say you were fast becoming a history addict."

She smiled and turned away. "I never had a reason to care this much."

Was there really any reason he couldn't be concerned about her walk with the Lord and just plain like the woman at the same time? He held out his hand. "Let's soak up some history."

Emily stared at his hand and closed her eyes. "Jake, I'm—"

"I know. You're leaving. Moving to California for some hugely important reason I can't know." He took the hand that rested on her hip and fit it into his. "But you're here now. Can't we just enjoy the moment and each other?"

Her lips separated, but her hand stayed tucked in his. With a shaky sigh, she shrugged. "I guess."

♔

This is insane. Holding hands with a guy she had no hope of ending up with wasn't any smarter than trying to trap one who didn't love her.

But it felt so good.

Emily tried to focus on the mission. They were looking for Elizabeth Shaw's headstone. "She died in 1851."

"All of the older ones are here in this corner so we can ignore everything over there." Jake gestured toward the trees that bordered the small cemetery. Way in the far corner, Lexi sat with her back against a tombstone, drawing in her sketchbook.

"Is she okay?"

"Just a little bent out of shape. She's twelve. Need I say more?"

"Did I do something?" Emily had tried to pass off Lexi's terse answers in the car as adolescent moodiness, but she'd seemed fine with everyone else.

"She's having a problem with you and Adam getting along so well. She's a twin—it's a different relationship than regular siblings."

"I can understand that."

Jake pulled her hand to his chest. "Guess I'll just have to keep you away from Adam. And with me."

"L-let's find Lizzy Shaw." What was wrong with her tongue?

"We need a system. Let's start at the corner and—"

"Found her!" Adam waved with both long, skinny arms then turned around. "Lex! Bring the crayons!"

183

Emily walked ahead of Jake. Lexi didn't move from her spot.

Bleached white and rounded at the top, the stone stood on a block of matching rock. The characters were shallow and weathered. Emily took a quick breath as she stared at a basket of apples carved beneath the curved top. Almost identical to the apple basket painted on the cellar door. "Elizabeth Yardley Shaw. Died December 22, 1851. AE 38."

Adam's head swayed slowly back and forth. "Three days before Christmas. Bummer."

"A year older than Mom." Lexi had materialized without a sound. She handed the notebook and plastic box of crayons to Adam and walked away.

Jake squeezed Emily's hand. "Somehow I'd envisioned this as a fun afternoon."

"It is. Ignore her." Adam ripped off a sheet of paper. "Do you guys know what AE means?"

"Age," they answered together.

"Of course it means age." Adam got down on his knees and took out a crayon. "But it comes from Latin. *Anno aetatis suae*—it means 'In the year of his—or her—age.'"

Emily ruffled Adam's wild curls then remembered she was supposed to keep her distance. "Who needs the Internet? We have you."

"Finally, somebody appreciates me." Adam held the paper against the headstone and 'Elizabeth' appeared in white amid his dark blue crayon strokes. "Did you know that the Kamchatkan Indians bred dogs for the purpose of devouring their dead because they believed that those eaten by dogs would be better off in the..."

Adam's voice faded in the distance as Jake dragged Emily, laughing too hard to walk straight, toward the parking lot, yelling "Ignore the boy!"

⁂

In spite of Lexi's drama and Adam's attempts to make them gag, it was turning out to be a great afternoon. Until a minute ago, when she'd wandered off in search of more Bottomleys, Emily's hand had nestled nicely in his. Jake followed several paces behind, more

engrossed in the way the breeze flitted through Emily's hair than in
dates engraved in granite.

She wore white pants that came to the middle of her calves, a
sleeveless blouse the color of Batman Bubblegum ice cream, and
white sandals with tons of skinny little straps. Thin gold chains
encircled her neck, wrist, and ankle. It was the first time he'd seen
her wear any jewelry other than earrings. The girl was transforming
before his eyes. The day she arrived in Rochester she'd resembled a
black-and-white cardboard cutout folded on the kitchen floor. Each
passing day infused a bit more depth and color.

He caught up with her and they walked in comfortable silence
along a row of time-smoothed gravestones. Adam showed off his
stack of rubbings then went off to find Lexi. Emily pulled out the
phone Jake had rescued and took a picture of Elizabeth Shaw's
marker. "It's haunting," she said. "Not in a creepy way, just strange to
think of the connections. This woman lived in my house."

Jake couldn't remember her calling it "my house" before. *Good.
Take ownership. Stay here.* Half an hour of hand-holding and praying
it out had convinced him once and for all to wave the white flag. He
liked her. He wanted to pursue something deeper than friendship.
If she snubbed him and rode off into the sunset in her ugly gray van,
he'd be trashed for a while. But not trying would drive him crazy.
"She probably helped design it—planned exactly where she wanted
each wall."

A featherlight fist cuffed his arm. "Are you familiar with the
serenity prayer, Mr. Braden?"

Jake rubbed his arm. "Yes, and I totally agree with the 'courage
to change the things I can' part."

Emily's laugh blended with the chirp of goldfinches from the
border of trees. "But my mind is not one of those things. I was
under no obligation to compromise with my contractor, but I let the
windows and the trim and the ugly old cupboard stay, and he should
be kissing my feet in gratitude."

Tempting. If there weren't children present. "When it comes
time to sell, you'll be the one kissing feet, Miss Foster."

"We'll see about that." She turned with a huff, walked several
feet, and stopped. At her feet stood a marble urn about ten inches

high filled with daisies. The inscription on the pedestal beneath it read:

ANGEL MARIE
APRIL 14, 2011
STEP SOFTLY. . .A DREAM LIES BURIED HERE

One date marked both birth and death.

Emily covered her mouth with one hand. Her body stiffened. Jake put his arm across her shoulders. "How sad."

She nodded and a sob ripped through her.

"Emily?" Jake turned her to face him then wrapped his arms around her. Her chest heaved, her shoulders shook. Hand against her hair, he pressed her close to his chest. *Lord, what do I do?* He held her until her sobs quieted. "Talk to me," he whispered.

Minutes passed. Finally she took a shuddering breath, let out a word he couldn't understand, and cleared her throat. "I was pregnant when I had the accident. I lost the baby."

His arms tightened. "Emily. I'm so sorry."

"It was too early to know"—she pulled away and swiped her face with both hands—"if it was a boy or a girl, but I know it was a boy. I just know." The sobs resumed.

Again, he pulled her into the shelter of his arms. The tears he'd witnessed, the sad, drained look, all made sense now. "How awful."

"I had no right—"

His chest tightened. "Lots of women ski early on in their pregnancies." Didn't they? He knew of one, the wife of a friend. "Accidents happen. You can't blame yourself."

"It wasn't an accident."

She shattered again. Jake felt like he was literally holding her together. Questions peppered his mind, but he didn't voice them.

He simply let her cry it out.

⸙

The crayon snapped in Lexi's hand. She stared at the bumpy red edges of the break, picked up a purple one and broke it, this time on purpose.

Emily was crying. And Jake was hugging her. Holding her like a child, his head resting on her hair—her short, wedged hair he was supposed to hate.

Who cared? Pansy would be home tomorrow. That was all that really mattered. That was all the family she needed anyway.

But she couldn't keep from looking at Jake hugging Emily. She'd never seen him with his arms around anyone other than her mom or grandma. Sure, he gave Tina a goofy kiss on the cheek when he saw her, but everybody knew that didn't mean anything. He'd brought the lady with the pretty hair to a family picnic once. She had a name from a book. Heidi. She was nice in a too-nice way, and pretty, but she whispered to Jake the whole time and hardly talked to anyone else. Adam told Jake he was glad when he dumped her. Adam said it, so Lexi didn't have to.

It probably wasn't going to happen that way with Emily. Jake looked happy and that should be important to her. But if things had worked out the way she'd planned, they'd all be happy. And Emily would be in California.

She hated the selfish person she was turning into. But it was really just her survivor instincts that made her like this. If nobody else was worried about her future, she had to be. Maybe Adam could just drift along like it didn't matter where they lived, but she couldn't. Of course they wouldn't end up on the street, but what kind of a life would they have living with Grandma forever? By the time they graduated from high school Grandma Blaze would be an old lady. Who wants to bring friends over if the person you live with keeps her teeth in a jar in the bathroom?

Maybe it was time she told Jake about her plan. He'd like it because it would be way better for him than living in an ugly black room in his mother's basement. He loved his niece and nephew as much as a lot of fathers loved their own kids, and he spent more time with them than any real dad she knew. And she and Adam wouldn't be any trouble. Adam would mow the lawn and shovel snow and she'd cook and do dishes. She'd even babysit to buy her own clothes.

It didn't have to be a really huge house. She could give up her dream room with its big arched windows and the bed that looked like a tree house. She wouldn't mind sacrificing if the three of them could be a family.

She snapped a green crayon.

She had to get Emily out of the picture.

ᪧ

October 15, 1852

"Venison stew." Hannah handed the bowl to the emaciated man as Papa covered his shoulders with a blanket. "It'll warm you."

"Thank you. God bless your kindness."

Papa sat on the bench across from the man who called himself George. "How long have you been on the road?"

"Since las' snow." He kept his eyes on the soup bowl. "Stayed on awhile near Springfield. Buried my little girl there."

Hannah's breath caught in her throat. "I'm so sorry. How old was she?"

"Only saw ten summers. Los' my wife las' summer tryin' to give birth once again."

Papa put his hand on the man's back. "I lost my wife to the fever last year, but I can't imagine the heartache of losing a child."

George's head swayed from side to side. "Shoulda stayed. My sister told me to stay. I left her 'n' my mother. I couldn't stand the thought of one more plantin', but maybe my Mariah'd still be here if I'd stayed. They'd'a brought the doctor so's not to lose her."

"Was it the fever?" Papa's eyes pooled with tears.

"Infection took my girl. They can take the strap to me. Won't stand for it with my own. Still, they wouldn'ta let her die. . .like I did."

Hannah took a step forward. "The infection came from a whipping?"

"Yes'm."

Fingernails biting the flesh of her hands, Hannah knelt at the man's feet. "You must not blame yourself. Not for one minute. You took your daughter away to save her from further beatings. You did the right thing. It was their fault." The figure in her mind, face distorted like an angry, hateful mask, arm raised to crack a whip,

188

resembled Liam's father. "The man who lashed her is the guilty one."

Papa raised his hand to still her. "Are you a God-fearing man, George?"

"Wouldn'ta lived long 'nuf to see my baby born if'n I weren't. Lawd's been good in spite of the bad."

"Then I think we ought to pray."

George folded large, work-worn hands. Papa closed his eyes. "Heavenly Father, we come before Thee with heavy hearts. Great evil has been done to this man and his family. We ask for Your peace to flood his heart and, Lord, hard as it is, we ask for forgiveness to flow like the breath we..."

Hannah clenched her hands together, but couldn't form words into a prayer.

"Amen." George wiped his face with both hands. "Miss Hannah, may I give you something?"

"You don't need—"

"I want you to have this." Scarred fingers reached into a pocket in his frayed coat. "I was workin' on a set of animals for my little girl. Noah's animals. Two by two." His gaze wandered far from the small room. He pulled out a tiny, intricately carved frog. "I'll keep the other one for 'memberance, but I want you to have this one."

As she held out her hand, it shook with the sobs she could no longer control. "I will pray for you when I look upon it. I will pray you will soon be reunited with your mother and sister. As a free man."

CHAPTER 21

Chances
Est. 1843
An Establishment of Fine Food and Spirits

Emily sat in a captain's chair at a table in the corner and read the history of the building on the front of the menu while she waited for Dorothy.

The original claim to the land on what was then known as the Pishtaka River was laid by Levi Godfrey, who built a log cabin on the site in 1836. Levi added a second story to the house and turned it into a tavern. People traveling from Lake Michigan to the Mississippi River would often share meals with his family and spend the night on his dirt floor. After the log house burned down, the property was bought by Peter Campbell. In 1843, Campbell built the present brick building, then called the Union House.

Emily laid the menu on the green place mat. She glanced at the entryway to the dining room and imagined Hannah Shaw walking in. She could see her in a floor-length blue dress like the woman in the picture on the wall, her hair braided and coiled at the back of her neck, a blue velvet bag swinging from her wrist.

Hannah would glance up at the pressed-tin ceiling as she laughed at some witty comment. Her eyes would follow the rough-hewn beam that separated the dining room from the bar, which may have been the tavern back then. Would she and her beau have ordered from a menu? Maybe they'd have only a few choices—roast lamb from a local farm, or fresh venison with seasonal, locally grown vegetables.

Would she and Hannah have been friends? How different her life would have been had she been born in Hannah's era, when women didn't have careers, live in their own apartments, or go on unchaperoned dates. They didn't ski, and recreational drugs were unheard of. Hannah's letters lamented the few choices open to women of her day. If only she could have seen the other extreme. *Hannah, you were so safe.*

Emily thought of the women memorialized in the English Settlement Cemetery. Many had lost children. Most probably experienced more loss than she would ever know.

But not at their own hands.

Across the room, a black-and-white picture of four men sitting on what appeared to be a dam, dangling fishing lines into the river, spoke of a time when life was never easy, but so much simpler. If she'd lived here in 1852, she'd probably be married with several children. Living a hard, simple, and probably happy life.

Dorothy's tiny frame appeared in the doorway. She waved then stopped to talk at three tables before sitting in the chair across from Emily. Her face rippled with concentric laugh lines. "Were you waiting long?"

"You're right on time. I came early to soak up the ambience."

"This part of the building was built a few years before your house. So Elizabeth Shaw and her daughter could have sat right in this very spot sipping tea."

"I was actually just thinking about that."

"We're all connected. I always picture history like holding a mirror up to a mirror. We're reflections of the people who came before us and the generations that follow, don't you think?"

What happens to the people whose reflections stop here? Emily glanced up at the fishermen and made herself present in the moment. "That's a beautiful way of putting it."

"Makes history not so dry. I was a teacher for thirty-seven years.

191

Always tried to help my students see the things that happened before us as still alive, just in a different time continuum." She tapped a crooked finger on the vinyl tablecloth next to her place mat. "Like your Shaw ghosts. Still alive, just not fully." A myriad of fine lines fanned away from twinkling gray eyes.

"Do you really believe there are spirits living there?"

"Well, I believe places hold memories, and if we know how to look and listen, we can learn magical things." Faded eyes narrowed. "So tell me what you've learned."

Emily's fingers tightened around her water glass. She took a long, slow drink. She cleared her throat, wiped her mouth, and was saved by their waitress.

The woman refilled Emily's cup and poured decaf for Dorothy without asking. "Ready to order, or should I come back in a few minutes?"

Emily looked at Dorothy. "You haven't had a chance to look at—"

"Oh, I know this menu about as well as I know my own name. I'll have the ahi tuna salad, Helen."

"Vinegar and oil?"

"Of course."

"Ma'am?" The server looked at Emily and for a split second she was conscious of being an outsider. There was no place in this world, not even back home, where she could walk in and order "the usual." She turned the menu over and pointed halfway down the page. "I'd like the chef salad with French and bleu cheese on the side, please."

The waitress headed to the kitchen, and Emily studied the scalloped edge of her place mat. In spite of all she might learn from sharing her finds with Dorothy, this wasn't the time. She'd already planned out the "reveal." She'd invite Blaze, Tina and Colt, and Dorothy for a preview of the cellar and the letters. She'd let Dorothy break the news to the state Historical Society and even invite reporters if she wanted. It would all play out on the day she listed the house and left.

She tried to match a bit of Dorothy's excitement. "The booklet about the English Settlement Church says they did extensive remodeling in 1967. Do you know if any of the original pews still exist?"

"Some of the members took pews. I imagine some of them are still around. Why do you ask?"

"There's a church pew in my attic with a carving of a cluster of grapes on the back."

"Really?" Dorothy licked her bottom lip. "I'd love to see it. It looks old?"

"Very."

"I'll ask around and see if anyone knows anything. Anything else?"

"On the back of the cellar door there's a very faint image of a basket of apples. It was hand painted and the carving on Elizabeth's headstone is so similar."

Dorothy leaned forward. "Doesn't seem like it could be a coincidence. There were fruit trees all around the house when I was young. It's very possible the Shaws planted the originals."

A faint chill shimmied down Emily's spine. "Jake took two layers of flooring off in the kitchen this week, down to the original wood. There are several paths worn in the wood—between the back door and the cellar and the cellar to a corner cupboard that appears as old as the house. I haven't seen ghosts, but it's so easy to imagine the family sitting in rocking chairs on the back porch or the women shelling peas in the kitchen."

"Mirrors."

Emily nodded.

"My son thinks I live in the past too much." Dorothy traced a bead of water down the side of her glass.

A flash of reproach warmed Emily's neck. Until this point she had looked at the woman as purely a conveyor of information. "How old is your son?"

The smile returned. "He'll be fifty next month. He lives in Chicago. Harry is my only child and he never married." She wiped the corners of her mouth with her thumb and index finger. "For me, the reflections in the mirror continue through my students and their children."

Emily swallowed hard. Not a one of her preschoolers would remember her in years to come. "What an incredible legacy."

They talked about teaching until their salads came and then

Dorothy began a monologue of Rochester history. She spoke of people long buried in the Rochester or English Settlement cemeteries as if they were "alive, but not fully."

Mr. Godfrey, who built the original tavern, had supported himself from the age of twelve. He brought his family to his little log hut in the spring of 1836 "to a humble home in a setting of surpassing beauty" along a clear stream banked with carpets of green and overflowing with wildflowers.

Before the first marriage ceremony was performed in Rochester in 1838, the groom, Philander Cole, traveled over twenty miles to Racine on foot to obtain his license. His new bride became the envy of every woman in the area for owning the first cupboards with doors.

When Mrs. Allen Stetson was thirteen years old, she rose before dawn every morning, fixed breakfast, and finished the household chores so she could accompany her father and brother to the fields. She was too fearful to remain at home alone because of the Indians.

Sunlight angled lower through the windows as Dorothy spoke. Emily slipped her hand into her purse and discreetly checked the time on her phone. An hour had passed and they hadn't yet made it to the middle of the nineteenth century.

The first church society was organized in 1837. They sometimes met in the tavern. Mr. Taggert, the first schoolteacher, cut willow switches on his way to school. Mail was delivered only once a week in the early years. A letter could be sent for six and a half cents.

Every bit of it was fascinating, but when Dorothy began to yawn, Emily feared they'd never see 1852. Pushing her bowl aside and folding her napkin, she took advantage of a yawn and stared up at the ceiling. "I love the feel of this place." As casually as she could manage, she added, "It mentioned on the menu that this building was a station in the Underground Railroad."

"It may have been. We know for certain that several places in Rochester were safe havens for runaways. You know about the Ela house?"

Emily nodded. "A runaway slave and his conductor stopped there."

A long-suffering look pinched Dorothy's mouth. "*Joshua Glover*"—

194

she formed the name as if speaking of royalty—"and his conductor, Chauncey C. Olin, got a fresh team from the Elas for five dollars and stayed for a cup of hot tea and lunch in March of 1854."

"Fascinating." Emily sipped her water with what she hoped was a casual air. "Do you think there's any chance my house was involved?"

"In the Underground Railroad?" Dorothy leaned forward. In a single blink, her eyes lost their tired look. "You're thinking what I'm thinking, aren't you? That letter from Missouri. Very mysterious, isn't it? What was the work they'd accomplished? I'd read that letter several times years ago but after meeting you I've been absolutely obsessed by it. Grace Ostermann was a bit of an odd duck. I asked her many times if I could go through her house looking for historical evidences and she refused every time. Almost as if she were protecting something"—her pupils widened—"or someone."

"Someone?"

"If I lived in a house inhabited by spirits of the past, I wouldn't too readily share them with the public, would you?"

"No. I guess I wouldn't. But maybe she was just a private person."

"Well, I can understand that, but since she's gone. . ."

Emily was sure she was expected to finish the sentence. She drained her water glass.

"If I could just look around a bit, get some pictures—"

Swallowing wrong, Emily answered with a cough. "What would you be looking for?"

Dorothy leaned yet closer, glanced left then right. "There could be signs that aren't obvious to the untrained eye."

"Like what?"

"That shed behind the house has been there as long as I can remember. It's stone, isn't it?"

"Just the bottom half. It's wood on top."

"Hmm. Could be the original foundation." Her eyes brightened. "There could be a tunnel. What if the the legendary tunnel actually existed, but on the opposite side of the river from—" She stared over Emily's shoulder. "Oh my. Isn't this awkward?"

"What?" Emily craned her neck. Three men and a woman followed the hostess to a table.

"You don't know her?"

"No."

"That's Jacob Braden's last girlfriend. Heidi something-or-another. They were quite the item for months."

Emily ordered her neck not to crank to the right, but it wouldn't obey. She stared at the woman who could have been a cover model.

"Never did hear why they broke up. They seemed happy enough—"

"Do you need more coffee? I do." Emily felt no qualms about cutting the woman off. She was here for a lesson in history.

But not Jacob Braden's.

⁂

Emily handed Adam a glass of lemonade and sat beside him on her front step. Upstairs, Jake and Topher taped and sanded drywall at an astounding speed.

Adam took a drink and wiped his mouth with the back of his hand. "What if Mrs. Willett just shows up here?"

"I'll tell her no one is allowed during remodeling."

"Watch her come over with a shovel in the middle of the night and start digging in your shed."

Emily laughed. "If she does, I'll rattle chains and make howling noises."

Adam's eyebrows took turns arching. "Maybe you won't have to. Maybe the real ghosts will scare her away."

"They haven't tried to scare us yet."

"That's 'cause we're cool." He lifted a book from the stack on the step and pointed to a two-page spread depicting Underground Railroad quilt symbols. "We should make some of these."

Emily scanned the page for the pattern of the quilt on her church pew. "I don't sew. Do you?"

"Actually. . ." He patted both of his pant legs then unzipped a pocket and pulled out a hinged metal Altoid box.

"You piece quilts with breath mints?"

"Funny." He opened the box and showed her two sewing machine spools of thread and three sizes of needles. "I could sew, if I had to. But I meant we should make these out of paper. They could be cards in a board game. The board could be a map with all

196

the Underground Railroad routes." He flipped to the beginning of the book and showed her what appeared to be a map of rivers of the eastern half of the United States.

Like veins flowing backward into arteries, several lines converged in southern Indiana and formed a thick northward line through Ohio and across Lake Erie, ending in Canada. One line verged off, following the Mississippi along the curves of Illinois then arcing northwest across Lake Michigan, Michigan state, and into Ontario.

Emily's breath caught in her throat. The line dissected Rochester and Grand Rapids, connecting two parts of her life she was trying to separate. She turned several pages, back to brightly colored quilt blocks, and focused on their beauty and not on their hidden meanings. "I have a box marked 'art supplies' in the basement if you want to run down and get it."

"Awesome." Adam pushed the book toward her and jumped to his feet. "We should be reading these books in the secret room."

"By kerosene lamp."

"Yeah. Can we?"

She hated trampling his enthusiasm. "It's too damp down there for my lungs."

"Oh yeah. I forget you're still sickly." He pounded his chest and wheezed as he opened the door.

The boy was good for her soul. Emily closed her eyes and lifted her face to the midmorning sun.

"Excuse me!" The voice was breathless. Footsteps pounded. Sherry Vargas ran across the street, both boys in tow. All three were barefoot. "Is there any chance you could watch the boys for a few minutes? *Some*body closed the drain in the bathroom sink to play with submarines and somebody else came along and left the water on. So we now have our very own swimming pool and—"

"Go! I'll watch them. Adam and I were just going to do some crafts anyway."

"Thank you so much." Sherry backed away, still talking. "I keep telling Tina I want to invite you over for dinner, but with work and the kids—"

Emily waved her away with a smile. "Go drain the lake. Maybe we can chat when you're done." The little voice that was supposed to remind her she wasn't here to make friends seemed to have contracted laryngitis.

Adam returned. "Hey." He greeted the boys. "You guys want to make some cool stuff?" He looked at Emily. "Maybe we should move to the back porch where we have more room."

"Good thinking."

"Always." He tapped his temple then hoisted the plastic bin to his hip and motioned for the boys to follow.

She couldn't explain why the craft supplies had made the trip around Lake Michigan with her. Maybe, like a pioneer woman hiding her favorite teacup in the flour barrel as she packed the Conestoga, she needed just one souvenir of her old life to take west. Glue sticks, round-tipped scissors, rulers, markers, copy paper, construction paper. The box transported her to a room with rainbow-shaped tables and miniature chairs. Primary colors, wooden blocks, puzzles, nap mats, cubbyholes filled with tambourines and maracas.

For a moment, she was Miss Em again, the teacher who made up silly songs and rhyming stories, who wore a clown suit for birthdays and danced the hokey-pokey with four-year-olds.

She'd told the other teachers she couldn't come back because she couldn't be the Miss Em the children were used to. They knew she couldn't lift or bend. They didn't know she couldn't spend her life loving other people's children.

As Emily walked around the side of the house, Topher waved through an open upstairs window and blew her a kiss. The boy was getting annoying. Jake had ordered her to stay out of the house while they were sanding. Whether he was more concerned for her lungs or her lips, she wasn't sure. He'd commanded her to sit in the sun and not lift a finger, but she'd just about finished scraping the porch spindles.

Three boys sat cross-legged on the porch by the time she joined them. She offered lemonade and opened the back door. Jake stood by the sink, downing a glass of water, the front of his shirt soaked with sweat.

"I'm sorry it's so warm in here."

He winked at her over the rim of the glass. "It's not all your fault."

Her only comeback was a smile and a shake of her head.

"Do that again."

"Do what?"

"The hair thing."

She whipped her head to the right. Her hair splashed over her cheek. "Like this?"

"Exactly like that." He took a step toward her and set the glass on the counter. His eyes said dangerous things.

She couldn't listen. "Michael and Russell are here."

"I see that." He took another small step.

"They want lemonade."

He brushed a rogue strand of hair from her cheek. "They won't dehydrate in the next two minutes."

Two minutes. If he was about to do what she thought he was about to do, two minutes could kill her. How long could a person go without oxygen before brain damage set in? Maybe it was too late. If she let him kiss her it would be proof she'd already been holding her breath too long.

Kiss and run, oh what fun.

She inched away while she still had the power to run. Any closer and she'd be rooted to the spot.

Maybe forever.

"I can't keep them waiting."

Jake's chin lowered a fraction of an inch. Dust-covered arms crossed his damp shirt. "But you have no problem keeping me waiting, do you?"

His arm brushed hers as he walked past her.

♔

"Do you know what a quilt is?"

Michael nodded. "Like on my bed?"

"Yes. Look at these pictures. Long ago people made quilts that told secret messages."

Russell leaned over the book. "Like codes?"

"Yep." Adam pointed to a picture. A white square in the center, surrounded by a wide red border. Triangles, pointing toward the middle, intersected each corner. "This one's called the Monkey

199

Wrench. It meant the slaves—do you guys know who slaves were?"

Michael shook his head. Russell nodded. "They were black people that bad white men stole and made them pick cotton all day long in bare feet."

Eyebrows raised, Adam looked to Emily with an expression that asked for help. Emily smiled and shrugged. "Those people had to work very, very hard and they wanted to be free to choose the kind of jobs they would have and where they would live. So some of them ran away." She turned to the map of Underground Railroad routes. "This is where Rochester is. Some slaves came from places like Mississippi and Louisiana and Alabama and tried to get up here to Canada where they could be free to live the kind of lives they wanted. But there were no airplanes or cars or buses so sometimes they had to walk for miles and miles. They walked mostly at night because there were men who were looking for them and they didn't want to get caught."

Adam patted the porch floor and grinned. "And sometimes good people would hide them in their barns or attics or in secret rooms."

The pupils of Michael's dark eyes seemed to widen. "I would let somebody stay in my room if bad guys were after them, and I would give them my Crocs and all my shoes."

"Me, too." Russell was not to be outdone. "And Mom would cook for them, and we would buy them clothes and maybe umbrellas and mittens. And guns so they could shoot the bad guys."

Clearing his throat, Adam drew their attention back to the Monkey Wrench square. "If the slaves saw this picture on a quilt they knew it was time to get their tools together and get ready to leave to go to Canada. They needed hammers and nails to build shelters along the way."

"And drills and saws," Michael added.

Russell punched his arm. "They didn't have 'lectricity in the old days."

It took every ounce of Emily's self-control not to scoop Michael in her arms and banish the embarrassed look on his face. "Actually, they probably did bring the nonelectric kind of saws and drills if they had them."

"See?" Michael stuck his tongue out.

"Adam, tell us about the other quilt pictures. *Quickly*," she whispered.

"This is a Wagon Wheel. It told them to pack all the stuff they would need on their trip. They couldn't bring a lot because most of the time they had to carry it on their backs."

Deep grooves creased Russell's forehead. "I would bring my basketball and my pillow and my boots."

Michael appeared deep in thought. "I would bring a sleeping bag and a flashlight and peanuhbutter cookies." His eyes widened. "I got an idea. We could really put stuff in our backpacks and pretend we were running away from bad guys and hide and everything."

"That'd be fun." Adam held out a fist and tapped knuckles with Michael. "And I know just the place we could hide." He responded to Emily's warning look with a deliberately blank look.

"Awesome." Big brown eyes turned on Emily. "Did you make cookies again?"

Her throat tightened, but only momentarily. She ruffled Michael's hair. "As soon as Jake's done making a mess in my house, I'll bake peanut butter cookies from scratch and you guys can help."

"Awesome."

Emily turned away. Her gaze followed the outline of the trapdoor and she smiled at the squabbling coming from the blue spruce. "Yeah. Awesome."

"The guy you met in the kitchen earlier? That was the old me."

Jake folded onto the floor of the now empty porch and picked up a glue stick. He didn't seem capable of eye contact.

"The old you told me about Jesus."

"Right. The guy in the kitchen was the guy I became after that, that I'm trying not to be anymore."

In spite of the twisted sentence, she had no problem deciphering. There were strange parallels in their lives.

He picked at a flap of peeling paint. "We haven't had a chance to talk since the cemetery, and I have no idea how you're doing about that or where your head's at about me, us, and besides that I was covered with drywall dust, and then I go and. . . It's just that you looked so amazing when you flipped you hair like that. That's not the only reason, I mean I don't come on to every beautiful woman, but you and I—" He groaned and ran both hands over his face. "I'm sorry."

How long could she stay angry at a guy for thinking she was beautiful? "All's forgiven."

"Does that mean. . .?" His eyes sparked.

"No."

"Fine." His sigh was probably heard in Burlington. "Does it mean I can take you to dinner?"

"Jake, I—"

"I know. We've had this conversation a few times now. Let me take you to Chances. For research.

She sucked in her bottom lip. "That's a line for the books."

"Did it work?"

"No. I was there with Dorothy yesterday."

"Great. How's this one? I need to take you out for your health. You shouldn't be breathing all this junk. Actually"—the wink made a reprise—"you should be living with me. It's not healthy here now that we're sanding."

A full-blown laugh shook her. "Your house is no longer a safe place. Besides, there's no room for me there anymore. I don't think Lexi'd jump at the chance for a roommate."

"Duh." His face sobered. "I feel really dumb that I didn't think of this before."

"Think of what?"

"We need to trade places. You take my room and I'll take yours. It makes perfect sense. I'll be here to work as late as I want and you'll be there to breathe clean air and help my mom with the kids."

His last few words closed her mouth on her protests. "There is some sense in that."

"I do, occasionally, make a little. So we agree?"

She shrugged. "We agree. If Lexi doesn't have a cow."

"Then I'll be back here at seven to pick you up for dinner and move your things when we're done. Feel up to walking?"

"That sounds nice."

"It does, doesn't it?"

She walked him to the front door, listened to the truck's engine start, sputter, stop, and rev again. He waved as he pulled away. She turned and leaned against the door frame, surveying what Jake referred to as the wreckage of her main floor. From the front door, she could see straight into the kitchen. The dining room wall was gone and the narrow kitchen door had been widened to an eight-foot opening. The decision to cave on keeping the original woodwork had been a smart one. The house kept its old-fashioned charm but was now entertainment-friendly. "You and I make a pretty good team, Mr. Braden."

As soon as her lungs were good, she'd be rolling up her sleeves, sanding, staining, and painting. She liked the idea of working next to and learning from Jake. Learning, so at the next house she could tackle more of the work herself. The thought did things to her stomach that she shouldn't allow an hour before he was picking her up for dinner. She walked out onto the back porch and put away tape and scissors. She leafed through a pile of construction paper quilt squares. Time with the boys had gone fast. Too fast. She'd slid into teacher mode as if she hadn't missed a beat, as if that chapter of her life weren't closed forever.

Even if she could handle it emotionally and physically, there wasn't enough money in it. She needed to make fifty thousand dollars a year for the next four years. After she'd made restitution, she'd have the luxury of choice.

As she closed the craft box, her phone vibrated. She pulled it out of her back pocket and stared at the screen. *Speaking of making money.* "Hi."

"Hey." Cara's first syllable was loud but slightly garbled.

"Not a great connection. Maybe you should call me back when you get to a better—"

"Is this better? I was lying down."

"A little. You sound funny. Are you sick?"

Cara answered with a deep laugh. "Not the contagious kind. Went to a gallery opening last night. I'm sleeping it off."

Two years ago that would have produced a laugh and a round of Can You Top This? But not a single morning-after story came to mind. *That was the old me.* She looked at the clock on the microwave and subtracted two hours. "It's four o'clock. Did you stay home from work?"

"Yeah. Not a problem. That's what I'm calling about. Work, I mean. Are you ready for this?"

Doubt it. "What?"

"I found you a job. A crazy-paying job that's, like, made just for you."

Emily's spine straightened. Was this Destiny disguised as a hung-over friend? "I'm listening."

"The gallery owner—did I mention she owns three others? Freaky successful. She has three kids under five and she's interviewing nannies. But she doesn't really want a nanny, she wants like a substitute mom, you know? And she's paying eleven hundred dollars a week and room and board is included. I told her to stop looking. She's never home so she wouldn't be interfering with anything. Her house sounds insane—built into the side of a hill in Sausalito. Can you imagine? You could play with kids all day long. All the good stuff of being a mom, but they wouldn't be yours. How cool is—"

It wasn't the first time she'd hung up on Cara.

♔

Upset as she was, she did the math.

Lifting her top layer of hair with a round brush, she spritzed it with hair spray and calculated the numbers one more time. Eleven hundred dollars a week times four was forty-four hundred a month.

With money like that she could even provide an expense card.

And all she'd have to do for it was play a role she'd never fill in real life.

If she'd wanted to take care of little kids she would have stayed right where she was.

But if she took the job she wouldn't have to gamble on the housing market, on making enough money on this house and the next.

She couldn't turn it down.

But what if there was a future for her right here?

She'd know by the end of the night. She would not say good

night to Jake without telling him everything he needed to know to decide if there'd be a second date. Even the slightest hesitation on his part and she'd know. And she'd program her GPS for Sausalito.

As she rolled another swath of hair onto her brush, her phone rang. She answered it without looking at it. If it was Cara, first she'd say "Sorry" then she'd say "I'll give you an answer tomorrow."

"Emily? It's Blaze. I'm calling for Jake. He's on his way out the door and he couldn't find his phone. Evidently he double-booked without realizing it. Lexi has a ballet rehearsal tonight, and I guess he promised to take her and a couple of friends out afterward. With all that's been going on lately, it's no wonder he can't keep things straight. Anyway, I'm so glad you're coming here. I know I'm a really poor alternative, but I was wondering if you'd like to come over early and hang out with me tonight. I'm looking for a reason to laugh and can't seem to come up with one."

"I'd love that."

"Good. I'll set out a picture of Jake and you can pretend you're with him."

With a hollow laugh, Emily said good-bye. Blaze was one sweet but pushy mama.

Maybe she'd have an extra picture she wouldn't mind Emily keeping.

She could pack it away in the Conestoga.

205

CHAPTER 22

Settling back in the end of the couch, Emily let out a sigh. She felt so relaxed here. As long as she kept her eyes off the eight-by-ten glossy in the middle of the coffee table.

Blaze had a flare for decorating and color. Gold walls, upholstered furniture in burnt orange, gold, and splashes of cobalt blue, and a perfect balance of stripes, florals, old, and new. "You have the coziest living room."

"Thank you." Blaze tucked her legs beneath her on the opposite end of the couch. "Abby helped."

"You must miss her so much. I can't imagine what that kind of loss feels like."

"I hope you never have to."

Emily sipped her coffee and looked away. Her gaze landed on the one spot she needed to avoid. Redirecting brought her to a wall of black-and-white family pictures. One showed Abby seated in a rocking chair. Blaze's arms wrapped around her shoulders from behind. Her face nestled next to her daughter's. "Imagine living in a time before photography."

Blaze nodded. "Memories fade. I'm so glad I have these."

The silence that enveloped them was peaceful and reflective. After several minutes, Emily nodded toward the wall. "There aren't any pictures of Jake the way he looked when I met him nineteen years ago."

"They don't exist. He burned them all when he 'turned cool.' His words, not mine. Believe me, there was nothing cool about him from my perspective. I was reeling from losing my husband and all I could do was sit back and watch as my sweet boy morphed into Dracula and then woke up one morning convinced he was Brett Favre."

"You seem to have a good relationship now."

"We do. I wouldn't have made it through Abby's death without him. He's a good man." The look she jabbed at Emily seemed laden with meaning. Smile lines sprouted at Blaze's temples. "There aren't any pictures of Topher when you first met him, either."

Emily put her hand over her face. "Jake told you."

"No." The lines deepened. "Topher told me. I practically raised that boy. He calls me Mom Two. He tells me way more than my own son ever has."

Emily shook her head. "I wish he'd quit acting like we were star-crossed lovers meant to be together for eternity."

"That's pretty much what he's been telling Jake at every opportunity, I think. He's harmless. He makes my boy laugh and I love him for that."

"And I'm supposed to be making you laugh."

Blaze closed her eyes, sighed, and stared down at Jake's picture. "We got word about Ben today. He only has to serve twenty-eight days altogether. They charged him with disorderly conduct." Blaze ran fingertips over her lashes. "We did some research. With the kids so close, and shooting across the highway, they could have slapped him with so much more. He could have been behind bars until after Adam and Lexi were out of high school."

"I'm so sorry."

"I guess we need to be thankful for temporary guardianship. Every day we can keep that man away from those kids is a gift." She grabbed a box of tissue from an end table as tears started in earnest. "Did you know that seeking permanent guardianship was Jake's idea?"

"I gathered that." She gave herself permission to linger on the framed picture. "You're right. He's a good man."

"I'm so proud of that boy. He's given up so much already."

"For the kids?"

Blaze nodded. "He'd just finished remodeling his own house when we found out Abby was sick. He had a girlfriend I think he could have gotten serious about. He was on his way to having everything a guy could want. When Abby died, he sold the house dirt cheap and moved back home. At the time, we thought the kids would be living here." She picked up her mug. Her lips lifted in a halfhearted smile. "In case you're wondering, none of us are heartbroken that his relationship ended. On the one-to-ten scale of maintenance, she was a twelve."

"Did he break it off?" The question put her at a thirteen on the scale.

Blaze gave an overly understanding smile. "Yes. Another reason I'm proud of him. To my knowledge he hasn't dated in months." She turned toward the window. Emily was sure she was fighting to keep the smile tame. "Anyway, a friend of his from high school is a lawyer. He's agreed to cut way back on his charges, but if we ever get to court and Ben decides to fight dirty, I have no idea what it could end up costing."

"Why is it taking so long?"

"There hasn't been enough evidence. The kids claim he's never hurt either one of them."

"You don't believe them, do you?"

Blaze shook her head.

"Won't this latest incident help?"

"We're pretty sure Ben lied to the police about how close the kids were when he shot Pansy. The neighbor didn't actually see it happen, and the kids would go along with Ben's story." A shaky sigh rattled from her throat. "Ben's threatened them with something to keep them from talking. I'm sure he has all along. If I press it, they both get mad. Too mad. They're hiding something."

"If Jake got guardianship, does he plan on living here or—"

The front door burst open. Adam bounded in, looked at Emily, and stopped in his tracks. His head cocked to one side like a puzzled puppy. "What are you doing here?"

"Having coffee with your grandma."

"I thought you and Jake were going out."

Blaze pointed to his shoes. "He forgot he'd promised Lexi to take her and her friends out after rehearsal."

"Huh? I thought Mrs. Benner. . ." He kicked his shoes off and into the corner, shaking his head as he did. "Hey, I've got an idea. Wait here." He ran toward the back hall.

Emily smiled. "What I wouldn't give for just an ounce of that energy."

"You and me both. And a few of his brain cells."

"He's amazing."

"He's in advanced classes at school. That's hard on Lexi. She gets good grades, but she has to work for them. Adam has almost a photographic mem—"

Adam bounced in, brandishing the thick pamphlet Emily had glimpsed in the van during their Pansy stakeout.

"Let's do this. Right now." He plunked onto the middle of the couch and put Jake's picture facedown on the floor. Emily's mood lightened. The pamphlet unfolded to the size of a road map. "The other side has all the stuff in Burlington."

The BuR SPUR of Wisconsin's Underground Railroad. The Burlington, Rochester, and Spring Prairie Underground Railroad Trail. Emily's eyes traveled from the map labeled "Out-of-Town Driving Tour" in the center to the pictures of buildings and numbered paragraphs framing the page. "There are thirty-two sites on this. If we start now, we'd be lucky to make it to the last place by breakfast." She ruffled his hair. The crazy waves invited it, and there was no sister around to get jealous.

Blaze shook her head. "It's suppertime. Let's wait till morning. I have a friend who volunteers at the museum. He's working on a book, so he's there on Saturdays. We can start as early as you want."

Adam didn't hide his disappointment.

"Well. . ." Emily stretched the word like a drumroll. "I suppose this means we should let your grandma in on our little secret."

"Cool. But not till tomorrow. She's making us wait, so we'll make her wait." He scrunched his nose and stuck his chin in the air. "I'm going to pack my camera and my digital recorder and my. . ." His voice trailed off as he ran down the hall.

Emily stood and picked up her cup. Blaze stretched to one side and then the other. "You asked about what would happen to the kids." She bent down slowly, picked up Jake's picture, and set it on a shelf. "I can tell you *my* plan for those kids." Her hands folded and pressed to her chest. "I plan to find that boy a woman who can love him and those kids with all her heart."

Lips parting, face warming under the direct stare, Emily froze.

With a loud whoop, Blaze clapped her on the back. "Told you I needed something to make me laugh! Your face did it!" Her arm slipped across Emily's shoulder, and she drew her close in a one-armed hug much like the one in the picture on the wall. "You've got nothing to worry about. Unless you're *the one.*"

⚜

On Saturday morning, Lexi crouched in the corner of her bed and grimaced at her friend Naomi. The door handle rattled. "Lex! Open up."

Naomi, sitting on the floor holding Pansy, held her index finger to her mouth.

"Alexis! What's going on? You hid my phone, didn't you?" Something banged against the door. "Mrs. Benner just called. *She* was planning on taking you to the recital last night. What're you trying to pull?"

Her door was locked, but all he'd need to open it was a paper clip. Pansy yowled and hobbled off Naomi's lap. How could the poor cat know that the man on the other side of the door wouldn't lay a hand, or foot, on her in a million years?

Lexi leaned over the bed and picked up Pansy. The bed groaned and she flinched. She should answer Jake. But she didn't have an answer. When she'd heard he was going out on a date with Emily, she'd had to act fast.

"You're grounded."

She heard footsteps. He'd given up easily. "He won't follow through." With his head full of Emily, he'd forget he'd grounded her.

The plan was Naomi's idea. Before Mom got sick, Lexi had never lied about anything worse than saying she forgot an assignment so she'd have an excuse to call Naomi. But even in the Bible people lied to protect somebody. Rahab lied to protect the two spies. Sara lied

210

to protect Abraham. Where would the world be now if those men had killed Abraham? Her Sunday school teacher said those were "special circumstances."

So was this. Lying to protect your family was a good thing.

She remembered how she'd felt the first time she didn't tell the truth. Mom was in the hospital again and Ben was in charge. He made Lexi fix supper. Adam read to her while she cooked and she forgot about the macaroni. It burned on the bottom and Ben got crazy mad, madder than they'd ever seen him. He hit Adam with the back of his hand and Adam banged his head on the corner of the cupboard. It bled all over.

That was the first time Ben said if they told anyone he'd call the social workers and they'd split them up and put them in different foster homes.

Jake had come over after supper to get Mom's hairbrush. He saw a streak of blood Lexi had missed on the white cupboard. She'd grabbed a napkin behind her back and wound it around her finger. "Cut myself grating cheese," she'd said. "It's not deep, but it sure did bleed." She felt like an actress. Jake believed her. That was as good as applause at the end of a school play.

Now she could lie good if she had to. Under special circumstances. But that didn't make her a liar.

The back door slammed. Jake wouldn't be coming back tonight. But Emily would. Lexi bent down and buried her face in Pansy's fur. "We need another plan." Even though she'd kept Jake and Emily apart last night, things hadn't worked out all that great. Grandma Blaze had invited her here. To stay. She'd kicked her own son out of his room.

Life was turning upside down. And it was up to her to fix it.

Rolling a strand of black hair around her finger, Naomi said, "You have to make Emily hate being here and think your family is horrible." She grinned and the lamplight reflected purple on her braces. "Let's invite her to our sleepover tonight and we can make up stories about how mean your grandma is and how Jake gets drunk and gambles and stuff like that."

Naomi was serious, but it struck Lexi as funny. She laughed, deep and creepy. "And we'll all tell seeeecrets."

The purple lamp made Naomi look ghoulish. Her nose and forehead wrinkled and she laughed freakier than Lexi. "No. Wait. We'd be way more believable if she overheard us talking when she thinks we don't think she's listening."

Goose bumps rippled up Lexi's arms. "Perfect. Grab that notebook on my desk and let's write it out." Lexi rubbed her hands together. A giggle bubbled up from somewhere near her toes. "Soooo perfect."

⚜

October 21, 1852

It felt good to laugh. They'd done so little of it together. Liam held one end of an eight-inch iron hook, Hannah gripped the other. "Tell Miss Baker the truth." He touched the tip of her nose, leaving a black mark. "Tell her I am promised to another."

"She'll ask who."

"A man does not so readily give up his secrets to a casual acquaintance. Especially one who is so cheap as to only purchase a two-penny pot hook. Tell her you pleaded on your knees but I wouldn't relinquish the name of my green-eyed, copper-haired, fair-skinned beloved."

Hannah giggled but her smile slipped away too soon. "Will we ever dance, Liam?"

He let go of the hook and looped his thumbs in the tie of his apron to keep his arms from doing what they longed to do. "This may go on for years, but our part in it will not. We'll know when God has released us, and it will likely be at the same time I become Jim's partner and can afford to support you in the manner to which you are accustomed. The Lord has been gracious to fill our days with purpose and not just longing. When that day comes, I'll stand atop the grist mill and tell the world that Hannah Shaw has agreed to be my wife."

Eyes misting, she looked beyond him.

"What are you thinking?"

"That you are a stubborn man." A lone tear dropped to the hem of her skirt.

"I would agree. About what in particular?"

"If Papa knew we wanted to marry, he would open his arms and his home. You earn enough money to contribute a share and then we would all be there"—her voice lowered, her gaze traveled to the street where Jim stood talking to a man seated in a buggy—"to do what needs to be done."

Oh Lord, how much more can I stand? He could easily imagine the three of them living happily together, but for however long he felt called to be involved in a cause that could find him nose to nose with the barrel of a gun, no one could know of his feelings for Hannah. No one could tie the two of them, the three of them, together.

His right thumb dislodged from its moorings and skimmed her cheek. "If, when I have a job worthy of you, it would help your father to have us live with him, I would be more than willing. He is more of a father to me than I have ever hoped for. Until then—"

Jim ran into the shadows of the shop, eyes blazing, a paper gripped in his fist. He thrust it at Liam. "I'm told I have to post this." He spat on the ground.

The paper rattled in Liam's trembling hand.

$2,000 REWARD $2,000
Offered by Mr. Jackson Harper of St. Louis County, Missouri
*for the return, **Alive** and in **Good Condition**, of his negroes:*
George, *31 years of age, six feet, one inch tall, 180 pounds in weight.*
He has very dark skin, numerous whip scars on his back.
Wearing an iron collar when he escaped.
He possesses the skills of a carpenter and wood carver
and may have secured employment in that trade.
$1,500 reward.
and Mariah,
his daughter, 11 years of age, five feet tall, 100 pounds in weight.
She has light skin and a very prominent chin.
$500 reward.
These two ran off March 5, 1852, and have been reported heading
for this vicinity. Anyone having any knowledge of the whereabouts
of either or both of these negroes is requested to contact

213

the nearest sheriff or federal authorities.
Reward will be paid upon confirmation of identity.
Warning
Willful withholding of information pertaining to the
apprehension of these fugitives is a violation of federal
statute and is punishable by fine and imprisonment.

Tears streamed down Hannah's face. Throwing the hook against the wall, she ran out.

CHAPTER 23

Emily stood in front of a glass case displaying high-button shoes. She looked at a wood-handled button hook and wondered again at the women who first lived in her house. What was a day like for Hannah Shaw, who stitched by candlelight and baked bread at sunrise? She imagined rising before dark, dressing in layers of heavy clothes. Did she wear high-button shoes all day or something more comfortable?

The wood floor creaked beneath Adam's feet as he paced from one museum display to the next then finally stopped by Emily. "What's that?" He pointed at a black metal hinged instrument with a handle like a pair of scissors.

"A curling iron. Our Hannah probably had one. They used to heat it on a stove or clip it onto the chimney of a kerosene lamp."

"Huh. You guys got it easy now."

Blaze's friend, a tall, gray-haired man, approached. "Can I answer any questions?"

Emily held up a booklet she'd picked up at the door. *Racine County, Wisconsin, Roots of Freedom Underground Railroad Heritage Trail.* "We're going to be doing the walking tour this afternoon. We're also researching information on Thomas and Elizabeth Shaw. They built a house in Rochester in 1847, and their descendants lived there until the 1940s."

"Shaw. Thomas Shaw." The man tapped his chin. "I seem

to remember something. Did he have any connection with the Burlington Academy?"

"I don't know. We really don't know much about the family."

"Can you stop back here when you finish the tour? I'll see what I can find. I know I've seen that name and it will bug me as much as you if I don't figure out where."

⚜

"Whoa!" Adam, running half a block in front of Emily and Blaze, used the pamphlet to point at a white house. "This is the Cooper House. So Cooper School was named after the guy who lived here, I bet. And it says Joshua Glover stayed here, too!" He rattled off the rest of the information and ran on to the next place.

Blaze laughed. "Can't you see him as a tour guide someday?"

"I could see him leading those wilderness survival trips where they live off grub worms and cactus juice."

"Could be."

They caught up with Adam in front of Lincoln School, built in the late 1850s as Burlington's first high school. In front of the building stood a monument honoring Dr. Edward G. Dyer. "I read about him," Adam said. "He hid runaway slaves in his attic at least three times and they all came back years later to thank him."

"I wonder how often that happened." Tears stung Emily's eyes as she pictured that kind of reunion. "Imagine being responsible for someone's freedom."

She knew what it felt like to take it away.

They stood in front of a two-story white house with a flat roof and white pillars. As Adam began his travelogue about the holes cut in the shed that once stood behind the Perkins house, Emily's phone buzzed. She pulled it out and looked at it. Susan. She was about to turn the ringer off when she realized that right now, with an excuse not to talk long, was a good time to answer. "Hi there." *Keep it light. Sound happy.*

"Hey! You busy?"

"Actually, I am. I'm taking a historical tour of the town just south of Rochester."

"Sounds boring. I just wanted to make sure you're doing okay.

216

You haven't answered my calls."

"Yeah. Sorry. I've been crazy busy with the house."

"Well, you're going to get a break next weekend."

Emily's stomach knotted. "Yeah. I'm looking forward to it." *Liar.* The thought of twenty-four hours with Dawn Anne and Sierra made her chest pound like a scene in *The Tell-Tale Heart.* "It'll be good to catch up with them."

"And me."

The knot spasmed. "What?"

"I can't let you three be together without me."

"But I thought they were coming to Michigan."

"They are. But Craig's got business in Milwaukee next week, so I'll fly over with him and drive back with Dawn Anne and Sierra. How perfect is that?"

"That's. . .wonderful."

A Susan pause followed—the time it took for her sister's bottom lip to form the pout that turned her husband and parents to mush—and made Emily glad there was a massive lake between them. "It's not, is it? It's because of the baby, isn't it? I knew it would be hard for you, but I thought you'd at least be able to be happy for us knowing what we've gone through and how much—"

"I am happy. It's wonderful. You're having a little boy. That's. . . wonderful. I'll see you Saturday then." She didn't bother with good-bye.

Blaze, who'd heard her half of the conversation, seemed to sense her need for silence and kept Adam engaged on the rest of the tour. Emily forced a smile as they walked back into the museum. The man held up a book. "I found something. Not much, but here in some of Dr. Dyer's notes there's an entry dated May 12, 1863, saying that Thomas Shaw brought his grandson Luke Keegan in with a serious case of poison ivy. He recommended an oatmeal plaster twice a day." The man smiled. "Don't suppose that tells you much."

She read the date again—1863. Dorothy had said Thomas had remarried and they'd had sons together. They would still have been children in 1863. Luke Keegan could have been the son of a stepchild. Or he could have been Hannah's. Emily cleared her throat, "We'll have to do some research on the name Keegan, I guess. Thank you." Eyes smarting again with tears she couldn't hold back, she turned and walked out into the sunlight.

Hannah, did you marry the man of your dreams? Did you bear him a son?

⚜

Black sheets. Black walls. Black thoughts.

Emily knelt on a rug that matched the rest of the décor and stretched toward a medieval-looking light fixture. It was just after nine, but her hips were feeling every concrete foot of the Burlington walk. She was exhausted, but if she didn't loosen up before getting into bed, she'd be calling for help to get out of it in the morning.

And just who would come to her rescue? She folded, head-down, lumbar muscles stretching as her imagination did the same.

Blaze's plan to find a wife for her son battled with Emily's plan to stay detached while she accomplished what she came here to do. Like a neutral referee, one thought stood between the two, arms akimbo, silver whistle blaring over the cacaphony. "Why," the ref shouted, "can't you have both?" If there was a woman in California willing to pay her eleven hundred dollars a week to watch her kids, there had to be similar opportunites in Milwaukee or Chicago.

She'd passed a test on her back porch with paper and scissors and two little boys—she could still love on kids without falling apart. She could move to a Chicago suburb or some ritzy area of Milwaukee, close enough to see Jake and the kids.

Reaching toward the black ceiling again, she took a deep breath of reality.

Money was only a part of the problem. She couldn't move one step closer to Jake without telling him the truth. All of it. No more flirting, no more soul-baring talks about everything but what really mattered. No more almost kisses. She'd avoid him until after her weekend with Sierra and Dawn Anne. And then she'd tell him. And then she'd leave. Unless. . .

With a low groan she stood, snapped the light switch, and crawled into bed.

Jake's bed.

And he was in hers.

She stared into the thick blackness and listened to the hum of cicadas through the screen of the small window. Last night a fan had kept the air moving in the concrete-walled room. Tonight the fan was gone and only the slightest whisper of muggy night air descended.

The battle continued in the dark. Lying on her back in Jake's bed, in a town where she wasn't supposed to know anyone, she felt like Gulliver in the hands of the Lilliputians. Each person she'd met threw a rope over an appendage. Adam, Lexi, Blaze, Tina, Michael, Russell, Dorothy. And the thickest rope, the one tossed over her neck, tightened in Jake's hand.

Lord, what am I supposed to do? The prayer formed on a half-asleep sigh. She had no right to come before the throne of God with a request for herself, but she was too tired to take it back.

♕

"What was her name again?"

The loud voice came from above and to her left. Emily opened her eyes. Only a pinpoint of light from her laptop on the floor in the corner eased the pitch blackness. She bunched Jake's pillow and turned onto her right side, rounding her stiff back as she curled into a fetal position. She must have been dreaming.

"Let's bring our shoes inside. They'll get all dewy." The distinct sound of a tent zipper followed. "Her name is Heidi."

That voice she recognized. Lexi. Outside her window.

"Why did they break up?"

"Because of me and Adam. Jake was crazy about her, and Adam and I adored her, but Jake thought spending time with Heidi took time away from us. And planning a wedding so soon after my mom died wouldn't be cool."

"But you're sure he still loves her?"

"Oh yeah. He keeps a box of her letters under his bed. I've seen it sitting out tons of times."

Emily sat up and hugged Jake's pillow.

"Wow. Unrequited love." An angst-filled sigh accompanied the wistful statement. "Beautiful, but so sad."

219

"I know." Lexi sniffed. Her voice was tight. "I just wish there was something I could do. I hate to see Jake so miserable."

"And think how Heidi must be feeling. Do you think she resents you for coming between them?"

"She's way too sweet for that. I know she only wants the best for us, but she has to be sad. They were MFEO." Lexi whooshed a sigh louder than the one before. "Let's go to sleep. Maybe we'll dream of something to do."

"Maybe. 'Night, Lex."

"'Night, Naomi."

MFEO? Emily's sleep-fogged brain processed slowly. And then a scene from *Sleepless in Seattle* came into focus. Meg Ryan reading a letter. . . "Can't wait to meet you in New York and see if we're MFEO."

Made for each other.

To which the other character replies, "It's like a little clue."

Moving as stealthily as the injured cat that probably slept in the tent outside her window, she eased back onto her knees on the black rug. Stretching in the middle of the night was sometimes necessary after a long day on her feet. Reaching up toward the ceiling, she curved her neck to the right then the left. Had she locked the door? No. Why would she?

She hadn't planned on snooping through Jake's things.

After a moment, her eyes adjusted to the blackness. The tiny blue light illuminated outlines, enough to keep her from banging her hip into the desk or knocking over the wastebasket. She padded across the cool floor and felt for the door handle. The button in the center of the handle slid in and turned without a sound and she tiptoed back to the rug.

On her knees again, an ethical battle ensued. She had no right to rifle through his things. Besides, what could she possibly gain from reading old love letters? She laughed at the irony. She'd been reading and rereading old love letters so often in the past week she'd memorized them. And she'd bought a small fireproof safe to protect them. The letters under the bed were a piece of Jake's history. If they still existed. And wasn't that all she really wanted to know?

Her hand slid under the bed and came out with a dirty sock. She wouldn't read the letters. She just wanted to know if he really still kept them. Her fingers skimmed a book. Bound in soft leather, it had to be a Bible. If she found the box, what would it tell her about Jake? That he still had feelings for the woman? That he was simply sentimental? Or maybe all she'd learn was that he never cleaned under his bed. She flattened on the rug. One fingernail scraped cardboard. Strange that she could tell it was a box just from the sound. Her chest tightened. This was Sierra's every waking moment. Had her senses heightened in this short time? Did she hear and feel things sighted people didn't?

Hooking her finger under the lid of the box, she pulled it toward her. In a week she'd know more about Sierra's world than she wanted to. One week to steel herself, two days in a hotel to pretend it was a patch of ice that changed both of their lives forever.

She slid the box over to her computer. The miniscule light brightened then faded. She tucked the computer in the crook of her arm and pointed the light at the box. It only needed to be bright enough to confirm there were letters inside. She lifted the cover. A thin purple ribbon fluttered into the box. Her stomach flipped.

She'd used the trick herself. In junior high, whenever she suspected Susan of reading her diary, she marked a page with a thread laid just so through a particular word. The thread wouldn't move unless someone opened the book.

So Jake had assumed she'd be nosing around. And now she'd have to face him. Should she 'fess up or wait until he found out? She picked up the ribbon and spread it across the open top. Shiny side up or down? A woman would always put it up. A man wouldn't care. She put it down. Her gaze skimmed the top letter. It was typed. That made more sense. Maybe they were e-mails he'd printed out. Who wrote letters these days? She thought of the "love" texts from Keith: HEY. THINKING OF U IN BLACK DRESS.

Hannah had no idea how fortunate she was to be born in an era where men used pens and weren't offended by flowery answers.

She didn't mean to read the first line. Or the second. She hadn't expected the light to be this bright.

Jake, my sweet darling,

    My lips still burn from your kiss. My heart beats like a herd of wild horses, and I can't wait until tomorrow when you hold me in your big, strong arms again.

Emily's upper lip curled. *Eeww.* The box was heavy. Were they all equally sappy? Hannah Shaw might have gotten away with it back when melodrama was the norm, but in this day and age it was simply weird. If this was the kind of woman Jake was after, she didn't stand a chance. She put the tampered box back in its place. Instead of crawling back into bed with jealous tears, she pulled the black sheet over her head and stifled her laughter. In Jake's pillow.

She fell asleep in seconds, but her eyes shot open after what seemed like only moments. Not a noise this time. A thought. A word. *Tomorrow.* The sappy letter said, "I can't wait until tomorrow when you hold me. . ."

When was tomorrow?

Kicking the covers aside, she eased out of bed and rewound her last few steps. Sliding the box, moving the ribbon, lifting the letter. No date. She set it aside. A picture lay on top. Jake, nuzzling the cheek of the dark-haired woman she'd seen at Chances. She turned it over. "Heidi and Jake forever" was scrawled on the back. She jammed it along the side of the box and looked at the second letter.

My sweet Jake,

    I'm so happy you changed your mind about liking that Foster lady. I know we can only meet secretly until you finish her house. Because I know how much you love me, I will wait patiently for the day when we can be together always.

                                    All my love,
                                        Heidi

Emily threw the purple ribbon into the box, slammed the cover, and kicked it under the bed.

Floating houses, the Golden Gate Bridge, art studios, sailboats, houses nestled into the side of the hill overlooking the bay—Emily looked up from her laptop, took a sip of latte, and breathed in the smell of fresh-baked cinnamon rolls. Artwork by a local artist covered the coffee shop walls.

A perfect setting for planning a future.

The time in the bottom corner of her screen gave the go-ahead. It was eight-fifteen in California. She'd catch Cara on her way to work.

The voice that greeted her was much perkier than yesterday's. "Hey, Em. Sorry about yesterday. I was a mess. Don't know why we got cut off."

Emily smiled at the surfer silhouetted on her screen, backlit by a twenty-four-karat-gold sunset. "No problem. Did you know Otis Redding wrote 'Dock of the Bay' in Sausalito?"

The squeal hurt her ear. "You're going to take the job?"

"I'm going to apply. Maybe she's already found someone."

"She hasn't. I was serious when I said I told her to stop looking. I guess you should send her your résumé and references, but honestly, I don't think she'll even look at them. The job's yours, girlfriend."

Emily leaned her chin on her hand. If she closed her eyes, she'd be on that beach, reclining in the sand, watching the last rays of California sun kiss the muscled bronzed back of the surfer. He'd turn and smile and say, "Hi, I'm Fabio. I don't want children, but I do want you." Relief giggled up in her like a shaken soda bottle. Anyone in the coffee shop who couldn't see her headset would label her a nut case.

No more concerns about the housing market. No more moving to a town and trying to figure out how to live in it without becoming part of it. The most obvious "no more" she'd have to deal with soon. But not until she had a guarantee in writing from her future employer whose name she didn't yet know. "E-mail all the info." She crossed her legs and a sudden familiar spasm grabbed just below and to the left of L4. She stood, stepped behind the chair, and pushed down on the top of the chair back with both hands. Emergency decompression. "Do you know the ages of the kids?"

"Yeah. Cute kids. She has a whole wall of black-and-whites of them at the gallery. They're on her website. She planned them exactly two years apart. Can you believe it? They were all born in the business lull right after Christmas. How's that for planning?"

"How old are they?"

"Oh yeah. The girl is five. One boy is three, the other's a year and a half."

A year and a half. Born right after Christmas. They could have been in the hospital at the same time. Straightening her arms elongated her spine. The spasm weakened along with her resolve. Flipping a house on her own—wielding a sledgehammer and carrying eight-foot slabs of Sheetrock—might be easier than pretending to parent someone else's children. Eighteen-month-old children needed to be picked up. And read to. And rocked. And snuggled. Massaging her low back, she slid back onto the chair. "Send me the info."

But not a picture.

CHAPTER 24

There's a new twist, Jake." Wayne Luther leaned against Emily's new countertop and pulled an envelope from the pocket of his sports jacket.

Jake's gut tightened. "What do you mean?"

"Ben started adoption proceedings before Abby died."

Steel bands wrapped around his skull. He took the paper. "If it wasn't final—"

"It could still work in his favor. Shows he was serious about being their dad, that he cared about securing their future."

Jake slammed his fist on the counter. "It shows he knew Abby might not make it and he wanted to secure the money!" He ran a paint-spotted hand over his mouth. "I don't need to be taking this out on you. You know how grateful I am for your help."

"Forget it. Kids still aren't talking?"

"I'm not asking. They've been poked and prodded like voodoo dolls. Family's supposed to be their safe place." Jake opened the fridge and handed Wayne a soda. "Don't we have enough evidence that the guy's a psycho?"

"Not necessarily. Every parent has bad days."

"He shot a cat!"

"With a toy gun."

"Come on."

Wayne popped open the can and took a drink. "Without the kids' testimony, it may not be enough."

"This wasn't the first time the neighbor called the cops."

"All Madsen's been cited with in the past is disturbing the peace. He hasn't caused bruises or broken any bones."

"Nothing we have proof of." Jake walked to the window, banged it with the heel of his hand, and shoved it open. Even with the front and back doors wide open, the kitchen was stifling. "I've seen bruises. It makes me sick to think what the slimeball threatened them with."

"Have you told them you're fighting for permanent guardianship?"

"No. I don't want to get their hopes up."

"Might loosen their tongues. Like you said, you're the safe place. They may feel more like talking if they know there's a plan."

"And what if the plan fails?"

Wayne ran a hand through short gelled hair. "I know. I've got kids. But you may have to risk disappointing them to make this happen."

A fat cardinal landed on a branch of the broken oak tree. Jake stared at the gash where the limb had ripped. The tender inner wood was no longer pink. "Maybe."

"Hey, I have to get home. I'll let you know if I hear anything." Wayne wrapped him in a quick hug. "Take care of yourself through all this. You doing anything for fun?"

Jake shrugged. "Trying my hardest to go out on a date."

Wayne's eyebrow rose. "Anyone I know?"

"Not yet."

"Well, let me know how it goes. A wife could definitely help your situation." Wayne laughed and waved. As he walked out the back door, something fell in the dining room with an echoing *thunk* followed by an even more sickening splash. A paint can. Spitting out a word he no longer used, Jake whipped around.

In time to see Lexi running out the front door.

He didn't see her. He couldn't have. Lexi stopped before she reached the corner and turned around. If Jake had seen her, he'd

be screaming for her to get back and clean up the mess. She ran
through backyards until she reached the pup tent she'd been living
in since Emily moved in. It wasn't a foot away from the basement
window anymore. She'd moved it to the middle of the yard the
morning after Naomi stayed over.

Their mission had succeeded. Emily had read the letters and
just this morning Lexi heard her talking to Grandma Blaze about
going to a hotel. Probably couldn't stand being in the same room with
the love letters. At this very moment, she and Grandma Blaze were
trying out a new cookie recipe for Emily to take to the hotel. That
was the reason Lexi had run to Emily's house in the first place—to
tell Jake how awful Emily's toffee bars were. The bars were awesome,
but Jake didn't have to know that. It was just one more step in a plan
that was working. In the nick of time, apparently.

She unzipped the tent flap and crawled in. It was so hot she
could hardly breathe, but it was a good place to hide and think over
everything she'd just heard. Putting in her earbuds, she listened to
Jesse McCartney singing "Body Language," a song Jake said she
shouldn't listen to. Maybe that was why the music didn't calm her
the way it usually did. She stretched out on her sleeping bag. In spite
of the heat, it felt damp and clammy. Or maybe it was her skin. She
got that way sometimes when she was scared or excited.

Right now she was both. Jake was trying to get guardianship! She
hadn't even told him her dream and he was making it happen. Unless
"you" meant Jake and Grandma. But then the other part, the part that
scared her, wouldn't make sense. *A wife could help your situation.* Did
that mean Jake was interested in Emily just because if he was married,
or looked like he was going to get married, the social workers or judge
or whoever decides those things would be more likely to let her and
Adam live with him?

So maybe he didn't really like Emily after all. Maybe he just
needed a woman, any woman, to agree to marry him. She thought of
something Naomi had said about wishing her mom and Jake would
fall in love and get married and then they could be sisters. Mrs.
Benner wasn't Jake's type, but if he was desperate to find someone,
he might consider her. She was an awesome cook. Her house was
always superclean. And she was funny, too. One time she got glasses

227

with fake noses for herself and Naomi and Lexi, and they drove around Burlington wearing them and watching people's faces. Jake needed somebody to make him laugh.

And it sure wasn't going to be Emily. Not if she could help it.

Her fingers fumbled with the zipper. She had to talk to Naomi. Fast. Sweat beading on her face, she popped out of the tent.

And came face-to-face with Jake.

✿

"What did you hear?"

Jake sat in a lawn chair drinking a no-longer-cold soda. He'd waited in silence, planning his questions, rehearsing a lecture. What was it about the red-faced girl with hair the color of her mother's that made him forget it all? He pointed to the empty chair across from him and Lexi sat down. He waited for her to answer.

She played with the fringe around a hole near the hem of her shorts. "I'm sorry I spilled the paint. I just turned around and—"

"It all went on the drop cloth."

Finally she looked up, sunlight sparkling on unshed tears. "You're trying to get permanent guardianship."

Jake nodded.

"Just you, or you and Grandma?"

"Just me. You know Grandma would love to have you."

"But it would be hard on her. I know."

"I haven't told you guys because I didn't want you to get your hopes up. We don't know how things will turn out."

"What if we just say we want to live with you and not Ben? Won't they listen to us?" A tear spilled from each eye and rolled slowly down freckled cheeks. Lexi swiped them away.

"They might. It sure won't hurt. But you're not quite old enough to appoint your own guardian."

"How old would we have to be?"

"Fourteen."

"What if Ben gets us and adopts us before that?"

"What they will listen to is you and Adam telling the truth about anything bad Ben has done to you. Any time he's hurt either one of you or said things to make you feel bad about yourself." He

228

crumpled the empty can and tossed it. "You need to start being honest, Lex."

"But what if he says bad things about you? What if we tell things about him, and then he tells things about you, and the court decides we can't be either place and splits us up and puts us in different foster homes?" Her face crumpled. Tears poured.

Jake's hands seized into fists. What kind of garbage was Ben filling their minds with? "Lex, there's nothing he can say—"

"He knows things about you. What if he tells the judge that you got tickets for drunk driving or that you used to be Goth and you took drugs and got in a car accident?"

Closing his eyes, Jake breathed away fear. He'd had two DUIs before he was twenty. The car accident wasn't his fault, though they'd both been drinking, and he'd smoked pot his first year in college then came to his senses and hadn't touched it since. Old stuff. None of it would affect his chances—unless Ben had a lawyer who tried to make his past an issue. What scared him was knowing that Ben wasn't as passive as he'd assumed. "Lex. . ." He tried to steady his voice, but it didn't work. "All of that happened years ago. I was young and stupid. No judge is going to take that into consideration."

"But it's all true, isn't it?"

Staring over her head at the little green tent, he sighed. "Yes. It's all true."

⚜

Jake stood on the second rung of the ladder in Emily's new master bath, twisting wires and sorting through all Lexi had said. And not said.

"Would the judge think you could take care of us better if you were married?" she'd asked.

He'd answered her honestly. "Maybe."

Lexi had smiled then. "I think so, too." And then she'd asked if they were done talking and ran off to call Naomi.

"The judge isn't the only one," he muttered as he stripped a wire for the ceiling fan. Every encounter with Lexi over the past few weeks deepened his conviction that he wasn't equipped to raise her

229

alone. Adam he could handle, but he'd had no experience with the weird hormonal stuff.

Connecting the two black wires, he smiled at the irony. For the kids' sake he'd tried to keep some emotional distance from Emily. Now, for the kids' sake, he felt almost compelled to pursue her. As he loosened a screw in the mounting base, he worked on his side of a conversation he hoped to have after supper. *I know you're leaving, but—*

The screen door banged downstairs. Jake sighed and mounted the antique-looking motor housing. He wasn't up for any more twelve-year-old drama. Slow footsteps probably meant she was in tears again. "I'm in here."

The sound stopped and he turned. The screwdriver slipped from his hand and hit the floor. "Emily. You scared me."

"Sorry." Her tone was flat, her face drawn.

He climbed down. "Hi." He wasn't sure what was supposed to follow that. "Do you like it? I can put the blades in so you can get the full effect."

She shook her head. "It's fine."

Fine. It was a code word with women. The word was as neutral as Switzerland. The tone of delivery meant everything. It didn't take a genius to break this one. Maybe the fan was okay, but nothing else was. And it was his fault.

He climbed down, wiped his hands on his jeans, and touched her elbow. She pulled away. He stuffed his hands in his back pockets. "I'm sorry about dinner the other night. Lexi—"

"I understand."

He waited, watching as her lips pressed against each other and her blinking increased. It was hard not to smile. He'd seen the exact same look on Lexi's face just hours ago. "I don't."

She looked at him. Probably involuntarily. Tiny ridges raised between her eyebrows.

"If you're not mad about me cancelling out of dinner, I don't understand what's changed since Saturday. If I said something or didn't say something, if I did something to upset you I—"

"I know about Heidi." Narrowed eyes turned on him.

Jake swallowed hard. What did she know? And why did it

matter now anyway? Only one person knew the things he wished no one knew, the things he'd confessed and repented and tried to forget. "Topher told you, didn't he?"

Her chin drew back. "No?" She said it as a question.

"Then how—"

She sighed with so much force he felt it on his neck. "It doesn't matter."

Doesn't matter how you heard or doesn't matter what kind of a relationship I had with Heidi?

"I need to talk to you about the finishing work."

No way was she going to throw a smoke bomb and then stand there as if she hadn't just clouded everything between them. "I can understand why my relationship with Heidi might bother you, but considering what you told me at the cemetery, I don't think you're in any position—"

"What?" Her eyes blazed. Her hands flew to her hips. "You're serious, aren't you? Because I made mistakes in my past I'm supposed to be perfectly cool with you asking me out the night after you're lovin' on some—"

"Whoa! Stop. What in the world are you talking about?"

"I'm talking about you and Heidi and disgusting love letters and—"

"Disgusting? Since when do you think the letters are disgusting and what does Heidi have to do with anything?"

"Not *those* letters, the ones under your—" Her mouth gaped. She spun around and headed for the stairs.

"Emily! Wait. You're not making sense. I haven't seen or talked to Heidi in over a year."

She stopped, teetered, and grabbed the railing. "You haven't?" She didn't turn around.

"I broke up with her before Abby died. What's this all about?"

A faint gasp echoed in the stairway. Her shoulders dropped and she sat down. "Jake?" Her voice was tight and hushed.

He walked down and sat one step below her.

"Did Heidi write you letters? Really mushy letters?"

He shrugged. "A few cards, I guess. She worked in our office. I saw her every day. Not much need for letters."

Her eyes closed. The slightest smile curved one side of her mouth. "I think I've been had."

⚜

"That's cruel." Emily couldn't quite mask the smile Jake's suggestion spawned. She reached overhead for the railing and pulled herself off the step. "You have to be sensitive to her feelings."

"You dare accuse me of not being sensitive?" Jake clapped one hand to his chest. "Look at it this way—Lexi needs a graceful way out. If we treat it like we thought it was a practical joke, she can laugh her way back into my good graces. Either that, or I kill her."

"Okay. I'm in. As long as you promise that after we get her, you have a heart-to-heart and convince her no one could ever take her place in your life."

"I promise."

This wasn't going the way she'd planned. "Heidi's" letters had steeled her with the strength she'd needed to march over here and tell Jake she was leaving. Yet here she stood, looking down at his perfectly disheveled hair, close enough to breathe in his earthy scent, laughing and conniving as if she weren't ready to say good-bye.

⚜

October 23, 1852

Sweat dripped from Big Jim's forehead. One foot tapped on a massive pumpkin as his fiddle rested on the knee of his breeches. Hands that seemed too large for such an instrument raised the bow again and coaxed the first few notes of "Miss McLeod's Reel" from the strings. Music filled the barn and Hannah's soul.

Across the room, Liam's gaze swept the crowd and found her. He wore what appeared to be a new white shirt. Had his mother stitched it just for this night? His smile drew her—a pull she wouldn't resist. Like the desert oases she'd read of, the space beneath fresh-cut beams, surrounded by newly raised walls, shut out the ugliness of the past few days and sheltered them, for these few precious hours, from the fear they'd face come nightfall.

She stepped beside her father as two lines formed, women on

one side, men on the other. Running damp hands along the paisley print of her skirt, she lifted her chin.

Just one dance.

Liam took his place and leaned forward enough to keep his eyes on her. As Hannah's shoes hit the sawdust, Dolly brushed past her, strode behind the women, and planted herself directly across from Liam.

Hannah froze. The music picked up. The couple on the end closest to her joined hands and glided down the aisle then turned in a smooth half circle.

Cheeks burning, Hannah stood out from the safety of the crowd, by all appearances rejected. Head still held high, she turned and pushed through the wall of spectators. Pretending not to care, not to hear the whispers, she forced her feet to walk until she reached the stinging safety of the cold, late afternoon air.

The reel no longer tempted her feet to dance, but neither would she allow them to run. It wasn't Liam's fault that he danced with the girl with the fat curls pinned to one side of her head, the girl whose mother detested all that he stood for. She would wait for him here, knowing he would come for her when the song ended.

And he did, at a run. "Hannah! You know that was not of my doing."

"I know."

He took her hand, pulling her into the shadow of the barn. "Come here," he whispered.

She slid easily into his arms. The sun was low, casting stretched-out shadows. "It will be dark soon. And the sky is clear. You'll be traveling tonight, won't you?"

He kissed the top of her head then lifted her chin. "I'll need a memory to warm me." His head bent. His lips touched hers—

A gasp, followed by stomping feet on hard-packed earth. "Hannah Shaw! You. . .traitor!" Dolly stood, hands on hips, eyes blazing.

Pulling away from Liam, she looked up at him. "Go inside. Let's not draw a crowd."

"I'll be close," he said, stepping around the corner.

"How could you?" Dolly took two giant steps until Hannah felt her breath on her face. "*I* claimed him."

Hannah laughed, not intended, but fitting. "You cannot claim what belongs to another."

"Belongs? What are you saying?"

Her hands dug into the fabric of her dress, her chin jutted forward. "Liam and I have been in love for many months."

"You lie!"

"I do not. I have a box full of letters in my closet to pr—" Her hand flew over her mouth.

"Then it's true, isn't it? Liam and your father are working together to—"

"*Hannah!*" Liam rounded the corner, took her firmly by the elbow, and marched her away from the squawking Dolly Baker.

CHAPTER 25

Emily was breathing hard and laughing when she fell into a seat at the coffee shop. Adam plopped into the chair beside her, equally breathless. They'd tied in a power walk from her house, probably because he'd held back.

Adam craned his neck, looking out at the street. "Where is she?"

Scanning the little coffee shop's midmorning patrons, Emily shrugged. "She'll be here." Dorothy's brief, urgent call said simply, "Meet me at the coffee shop in five minutes."

"This is so cool."

Emily pulled out a twenty-dollar bill and slid it across the table. "Get me a regular coffee and a turnover and whatever you want."

As she watched the front door, she added to the mental list of things she should have told Jake yesterday. But the laughter had felt so good and telling him now would put a damper on his get-even-with-Lexi scheme.

Adam returned with two blueberry turnovers just as Dorothy walked in.

"I got to thinking about that letter Hannah sent from Missouri, so I contacted a friend"—words tumbled out as Dorothy pulled out a chair—"in St. Louis and told her about it and she and her husband drove down to Fredericktown and started asking around. Look what they found." She shoved a curling scroll of shiny paper, the kind used in old fax machines, across the table. Adam secured the corners with salt, pepper, and the turnover plate.

"My friend Delores talked to a man who does Civil War reenactments, and he got her in touch with a lady who's writing a book about several families in the area, and she directed Delores to the Dillard family who are shirttail relatives to the Greenes and a Marvin Greene, who is five generations down from the woman this letter was written to, let her copy this letter and said he might have more written by this same man." She stopped for a desperately needed breath. "Read it." She dabbed her flushed face with a tissue. "This is like a puzzle, isn't it? We had one piece, and now we add this. If only. . ."

Adam's toe did a steady tap on Emily's shoe as she tried to read over Dorothy's endless words. What would happen to the woman's blood pressure when Emily revealed the other pieces to the puzzle? With discreet finesse, Emily let her hair fall over her cheek and slipped her finger in her ear. With the commentary muffled, she read:

Rochester, Wisconsin
June 27, 1854

Dear Mr. and Mrs. Greene,

With some distress I write this letter, hoping not to alarm you, but that you may put my mind at ease. I have received a good word that is of great importance to a mutual friend of ours, but our friend has not answered the letter I posted on April 21. Something in her most recent letter leads me to believe she may have departed in search of the good news I wish to report to her. I do hope I am wrong and she is safe and sound with you and her father. If they are not with you and you know where I might find either of them, please answer as soon as you are able.

James P. Thornton

Adam squinted. "I don't get it."

Dorothy clapped her hands. "Neither do I. But isn't this delicious? A true mystery. James P. Thornton is Big Jim, the blacksmith, so we've solved one little part. But what is the good news and who is the friend?"

Hand sliding over his mouth, Adam grabbed the crumpled dollar bills on the table. "I'll get you some coffee, Mrs. Willett." With that, he jumped up and bolted to the counter. All, Emily was sure, to keep from laughing or blurting something he shouldn't.

Emily stared at the little woman on the other side of the table. Dorothy knew people. She had connections and resources that could prove invaluable in discovering if Hannah and her man were ever reunited. But could she be trusted? Emily traced the outline of a purple iris on the side of her cup. Should she take a chance? "Dorothy, if I told you something in confidence, something very, very important, could I trust you to keep it to yourself?"

"They talked to you, didn't they? I knew they would."

"They? They who?"

"The ghosts. Hannah, Elizabeth. . .you've heard them, right?"

Adam returned at just the wrong time. Though he clearly tried to temper his reaction, coffee splashed over the side of the cup, just missing the fax. "You heard the ghosts?"

"No." Emily couldn't look at him and maintain any level of composure. A gulp of coffee scalded her mouth, but quelled the laugh spasm. "We found other letters. In the house."

Dorothy shrieked. A bald man at a table near the window mopped coffee from his newspaper. "You okay, Mrs. Willett?"

"I'm fine, Ernie. I just heard some good news."

"Good news is meant to be shared." The man winked at her.

"I know." Dorothy sighed. "Just not quite yet." She turned back to Emily. "Oh my." She fanned her face with a napkin. "May I see them?"

"Of course." *And maybe I'll throw in a little extra surprise.* Should she have portable oxygen on hand if she decided to show her the cellar?

"We haven't had a new discovery for quite some time. When Madison hears. . .eventually. . ." Dorothy shielded her mouth with her hand. "You do plan on making them public, don't you? I won't tell a soul what's in them or who wrote them, I promise, but at some point. . ."

"Yes. Of course. But don't you think we should keep it quiet while we solve a bit more of this puzzle?"

"Ooh." Faded eyes seemed to draw color from the excitement. "Yes." She glanced at the bald man. "Absolutely." One finger crossed her lips. "Mum's the word, my dear."

☙

Adam held Mrs. Willett's car door open as she said good-bye to Emily for the fourth time.

"You talk to your lawyer and I'll talk to mine and as soon as you get the papers drawn up I'm ready to sign." She finally sat down in the car, but before Adam could close the door, she popped out again. "Don't worry about landscaping. It will be a good reason for my son to come home."

"All right." Emily waved from the front step. Her arms must be getting tired. "Good-bye."

Five good-byes. The lady finally lifted her foot off the ground and Adam added his good-bye, closed the door, and walked quickly away from the car. He didn't really think Mrs. Willett looked like she should be driving. She'd practically passed out in the hidden room, but he had more important things on his mind.

"So, you sold your house."

"Can you believe it?"

He couldn't tell if Emily looked happy or not. Maybe she was just in shock at how easy it was. Or maybe she was changing her mind. He hoped so. He stepped onto the first step and announced his idea. "We have to go to Missouri. We have to figure out what Hannah and her dad were doing there and what happened to them."

"We do?"

"Yes. We have Mrs. Willett working on things here, so we need to go down there and see what we can dig up." He stood a step lower than Emily. Looking up at her, he used what Grandma Blaze called his puppy dog eyes. If his grandmother couldn't say no to them, maybe Emily couldn't either. "Pleeease?"

Emily burst out laughing. "*I'm* not the one you have to convince! I think it sounds like a blast, but I don't know who would go. Your uncle probably couldn't leave his jobs and your grandma might not feel up to it and—"

"Just you and me. And Lexi if she quits being stupid."

"Your grandma has temporary guardianship. I don't know if you can even leave the state legally. And they're not likely to let you go all that way with someone they hardly know."

"So we convince Grandma to go. We can get a hotel and she can stay there while we hunt around if she's not feeling good."

"Hotels cost money."

"Then we can take our pop-up."

"You've thought of everything."

"Everything. Come on, let's go talk to—" He didn't bother finishing because Jake's truck drove into the driveway. "Don't tell him," he whispered.

"You can't plan—" She quit talking when Jake slammed the truck door and waved.

"What are you two up to?"

"Conspiring." Emily smiled at him with a goofy look on her face. They were getting married. Definitely. "Adam is hatching a plan."

Great. Just blurt it out. This is where his plan died.

Jake put his hands on his hips. "What kind of a plan?"

Here goes nothing. "Mrs. Willett talked to a lady in St. Louis who knew a guy who had a letter." He rubbed his hand on his forehead and looked at Emily. "You tell him."

Emily told it way faster than Mrs. Willett. "So now Adam thinks some of us need to go to Missouri to search out more information."

Jake smiled at her with the same goofy look. "Sounds fun."

What?

"I don't think I can get away, but my mom might jump at the chance to do something adventurous."

Seriously? Jake wasn't going to try to talk them out of it?

Jake grinned. "It would be good for all of you. But you'd need to go before"—he bit his bottom lip—"you need to be back here to work on the trim."

Something was weird there, but Adam didn't try figuring it out. "Yes! Let's go talk to Grandma! I'll map out our route and put it in my GPS and find campgrounds, and we should talk to the guy with the letters and see if we can..." He was halfway across the road when he realized Emily was still on the step making goo-goo eyes at Jake. He laughed and kept on going.

⚜

Vacation with Emily? Lexi threw her shoe at the giant purple penguin in the corner. Emily finally moved out and then invited herself along on a family vacation? The other shoe bounced off the wall and landed on the bed. Pansy looked up and gave her the evil eye. Even her cat was against her.

Plopping onto the purple spread, she stared at the phone she'd grabbed as she stomped through the living room. Naomi's mom would invite Lexi to go with them on their trip to Wisconsin Dells. Mrs. Benner was like that.

Visions of boat rides, water slides, and candy stores danced in Lexi's head as she dialed. Mrs. Benner answered.

"Lexi, how are you?"

"Not the greatest."

"What's the matter, sweetie? Anything some chocolate chip cookie dough could fix?"

Lexi smiled. "It would sure help."

"What's going on?"

"My grandma's making me go on a trip next week with her and Emily." Naomi told her mom everything—Mrs. Benner knew about Emily.

"And you don't want to go, do you?" There was a slight pause. "I wish we could take you with us. We're taking my mother and it's kind of a family trip, you know. Here, talk to Naomi. She'll cheer you up."

"Hey, Lex. What's up?"

The picture she painted for her best friend made her eyes burn. "Can you imagine? Stuck in the car for hours and hours with my grandma and Emily blabbering in the front seat and Adam reading to me about UFOs or one-celled animals or plant moss the whole time? I'll go crazy."

"I wish you could go with us. I asked a couple days ago just 'cause it would be way more fun with you there. My mom's being weird."

240

"This stinks for both of us."

"Yeah. I'm downloading a ton of cool music. You should, too. You can plug in and shut them out."

"I don't want to shut out, I want to get out! How can I get out of going?"

"Get sick."

The two words were prettier than any music she'd ever put on her iPod. "Yessss. That's why you're my BFF. You're a genius."

"I know."

"What should I get? Bronchitis? Tonsilitis? Something I can fake good without making myself throw up."

"It can't be so bad that they want to take you the doctor, but something contagious. How about poison ivy? There's tons of it down by the river."

"Nah. I had that when I was ten. Mom put stuff on it and still made me go to school."

"I faked a fever for a couple days by rubbing the thermometer on my bedspread really hard."

"My grandma has the kind you stick in your ear. I got it to a hundred and three once by holding it on my lamp, but then Mom stuck it in my ear and I got grounded for trying to get out school."

"When I was five I drank my grandpa's prune juice and I couldn't get off the toilet for a whole day. My stomach hurt so bad I couldn't even stand up straight."

"That might work." A day of horrible stomach cramps would be way better than a week of Emily acting like she was part of the family. Then again, who would know if her stomach actually hurt? "Only I don't think I need the prune juice."

"Let me hear your best stomachache sound."

Lexi groaned and flopped back on the bed. Pansy yowled and Naomi laughed. "Perfect, Lex. It's gonna work."

CHAPTER 26

Emily sat in the lobby of the Hampton Inn, her gaze volleying between the door and the clock. Ten minutes to wait. Maybe less, but not a minute longer. Dawn Anne was a stickler for staying on schedule. After their first girl trip, Emily and Susan had started calling her "Mom" right along with Sierra. Dawn Anne set their alarms, told them when to be quiet and go to sleep, and doused them with water if they refused to crawl out of bed.

Disney World, San Antonio, Las Vegas, the Black Hills, and Apostle Islands. They'd seen the country together. When Dawn Anne's husband got a job in Denver, Emily and Susan had flown out for a skiing trip at least once a year.

They were an eclectic foursome, but their temperaments meshed. Dawn Anne got them to the next stop on time. Susan forced them out of indecision over maps and menus. Sierra provided their excuse for Magic Kingdom, M&M World, and the San Diego Zoo.

And Emily? She clamped her forearms over her churning stomach. Emily was the tension-tamer, the practical joker, the witty commentator, the one who sang her silly preschool songs and made them laugh. What would her role be now that laughter was inappropriate?

She'd awakened at six with a stress headache. Percocet dimmed the pain, but the stress found a new target in her belly. Perspiration dampened her top lip. One minute her skin was hot, the next cold and clammy. Did any of them think this was going to be just like old times?

Pushing to her feet, she pulled out her phone and found a number she'd put in her contacts list last night. A Realtor in St. Louis. While she was looking up information on Missouri, an ad for foreclosures had popped up. She'd found one dirt cheap that claimed to be structurally sound. St. Louis. One step closer to the Pacific.

Unless her talk with Jake turned out different from any scenario she'd envisioned yet.

The automatic front doors slid open. Three women she barely recognized walked through. One, hand on a rounded belly, wiped away tears of laughter. Next to her, a tall, tanned woman practically doubled over as she laughed. Behind them strode a dark-skinned girl with sleek black curls and the long legs of a dancer.

And a guide dog.

⬥

"I love this house." Dawn Anne ran her hand across the granite countertop. "I want to buy it."

Still in awe of the easy banter, Emily shook her head. "You'd never leave Colorado."

"Actually. . ." Dawn Anne smiled and nodded toward Sierra, kneeling on the floor beside Beacon. "It appears we will. If our rising star lets her mom and dad follow her to Julliard in the fall."

Susan gasped. Sierra pumped the air with her fist. "I got a full scholarship and I can start a year earlier than I thought!"

Emily grabbed the edge of the counter to steady herself. Dawn Anne's hand grasped her elbow. "You okay, Em?"

She felt the color seeping from her cheeks. "Scholarship? How? I thought. . ."

Sierra stood, one hand on Beacon's head. "Crazy, isn't it? I auditioned a month ago." A wide grin accentuated high cheekbones. "I thought that dream was dead, but Mom found a dance instructor in Denver whose daughter is blind. She's amazing. It's hard, but I just needed to learn new tricks, like being really precise in my counts. It's kind of a cool faith builder." Joy lit unseeing eyes. "My instructor told us about a foundation that awards scholarships to handicapped dancers. Well, deaf and blind dancers. Pretty hard if you only have one leg." She burst into giggles that spread to her mom and then Susan.

"A full…" Emily's voice barely made it over the sound of sanding and men's laughter from upstairs. She rubbed her hand along the granite countertop she leaned on for support. So all of this work was for—

"What say we go get some food for those hardworking hunky men upstairs? And us." Susan patted her tummy. "This little guy demands feedings every three hours." Her eyes darted to Emily.

Numbly, Emily nodded. "Why don't you two go. Sierra and I can walk the dog." Not that her legs were stable enough to cross the room at the moment.

Dawn Ann and Susan grabbed purses and left. Emily stared at Sierra. "Congratulations. I thought you were focusing on piano." Her voice faded. "This is amazing. Dance has always been your first love."

"Yeah. I used to think I couldn't live without it. I found out I could, but how cool is it that I don't have to?" She blinked several times. "God is so awesome."

"Yeah." Emily's numb brain didn't know where to take the conversation from there.

"Tell me more about your house."

"Can you keep a secret?" The question blurted out. She hadn't planned it.

"Better than anyone."

"This house was a stop on the Underground Railroad."

"Really?"

"There's a room off the cellar and we found old letters that give proof it was used to hide slaves."

"Why is it a secret?"

"I don't want this place turning into a circus while we're trying to finish the remodeling. I want this work done…soon." Voicing it brought the truth home with breath-stopping force: none of her self-imposed deadlines mattered anymore.

"Show me the room."

Emily hesitated. "Okay. It's this way." She touched Sierra's arm.

"Tell me everything."

"Run your fingers along the edge of the door. I've counted at least six different colors of paint."

Sierra caressed the wood. "It's like feeling history."

Feeling history. "It is. There's a built-in cupboard in the corner by the window. I stripped it and refinished it. It felt like going back through time, each layer of paint represented an era, or a season in someone's life. I tried picturing women at the turn of the last century or in the forties or sixties. The cupboards are all new and I need to sand down all the trim, but I don't want to do this door."

"You should leave it. The lady who's buying it might like the slice of history."

"Maybe I will." She opened the door. "Here, on this side of the door you can just barely make out a faded painting or stencil of a basket with a handle. The basket is full of apples and one apple is sitting beside it."

"Does it look really old?"

"Yes. And the cool thing is, there's an almost identical picture carved into the tombstone of the wife of the man who built this house."

"Wow." Sierra rubbed bare arms. "Goose-bumpy."

"I know. Grab the railing. It's rough. Be careful you don't get splinters. I'll go first and you can put your hand on my shoulder. There are eight steps."

"Must be a low ceiling."

"It is. The walls are stone. Huge, square stones. The floor is rough cement, looks like it was spread with a hand trowel, not very level. There's one tiny window with a ledge under it. When we go back upstairs I'll show you what I found there. Three more steps."

"It stinks down here. No offense, but it's kind of reeky."

Emily laughed. "It's damp. I'm sure being so close to the river doesn't help. Straight ahead are shelves. When Cara's great-grandmother lived here, they were packed full of canning jars. Tomatoes, beans, beets, corn, you name it."

"Bet that was pretty."

"It was." Emily swallowed hard. "Very colorful. That had to be such a good feeling, to know your family would have food for the winter because of the work of your hands."

" 'I sing for joy at the work of Your hands.' " Sierra's clear, sweet voice filled the cellar, ending in a giggle. "Sorry. Couldn't help it."

"Don't ever apologize for singing. You have a beautiful voice."

"Thank you. Dillon likes it." The giggle returned.

"That boy is head over heels for you, isn't he?"

"Yes. And the feeling is very, very mutual. Now back to the tour."

"The shelves are full of my stuff now. Plastic bins of winter clothes, things like that. The whole shelving unit was sagging to the left when I first got here. Jake fixed it and—"

"That boy's head over heels for you, isn't he?"

Emily coughed. "As I was saying, while he was fixing them, we discovered that the wall behind the shelves is attached to the ceiling by wheels in a track, like a barn door."

"And it's hiding the room?"

"Yes. Here, you can open it." She guided Sierra's hands to the edge of the wall.

"There's just enough room for my fingertips. So you really can't tell it's a door when you look at it?"

"It just looks like a wall. There's one step down into the room."

As the door slid away, Emily felt for the flashlight she'd left on the shelf. It wasn't there. She looked up at the single bulb hanging over the stairs and the weak afternoon light struggling through the mud-spackled window, and helped Sierra down the step.

"There are wide benches on your right and left and straight ahead. The one on the right has a hinged lid with room for storage underneath. Sit down on the bench to your right and feel around with your right hand."

Sierra released a quiet gasp when she found the carving. "*M. . .A. . .R. . .*is this an *I* or a *T*?"

"*I.*"

"Mariah." She traced the date. "Do you know how many people they hid here?"

"No idea. The letters refer to parcels. Everything had to be in code. This area wasn't as well-traveled as routes through Ohio. From here, people were taken to Lake Michigan, and steamboats took them either directly to Canada or to Michigan and then Canada."

Sierra's silhouette was barely visible. The girl felt the wall behind her then slid her hand along the bench. She swung her legs up and lay down. "Did you know my dad can trace our family back to a runaway slave?"

Emily's head jerked up. "No."

"Yeah. Like six generations back. Jeremiah Humphries. He and his wife and a bunch of kids were owned by a tobacco farmer. Jeremiah escaped and promised to come back for his family, but the Civil War started and he couldn't get back for years. By the time he did, his wife and two of the kids had died in some kind of epidemic. But he brought the rest back up here to Michigan where some people had hidden him and helped him get to Canada."

"That's how your family ended up in Michigan."

"Yep. Jeremiah's daughter was my great-great-something-grandmother. It's weird to think that someone I'm connected to by DNA hid in places like this. Can you imagine it? Being all alone and not knowing who you could trust, and missing your family and facing wolves and snakes and who-knows-what just to get free?"

"I can't imagine it."

"Would you do that? Would you go through all that just so you could be free to make your own choices and stuff?"

Emily paused. "I hope I would. What a heritage you have. Sad, but amazing at the same time. You come from strong stock, girl. Maybe that's why you're so tough."

Sierra laughed. "I'm not tough."

"Look at you," Emily whispered. "Dancing—" Her voice thickened and she couldn't go on.

Sierra sat up. "And look at you, going through all those surgeries and now you're flipping a house."

"I don't have your spirit. You lost so much more than I did. You should be angry and bitter and—"

"Don't you believe God is totally in control of everything?"

"I can't believe that." *I was in control. If you only knew. I determined your fate.*

247

"Haven't you seen good stuff come out of what you went through?"

"No." Emily pressed both hands to her face.

"I think you're wrong." Sierra's soft words filled the darkness. "I don't think I lost more than you, Em. I think you lost the most precious thing a woman can lose."

Emily's tears ran silently until Sierra got up and sat beside her and put her arms around her. This was wrong. So wrong. She pulled away. "I deserved. . ." The words slipped out unbidden.

"No! Emily, that's not true. Is that what you think? God doesn't work like that."

The dank air left the room. She couldn't make her lungs expand. Breaths came in shallow pants. Her heart raced.

"Emily." Sierra reached out, felt for her arm, and grabbed on to it. "You know I forgave you, right? I mean, we never talked about it, but you know I don't hold it against you, don't you? We all make mis—"

"What—" Her head felt light, her skin clammy. "What do you know?"

"That you were partying with some people and you took drugs before we—"

A tight, strained gasp escaped. "When did you. . . ?"

"Em, we've known all along. The people you partied with talked to Mom at the resort and—"

"She didn't report it."

"No. Of course not. She didn't know if you were even going to live and you lost the baby and—"

"You knew? And you still. . ."

"Still what? Still love you?" Sierra's grip tightened. "I was angry at first. Depressed and hopeless, screaming at God, asking 'Why?' And then He showed me that 'Why?' is a stupid question we have no business asking. If anyone should have screamed 'Why?' it was Jesus. But He didn't. He trusted His Father and look what happened."

"But you're not Jesus. You were a child with a beautiful future stretching ahead and—"

"Stop." Sierra's command was tinged with irritation. "I'm still going to have a beautiful future. Sure, there's a lot I'll miss. Life is hard this way, but what I'm not going to do is"—she slammed her hand on the bench—"I'm not going to be a slave to this! I'm not going to go through life like I've got chains around me. God could have stopped you from taking Ecstasy. He could have stopped me from putting on my skis. I don't know why He didn't. I'll never know why. What I have to do is let Him guide me, just the way I took your arm going down the stairs. And He's doing it. I can still dance, Em! I have a wonderful family and friends and now I have a boyfriend. I'm blind, but I'm not locked in a little room like this with no way out." She pulled her hand away. "And you shouldn't be either."

The words stung. Emily closed her arms over her chest.

"Can I pray for you, Em?"

She wanted to say no, wanted to run from the black room. But she said nothing. And Sierra prayed.

"Lord, we know it is never Your will to keep us in darkness. You are the One who leads us into the light of Your love and mercy and forgiveness. Emily knows You have forgiven her. Help her to embrace that truth with every cell of her being. Grant her the courage to step out of the dark and walk in the freedom of Your light."

October 23, 1852

"Can you swim, Isaiah?"

"No, sir."

Liam stared at the tightly curled black hair of the man who sat on the bench with his head bowed. "Are you well enough to run if you need to?"

Isaiah nodded, lifting his face to the lantern Hannah held above him. "Do you know what a gazelle is, Mr. Liam?" His voice undulated in a way not common to the runaways they'd met thus far.

"I have read of them."

"There were many where I grew up. When I was a boy, my father called me Gazelle. He said I bounded through the woods like an animal with winged feet." His smile failed to touch sad eyes. "I am older and sorrow has taken strength from me, but in here"—he thumped his chest with a large, open hand—"I am still a young gazelle."

Liam nodded and returned his smile. "I hope you will not need to run tonight, but it is a comfort to know you have wings on your feet."

Hannah's father put a hand on Isaiah's shoulder. "You need to be off now. My daughter and I will pray for you throughout the night and in the days to come. Godspeed."

A single tear slid down Isaiah's cheek, reflecting the flickering lantern flame. "I'd be grateful if you would lift a prayer for my wife."

"Of course."

Hannah raised the lamp. The halo of light widened. She looked up at Liam, eyes shimmering. "Isaiah's wife is still on the plantation, expecting their first child."

Lord God. Liam shook his head. He couldn't imagine leaving Hannah in that condition. "That must be so hard." His words were weak, inadequate.

"She is blessed to be a cook. She works in the house, not in the fields. But if she bears a son. . ." Isaiah stared between Liam and Hannah, his eyes on some point far beyond the cellar walls. He didn't need to say more. Liam had learned enough to know a man-child would be sent to work in the fields when he was barely old enough to walk.

Liam picked up the bag of food Hannah had prepared. His elbow touched hers. His arms burned with the desire to hold her, to kiss away the fear that chiseled grooves between her eyes. Instead he put one hand on the ladder and nodded toward the lantern. Reluctance tightening her face, she blew it out.

Blanketed by darkness, he climbed the ladder and slid the stone aside. Leaning down, he offered his hand to Isaiah, ushering him into a starless night.

CHAPTER 27

Branches tapped against the attic window, picking up tempo as the wind increased. Gray clouds roiled above the river. Emily sat down on the church pew. Reaching up, she directed the light from her secondhand floor lamp onto the cross. She hadn't once touched the Bible, but now it nested on the folded quilt. Jake had moved it, probably read it. Curiosity had tempted her often. How old was it? Had it belonged to Hannah? Nana Grace? Was there an inscription or favorite passages underlined? Maybe even a family tree with answers they'd been seeking. But she hadn't opened it. Hadn't touched it. Maybe now was the time.

Tiny raised bumps textured the cover. Water spots dotted the faded red edges of the pages. Tears? The book crackled when she opened it to the first page. THE HOLY BIBLE CONTAINING THE OLD & NEW TESTAMENTS PRESENTED TO FRANKLIN AND GRACE OSTERMANN ON THEIR 15TH ANNIVERSARY—JUNE 4, 1956. WITH ALL OUR LOVE, MOM AND DAD

She turned to the copyright page. REVISED STANDARD VERSION. TRANSLATED FROM THE ORIGINAL TONGUES BEING THE VERSION SET FORTH A.D. 1611. REVISED A.D. 1881–1883 AND A.D. 1901 COMPARED WITH THE MOST ANCIENT AUTHORITIES AND REVISED A.D. 1952

Closing the Bible, she stared at the faded gold imprint. HOLY

BIBLE. Grace and her husband read from this. Hannah and her parents may have sat in church in this same pew, reading the same words from an older printing. She fingered the end of a red satin ribbon sticking out of the bottom and opened to the marked page. She began reading on the left, at Psalm 139. *"Whither shall I go from thy Spirit? Or whither shall I flee from thy presence..."* She read silently, but stopped suddenly at the eleventh verse. She read the next two verses to herself then whispered them aloud.

"If I say, 'Let only darkness cover me, and the light about me be night,' even the darkness is not dark to thee, the night is bright as the day; for darkness is as light with thee."

"Oh God..." Those were the only words that formed for several tear-filled moments. "Forgive me for thinking I could hide from You."

She blinked to clear her vision and tears spilled onto the page. "For thou didst form my inward parts, thou didst knit me together in my mother's womb." Her chest heaved. Her breath shuddered. A picture flashed in her memory. A red Bible. Susan had taken it out of the bedside table at the Denver resort and used it to flatten a coffee-stained receipt. As she did that, Emily tucked her Live Strong shirt into ski pants and fastened suspenders with fingers that wouldn't cooperate. *God, if only You'd made me read this then. I would have thought about the baby, thought about the danger.*

It wasn't true. The stark horror of the truth doubled her over. She was going to be sick or faint. She set the Bible on the pew and slid to her knees, head bent to the floor. *God, forgive me. I did think.*

She saw the hand held out to her as clearly as if she were back in the hotel room, pouring her heart out to people she'd known less than a week. She saw the little blue pill on the palm of the hand. *Take this and forget about the jerk.* She took it. *Maybe it will make this all go away.*

Her fingers curled on the gray linoleum. Her breathing was too fast, too shallow. Her lips tingled. She couldn't remember what to do to stop it. *God, I was so hurt, so lost. I wanted the pain to go away for a little while.* When Sierra asked her to go skiing, she thought the Ecstasy had worn off. Her heart rate had slowed and she thought she was clearheaded. She hugged Susan before she left the room.

Something she never did. She hugged Sierra when they met in the hall. It seemed so natural.

On the lift, the breeze on her face felt like bubbles. The snow sparkled like tiny Fourth-of-July sparklers dotting the hill. Snow-covered trees seemed soft and fluffy, as if she could stretch across their tops and feel weightless. She'd grabbed Sierra's hand just before they reached the top of the mountain. "I'm not mad at Keith anymore. I'm going to call him and tell him I forgive him."

Sierra knew about the breakup, but not the pregnancy. No one knew but Keith. "Are you sure that's a good idea?"

They hopped off the lift. "Of course it's a good idea. It's a wonderful idea. I forgive him. Who could stay mad on a day like this?" Her last words before pushing off were, "Look at the sun on the snow. It's a beautiful day and life is beautiful!"

Emily stared at the cross. She didn't know who'd put it there, or why, in a house otherwise stripped bare, someone had chosen to leave this sanctuary as it was. Maybe Cara's parents had hoped this place would draw their children back to the Lord. Maybe Nana Grace had requested it never be disturbed. Whatever the reason, Emily knew that God had orchestrated this moment, this place of refuge, for her.

Six months ago, she'd planned her death. She'd written letters to her parents, her sister, and Sierra. She'd sat on a dock at the Clinch Park Marina in Traverse Bay, alone on a cold, moonless night, and emptied sleeping pills and pain meds into her hand. Two hours passed. Her body grew numb to the cold as she watched her breath crystallize over the pale yellow ovals and pink-and-blue capsules. But just as she raised her hand to her mouth, the northern sky lit with streaks of green and tinges of purple that shimmered and danced over the water.

She'd known then that God had put her in that place at that time to witness His handiwork and choose life. And she knew now that He'd put her in this place to make another decision. *"Emily knows You have forgiven her. Help her to embrace that truth with every cell of her being. Grant her the courage to step out of the dark and walk in the freedom of Your light."* She stared at the cross. "I don't know how."

Trust Me.

Not words, not voice. The message embossed her spirit. She knelt by the bench. Her mouth formed the lines of the psalm. *"I praise thee, for thou art fearful and wonderful. Wonderful are thy works! Thou knowest me right well; my frame was not hidden from thee, when I was being made in secret, intricately wrought in the depths of the earth."* The words swam. *"Thy eyes beheld my unformed substance; in thy book were written, every one of them, the days that were formed for me, when as yet there was none of them."*

There were no days formed for her child.

Not this side of heaven.

She could spend the rest of her life in shame and regret—in darkness—or she could choose to trust.

And step into the Light.

👑

Emily awoke on the cold square of gray linoleum. Rain beat hard on the roof. Wind rattled the window. It was nearly dark. She rose to hands and knees, arching her back out of habit, though nothing hurt. A month ago, lying on the hard floor would have stiffened her for days.

Rubbing her arms, she pulled the quilt from the pew and wrapped it around her. Her fingers skimmed a faded rose and stilled at the edge of a petal near two embroidered letters. She stood and moved the lamp.

HS. "Hannah." She breathed the name. Lifting the quilt as if it were made of tissue paper, she held it high, stretching her arms wide. She thought of Adam's words, "The rose wreath is a symbol. It means someone died on the journey." All this time, she'd imagined Nana Grace's gnarled fingers making the tiny stitches. Had Hannah made it after her mother died or when the love of her life hadn't returned home? Had her tears dampened the fabric as she traced leaves and petals, or had memories coaxed a smile as she worked?

Emily sat on the pew and draped the quilt over her knees. *Someone died on the journey.* Hannah's grief produced a thing of beauty. Emily turned her eyes to the cross. *Lord, can You make something beautiful from mine?*

CHAPTER 28

Emily sat beside Jake on her front step. She swatted a mosquito on her arm and missed then smashed one on his bare knee, leaving a bloody streak. It was the first time she'd seen him in shorts. Now she'd not only gawked at his tanned legs, she'd touched one. "You don't think this is too mean?"

"It's giving her a taste of her own medicine." He smacked a mosquito on her forehead.

"You're sure it won't backfire?"

"Positive. I casually worked Heidi into a conversation with Adam the other day. I asked him what Lexi thought of her." Jake's eyes glinted with mischief in the glow of the light above the door.

"And?"

"Lexi told him Heidi looked like a freak from a wax museum, had the personality of the White Witch of Narnia, and hung on me like an octopus with a million tentacles."

"I should have introduced myself to this old love of yours when I saw her at Chances."

"She is not an old love. She is an old mistake."

"So you're no longer drawn to ice queens?"

"I've changed my criteria a bit."

"You do realize that no one will be good enough in Lexi's eyes."

255

"Yeah. Could you explain that to me from a female point of view?"

"Women of all ages compete for men's attention. Dawn Anne said she and Sierra started fighting over her husband when Sierra was only three months old."

"That's insane."

"It should make you feel very special." She clapped her hands, killing two bugs with one blow.

"It makes me feel like I will never, ever understand women."

"That's a given."

Jake fingers grazed her cheek and tucked a strand of hair behind her ear. "I'd like to try understanding one of them. Maybe, with a little help."

"If we wait too long she'll be asleep."

"Can we continue this conversation later? You're leaving tomorrow for a whole week, you know."

"Maybe. Go home, take a bath in bug spray, and wait"—she deepened her voice to her best imitation of Topher—"for me to call ya', Cob."

Jake's face lost every trace of softness. "Yeah. Sure. Whatever, bro."

With an eye roll and a wave, she walked into the house, watched the time on her phone morph from 10:14 to 10:15, and poured a glass of tea while she waited for 10:20. Jake hadn't called her, so everything must be in place.

⟡

"Go back to bed. You'll feel better in the morning."

Lexi shook her head and folded both arms over her belly. "Feel my head, Grandma. Is it hot?" The heating pad under her pillow was another one of Naomi's genius ideas.

Adam threw his backpack on the couch and shoved a book in it. "She's faking it. She's just trying to wreck all our plans."

"I am not. I really want—" Grandma motioned for her to lean down to where she sat in the recliner so she could feel her head. Her expression changed from annoyed to concern. Yippee for heating pads.

"You do feel warm. Adam, get that bottle of ibuprofen out of the first-aid kit in the clothes basket in the kitchen."

Lexi shot a told-you-so look at her brother as he stomped past her. She took the medicine Grandma gave her, hoping it wouldn't hurt her if she really didn't need it, and walked off to bed, moaning softly on her way. "I'll try to sleep."

She went to the bathroom first. Grandma wore a ton of makeup. There had to be something gray in her drawer. Sure enough, eye shadow just the right color for a nice shadow *under* her eyes. After an appropriately long time, she staggered out, leaving the fan on in the bathroom, and walked down the hall, touching the wall with one hand for support. She was beginning to convince herself she was sick.

Positioning her pillow to cover the heating pad, she lay on her back and turned the bedside lamp toward the wall. A little light was necessary to show off the circles under her eyes when Grandma came to check on her. Every few minutes, she put her hands under the pillow. When they were hot, she pressed them to her face.

Hard as she tried to keep her eyes open and her face warm, sleep was hard to fight. She'd almost given in when the sound of a hammer woke her. Right outside her window.

"Sorry, Topher. Just had to pound a piece of siding back into place before it rains again. Thanks for calling back."

Lexi was wide awake now. Her uncle picked weird times to fix things.

"Yeah, I'm serious. Go figure, huh? All this time I figured she hated my guts, and then she sends this amazing letter.

"Read it? I don't have to. I memorized it! 'My sweet Jake,' it starts. How cool is that? Yeah, I know. 'I'm so happy you changed your mind about liking that Foster lady,' she says. No, I didn't really change my mind. I still really like her, but, hey, she's moving to California, you know? If Heidi still loves me, man, I can't take a chance on losing her again. She's the best thing that ever happened to me. Do you realize how close we came to getting married? Yeah, I know, she'd be the perfect mother for the twins. She's warm and funny and she just gets kids. Okay, here's the rest of it—'I know we can only meet secretly until you finish her house. Because I know how much you love me, I will wait patiently for the day when we can be together always. All my love, Heidi.'"

A cramp gripped Lexi's stomach like a hand crumpling a soda can.

"I'm not wasting any time, bro. This time I'm not going to let her get away. I'm calling her as soon as I hang up." A loud sniff echoed through the window. Jake was *crying*? "I'm proposing to her tonight."

Lexi broke into a cold sweat. She felt the blood leaving her head. The room swayed. She had to stop him. Now. Throwing off the covers, she flew out of bed, yanked open the door, ran down the hall and through the living room. She made it to the kitchen door before Grandma yelled.

"Lex! Stop!" Her recliner creaked as it snapped upright. "She must be delirious."

"I doubt it," Adam answered.

Lexi didn't stop. "I'm fine. I'm all better." It didn't matter now if they knew she wasn't sick.

A week with Emily would be a million times better than Jake marrying the White Witch.

👑

Lexi swiped a tear as Grandma stomped back into the house. She hadn't heard the end of this. She glared at Jake. "It's not true?"

"Not a word of it."

"Then why. . .?" A branch snapped. Emily walked through a space in the shrubs. Lexi's skin suddenly felt like the worst sunburn anyone had ever gotten. Naomi and her stupid ideas.

Emily sat down in the empty chair on Jake's left. Jake patted the chair on the other side. "You needed to see what it feels like."

Lexi couldn't look at either one of them, and she sure wasn't going to sit down. Everything in her wanted to be mad, but it was all her own fault. "The letters were Naomi's idea."

Emily smiled. "They were very creative." She didn't say it nasty. It would be easier if she was nasty. "Very convincing." Emily leaned forward. "Lexi, I understand why you wrote them."

She did? "You do?"

"Of course. Your family is special to you. I went through something kind of similar when I was a little older than you. My sister brought her best friend along when my family went on a cruise. I'd been looking forward to it for months, and all of a sudden Dawn Anne, this girl I didn't even know, who was ten years older than me, is barging in on our family time. I spent the whole nine days of the cruise watching grown-ups play shuffle board. Dawn Anne stole my sister from me and I hated her for it."

Emily didn't really look like the kind of person who would use the word *hate*. Lexi moved the chair a few feet back and sat down. "Really?"

"Really. So I understand why you wouldn't want me around."

"Did you do anything to that girl?"

Emily laughed. "I put a jellyfish in her bed."

Jake's eyes looked like great big marbles. "Those things sting!"

"It was dead."

"Eeww." Hard as she tried to hate Emily, it wasn't working. She wasn't a bad person. She just didn't belong here. "What did she do?"

"She totally freaked. She and my sister didn't go to bed until after midnight, and Dawn Anne's screams woke the people in the state room next to us. It got really ugly."

"Did they ever find out you did it?"

Emily shrugged. "They couldn't prove it and I didn't 'fess up, so they couldn't punish me. I was in my twenties before I told them the truth."

"For real?" Not only did she not hate Emily, she just might become her new hero.

She still didn't belong here.

But maybe it was better to let her think they were friends.

⚜

"That went well."

"I thought so." Emily ran her thumb along the ridged aluminum arm of the lawn chair angled to face Jake.

"You totally won her over when she found out what a nasty kid you were." He leaned forward and took her hands. "I'm glad you grew up."

259

Heat slithered from her palms to her shoulders. Though the color of an icy mountain lake, his eyes were anything but cooling. She breathed deep, pulling the night air into her lungs. She needed to keep her head clear. "Jake."

His eyes closed briefly. His grip loosened. "Just once, could you say my name in a different tone?" He sat back in the chair. "I bet you were really good at playing Red Light/Green Light, Teach."

Pulling her hands free, she stood. His sarcasm was justified. "I know. I know I'm sending mixed signals."

"Emily." He whispered her name and started to stand.

"Don't." She held one hand up. "I need you to listen without saying a word. I need you to hear all of it." Wrapping her sweater tight across her chest, she turned to face the house. Looking at him, she'd never get through it. She told him about the day of the accident, the people she'd met, the little blue pill.

"So you blame yourself for what happened to Sierra."

Emily nodded.

"And for losing the baby." Again, he said her name. Again, she raised her hand.

"My injuries. . ." She pressed one hand to her temple and stared at him. She needed to see his reaction. "I hemorrhaged internally. The only way they could stop it was to do a hysterectomy."

His eyes narrowed. His lips parted. He stood and took a step toward her, as she knew he would. She expected his arms to engulf her, expected words of sympathy. She steeled herself as he did what she knew he would and tried, with every ounce of strength she possessed, not to savor the warmth and hardness of his chest or the sense of being cared for and protected. Of being home.

⚜

The pain was physical. As he pressed his face against her hair, the ache in his chest grew. "I'm so sorry, Emily."

She didn't conform to him, didn't soften in his arms. And then it hit him. All her red lights were about this moment, about his reaction to this reality. His eyes closed. He breathed deep of her spicy scent. Emily couldn't bear children. If he stayed with her, he would never know what it meant to father his own child. Was this

260

what God was calling him to? If he married her and gained custody
of the kids, Emily would have a ready-made family. She would have
someone to shower with maternal feelings. But he would never
know what it was like to hold a son who looked like him, to pass on
his name, his genes.

Emily's hands rose and pressed against his chest. "It's okay, Jake.
I'm okay." She looked up at him, eyes clear, not tear-filled. A faint
smile tipped one corner of her mouth.

He pulled his arms away to brush the hair from her face. Emily
shook her head. Her hand rested on his arm for just a moment, like
a butterfly landing then taking flight. Then she turned. And walked
away.

He didn't follow her.

♔

October 23, 1852

Isaiah's deep, hushed voice sang into the thick blackness. "Wait not
for tomorrow's sun. Turn, sinner, turn O!"

Liam's paddle adjusted to the rhythm of the song. It was hard
work, going against the current, but his arms took to the task
without complaint. An hour ago he'd been grateful for the blackness
that shrouded them, but the clouds had shifted, exposing the moon.
He gave thanks for just enough light to navigate the chain of lakes
ahead. They were almost halfway to the bend in the river where he
and Isaiah would part ways.

"About an hour," he whispered when Isaiah paused between
verses. An hour until Isaiah's song would have to cease and he'd
need to flatten himself on the bottom of the canoe, under the pile of
flour sacks and next to two dead beavers.

How strange this past year had been for a farm boy who'd
never had hopes of doing anything but buy his own land, find a
good woman, and support a family. Yet here he was, training to be
a blacksmith, more in love than he'd ever imagined a human being
could stand, and part of something so much bigger than himself.
He and Big Jim and the Shaws had only played a small role, but it
was a necessary part. They hadn't helped many, in the whole scheme

261

of things, but some were children with hope-filled futures ahead. Some, like Isaiah, hoped to gain their freedom in order to return and help their loved ones break free.

If he harbored anger at being called to this mission instead of raising a roof on his own land with Hannah by his side, the anger was aimed not at God but at men who thought it their right to own other men and at those who tolerated such evil. Liam took a long, slow breath and let the words of the gospel song sooth his ire. "Turn, sinner, turn O!"

Liam stayed close to the shore and out of the splash of moonlight that lit the glasslike lake. He rounded the curve of the north shore and navigated the narrow channel that led him back onto the Fox. The Pottawatomi called this river *Pishtaka*. Buffalo. At times during his nights on the river, Liam imagined what it had been like before settlements dotted the river named for those majestic beasts.

"Wait not for tomorrow's sun. . ." Isaiah's rich voice soothed them both. "Turn, sinner, turn O! Wait not for tomorrow's sun, turn, sinner, turn O! Tomorrow's sun will sure to shine, turn, sinner, turn O!"

"Good words, Isaiah. I'm trying to put them to memory."

A dog barked. Too close for Liam's comfort. Not a wild dog, from the sound of it. A hunting dog, nose to the ground. "Get down."

The barking grew louder. Liam stopped paddling, holding the end of his paddle against the current. The noise stopped abruptly. The canoe drifted in the silence. Gooseflesh rose on Liam's arms as he strained to hear anything that didn't belong with the chirping of crickets.

Movement. On top of a small rise above the east bank. Moonlight silhouetted two men and a dog. Two men, and two muskets. Hunters? Liam's heart slammed his breastbone. His breathing came in short, strained gasps. Dipping his paddle straight down, he searched for the river bottom. There, five feet down. But was it deeper toward shore? And, large as he was, would Isaiah be any match for the current?

"Mr. Liam?" Isaiah whispered, fear tightening his voice. "I'll not put you in danger."

"The water is up to your shoulders here. You're better off fighting the river than those guns." Liam paused, taking only a heartbeat to make a decision punishable by death. He lifted his pants leg and pulled out the only thing of value Da had ever given him—a Colt revolver. "Keep it dry," he said, handing it to Isaiah.

"No, Mr. Liam, I cannot—"

"Hide on the bank. If I'm not back for you in an hour, stay close to the river and head north. There's a farm, just west of the sharp elbow in the river. There'll be a single lantern in the barn window. You'll be safe there."

Gaze fixed on the shadowy figures on the hill, Liam rode with the canoe as it rocked. Isaiah made a small splash. An involuntary gasp escaped as the cold water hit and his feet scrambled to find the bottom. *Lord, bring him to solid ground.*

"Ho! Stop!" The voice—loud, angry—rolled down the riverbank.

Liam lifted the paddle, dipped it in the opposite side, moving toward the voice and the guns and away from Isaiah. "Hello!"

The dog howled and broke into a run. Reeds rustled as he neared the water. One man followed, the other stayed on the hill, with full view of the river. Liam prayed the darkness would conceal Isaiah's wake. He waved. "What are you hunting on this fine moonlit night?"

Man and dog reached the bank at the same time. "Sheriff Hiram Brown." The man tapped his chest. Moonlight reflected off a silver badge. "Question is, who are you and what are you doing out here?"

Bounty hunters. The man probably wasn't a lawman at all. "Checking my traps." Liam eased up to the bank and grabbed onto a tree limb. "Liam Keegan. I work for the blacksmith in Rochester. Smith by day, trapper by night." He fought to keep his tone light and casual. "What're you looking for, Sher—?"

The dog shot through the sheriff's legs and leaped into the canoe. His yowls ricocheted off the trees as he sniffed and scratched, his tail waving like a surrender flag.

"What's in there?" The sheriff lifted the gun and cocked it. The sound reverberated across the water.

"Beavers. Have a look." Out of respect for the firearm, he didn't turn around. If any sign of Isaiah was left, he'd know soon enough. But the carcasses would explain the hound's frenzy. The dead animals might well be Isaiah's saving grace.

The sheriff picked up a stick and poked the bags and the animals. "Enough room for a man to hide."

"I suppose." Liam tried to add boredom to his voice. Maybe a touch of frustration. What would he be feeling if, in fact, he were only out here checking his traps? "Are you looking for a man?"

"We are."

"What'd he do?" The more ignorant he sounded, the more believable he might appear.

"Ran off from his master."

"Ah. One of *them*. There a reward?"

"One thousand dollars."

Liam lifted his brows. Not that they'd be seen in the dim light, but he needed the appropriate mask. "A tidy sum. I'll certainly keep my eyes and ears open."

The sheriff called his dog out of the boat. For what seemed like an interminable time, he stared at Liam. Finally he touched the brim of his hat. "We're camped up yonder. You hear anything, you come find us."

"Will do, sir. Hope you find him." The last words threatened to choke him. He pierced the water with the tip of his paddle and kept heading upstream, mouthing words as he paddled. "Tomorrow's sun will sure to shine. . ."

CHAPTER 29

Holding the Percocet bottle up to the thin dawn light streaming onto the gray linoleum, Emily counted the pills and tucked the bottle in the toe of a shoe. Just in case. She zipped her bag and lowered it through the attic hatch on the end of a rope she'd found in the shed. There was no man in the house to hoist a tote bag on his shoulder the way he'd once carried her.

He hadn't come after her. She'd spent the first three hours of the night on the church pew, wrapped in the rose wreath quilt, praying, reading, and listening. For her phone to ring, for a knock on the door, or the sound of a key in the lock. Around one a.m., she decided to call Blaze at first light and tell her she wouldn't be making the trip to Missouri. And then she'd found a half page torn from Jeremiah and stuck in the Psalms.

"I will fulfill to you my promise and bring you back to this place. For I know the plans I have for you, says the LORD, plans for welfare and not for evil, to give you a future and a hope. Then you will call upon me and come and pray to me, and I will hear you. You will seek me and find me; when you seek me with all your heart."

Could God's promises to the exiles of Israel apply to her? An unexplainable peace had wrapped around her, more comforting than the arms she hadn't wanted to walk away from. As she folded the quilt, it took on new meaning.

265

Something died on her journey—shame, and the guilt she had no right to carry. She'd crawled onto her bed and slept for five straight hours without waking, without a pink-and-purple pill. When she woke, it was with anticipation. She would laugh with Blaze and Adam, hopefully stay on Lexi's good side, see a part of the country she'd never seen, and maybe find out what happened to Hannah.

The soft-sided bag hit the floor, and Emily let the rope drop. Slinging her purse over her shoulder, she turned off the lamp. She was halfway down the steps when her phone rang. "Let it be him," she whispered, laughing at the pathetic voice that sounded like a song from her grandmother's Vicki Carr album. "Hello."

"Emily, it's Blaze. We have a problem."

"What's wrong?"

"Ben's out. They let him out a week early."

Emily dropped onto the top step. "Do the kids have to go back to him?"

"Not yet. There has to be a hearing first. He got home last night. Claims he's a new man." A gutteral laugh sent a chill down Emily's back. "I told him what we were doing this week and he says if we go he'll have us arrested for stealing his camper."

"Is it his? Can he do that?"

Blaze released a long, controlled sigh. "Probably. The pop-up is ours, but I can't find any proof. I paid cash for it maybe six years ago. Abby borrowed it for their last vacation and we just never got it back."

"Forget camping then. We'll stay in cheap motels. I'll pay—"

"You have no idea how tempted I am to take those two and run. Just start driving and never turn back. If I thought I'd get away with it. . . But leaving for a week could hurt them. Even if all Ben ends up with is visitation rights, he'll take it out on them." Her voice reduced to a husky whisper.

"But you can't cave in and let this guy—" Emily clamped her hand over her mouth. This was not her business. "Do the kids know?"

"Not yet. I haven't told Jake yet either."

Emily's gut tightened. *Counter with a positive.* "Adam will be crushed." It was the best she could do. At least it took her thoughts off Jake.

"I know."

"Let me come and get him, okay? I'll take him out for breakfast and we'll go to the Rochester Cemetery or something. Lexi, too, if she's interested."

"Thank you. That would help." Her voice cracked. "But first we have to empty the camper and take it back before. . ." Her sobs vibrated in Emily's ear.

"I'll be there in two minutes."

⚜

He'd spent the night curled on one end of Topher's couch. On it, not sleeping on it. Bart the Dog snored on the other end. The crooked clock on the shelf next to Topher's beer can pyramid cuckooed five times. Jake threw a sock, hooking the ugly yellow bird before it could retreat and give one last annoying squawk.

"You look like something Bart dug out of last week's trash."

"Feel worse."

"So? Who won? You or God?"

Jake laughed. If anyone understood wrestling with God, it was the shirtless guy scratching his belly with one hand, eating a breakfast burrito with the other. So far, Topher was winning his battle.

"He did. I think." He sat up, grabbed a sock off the floor, and shoved his foot into it. "I don't know. Maybe Emily won."

Topher perched on the arm of the cracking vinyl recliner. "Don't rush into this if you're not sure."

"I'm sure I don't want to let her go."

"But not having kids is huge, man. Adam and Lexi will be gone in what? Six years?"

As if they hadn't dissected the subject to death last night. "I'm not okay with it." He stood and rescued his other sock from the cuckoo bird. "But she's not either. I'm not okay with Abby dying, but it is what it is. Sometimes life stinks. The fact is, I want her more than I'm disappointed about not having kids with her. Does that make sense?"

"Yeah. It does." Topher took the last bite and grinned with his mouth full. "Ah shink yer"—he swallowed and wiped the back of his

267

hand across his face—"making the right decision."

"How so?"

"You've never been like this with anyone else." He held his hands up, pointed his fingers at his ears, and wiggled them. "You get all sparkly with this chick."

"Sparkly?" Jake bent, grabbing the nearest weapon. A foam cheese-head hat left his hand and bounced off Topher's forehead. Topher didn't blink.

"Yeah. And besides"—Topher stood and walked to the doorway leading to the kitchen—"she's a crazy good kisser."

⚜

Jake's voice bounced back at him from the bottom of the attic stairs. Emily wasn't home, but her packed bag sat on the second floor landing. They hadn't left yet. Her van was still hooked to the camper in his parent's driveway with Adam's "Missouri or Bust" sign in the window. Parked right where he'd seen it last night when he circled town a dozen times before crashing on Topher's couch.

The bag looked like it weighed a ton. Had she gone in search of someone to help her get it down the stairs? He pulled out his phone and checked it then shoved it back in his pocket. He wouldn't be top on her list of people to call for help. Hefting the strap onto his shoulder, he clomped downstairs and set it by the front door.

She was probably at his house. At *his mother's* house. How long would it be until there'd be one he could call his? His gaze followed the floor planks from the front door to the kitchen. As much as it still galled him that he'd been powerless to defend the dining room wall, he had to admit the space made more sense this way. He could visualize a flat screen to the left of the door and a couple of overstuffed leather couches. He could keep his eyes on the game while dishing up his killer chili.

He plopped onto the floor and leaned against the outside wall. It was the perfect spot for a recliner. Leather, but not dark brown like the couches. Maybe a light tan. He'd angle it so he could see the flat screen and still be able to talk to the people on the couches.

And just who would those people be? If the Packers went to the Super Bowl, who'd be gathered around, scooping up his five alarm chili with homemade tortilla chips? Topher and his crew? Emily and the kids?

Fingers splayed, his hands rested on the floor, his right one only inches from the setting of the scene he'd rewritten so many times. Emily on the floor in tears, Jake the hero kneeling beside her, saying all the right things. Things that made her melt into his arms. He leaned to the side, as if she were there, as if he could slide his hand over hers. Closing his eyes, he imagined the magic words. *Whatever it is, you can tell me. I'm here for you and—*

The front door opened. Emily stared at him, down at her bag, then back at him. "What are you doing?"

Feeling like a fool and hoping it didn't show, he said, "Just trying to get a feel for the place."

A small but real smile tipped her lips. "That's my line. And you didn't fall for it."

"No, I didn't. What was going on that day?"

"I saw Michael running after the ball. I knew I couldn't move fast enough to stop him." That was the extent of her answer. One shoulder rose then lowered.

"It made you feel helpless."

She nodded.

"Like the accident?"

"Yes," she whispered. "But then you yelled for him and. . ." Her gaze latched on the dining room window. "So what's your story?"

"Feeling a little helpless myself, I guess." He patted a spot on the imaginary couch. Not too close, but not so far that he couldn't touch her. If she let him.

She sat and folded her legs under her. *Comfy? Need a little more chili?*

"I'm just kind of lost as to how to explain to a girl I'm intensely drawn to why I didn't say anything when she really needed an answer."

Blond wisps tapped her cheek. Again, that hint of a smile. She held his gaze. "I didn't expect an answer."

Jake tipped his head. Something was different about her.

"I spent a good part of the night talking to God," she said. "And listening."

"We have that in common. What did you hear?"

She fingered a crumb of dry plaster. It crushed between her fingertips. "Hannah made the quilt. I found her initials on it."

"It's that old?"

Emily nodded. "I wish I knew who she made it for. All those tiny, intricate stitches. Hours and hours to commemorate someone." Her chin lifted. Blue eyes shimmered at him, into him. "She made something beautiful out of her grief."

He held out his hand, palm up. She looked down. A tear dropped to the center of his hand. She covered it with hers. He wiped the tear track off her cheek with his free hand. "What will be your something beautiful?"

"The rest of my life maybe."

"I like that." He closed his hand over hers.

"I thought I couldn't start living until after I'd made restitution."

"To who? Sierra?"

"She was supposed to be in New York this year. She had a partial dance scholarship to Julliard. Dancing was her life, all she ever wanted. I thought she'd lost that forever, but she's an amazing pianist and I wanted to earn enough to pay her tuition."

"That's the thing that was going to make you feel like you could start living?"

"It was. But Sierra's still dancing. She has a full scholarship to Julliard. She's living. And I'm not." Her chest shuddered with a rasping breath. "Last night I gave myself permission to live. I can't undo my mistakes. I can't." She fell silent. Jake was sure she was cataloging mistakes. "I can't make anything right. But I have to start living like I'm forgiven."

Jake traced the veins on the back of her hand with his finger. "I realized something during the night, too."

Emily's lips separated. The tip of her tongue pressed her upper teeth as if preparing to tell him to stop. "Jake, you don't—"

He held up his hand. "Life isn't fair, but God is good. That's what I came to last night. I don't know if there's a future for us, but I want to find out." He covered both of her hands with his. "I need you to know that your news isn't going to cause a problem for my part of us."

Her eyes closed.

"What are you thinking?"

"That things that seem too good to be true usually are."

"But not always."

"But there are so many things..." Another tear fell.

"Like what?"

"Like you're so good with kids. You need to be somebody's dad."

"I don't have to father a child to be a dad."

"I told a Realtor I was ready to put an offer on a house in St. Louis."

"You can get out of that. And if you decide not to, I have a phone. I talk. I text. I e-mail. I drive. I fly. I might even want to spend some time remodeling a house in Missouri. Anything else?"

"I have an apartment waiting for me in California."

"I'll bring my kayak."

"You have Adam and Lexi to worry about."

"I'll bring my kids." He brushed a strand of wheat-colored hair off her cheek and tucked it behind her ear.

"You hate short hair."

"Past tense." The side of his thumb skimmed her cheek. "That was the old me."

"You..."

His left hand cupped the other side of her face and he leaned toward her. "Really like you," he whispered an inch from her lips. "Really, really..." The rest was lost as his lips pressed against hers. Soft, warm, lifting him somewhere far beyond like.

CHAPTER 30

Lexi kept several bike lengths between her and Adam as they wound through the woods, Emily at the head of the pack, Jake following as close as he could without actually sharing the stupid bike seat with her.

Missouri would have been torture, but at least she wouldn't have had to watch Miss Who Needs a Prince turning her uncle into a pile of cooked spaghetti. Jake acted like an idiot around her—all "Don't overdo it. Let's take a break" and "I'll rub your back." Gag. Even from way back here, she could tell what he was saying just by the way his bike helmet tipped to one side and her shoulders shook in a lame giggle. Disgusting. Lexi made a vow to herself to never act like a toddler if she ever fell for a guy.

But she had bigger things to worry about than breaking up Jake and Emily. That plan was nothing compared to the new one. *If Adam doesn't cave.* Her teeth clamped together and she tightened her hold on the hand grips. The monster was back, overtaking her brain. Grandma said it was hormones. But it wasn't. It was Ben.

The trial was in two days.

She slowed down as they came to the bridge, listening to the rattling boards as the other three crossed. Lexi stopped in the middle and stared down at the calm green river. She liked it better when it looked like she felt—all rushing and foamy, sweeping things

272

downstream in its hurry to get away.

The trial was in two days. The day before their birthday. *Happy Birthday, kids, you get to spend the next five years with Blimpo.*

Adam was the one who came up with the plan, but for the first time ever, she wasn't sure she could trust him. They'd been stashing food in their backpacks for a week now and no one had noticed. Last night, Grandma had walked in and caught her sewing a carrier for Pansy out of a pillowcase. She had no choice but to tell her what it was. Grandma thought it was cute. No suspicion at all. The really tricky thing would be tomorrow night—breaking into their own house to get Mom's emergency money without waking Ben.

That's where Adam's smarts came in handy. He'd found a six-pack of beer in Grandma's basement. The dust and cobwebs meant it was old. Maybe it belonged to their grandpa and was older than they were. Adam's plan was to leave it by the back door with a "Welcome Home, Ben" sign on it. Adam didn't know if six beers was enough to make him pass out, but it should make him sleep sound. If they were lucky, the beer might be old enough to make him really sick. And die.

But Ben wouldn't die—or even sleep—if Adam chickened out. He was starting to say things that scared her like, "Let's just wait and see what happens. We can always take off on Monday after we know."

But what if they didn't get the chance? What if Ben won and they got handed over to him without warning? If Adam would just stick to the plan, things would work out. They'd sneak in late Sunday night, get the money, then get up really early Monday morning, before light. They'd leave a note for Jake and Grandma saying they were fine and they'd call home at six o'clock to find out what happened at the hearing. If Jake won, they'd come home. If Ben won, they'd disappear and hide out somewhere until Jake could find a new place—maybe Missouri, Adam said—where they could all live happily and no one would tell Ben.

That was another reason Emily being around was messing things up. Grandma's best friends wouldn't tell on them. Jake could talk to Topher and Tina and Colt, and they could come to visit and they wouldn't tell anyone. But Emily acted like the kind of person who had to do the right thing all the time, even if it meant wrecking somebody's life. Besides, if she told on them she'd get Jake all to herself.

Lexi couldn't worry about Emily right now. But she didn't have to hang around and watch. She got back on her bike and rode hard until she passed Adam. "I'm heading home," she said as she pulled up next to Jake. "I'm not feeling so good."

Emily slowed to a stop, and Jake fell in behind her like a trained puppy. "Do you think you're coming down with something?" Emily reached out and put the back of her fingers against Lexi's forehead. The way Mom used to.

Lexi drew back. "No." She faked a smile and shrugged, trying to look embarrassed. "Just girl junk, you know?"

"Oh yeah." Emily smiled. "I know."

No you don't. You don't know at all. Lexi hopped back on her seat and pushed the pedal. *You have no clue. Because you're the girl junk making me sick.*

⚜

"Guess I'll leave you two alone."

Adam got on his bike, but not before giving Jake a conspiratorial wink. Emily shook her head. "Did you pay them to leave?"

"You'll never know." Jake propped his bike against a tree just off the trail. "Let's walk a bit. Back to the bridge."

"I'm fine. My back's great. You're being overprotective. I don't need this many breaks."

"But I need to hold your hand." He unlatched his chin strap and wiggled his eyebrows. "And the rest of you."

Face warming like a teenager, Emily swung her leg over the seat and leaned her bike against his. "You unnerve me sometimes." She hung her helmet on the handlebars and held out her hand. "Do you know that?"

"How so?"

"When you say something like that and don't mean it to mean what it sounds like."

"Say that again. Faster. I dare you." He steered her onto the path. Sand and fine gravel crunched under their shoes.

"I'm used to guys who. . ."

"Mean what they sound like they mean?"

"Yes."

"Don't think I don't want to do what it sounds like I say I mean."

Emily stopped. Her eyes filled with laugh tears. "Thank you." She gave free rein to the laugh. "It's nice to be wanted by someone who won't do what he wants to do."

Jake dropped her hand and slid his across her back. "It's nice to be with someone who likes to be wanted by someone who won't—"

"Stop!"

"Am I unnerving you again? I like that. Not sure I've ever unnerved anyone before. And speaking of nerves. . ." He stopped and turned her to face him. "Do you know what a beautiful distraction you've been this week?"

"Distraction?" She hovered for a long, dizzying moment on the current generated by his hands on her back. The grin that backlit his eyes drew her like a weak-willed moth. "That's all I am to you?"

"Yep, that's all." He rested his forehead on hers. "Just something to consume me with dreams of a possible future so I don't get consumed with thoughts of the possible future."

Closing her eyes didn't stabilize the fantasies spinning in her head. She took his hand again and they walked in silence to the bridge. Grasping the rust-orange railing, she followed the tree-lined curve of the river. The water barely made a sound, so different from her first glimpse of it. Like her, it was peaceful. Unlike her, it was calm and steady.

Her present life felt like a photograph of a moving object, blurry and out of focus, yet fascinating. Not all of her brain chemicals had gotten the message that life had done a one-eighty. She still woke every morning feeling physically and emotionally stiff. And then she'd remind herself Sierra and Dawn Anne knew and forgave her, God knew and loved her anyway, Jake knew and couldn't seem to keep his eyes, or his self-controlled hands, off her. Catching up to her new reality would take time.

A red-tailed hawk swooped low over the water. Farther down the bridge railing, two gray squirrels chased each other. Thoughts of a possible future swooped and scampered along with the wildlife.

The whole morning had been a game of Let's Pretend. Anyone who passed the four of them on the bike trail would have thought they were one small, happy family. *Lord, can it be?* She leaned into the arms circling her from behind. "How do you think the kids are doing?"

"They're scared. Adam's like me—he hides it by being the funny guy. Lex is hard to read. Must be that girl junk."

"It does get in the way. Have the authorities asked them what they want?"

"The kids haven't told us, and with all the privacy stuff, we can't ask what they've said."

"You know they want to be with you."

"But are they too scared to be honest? Mom's told them it will help if they detail everything Ben's ever done, but you can see the fear in their eyes. What if Ben still has access to them if I get guardianship? Can you imagine how freaked out they must be?"

Emily turned in his arms and stared into troubled eyes. "Two more days and you'll know."

"Yeah." His lips skated the length of her nose. "You're coming with me, aren't you?"

"To the hearing? Is that allowed?"

He nodded.

"Of course."

"Know what?"

"What?"

"I'm glad we decided to live while we're waiting for life to begin."

Lifting her lips to meet his, Emily murmured her assent. "Me, too."

Lexi pulled the plastic wrap off the gigantic bowl of potato salad and carried it out the back door and down the steps. Her feet acted like they were magneted to the ground. This didn't feel like a fun Sunday picnic.

A car door slammed. Naomi, all tanned from the vacation Lexi should have gone on with her, ran up and hip-bumped her. "You shoulda been with us!"

"Tell me about it."

Naomi bounced her curls in the direction of the grill where Jake flipped burgers and Emily turned the hot dogs and brats. Like that took two people. "Your plan's not doing so great, huh? Or did you decide you like her?"

"Never."

"She seems really nice. And she and Jake kinda look like they belong together. I bet if you gave her a chance—"

"Don't you get it? Doesn't anybody get it? It doesn't matter that she's nice. She'd wreck everything, mess everything up. And what about our plan? Your mom's coming, isn't she? That's why she was invited to this stupid thing."

Naomi looked down at the daisies on her toenails. "I got some bad news." Her nose wrinkled like it did when she smelled peanut butter. The news couldn't be all that bad—something she didn't like, but didn't hate either.

"What?" Any news would get her mind off tomorrow. And tonight.

"Are you ready for this?"

Lexi rolled her eyes. "I won't know until you tell me."

"My mom's got a boyfriend. She's been e-mailing the guy she went out with in high school and I didn't know it, but our vacation was at the Dells so my grandma and I could meet him. It would have been so cool if it woulda worked out for you and me to . . ."

Lexi was good at smiling on the outside. It didn't take much work at all anymore. Naomi followed her into the house and babbled while she took the cheese out of the fridge and arranged it on a plate. She babbled while she opened three bags and dumped them in bowls. She was still going on and on about the boyfriend and his two gorgeous teenage sons and his big house up north when they sat down to eat.

⚜

Emily hung the clean barbeque fork on the grill and pointed at the circle of chairs around the campfire. "Let me try this again. The three who are standing are Amy, Kerry, and Luis. Rich and Dom are on the bench, and the guy in the blue hoodie is Wayne, your lawyer.

I already knew Topher, Colt, and Tina, and the guy in the Brewers hat is. . .uh. . .on the tip of my tongue."

"Ralph. He installed your toilets. You shouldn't forget his name."

"You're right." She rested her head on his shoulder, thinking for the hundredth time this week that he was the perfect height for her. "This was a good idea. Everyone needed a distraction."

"Everyone else needed one. I already have mine."

"Nice to be useful."

"Oh, you are." He nuzzled her ear with his nose. "You are definitely useful."

"Uh-oh. Interruption at two o'clock."

Tina walked toward them, carrying a folded lawn chair. "We need to go pick up the kids and get them to bed. But first I want a tour of Emily's house." She aimed her I-told-you-so grin at Jake. "Can I steal her for a minute?"

Emily yawned. "I think I'm ready to call it a night." She raised up and kissed the frown off Jake's lips. "Send them home and get some sleep."

"Yes, ma'am."

They were barely out of earshot when Tina whispered, "Well? Is this a kiss-and-run or a kiss-and-stay-forever?"

"It's not a kiss-and-run. I don't know about forever yet."

"But you want it to be, don't you?"

"Yes."

"I knew it."

Emily tuned in and out of Tina's monologue about how she knew Colt was "the one." The reverie continued until Emily opened the front door and turned on the new overhead lights. Tina let out a respectable gasp. "It's amazing. So new, and yet you kept all the old feel."

"Thank you. That could have been the tagline on my spec sheets, but with Dorothy buying it. . ."

Wide brown eyes flashed at her. "You're still selling? Only if you and Jake don't work out, right?"

"No. I mean yes, I'm still selling. If Jake and I. . .we'll figure it out if that time comes."

Tina's long-legged strides loped through the dining room and into the kitchen where she continued to gush, not just about the house, but about how perfect it would be for a family of four. She headed for the stairs. "How could this not be your destiny, girl? Four bedrooms. One for Adam, one for Alexis, one for you and Kiss-and-Stay, and a nursery for the cute babies you guys will have." Tina rubbed her bulging belly. "They'll be buds."

Happy place. She thought of Jake's nose on her ear, his whispers sending chills skittering up her back. She had more happy thoughts than she'd ever need. She flipped on the bathroom light switch. "Jake said he found this light fixture in your barn."

Tina squealed. "That used to be in my grandma's dining room! See? It's a sign. If you keep the house, I can come sit in your bathroom and feel like I'm having Thanksgiving dinner with Gramsy."

The heart-stab from the nursery comment dissipated. Laughter was the only option. "If I were staying here, I'd keep a gravy boat on the counter just to make you feel at home."

Tina's eyes grew uncharacteristically serious. "Walk me back."

She had no idea what possessed her to agree. Tina was silent until they crossed the street.

"Jake won't ditch *you*. You know that, don't you?"

She'd shared almost nothing of her past with Tina. Was it that obvious?

"Maybe I'm wrong, and it's none of my business, but if you're holding back because you think he's going to dump you, you're dead wrong." They reached the redbrick house. Colt sat in the car in front. Tina gestured to the side of the house. "Now go get one more good-night kiss." With a quick hug, she sprinted toward the car.

Emily was a step from the backyard when she heard her name mentioned. She stepped back and crouched close to the edge of the house.

". . .did what I told you." The lawyer's courtroom voice carried around the corner. "You tell them you're getting married and you've got a major leg up over Madsen. I'm telling you, man, she's your lottery ticket. With Emily in your pocket you got this sewed. . ."

The last thing she heard before she ran was Jake's laugh.

࿇

November 2, 1852

"Must I come?" Hannah offered Papa a spoon of cooling apple Betty.

Papa shook his head. "It would look odd if you didn't accompany me." He slipped one arm into the frock coat he wore only for church or business, or supper with cousins he'd rather not see. "We cannot be guided by fear, Hannah."

Her mouth puckered. She should have used more sugar. "The way Cousin Jonathan looks at us, it's like he knows. He knows what kind of man you are. How could he not suspect that you are actively involved? I don't like this. Why are they back so soon? I feel like we're walking into one of Liam's wolf traps. Only *they're* the wolves who should be trapped!"

Papa's eyebrow rose high. "Funny you should bring up Liam."

"What do you mean?" Hannah ran a finger under the high, and suddenly too tight, collar of her calico dress.

"Put on your coat." He lifted it from a hook by the back door. A hook made by Liam. "We'll talk as we walk."

Her fingers trembled. She counted buttons. Twenty-four. She slipped damp hands into gloves and followed Papa out the front door and down the steps. He said nothing until their shoes echoed on the planks of the bridge.

"There are rumors."

"Abou—" Her voice rasped, disappearing beneath the rush of water and the echo of their footfalls.

"About you and Liam." His voice was stern, without a trace of approval. "Mrs. Baker came into the store this morning. Apparently Dolly has shared some things with her I assume you told in confidence."

Bile rose in Hannah's throat. Clamping a glove over her mouth, she prayed the spoonful of apple Betty would stay down. "Wha— what did she say?"

"That your father is dumb as a post."

"She did not!" Relief tumbled like the dark water at the tease in his voice.

"No, she did not. But clearly I am. Would you like to tell me what I am too obtuse to figure out on my own?"

Hannah stopped beneath the gas lamp in front of the bank. She needed to see her father's face before answering. What she saw was not disapproval, but a hint of fear—the very emotion he'd just told her they could not be guided by. "We are in love, Papa."

"The feeling is mutual?"

"Very much so."

Papa's eyes closed briefly. "What are his intentions?"

"The highest. You know him. He—"

"I thought I knew him. Go on."

"He won't ask me to marry until he is making more money."

Papa nodded, took her elbow, and they walked to the door of the Union House. "I imagine there is more to it than that. He is, as you say, a man of the highest intentions. He is protecting you, Hannah."

"From what?"

"From being linked to him as a coconspirator should he ever. . ." The sentence went unfinished. "I'll not allow that. There is far too much danger in being seen with him."

Her breath stopped.

As Papa grasped the door handle, he smiled. "But if that boy would like your father's blessing to court you secretly, he'd best come and ask for it."

Hannah gasped. The apple Betty rose again then settled back where it belonged, but there was no way her belly would calm enough to allow her to eat.

Cousin Jonathan stood as they approached the table. Hannah hugged him with more exuberance than ever before. His mind-reading stare and evil politics wouldn't touch her tonight. As always, he tolerated the embrace as well as he would a bucket of ice water. Hannah kissed Victoria's powdered face and tried not to sneeze as she sat down.

"We took the liberty of ordering." Jonathan motioned for the innkeeper's wife.

Hannah slid the ivory napkin from her plate and twisted it in her lap. Liberty? *You dare use that word?* She concealed her ire with a tight smile. "How was your trip?"

"The new road is a marvel." Jonathan fiddled with his collar as he prattled on about the wonders of the plank road stretching from Janesville to Racine. Papa joined in.

Hannah stared at the pressed tin ceiling, hearing nothing, as she imagined Liam shaking like a schoolboy when he came to Papa, hat in hand, asking for permission to court his daughter. The secrecy only added to the romance. *Liam, wait until you hear what—*

Two men pushed past the innkeeper's wife. She stumbled. Water doused Hannah's sleeve. She jumped out of her chair. The tallest man, unshaven and streaked with dust, pointed at her. "It's true," he whispered, turning to Jonathan. He took a step toward her. Hannah gasped. "We didn't find the letters, but we found something else. There's a room in the cellar. *Not* for storing potatoes."

Hannah clutched her stomach. Dolly was the only one who knew of the letters.

The man grabbed her arm.

"Leave her be. She's just a girl. It's him you want." Jonathan pointed at Papa and the two men advanced. Three men rose from the bar and yelled at the men to step away from him.

There was nothing she could do for Papa. With all eyes on her father, she slipped around the ruckus and ran outside. She ran and didn't look back until she got to the back door of the blacksmith shop. *Please, someone be here.* She knocked. One knock, followed by two. *Please.* The door cracked open, showing a sliver of Jim's face, then flew open. "Hannah! What is it?"

"Two men. They got Papa. I need your horse. I have to warn Liam."

"What men? What did they say?"

"I can't. . .explain now. Your horse. . .please."

"Can you ride?"

"Yes." She hadn't ridden a horse since they'd moved into town, but it would come back to her. It had to.

Big Jim moved like a man half his width. In five minutes she had mounted his massive roan and was flying over the bridge. The shoed hooves clamored like church bells ringing out danger.

Father God, protect Papa. Her mind scrambled to picture the cellar room. What had they found? What proof that could hold him? It was a storeroom, swept clean since the last guests, and lined with barrels of apples. No different from any other cellar.

Unless they lifted the barrels and the lids of the benches, dug beneath the burlap sacks, and found blankets and bandages and clothes of every size. *Oh God, hear my prayer. If they have not found those things, blind their eyes.* She thought for a moment of turning back, of taking the clothes and stuffing them in the walls with the letters. But time was precious. All that mattered was Liam.

A half moon crouched between tall, skinny pine trees. The sky was deep blue, the color of the velvet dress Mama was buried in. An hour from now she might not find her way home. She might not want to go home. She willed her thoughts to fill with hope, but nothing slowed the tympani of her pulse as the horse pounded the dirt.

The church roof, silhouetted against the night sky, marked her turn. *Mama, can you see me?* Shadows slithered around the gravestones. Hannah shivered and turned her eyes back to the disappearing road. It wasn't far. A mile, maybe two from the church. Please, let there be lights lit. A plot of cut corn to her right, and then the house, small, low, far from the road. Firelight glowed from a tiny window. Hannah slowed the horse.

She'd never been to Liam's house. Never even seen his mother. She needed an excuse for being there. Papa. She'd say her father was hurt. No. . .Jim. Big Jim needed him. That would make sense. She knocked. Heard footsteps.

The door swung open and a wild-eyed man stood in front of her, a squat brown jug swinging from one finger.

"I. . .I need to talk to Liam."

The man laughed. "Sure 'n' you would, lass." He stepped onto the porch. "Not nearly as much as you'd like to talk to his da, now, would ya?" The wind whipped at the stained muslin shirt that hung to his knees.

Hannah took a step back.

"You'd be the shopkeeper's daughter now, I believe," His hand lifted to the tie of her bonnet.

"Leave her be!" Liam shoved into him. The older man's scarred, dirty hand flew back and clipped his jaw.

Liam reeled. "No more! That's the last time you lay a hand on me, old man." His fingers curled into a fist.

The sound of his knuckles smashing into his father's face was the last thing Hannah heard as her legs gave way beneath her.

CHAPTER 31

Draw up the offer. I can be there by—"

Emily smashed the brake pedal. The hand that held the phone jutted out to stop a plastic bin sailing across the others jammed into the back. As the light turned red, the van stopped, partway into the intersection. Thankfully, there were no other cars on the road this time of night. "Sorry," she apologized to the Realtor's voice mail. "I can be there when you open."

She closed the phone and it rang in her hand. "Hello."

"Miss Foster. Mike Ross with Southwest Realty. So glad you called." The man seemed to gulp on the last word as if salivating over the sale.

"I had no intention of waking you, Mr. Ross. I thought I'd called the office number, not your cell."

"One and the same, and no worries. Realtors never sleep. I'm on the job at two a.m. the same as two p.m." He laughed. She didn't join him. "Do you want to meet at the house? I imagine you'd like to see it before we finalize the offer."

She'd look like an idiot if she said no. "That will be fine."

"At the house at nine, then."

"Yes. See you then." Pulling into a gas station, she programmed her GPS for the next place she wouldn't call home.

A person could get lost in St. Louis, blend in with the crowd.

285

No one would notice the house in the middle of the block was no longer for sale. No one would care.

Useful. Why hadn't that triggered an alarm? "You are definitely useful." She quoted Jake to the clear plastic bin on the seat beside her. A construction paper quilt block stared back at her. Tumbling blocks pattern. A symbol meaning it was time to pack up and go.

⚜

Adam fingered the key in his pocket. He'd taken it off the ring so it wouldn't jangle. He waited while Lexi hid her bike next to his in the brush. The air was warm, but he couldn't stop shivering. Thin cirrus clouds slid across the waxing moon. It was too bright out.

The house was dark. No light from the TV, thank God. The beer should help, unless it made Ben have to go the bathroom. Why hadn't he thought of that? He should have found a way to slip him sleeping pills. He wiped his damp hands along his pants. His pockets were bulging, already stashed full for whatever they might need tomorrow. They'd both brought their backpacks, just in case. His GPS was still programmed for Fredericktown, Missouri. If Ben heard them, they might have to start running now.

He'd told Lexi to stay home, but she was acting like a mom again, all scared of him going alone. He didn't want her here. By himself he could slip in and out walking silent like an Indian. If Ben even snored too loud, Lexi would probably scream. At least he'd talked her out of bringing the cat. When they left for real in a few hours, there'd be no talking her out of it. "Leave your pack here," he whispered.

"Not if you're bringing yours."

Adam sighed hard enough to hit her in the face with his breath. "Fine. But leave it by the back door. You'll make too much noise. I might need stuff from mine." A rope, for instance, to lower out of an upstairs window. Or tie up Ben.

They walked in the grass along the driveway. Ben's room was on the opposite side. When they reached the back door, Adam pointed to Lexi's pack. She stuck her tongue out at him but took it off. He slid the key in the lock then stretched his shirt sleeve and wrapped it around the handle to absorb the sound. It muffled the *click*, but the

286

noise still made his heart skip a beat.

Blinds swung on the other side of the door as he eased it open. He signaled to Lexi not to close it. The floor sqeaked under their shoes as they padded slowly across the kitchen. The room smelled of old pizza and old beer. Lexi was hoping the beer was poison. It smelled like it.

The carpet in the dining room silenced their steps. Adam held his hands out to avoid bumping anything. As his little finger grazed a chair, he heard a sickeningly familiar noise, not where he'd hoped it would be. Ben was sleeping on the couch.

Lexi let out an almost but not quite silent gasp. He shot her a shut-up look and tiptoed to the stairway. The upstairs nightlight glowed enough to show dim outlines. The steps groaned like an old man in pain. Adam stopped after each one and held up his hand, listening for Ben's snore, all the while planning how they'd escape if Ben woke up. At the slightest sound, he'd find something to tie the rope around near a window.

He handed her his penlight and stood back and let her go in first so he could guard the hallway. Moving in slow motion, he reached in his backpack for his hammer. All he'd have to do was swing it and Ben would back off.

Lexi opened the closet door. Adam shot a thumbs-up sign into the room. She did good. That was the part he'd been most worried about. She didn't turn the light on until she was halfway into the walk-in closet. Smart girl. She'd listened to his instructions after all. He heard the dresser drawer jerk open. Not far enough, he could tell by the sound. He waited, tiptoed to the stairwell. Snores still rumbled.

"Adam!" Lexi's whisper was way too loud. He ran into the room. She pointed the light at the drawer, open about three inches. Not wide enough for the box. "Stuck," she mouthed.

He bent close to her ear. "Can you reach the box and open it?"

She shook her head. "I tried."

Adam pushed her away, got down on his knees. Clothes hung around his face. He'd never been claustrophobic before. He motioned for Lexi to close the closet door. His pulse pounded in his ears. Taking a deep breath, he grabbed both handles and tugged.

The drawer moved with a wrenching sound, slamming Adam onto his backside. He smashed into Lexi, who hit the closet door with a thud. The entire front of the drawer landed on Adam's legs. "Go listen." He forced a whisper. His throat felt like it was closing. "See if he's still sleeping."

Lexi, wide-eyed, shook her head. "I can't."

Adam looked inside the drawer and saw the box. He heard the end pop off Lexi's inhaler. The spray, and her deep breath, seemed magnified in the small space.

"Then get out of the way." He shoved the drawer front at her and grabbed the flashlight. He stood, but as he reached for the door, it swung open.

Lexi screamed and pointed the flashlight in Ben's face. Adam glared at the man whose arm shielded his face, whipped around, and jabbed his hand into the box, pulling out a wad of cash and stuffing it in his shirt. His hand crept across the floor until he felt his hammer. In one fluid motion, he slammed the hammer on Ben's bare foot, grabbed Lexi's arm, and shot past the cussing hulk. He ran halfway into the room. Lexi didn't. As he reeled around to see Ben's fat hand on Lexi's arm, his GPS flew out of his backpack.

Ben laughed. Deep and wicked. "Going somewhere?"

⚜

Victory Drive. How ironic.

Emily stared at the blond cupboards, harvest gold appliances, and white Formica countertop. "Cheery," the Realtor called it as he inched the pen closer.

"It has potential." *Unlike my life.* After twenty-four hours without sleep, twelve of them spent ranting and driving too fast, she'd developed a twisted sense of humor about her serial gullibility. As she reached for the pen, she noticed Mr. Ross's watch. Just like Adam's. Her heart squeezed. Adam would be crushed when he found out she'd left. This would be just one more loss in his life. The trial would begin in less than an hour. *Oh, God, don't let Ben get those kids.* Maybe she should have stayed, played the part just for them. She hadn't stopped to think.

"Miss Foster? Any questions?"

"No. No." She signed her name, slid the papers across the table, and stood.

"I have a good feeling about this. We've got motivated sellers, and I think before you know it you'll call this place home."

Not a chance.

She had one hand on the door handle of her van when her phone buzzed. She pulled it out, afraid to look at the screen.

Jake. Wondering where she was. He'd be there to pick her up for the hearing. He'd be wandering through a more-empty-than-usual house, wondering why she'd left. She pushed the button to make it stop vibrating.

She backed onto the street, took one more look at the tan house with white trim, and tried to feel something. Satisfaction, hope, anything. Nothing surfaced.

"In two-tenths of a mile, turn left."

She was going to Fredericktown. In the past few exhausted hours, the need to find out what happened to Hannah became demanding. With no answers for her own life, she could live vicariously through someone else's.

An hour later, a she passed a sign for Bonne Terre/Farmington, her phone rang again. "Sorry, Jake." She mashed the button again and threw the phone back on the passenger seat. Seconds later it buzzed again. An envelope showed in the window. A text message she would look at. If, by some remote chance, he was calling to apologize, to grovel maybe, it might lift a smidgeon of her mood. Or make it worse. She'd look at it when she got to a stop sign. Not before.

Two miles down the road, it vibrated again. Another call. "Sorry. All done being useful."

Her pulse picked up speed at a STOP AHEAD sign. Slowing the van, she pulled to the shoulder. No sense being in the middle of the road if she was going to have a breakdown. Or break something. She held her breath and opened her phone.

ARE KIDS WITH YOU? MOM'S FRANTIC.
ANSWER. PLEASE.

CHAPTER 32

In one mile, take ramp right."

The techno-British voice of Adam's GPS used to be funny. From the backseat of Ben's smelly Suburban, Lexi glared at it through tears, wishing she could smash it.

"Are we having fun yet?" Ben's words slurred. The right front tire vibrated on the rumble strip.

He's gonna get us killed. She fought the urge to grab Adam's hand. She turned to him and he nodded. He was being brave for her, and she knew his thoughts were racing, trying to come up with a plan. His foot jiggled a small flowerpot. One of them had fallen out when they stopped at the restroom and Ben had sworn up a storm. His stupid plants.

Adam's hands kept going to his pockets, but Ben had made him empty them. All his stuff, including his knife, was in his backpack, too far back to reach.

Ben had stood and watched while she and Adam hauled the way-back seats out of the Suburban. "You want to go camping? Let's go camping," he'd said. "Nice little birthday trip."

He was drunk. But not drunk enough. Either one of them could outrun him, but Ben did what he always did—he threatened. If one of them left, or screamed, or tried to grab the phone, he'd hurt the other one. The whole time they'd packed the SUV, he'd had his fat hand on one of them. When they stopped at a rest area, he grabbed Adam's arm before he let her out of his sight and stood at the open door, watching her go in and out of the stall. Then he took Adam with him into the men's restroom and made her stand close enough to answer him when he called her name. Lexi put her hand over her mouth. What would he do if she threw up all over him? Maybe it would be the perfect distraction.

The headlights reflected off a sign that said thirty-two miles to St. Louis. Ben waved at the sign. The tires on his side swerved over the white line. A car horn blared. "So what's in Fredwhatever, Missouri, that you're so anxious to see?"

"Letters." Adam spat out the word.

Ben laughed. "Stupid kid." He let go of the wheel to scratch his head then jerked it back.

Lexi's forehead knocked against the window. "The police are probably already looking for us." Her hand slid into her sweatshirt pocket and wrapped around her inhaler. Would it sting if she shot it in his face?

"They won't look until a person's gone for twenty-four hours. We'll be in Texas by then."

"That's not true. Not with kids."

Ben swore and called Adam a stupid kid again. Lexi wondered when the last time was he'd called Adam by his name. She wrapped her arms tight across her stomach. "He's not the stupid one," she whispered, then raised her voice. "You coulda won custody, you know. Now you're gonna get slammed in jail for a long, long, long time."

It was the first happy thought she'd had all night.

"What happened? Where are the kids?"

Emily's voice quivered. Jake cupped one hand over his ear to hear her over his mother's crying and Wayne and Topher on their own cell phones. As he grabbed the piece of notebook paper from his mother, a squad car pulled up in front of the house. He crossed the kitchen in two strides and walked outside. "They're not with you?"

"With me? Why would they be with me? What's going on?"

"I don't know." He ran his hand across his eyes. "They're gone, you're gone, Ben's gone. You tell me."

"How could you think—"

"I'm not thinking!" He slammed his fist on the top of the grill. "Mom said maybe you ran off with them like she said she wanted to, thinking you were helping—"

"No. I would never—I left because of what your friend, your lawyer, said last night about me being your lottery ticket."

"Oh man. Em. . .it was all a joke. I told them things were getting serious with us and he made this big thing out of it. You have to know I'm not like that."

"But you were desperate and. . ." Her voice cracked. He could hear the tears.

"Where are you?"

"South of St. Louis. Could Ben have taken them? That doesn't make sense. How do you take two kids?"

Jake clenched his eyes against the sting. "They were gone this morning when we got up. And Ben's not home. His car is gone. We found a couple of things. That sign Adam made—*Missouri or Bust*— was on the kitchen floor over there. There are triangles drawn on the back—like those quilt symbols you made with the kids."

A small gasp came through the phone. "Hold on. I've got the book here." He heard shuffling. "I've got it. How are the triangles arranged?"

He held the paper in the sunlight. The markings were reddish brown, the lines smudged, like they'd been drawn with a finger. In the morning heat, a faint scent wafted from the paper. Cinnamon. *Adam. God, let this please tell us something.* Tears blocked his vision. He blinked them away and took a deep breath. "Two opposite corners are shaded. . .triangles. The other two aren't. There's a square in the middle made of two white and two brown triangles that meet in the center."

Pages shuffled. "Are there four white and four colored all together?"

"Yes."

"It's. . .if I got it right, it's called broken dishes. It says it refers to a signal that involves broken crockery at some future landmark."

"Broken crockery? That doesn't make sense."

"But maybe it will. Tell the police. Have you talked to them?"

"They just got here."

"Tell them. I don't know what it means, but tell them."

Topher opened the back door and waved for him to come in. "I have to go."

"If there's anything..."

"I will."

⁂

The crunch of gravel under the tires woke Adam. It was light out. He'd told himself to stay awake. "Where are we?"

"We're camping. We're going to have fun. It's what families do."

A picnic table outside his window was the only sign of civilization. Ben had backed the Suburban onto the cement pad of a campsite. From the backseat, all Adam could see was trees. No campers. No tents. Nobody camps on a Monday. Still, there had to be someone around. "I have to pee."

"Wake up your sister. We'll take a walk. Holding hands like happy families do."

When they came back from the bathroom, Ben sat on the picnic table bench with his elbow on Lexi's hand. "Get out the food." He looked at Adam and pointed to the back of the Suburban.

Adam nodded. This was his chance. At the very least he could pull his backpack closer to the door so he could grab it later. Ben had to fall asleep sometime. As he opened the door, he realized his hands had quit shaking a long time ago. He wasn't scared anymore. Maybe God took it away, or maybe he was just too mad to be scared. They'd get away, he knew they could. He just had to be smart and wait for the right time.

"Bring me that green bag."

Adam stared at the green bag. "I think I put it in front with the cooler."

"Get it."

The bag didn't weigh much. He picked it up by the loop handles and tossed it over the back of the seat, praying it wouldn't make a sound. It didn't. Before he shut the back door, his hand slipped into his backpack and pulled out his knife. Was Ben really dumb enough

293

to think he wouldn't try? As the red plastic hit his palm, the idea flashed like a picture in a book. He walked along the side of the car, opened the passenger side door, and the knife.

He crouched low over the seat. *God, let this work.* He jammed the thin, tapered file into the ignition as far as it would go then yanked it to the side as hard as he could. It broke. Thank God. With the half inch of file left, he shoved the piece of metal in deep. Irretrievable.

Reaching between the seats, he snagged the green bag.

Ben had his hand out, ready to grab it when he walked around the back of the Suburban. "Got a little treat for my kiddies." He took the bag and pulled out a bottle.

Adam recognized the green liquid.

NyQuil.

Emily paced between two double beds and an old TV, back and forth from window to door, willing her phone to ring. She'd gotten the room because she was too scared to drive home after so long without sleep. Now that she was here, she wished she was on her way. Strange that *home* was the word that immediately came to mind.

"Lord, You know exactly where they are. You see them. Keep them safe. Don't let them be scared or—" Her phone rang. She flipped it open without looking at it.

"We found something else. Might be nothing." Jake was hoarse, but there was a lift to his voice she hadn't heard the last three times she'd talked to him. "The police found what looks like GPS written in the dirt by Ben's garage. They checked to see if Ben had a GPS on his phone and he doesn't. All I can figure is Adam was telling us he has his, but that—"

"He had all our Missouri destinations programmed in!" Her heart thudded against her ribs. "Fredericktown, Johnson's Shut-Ins State Park. It's a long shot, but maybe they're down here."

"I'll tell the police to contact the Missouri highway patrol. And I'm heading down there. I can't sit here and do nothing."

Emily grabbed the handle of the overnight bag she hadn't opened yet. "Give them my phone number. I'm going to Fredericktown." She tucked the phone under her chin and latched her computer case to the bag. "Wait. E-mail me pictures of Adam and Lexi. I'll make copies here. I'll stop at every gas station and rest area and—"

"Emily?" His voice was rough, raw.

"What?"

"I love you."

The line went dead.

⚜

"Adam! Wake up. We have to go."

Lexi's voice seemed far away, like he was underwater. His head felt huge and heavy. His tongue was thick. He opened his eyes. The sun was low, shooting orange rays between the trees. His back hurt. He was lying on cement.

"Wake up before he gets mad." Lexi shook his shoulder.

"What are we doing?"

"Driving. I don't know where. He keeps talking about Texas."

Adam sat up. Everything around him seemed fuzzy, out of focus. Ben sat on the bench, his belly showing through an open "V" at the bottom of his shirt. He had a beer in his hand. The grass was littered with cans. The bench bowed beneath him and groaned when he stood. "Got you to Missouri just like you wanted. Seen enough?" His sick laugh echoed off the trees. "Get in the car."

Muscles seized in Adam's gut. "Lex," he whispered, "when I say run, you go, fast as you can. I'll find you."

"No!" she mouthed back.

"Do what I—"

A loud roar shattered the air. "Stupid kid!" Ben slammed the car and swore. Over and over as he thundered toward them.

"Now. Run!"

Lexi stood, looked from him to Ben, and nodded. One foot left the ground. And Ben grabbed her.

Adam swung around, looking for a rock. Anything to throw in Ben's face. He lunged for the NyQuil bottle.

And a fist slammed into the side of his head.

⚜

Lexi screamed. Adam dropped to the ground. His head hit the

295

cement with a sound that made her scream again.

"Shut up." Ben put his fat, smelly hand over her mouth and kicked at Adam. "Get up, you—" A tiny river of blood trickled along the cement from Adam's hair.

Lexi screamed against the hand, tried to bite it. She lashed out with feet and elbows and clawed at the arm that clamped her like a vise. *God! Help!*

Ben swore. His heart hammered against her back.

Stars shot in front of her eyes. Her vision dimmed like she was walking into a tunnel.

Huffing and snorting, Ben dragged her toward the woods. Lexi blinked hard and took two deep breaths. She couldn't faint. She had to think, had to leave a sign for Adam. He knew how to track like the Indians did. He'd come after her. Her eyes clamped shut against the picture of him lying on the ground. The blood. *Mom! Can you see him? Help him. God, don't let him. . .* She wouldn't let herself say the last word.

The brush was thick between the trees. She kicked a rotted limb. It broke apart. She dragged her shoe across a fat mushroom, breaking the top off. Ben was slowing down. Lexi pretended to stumble and hooked her toe on a bunch of white flowers, smashing them to the ground.

They were heading uphill. Ben's breathing got harder and harder. If she could make him loosen his grip, just for a second, she could run. She kept her eyes on the trees, watching for a path, but the sun was dipping below the hill and it was getting harder and harder to see. Suddenly, Ben tripped. He let go of her. She fell, stabbing her hand on a stick. Her inhaler launched out of her pocket. She gasped in pain and a fat hand clamped around her ankle.

Ben laughed. Sweat dripped from his red face. "Guess you're staying here for the night. Alone." He sat up, crossing his legs like a statue of Buddha. With one hand, he unbuckled his belt. "Scream and I'll kill you, too."

☙❧

"The ranger found it just a few minutes ago."

Jake shouted at the phone over the rush of cool air through

the open windows of his truck. The air conditioner blew full force, but every time he closed the windows the cab felt stifling and he couldn't breathe. "Smashed flowerpots all over the cement pad at the campground. And the van was disabled. A piece of metal shoved into the ignition."

"Adam?" Emily's voice held the same near-hysterical timbre he heard in his own. A bizarre mix of fear and pride.

"Had to be. What a kid, huh?" He wouldn't tell her about the blood. Not a lot, they'd said. What did that mean? Someone was hurt. *Please let it be Ben.*

"Yeah." She blew her nose. "Okay, I got Johnson's Shut-Ins State Park on the GPS. I'll get there a little after eleven. Will they let me in that late?"

"I talked to the head ranger personally and told him you'd be able to help the search. State troopers will be there. They have people at every entrance. Someone will meet you at the gate. I should get there a little after you." *If I don't get stopped.* The speedometer needle hovered around eighty. "I'll try to call, but they said we might not have cell phone reception in the mountains."

"Okay." Her voice quivered. "The temperature's dropping."

"I know. We'll find them soon."

"Bye." She ended the call.

Before he could tell her again that he loved her.

Lexi shivered and curled into a tighter ball. She was freezing. Her shoulder ached. The belt around her wrist tightened whenever she moved. Her right arm, hanging straight over her head by the belt, was falling asleep again. She'd have to stand and get the circulation back, but her legs were so tired. The fingers on her left hand were raw from picking at the leather, trying to dig through it. The knot was beyond her reach. It was a long belt.

A coyote howled. Lexi pressed into the skinny tree that offered no shelter. Dogs yelped after the howl. *Keep them away.* Her fingers curled around the stick she'd found earlier. The one she wished she could use on Ben.

He'd lumbered off, telling her not to make a sound because he'd be close. She could tell he thought she'd beg him not to leave her alone. Stupid. She'd listened until she couldn't hear the shuffle of his feet. But she didn't dare scream yet. He moved too slow.

A faint breeze rustled the leaves. The air grew colder by the minute. Her chest tightened. She'd given in and begged him for one thing—her inhaler. He'd only laughed. And thrown it into the woods.

♔

November 2, 1852

Hannah's head bounced on Liam's shoulder as he carried her. Curled cornstalks brushed her arms like fingers of the dead. "Put me down."

His steps slowed. He stopped and turned. "Da's too drunk to follow this far." He set her on her feet but didn't let go. "Why are you here?"

"Men. With Jonathan. They've got Papa. They let me go. They don't think I'm involved, but they'll be after you." She commanded her voice to steady and willed away the black spots that threatened again. "It's my fault. They went looking for the letters and found the room."

"What letters?"

"Yours. Mine. I never destroyed them. I should have listened to you. I let it slip to Dolly. About the letters. She overheard you and Daddy talking. She must have told, but they didn't find the letters. Not yet. There's nothing but Dolly's word to link you to Daddy unless they make him. . ."

Shock registered on his face. Shock, then fear. His eyes closed.

Her heart pounded. "I'm sorry. So sorry. I should have known better. I never should have—"

Liam pressed a finger to her lips. "What is it your father says? 'We will not speak of what might have been.'"

"We have to leave. We'll go to Canada until Jim gets word that it's safe to come back."

Liam's arms straightened. He held her away from him. "We will leave. But not together. You will go to your aunt's and I will go to Canada, and when it is safe, I will come to Boston for you."

298

A sob tore from her throat. "No! I will not. I'm not a child, Liam. Stop treating me like one. I know there are dangers, but I am strong. I can face anything if I am with you."

His smile, barely visible in the darkness, warmed her. "All right then. Go home and pack your things and I will be there at midnight. Watch for my lantern on the river." He slipped the bonnet from her head. His hands dug into her hair and he kissed her as though he would never see her again.

CHAPTER 33

The strap of his backpack hooked a branch. Adam yanked it free. He turned back too fast and the ground tilted again. He prodded the spot where his bandana was folded under his cap. It didn't seem any damper than the last time he'd checked. As he turned, the LED light clipped to the bill of his cap illuminated a patch of trampled chicory flowers. At first he hadn't been sure Lexi was marking the trail on purpose. But there were too many signs. Maybe all the times he'd read his survival books out loud, she'd actually been listening.

What he didn't know was whether or not she was alone. If Ben was following her or dragging her, he could be reading the signs wrong. Maybe it was Ben, running like a fat bear, trampling everything in his path. Maybe Ben was running scared and Lexi had gone for help. If he hadn't broken the file off in the ignition, Lexi could have driven to get help. She knew enough about cars to do that. All he'd been thinking about was keeping Ben from taking them anywhere else. Far off, a coyote howled. The sound was followed by yapping. *Don't get scared.* Panic was the biggest mistake people made in the wilderness. He wouldn't allow tears. He had to find Lexi.

He busied his mind with things that would keep him from panic. He imagined being a runaway slave fleeing to freedom. In his head, he sang some of the Negro spirituals from one of Mrs.

Willett's books. *Go down, Moses, Way down in Egypt land, Tell ole Pharaoh, To let my people go.*

He dropped a chunk of flowerpot and kept walking. No one would see the broken pieces at the campsite until morning. It would probably just look like an accident. Nobody would report it. The quilt square he'd drawn back home wouldn't mean anything to anyone but Emily, and who would think to show it to her? It just looked like splotches of cinnamon on a wrinkled paper.

Doubts whispered through the oak branches, growing louder with each silent step on the leaf-padded ground.

He stopped and knelt by a patch of matted grass and set a piece of flowerpot in the center.

⚜

A branch snapped. Lexi's pulse pounded in her neck. The thing was getting closer. Were there bears? A fat raccoon waddled past. She made herself think of rabbits and squirrels and fuzzy, harmless creatures. A wheeze whistled from her throat. She tried to quiet her breathing, but the harder she tried, the louder it got. Slow. Calm. Fear would make it worse. She tried to pray, but no words came to mind. She pushed herself to a stand. The stars came back. Bending over, she rounded her shoulders and rubbed the sore spots between her ribs. Adam had read about it once. Acupressure.

Another sound. Footsteps. She held her breath.

"Lex?"

So faint. Had she imagined his voice? "Adam?"

And then he was there, grabbing her arm, hugging her.

"Adam!" She wrapped her arm around him. "Ben might still be close," she wheezed.

"Where's your inhaler?" he whispered in her ear as his hand followed her arm up to the belt.

"He threw it."

He rummaged in his backpack and handed her a candy bar. "Theobromine. Remember? Relaxes bronchials." His knife snapped open and he sawed through the belt in seconds.

As Lexi's arm dropped to her side, a deep, gravelly laugh boomed down the hill and ricocheted off the trees.

꙰

Walk faster. Emily gripped a chunk of terra-cotta flowerpot she'd picked up at the campsite as she swept the woods with a flashlight beam. She craned her neck to the left, and her toe caught in a tangle of roots. She lurched forward, grabbing a sapling and catching herself, but wrenching her lower back as she did.

Faster. She'd seen the blood on the cement slab. The ranger had tried to hide it from her and now she wished he'd been successful. She couldn't dismiss the image. Her teeth dented her bottom lip as she kept her screams inside. The ranger's reluctant assent to her joining the search was based on her promise to not make a sound.

Twelve more steps, gradually uphill, and her back cramped. She thought of the paisley cane at the bottom of the river as she painted the ground with her light, finally landing on a piece of wood the right length for a walking stick. With the stub of a branch, about three inches long, sticking out from one end, it looked like a long-barreled rifle.

"Why is it that you can hunt possum in the dark of night and paddle the river by day and I must stitch by candlelight and bake bread at sunrise?"

Hannah's words occupied her mind and took the edge off her fear. She'd walked a dozen more steps when a light flashed at her. She held her breath. "Miss Foster?" The ranger's hushed voice restored the cadence of her pulse. As he neared, the beam from his headlamp dipped toward something red in his hand.

Lexi's inhaler.

"Oh God." Emily's hand flattened against her chest. "Lexi has asthma. This cold air. . ." She stifled a sob. Her fingers closed around the inhaler. She slid it into her pocket next to the pottery piece. The ranger nodded and walked away.

Minutes passed. Lightning flashed through the dense trees. The wind picked up. It smelled like damp earth and something else. Something out of place.

"Chocolate!" She whispered it out loud without thinking. A faint sound filtered through the brush.

Wheezing.

"Lexi! Where are you?" Her voice echoed. A louder wheeze answered. "Lexi!"

"Em—"

Her hand shook, her light swung wildly. She froze as it hit an expanse of white. A man. Ben. Huge arms wrapped around Adam and Lexi, fat hands curled over their throats.

"Let them go. Now. Or I'll. . ." She raised the walking stick to her right shoulder and aimed it, and the flashlight, at Ben Madsen's eyes. "Let them go or I'll shoot." The words hissed from her.

Wild eyes opened wider. Ben's. Adam's. Lexi's. And her own. Her throat constricted. Black dots danced. "Now." The fat fingers straightened and lifted slowly away. His arms stretched to the sky and Adam and Lexi ran toward her.

"Don't move!" The ranger's voice split the darkness.

And Emily's legs gave way.

❧

"Emily!" A wheezing sob ripped from Lexi as Emily slumped against Adam. Never in her life had she been so happy to see someone she thought she never wanted to see again.

Emily wrapped her in a one-armed hug and the strength seemed to return to her legs. "Here." Emily opened her hand.

Lexi grabbed the inhaler, took two long puffs, and fell into Emily's arms next to Adam. Nothing, in over a year, had felt so good.

A radio beeped in the hand of a man in a uniform. A staticky voice from the radio said, "The kids' uncle is here."

"Put him on." He handed the radio to Emily.

Emily laughed over her sobs. "We found them. They're fine." She rested her head on Lexi's.

Adam leaned toward the radio. "Emily found us, Jake. She found us." His voice cracked and he turned away.

"Thank God." Jake's voice was like music. "Thank Emily."

"Yeah." Lexi nodded against Emily's neck and hugged her tighter. "Thank *you*"— she laughed through her tears—"muchness."

303

CHAPTER 34

Emily's new walking stick echoed against the hillside as they followed the boardwalk in Johnson's Shut-Ins State Park. Jake wrapped his hand around hers and lifted his face to the sun. Lexi sprinted ahead while Adam spewed facts about the reservoir breach that destroyed a portion of the park in 2005.

"One-point-three billion gallons of water. Imagine what that sounded like. It ripped out a chunk of the mountain and totally destroyed the old campground." His mouth twisted in a grimace. "That would have been a worse camping trip than this one."

Jake winked at Emily and she answered with a squeeze to his hand. "Unbelievable," she whispered.

"Mm-hm."

A nurse at the hospital had warned them that the kids might show signs of posttraumatic stress. So far, they weren't displaying anything but relief.

"Imagine looking out your tent flap and seeing a wall of water pushing a ten-foot-wide boulder right at you. Bummer."

"Ignore the boy." Jake laughed. Emily's look said she hadn't missed the huskiness in his voice.

Lexi turned and gestured with a wildly arcing arm. "Come on. Can we get wet?"

Jake nodded. "You've got an hour. We're meeting Mr. Greene at two."

The twins ran ahead. Emily led the way to a flat-topped rock ten feet above the rocky riverbed and pulled Jake down next to her. "You're going to be one of those *Wild at Heart* kind of dads, aren't you?"

With feigned innocence, he took the stick from her and leaned over for a lingering kiss. When he pulled away, Emily giggled. "We got caught." She gestured toward Adam, standing on a rounded boulder with his hands on his stomach and his tongue sticking out in the universal sign for gagging.

Lexi, sitting in an enormous hole in the rock carved by the east fork of the Black River, shot a thumbs-up and grinned at them like a girl with nothing more on her mind than the rush of water over bare legs.

Jake pulled Adam's Swiss Army knife from his back pocket. He pulled out blades, smiling at the broken stub of the blade that had prevented Ben from taking the kids to Texas. He hunted for the one he'd used during the restless night in the motel.

Even though everyone was safe, he'd been unable to sleep. Hours of adrenaline and the weight of future responsibility had him pacing the floor while Emily and Lexi slept across the hall and Adam was under observation at the hospital. And then he'd remembered the stick in the back of his truck. Emily needed a remembrance of her courage, of the moment she'd pointed it at Ben. Did she see God's faithfulness in what had happened last night? Instead of requiring restitution from her, He'd given her a chance to set someone free.

He smiled at her and carved a curled tail on the *y* in *Emily*.

Adam leaped to another rock and Emily stiffened. "That child had a ton of stitches in his head last night and here he is rock climbing."

"What doesn't kill you makes you stronger."

An adorably exasperated sigh hissed through her lips. "I'm buying you a stack of parenting books."

He tipped his head toward hers, breathing in a sweet and spicy medley of deliciousness. "You taught kids their age. You could teach me all I need to know."

She was quiet for a moment. "Teaching is different from parenting."

Jake folded the knife and slid his arm around her shoulders. The words he wanted to say were premature. "I'll need your help with the girl stuff," he said instead. If it were up to him, he'd tack a "forever" onto it, but she hadn't said a word about the house in St. Louis or about heading back to Wisconsin. For all he knew, she was on her way to California and this majestic place with the rush of dozens of waterfalls in the background was the setting for their farewell scene.

She's waiting on you, lame brain. The thought came in Topher's voice. Jake smiled and pulled her closer. "So about that trim you're going to refinish in the dining room. . ."

Emily laughed. "Subtle." She turned until her lips were once again an easy kissing distance from his. "You can ask, you know."

"I'm too scared of the answer." He took an exaggerated breath. "Are you coming back home?"

Blond strands trailed across her cheek. "I've been thinking about that."

He didn't like where this was going. "And?"

"I want to do something significant with the money from the house."

"Like what?" His voice rasped. From the moment he'd heard her on the ranger's radio last night, he'd lost his grip on his emotions. "What are you thinking?"

"Maybe some kind of art scholarship for handicapped kids. Or maybe. . .I can't believe I'm saying this. Maybe starting a preschool."

Jake nodded, knowing his voice wouldn't cooperate. She'd changed so much from the cardboard girl he'd first met.

"I can't decide if I should withdraw my offer on the house in St. Louis or go ahead with it. It's an amazing deal. It would be a smart investment, but"—she touched her forehead to his—"I hate the thought of breaking in a new contractor."

The sparkle in her eyes banished every ounce of tension in his muscles. He laughed and realized his AWOL voice had returned. "Braden Remodeling has been known to do some long-distance work, but there would have to be some major restrictions in the contract."

"Such as?"

"Such as Braden would have to go halfsies on the purchase of the property."

Emily blinked once, then again. "That's quite a long-term commitment."

He leaned into her lips. "Not nearly as long as I'd like it to be."

Her lips touched his then jerked away. "Wait a minute. That means Braden would expect to go halfsies on all decisions."

"You betcha." His eyelashes swept her cheek. "But no worries. I'm starting to like tearing down your walls."

✿

"I'm so sorry." Kalisa Harris set a netting-covered infant car seat on the garage floor and brushed a shiny black curl off her forehead with a tapered, manicured finger. She gestured to the cardboard boxes overflowing with newspapers, yellowed documents, and old photographs. "Marvin Greene's granddaughter called me from the hospital and asked me to meet you. She didn't have time to explain much, but said you could look through the boxes. I can scan and copy anything you find." She shrugged apologetically.

Jake smiled at the woman. "What are the doctors saying about Mr. Greene?"

"It was a mild stroke. His prognosis is good."

"That's a blessing."

"Amen to that." Kalissa lifted the car seat and stepped out the door. "My other daughter's playing in the backyard. I'll check on her and then I'll be back to see if you need anything."

"Thank you so much for—" Emily stopped mid-sentence as sunlight glinted on something that hung from a fine gold chain on Kalissa's neck.

A gold frog.

A chill skittered down Emily's spine. "May I look at your necklace?"

Kalissa grinned. "Of course. There's a story behind this." She set the car seat down, unlatched the clasp, and laid the frog in Emily's hand.

Lexi drew close and gasped. "That's exactly like yours, Emily."

Kalissa smiled. "Couldn't be exactly like this one. I made this from a mold I cast of the original, which is made of wood."

From the chunky, raised bumps along the spine to the sharp

307

angles of the bent legs, the frog looked so much like the one in the treasure can. She turned it over and echoed Lexi's gasp.

"An *M*!" Adam lowered his head until his hair brushed Emily's arm. "Weird."

"This"—Emily's hand quivered—"mine has an M on it. It's the same size and carved ex—"

"Where did you get it?" Kalissa's eyes sparkled with the excitement that infused the whole garage.

Emily told her about the house, the treasure can, the room, and the letters.

Kalissa sank onto a stack of boxes. "I apologized when you got here because I didn't think I'd be much help to you." Wide brown eyes stared in shock. Her lips parted. "It appears I was wrong." She smiled. "Would y'all like to follow me across town to my—"

"Mama!" Footsteps rounded the garage. A little girl with thick black braids stopped short then wrapped herself around Kalissa's legs. Kalissa bent and picked her up. "I'd like you all to meet my daughter. Hannah." She leaned over and pulled the netting from the car seat. A mass of black curls crowned a round little head. "And this is Mariah."

꧁꧂

Kalissa handed the baby to Emily, then set glasses of sweet tea on the kitchen table. Outside, on the expansive deck, Adam and Lexi blew bubbles with four-year-old Hannah. Kalissa sat down across from Emily. "I became obsessed with my family tree while I was in college. My search led me to the Greenes. And these." She tapped a stack of papers in plastic sleeves.

"My maiden name is Johnson," she said. "My great-great-great-great-great"—she held up one finger with each great—"grandfather was a slave. George Johnson. He fled Missouri with his young daughter, Mariah, in 1852. Mariah died along the way. Your Hannah and her father hid George and helped him get to a ship that took him to Canada. Sometime later, Thomas and Hannah Shaw came here to Fredericktown to help George's mother and sister escape. They stayed with Robert and Isabella Greene, who donated the money that Hannah, all by herself according to the

308

accounts I've read, used to buy the women's freedom. They say she..."

Emily sat mesmerized—by the story, and by the smooth, dark skin of the child in her arms. She ran her finger across the infant's velvet cheek. *Like feeling history.* She thought of Dorothy's words— *We're all connected. Like holding a mirror up to a mirror, we're reflections of the people who came before us and the generations that follow.*

Jake reached over and touched Mariah's hand, looking into Emily's eyes. Searching. She smiled at him, hoping he read joy in her eyes. He turned to Kalissa. "Do you know anything more about Hannah?"

"I know"—she slid the papers across the table—"she lived a long and happy life."

Emily looked down at bold, familiar strokes. The letter was headed, *Rochester, Wisconsin, December 16, 1881.* Her breath froze in her throat. "It's him." She scanned to the bottom. "Liam," she whispered. "His name was Liam."

Jake read quietly:

Dear Mrs. Greene,

It is with deepest joy that I wish you a blessed Christmas. Hannah and I are enjoying health and hope you are well.

It has been a tumultuous year for us. Our first grandchild was born in October, a week before Hannah's father went on to Glory. He will be sorely missed.

The good Lord allowed Thomas to see some of the fruits of his labors before taking him Home. George Johnson and his wife spent two weeks with us in September. You can imagine the tears as we joined hands in our cellar room and lifted prayers of thanksgiving. By way of gratitude, George lent some beautifying touches to our chapel with his woodworking skills. He still grieves the loss of his first daughter, but God blessed him with four children. Because of you, they were born into freedom.

May the new year be filled with blessings for you and yours,
Liam and Hannah Keegan

❦

Emily pulled a branch laden with almost-ripe apples close to her nose, breathing in the sweet, sun-warmed smells of August. Two little boys sat under the tree, eating the last of the peanut butter cookies.

From several yards away, Cardinal Bob cocked his head and stared at her. As she waved at him, she leaned on the gun-shaped walking stick and ran her fingertips over her name and the engraved date. Like portly Mr. Bottomley in Dorothy's book, she carried it as a fashion statement. And a reminder.

"I'm going inside, boys," she yelled.

"To make more cookies?" Michael's brown eyes peered at her from his apple tree hideaway.

She laughed. "Tomorrow. How about oatmeal this time?"

His nose wrinkled. "Uh-uh. Peanuhbutter."

"I kind of thought you'd say that."

She walked through the front door. The new floor plan never failed to make her smile.

Dorothy would be happy here.

And Emily would spend the rest of her life fighting a new kind of regret. Too late, she'd realized her flip had become home. Vanessa would probably say home was just a state of mind. If she could feel it here, she could feel it anywhere. Was there a mantra for convincing herself that was true?

In the kitchen, she picked up the treasure can. Several Squiggles had occupied the can, but Michael had recently declared, "Frogs *hiberate* in really hot summer." She opened the zipper bag and placed the treasures, one by one, back in the can. All but the tiny carved frog that sat on the windowsill above the new sink. The wooden Squiggles would leave with her.

She opened the cellar door, running her hand over the rough edge. *Like feeling history.* Dorothy agreed the door should remain as is.

She walked down the creaky steps, across the uneven floor, and opened the sliding door. Jake had oiled the wheels and they slid easily. Without picking up the flashlight, she stepped down into the room and sat on the bench, setting the can next to the carved inscription. In a few days, when she moved out to divide her time between St. Louis and the apartment above Tina's garage, the can would stay. The treasures belonged to her imaginary friends whose memories lived in the walls.

Footsteps sounded overhead. "I'm down here!" she yelled. At that moment, her phone vibrated.

Dorothy. Her finger moved slowly to answer the call. She wasn't in the mood to listen to more plans for wall colors or room arrangements. "Hi, Dorothy."

"Emily? I—oh, is Jake there yet?"

"I'm in the cellar, but I think he just got here. Do you want to talk to him?"

"Well..."

"We're coming down!" Adam called from the kitchen. Laughter and footsteps followed. Breathless twins tumbled in. The rip of Velcro sounded and an LED light lit the room.

"Just a minute, Dorothy." She looked at the kids. "Is Jake with you?"

"Yeah, but we gotta ask you something before he gets here."

"I'm on the phone."

Lexi bent over, hands on her knees. "This'll only take a sec."

Heavier footsteps sounded overhead. Adam nudged Lexi. "Hurry."

Lexi nodded and gulped air. "It's like this. Jake wants to help you more with your house in St. Louis, but he's stuck with us, but Adam and I decided it would be really good for us to get away from here for a year after all that's happened and St. Louis sounds like a cool place to live so we decided we should all move there and since you're a teacher we were thinking you could homeschool us and it kinda wouldn't work unless you"—she looked at Adam and he nodded. The cellar steps creaked. Lexi scrunched her face. "Would you"—they said in unison—"marry us?"

"Alexis!" Jake appeared in the doorway, nailing Lexi with a horrified look.

Mouth agape, Emily looked up into lake-blue eyes.

311

The stunned look slowly melted from his face. He shrugged, shook his head, and grinned. "Well. . .what they said."

"Uh. . ."

Tears brimming his eyes, Jake reached out for Lexi's hand then Adam's. In one fluid motion, all three were on their knees at Emily's feet.

"Emily Foster, will you do us the honor of making us the happiest family in the whole world? Will you marry us?"

Mouth still wide open, Emily nodded. "Yes. *Yes.* To all of you!"

Jake stood and pulled her to her feet. He held her gaze for a heart-stopping pause then bent and pressed his lips to hers. Her arms slid around him.

Adam covered his eyes. "That's disgusting."

"Hello? Hello? Emily?" The muffled voice came from somewhere behind Jake's right shoulder.

"Dorothy!" Emily pulled away, laughing, and put the phone to her ear. "Dorothy, I'm so sorry."

"No, it's me who's sorry, dear. Jake just left here and he said I should call you while he was there with you and—oh, I know it's too late, but Jake just showed me how he could knock out just one wall and make my house so much like yours that it. . ."

Emily narrowed tear-filled eyes at the man whose grin hovered inches from the phone. "It would feel so homey that it just wouldn't make sense for you to move, right?"

"Y-yes."

"I understand that feeling, Dorothy. I'll let you out of the contract."

"Oh dear, thank you. I'm so sorry for any inconvenience this—"

"No inconvenience, Dorothy." She traced Jake's lips with her fingertip. "None at all." She nestled into waiting arms.

Safe. Warm. Home. Where she belonged.

Becky Melby has been married to Bill, her high school sweetheart, for 40 years. They have four married sons and eleven grandchildren. Becky has co-authored nine books for Heartsong Presents and is working on her third novella for Barbour Publishing. *Tomorrow's Sun* is the first of three stories in The Lost Sanctuary series. Becky's favorite pastimes are spoiling grandkids and taking trips with Bill in their RV or on their Honda Gold Wing. To find out more about Becky or her books, or to let her know your thoughts on *Tomorrow's Sun*, visit www.beckymelby.com.

Discussion Questions for *Tomorrow's Sun*

1. Long before Emily arrived in Wisconsin, she decided not to make friends there. Have you ever entered a situation or relationship determined to guard your heart and keep everyone at a distance?

2. Jake had his own boundaries in place because he thought a relationship would take his focus off of gaining guardianship of the twins. How different would his interactions with Emily have been if he'd been able to trust God with the details of his future? Have you drawn boundaries around any part of your future? What would it take to leave it in God's hands?

3. Jake blames Ben for much of what has gone wrong in his life. That's a very normal, human tendency. If there is a person who has hurt you or seemingly changed the course of your life, how are you dealing with it? In light of this, do you find the promise found in Romans 8:28 comforting, or very difficult to accept? Have you experienced good things coming out of bad situations?

3. Have you ever discovered a "secret" room, a lost treasure, or old letters in an attic or basement? Have you moved into a house that held clues about previous owners?

4. Hannah's faith appears so strong even in the face of great danger. In what ways might it have been easier to trust God in a "simpler but harder" era? What "faith advantages," if any, do we have in this age of information?

5. Emily has a full "toolbox" of techniques for quelling panic. What "tools" have you found helpful in anxiety-producing situations?

6. The letters and the secret room begin to erode Emily's "wall", and she embarks on a mission to discover more about the letter writers. Adam longs to be involved in "something like the Underground Railroad." What causes exist today that Christians are, or should be, championing? Are you involved in something "significant," or do you long to be? What is God calling you to do that you haven't acted on yet?

7. In her pain and fear, Lexi lashes out just like her injured cat. Do you have regular contact with a coworker or family member who responds to the world like a porcupine—bristly and unapproachable? How does (or would) knowing the painful events in this person's life soften your reactions?

8. Jake and Lexi sit side-by-side in church, hearing the same music. One responds in joyful worship, the other can barely utter a word. How do the events in your daily life color your attitude toward worship? We know God is worthy of our praise no matter what our circumstances, so how can we more readily respond to Him simply because of who He is?

9. Emily's driving force is her need to make restitution to Sierra. In what circumstances does God ask us to make restitution, and for what purpose? The Bible tells us in many places that God's forgiveness doesn't come with a "to do" list we must check off before experiencing His grace. Emily could not escape the knowledge that her choices resulted in Sierra's handicap, but what would her mind-set about her own future, and Sierra's, have been if she'd accepted God's forgiveness and plan for her life earlier?

10. What was your initial reaction to Jake's lack of response when Emily told him she couldn't have children?

11. Second Corinthians 1:3–4 speaks of God comforting us "in all our troubles, so that we can comfort those in any trouble with the comfort we ourselves receive from God." We see this principle played out in the lives of Hannah and her father. Familiar with grief after Elizabeth's death, they minister to George and Isaiah with tenderness. Do you know people who, like Emily, have experienced miscarriage, infertility, or the loss of a loved one who are able to comfort others in the way they have been comforted?

12. Hannah acknowledges that Liam left without her because he didn't want to endanger her. Has there been a time in your life when you were on the giving or receiving end of a selfless love that "doesn't feel like love"?

13. God's faithfulness to His children in spite of their actions is always humbling. Emily's choices hurt Sierra. Describe how Emily must have felt when she was allowed to take part in rescuing Adam and Lexi.

14. What do you think the future holds for Jake, Emily, Adam, and Lexi?

If you enjoyed
TOMORROW'S SUN
be sure to look for

YESTERDAY'S STARDUST
Lost Sanctuary
Book Two

Available Summer 2012